Art Feldman was a master behind the wheel, in complete control of the machine. Every ride in his 1957 Chevy was a pleasure, every turn effortless, every acceleration smooth, every stop completely controlled. Some motorists around him would timidly creep along. Others would swerve from lane to lane, peel out from a stop, screech to a halt. "Sunday drivers," Vivian would say, mimicking a phrase Art used many times to characterize those who took their car out for a drive only on the one day they weren't busy riding the subway to work. Because they did not regularly practice the art of driving, they could not develop the skills necessary to handle a powerful vehicle through New York traffic. Let them stay in the right hand lane, out of others' way. Let them publicly acknowledge their inferiority, and they will not be scorned. If they found themselves trapped behind any one of the city's thousands of double-parked cars, too bad. They can wait for an opening that will let them escape. If they had the foresight and requisite technical skill, they wouldn't have gotten themselves into that position to begin with. If they venture into heavy traffic, they better know what they're doing. If they don't, they place others' safety at risk, and they will richly deserve the verbal abuse that will be hurled their way. "*Putz yoineh*!" was Art's Yiddish favorite. We kids preferred, "Where did you get your license? In a Cracker Jack box?" We tossed around these imprecations from a position of comfort. We were in good hands with Art behind the wheel. We didn't mean any real harm. It was nothing personal. Just make sure you can handle yourself before you get behind the wheel in New York.

Yes, Art could really handle a car. Maybe it was all the miles he put on driving as a traveling salesman, or maybe it was something he acquired out of necessity, handling that heap of a 1939 Plymouth he was given by his sister Ida. But I think it was something he was born with. That hand/eye coordination an athlete has can't really be learned, can it? You can get better with practice, sure, but if you don't have the natural talent to begin with, there's just so much you can do with fine-tuning.

Art wasn't a mechanic, though. Open up the hood of the auto and there wasn't much he could do except check the oil, and I don't think I ever saw him do that either, come to think of it. All the gas stations were full-service in those days, and they would do that for you. Art was never a do-it-yourself kind of guy. You see, he never had much of anything that he could do it himself with. Never owned a home, never owned a car except that old Plymouth, and that shouldn't really count because it was given to him. Art didn't grow up in a family that could show him that kind of stuff either. There were his mom and dad and seven kids all packed into one apartment in the South Bronx. His family didn't have a car. You could get by easily without one in New York. All his dad owned was his sewing machine, but he knew had to use that pretty well.

Art was really good with people, though. That's a real plus if you're a salesman. He could talk to anybody. Not that he was one of those guys who was always on, running his mouth. No, Art could listen too. He was a good listener, and he remembered what he heard. That might be even more important for salesmen. Another thing — he was good with languages. He got good grades in Spanish back in high school, and he put it to good use selling in New York. Many of his customers were Puerto Ricans, and he could hold a casual conversation with them. People appreciate it when you make the effort to speak their language.

Art was a friendly guy. In fact, he was more of a friend than a parent to us kids. Maybe that's not so good, but you have to remember that Art was gone a lot, selling out of town, and when he was home it was good that he was a pal. When you come right down to it, we didn't know him very well all those years he was selling, but what we do remember was mostly good memories. He would wake up in the morning on the trundle bed my parents used in our living room, and he would start doing those leg raises that were supposed to be good for his bad back. And each time he raised a leg, he would give a yell like it really hurt, but I don't think it really hurt much. He was just waiting for Vivian to react. After a few yells, Vivian would always say, "Feeding time at the zoo," and they would both laugh. It was a game they played, and we liked it.

Art would tell us jokes, and even more important, he could take a joke. One example, Art hated peaches. Not the fruit itself, but he really hated the feel of the fuzz on the outside of a peach. So, for a joke, we would sometimes put a peach inside one of his slippers. He'd get out of bed in the morning and as soon as he stepped into that slipper with the peach, he'd hop around and make a big fuss. I don't think he was really that upset, but he knew we'd get a kick out of it. That's the kind of guy he was.

Now, no one's nice and friendly all the time. Fortunately, there were some places you could go and release all your natural anger and aggression. If you were at a baseball game, you could be a little more vicious and it was acceptable. Art took me to my first game at Yankee Stadium in 1956, and I was ready. I had absorbed the necessary vocabulary by watching games on WPIX channel 11. When there wasn't a very big crowd in attendance, you could clearly hear individual fans hurling insults at the visiting team. Announcer Mel Allen would try to talk over the profanity with some success – he had a powerful voice, and he didn't leave the fans much dead space in which to insert their verbal contributions, unlike the more low-key, gentlemanly Red Barber, the veteran Dodger broadcaster who came over to join the Yankee team later in his career. One time, during a rain delay, one of the kids in the crowd leaned over a railing and pushed Mel's Panama hat off his head and down into his face. Mel grabbed the kid by his shirt. "Why'd you do that, son?" Mel asked in a semi-threatening manner. The camera cut away quickly. Some scenarios weren't fit for public consumption, even during a rain delay.

Now I wasn't going to bother Mel Allen or anyone associated with the home team Yankees. But I was fully prepared when the visiting team came to bat. "Stick it in his ear!" was what I shouted when the first opposing batter stepped up to the plate. It turned a few heads. "It's his first game," Art explained to the curious fans around us. There was a smile on Art's face and a hint of pride in his voice. Here was his 10-year-old kid, and he had already assimilated enough New York City toughness and confidence to hurl that kind of abuse at the visiting team. He must be doing something right.

2

The collection of purple clouds on the mimeographed sheet was meant to highlight the stratospheric accomplishments of the sales team members at Worldview Encyclopedia. Only those who met or exceeded management goals were honored by having their name and week's earnings placed inside a cloud. And there it was. "Art Feldman, $320", second cloud from the left. Three hundred and twenty dollars in one week was pretty good. Things were looking up. This would probably mean no screaming arguments about money this week. Actually, you couldn't really call them arguments, because it was my mom who did all the screaming. No one would believe that Vivian Feldman (nee Simonson) could yell like that. In fact, when neighbors in our Bronx apartment building heard the shrieks, they invariably guessed it was coming from some other woman in some other apartment. It couldn't be Vivian Feldman, so self-possessed and proper in her appearance. It must be one of those angry, bitter harridans who was venting her spleen.

Vivian Feldman was a lady, and a good-looking woman. By every indication my dad was in love with her. And even if there weren't many indications, why else would he put up with her temper? They never spoke about how they actually met, but they both grew up in the South Bronx and were married when they were in their early twenties. My older brother Harry came along when my mom was 22 and dad 23. There was some talk about their having to get married and that maybe there wasn't any marriage until after Harry's conception or birth, but who knows? Today this wouldn't be much of an issue anyway. The real question was did Vivian love Art? Well, she stayed with him for thirty-one years, right till the end. Plus she's lying next to him for all eternity up in the cemetery north of the city. She had plenty of time to change that arrangement if she wanted. Sure, she rarely showed much outward affection, and of course there was that insane temper. But there had to be more to the relationship besides her wanting to get out of her house and away from her tightwad, paranoid father.

Anyway, now there would be no need to borrow money from the Kaplans who owned the candy store downstairs. At least not this week, because Art Feldman had his name in the clouds. Harry said Art was really flying high during the Second World War when civilian working men were in short supply. Art got draft notices a few times but never had to actually serve because he was always just a bit too old, and had a wife and a kid. He landed a job as a foreman in a hat factory. But after the war was over, and the soldiers began returning, they started getting their old jobs back. The manager told Art that the foreman's job wouldn't belong to him anymore, but he would be kept on as a regular worker. Vivian said that would be a disgrace. Art shouldn't stand for it. Harry said Art wanted to stay, but he yielded to Vivian's demand that he quit. He had to look good in her eyes. That was most important. Art, with his 11th grade education, never had a solid job again. Just a bunch of fly-by-the-seat-of-your-pants sales gigs for outfits nobody ever heard of. No salary, strictly commission. Sometimes pots and pans, sometimes encyclopedias, sometimes *yoisele goniffs* which is what the Jewish guys called crucifixes. It didn't really matter what the product was. You needed a good lead and a quick spiel. Sometimes the C's (coloreds) seemed like the best customers, sometimes it was the PR's (Puerto Ricans), sometimes the JW's (Jews). It depended on who you talked to, who was getting the most orders. And if you weren't getting any orders, you could just write up a bunch of bogus orders with fake addresses. When they went to deliver the merchandise, they'd find out it was a vacant lot. But the guy who wrote the orders would be long gone. He collected his commissions and left quick.

Art wasn't that way. He was a nose-to-the-grindstone kind of guy. He'd work nights and Sundays sometimes too. Me and my younger brother would cruise along with him occasionally in the new Chevy he got every year – the best and only perk that went with being a Worldview Encyclopedia salesman. My brother liked to play with the car radio, and I'd like to see all the different parts of the city. Seems like my dad would always shout out to one of his co-workers he would see out making calls too, someone like Sy Lieberman, a tall heavyset man with wavy black hair who resembled Sid Caesar.

He'd be carrying his brief case as he strode across the street, a man on an important mission. And these calls were important, very important. What could be more important than putting a roof over your head and food on the table?

3

Art's father, Joseph Feldman, emigrated to the U.S. from Romania as a young man in 1901. I used to speak with him when I visited New York in the 1970's. He was in his 90's and living with one of my aunts.

"McKinley was president. Not a *mensch*. He wasn't for the working man. I came here with only the shirt on my back. I needed a machine so I could earn a living sewing. You understand? Do you think my uncle or my cousins would lend me one? I had to scrape and save to put a down payment. Ah, what's the use talking about it? I made my way, earned a living, brought your grandma over. You live and learn."

Nixon was speaking on TV as we talked, denying reports that we had any troops in Cambodia fighting the Viet Cong. Joseph turned to yell something in Yiddish at the screen, and my aunt started laughing. I asked what was so funny. "Grandpa said he should have so many zits on his face." Joseph had voted for McGovern. "Nixon?" He shrugged his shoulders and extended his arms forward, palms up – the universal Jewish gesture indicative of one's utter inability to make sense of an incomprehensible universe. Only the old Socialist grandfather and the New Left grandchildren would go for McGovern. All the remaining family members between the ages of

25 and 90 went for Nixon, the Republican landslide victory explained in microcosm. Joseph couldn't understand it. He must have thought that the country had turned a page when FDR coopted much of the Socialist Party platform during the Depression. Joseph wasn't happy about that initially. He wanted Norman Thomas to win the presidency or at least get credit for programs like Social Security and Unemployment Insurance. But at least socialist ideas had entered the mainstream and were being accepted by a large majority of citizens. Now they were electing a Nixon, a former henchman of red-baiting Joe McCarthy? How could it be? What is happening?

Joseph was already a Socialist who had shed most of his religion by the time he established himself as a tailor on New York's Lower East Side. He learned English by interacting with his co-workers and customers, but at home Yiddish reigned, and his wife who raised seven kids, spoke nothing else, even after they left the ghetto and moved to more spacious quarters in the Bronx. Now, his wife gone, Joseph lived with Ida, his second eldest daughter, and her husband Aaron Topler. Joseph got along with them fairly well although he never quite forgave Aaron for dropping his original surname, Trotsky. It was probably an unnecessary move, for Aaron was a mild-mannered electrician who would never have been mistaken for a Russian revolutionary. Still, Aaron didn't want to take a chance. First-generation Americans like Aaron were frequently anxious to disassociate themselves from radical politics. The same was true of their religion, or at least the more Orthodox manifestations of it. Seeing the Hasidic Jews with beards and sidelocks, dressed in black gabardines and velvet hats with ritual fringes hanging over their trousers, was reminiscent of some 18th century cult. It branded them as outsiders, uninterested in assimilation. It was repellent to many first generation Jews who thought of themselves as real

Americans. Joseph might vote for Socialist Norman Thomas; they went with the Democrats.

Joseph ran a tight ship. Every kid had role to play, and they didn't need to worry about finding out what that role was. It was assigned to them. The three daughters were born first, and Rita, the oldest, was the beauty. She had blonde hair and fine features. Joseph would dress up on Sunday and parade down the street with Rita on his arm. She was his pride and joy. Ida was the housekeeper. It was her job to help Grandma Claire at home. She also was grandma's translator and intermediary when bargaining with the English-speaking merchants. Fran was the sick one. She had diabetes, and had to be cared for. God forbid she should get really sick and die.

The four boys came next. Sol was the shrewd businessman who would guarantee the financial success of the family. Neither Joseph nor Sol anticipated the Depression greatly complicating their plans. Art was a worker. When the Depression hit, he was told to quit high school in the 12th grade, and find a job somehow, somewhere. They needed an extra paycheck. Saul, like Fran, was the sick one. He didn't have a chronic illness, but always came down with a bad case of whatever was going around – mumps, measles, chicken pox, the croup, the flu. He had to be taken care of. Thank God, like Fran, he survived childhood. David, the youngest, was the student, and the only one who attended college. It wasn't that he was possessed of any greater amount of native intelligence or academic ability than his siblings. He just came around at the right time. By the time he was in high school, the family had begun to dig their way out of the economic collapse. There were no more kids on the horizon, so why not invest in this last one? David became an engineer.

Art was on the track team in high school. A wiry 5'6", 125-lb. sprinter. He won some medals too, but Saul had stolen them, as he told it. I never got around to asking Uncle Saul for his side of the story. In any case, the fastest sprint Art ever made might have been unleashed on the day he pushed little David out of the way of a truck that was speeding down Intervale Avenue. Art took the hit instead and suffered a broken femur. When he returned home from the hospital, they threw a block party in his honor.

4

We had just arrived at the Tuxedo on 186th Street to catch a couple of Italian films, Angelo and me. We both had acquired a taste for foreign films recently. We had seen more than enough of the Hollywood blockbusters that packed the Loews Paradise and The Valentine on Fordham Road. We were high school honor students getting our first taste of world literature in English class. We were learning about the vast contributions to western culture made by philosophers and authors throughout Europe from the Renaissance on. We were bound for college where we would, no doubt, become even more sophisticated. What better way to announce our entrance into the intelligentsia than to patronize the Ascot Theater which specialized in foreign-language cinema? The surroundings were cramped, the floors sticky, the seats rickety, the air smoky, and the carpet stained and littered but what did that matter? If the restrooms had running water, that was all the comfort we required. We weren't interested in cleanliness, glitz, and a palatial atmosphere. We even scorned movies in color. Truth, beauty, conflict, and humor appeared more boldly in black and white. Elaborate scenery, refined costumes, and soaring musical scores were irrelevant to us, even undesirable.

Italian movies were a natural choice for Angelo, since he could make out the dialogue without the aid of subtitles. His folks were Italian immigrants. It was going to be a double feature – early Fellini. Challenging as hell intellectually, perfect for good conversation later over a pack of Phillip Morris Commanders and a bottle of Ruffino Chianti. As we passed through the red-carpeted lobby, I noticed a familiar figure poised to take our tickets. "Hi Grandpa!" Sam Simonson in a blue blazer, white shirt and red bowtie, glanced up uncomprehendingly but quickly concentrated on the task at hand again, grabbing and tearing our tickets, returning the stub to us. Angelo was surprised at my salutation. It wasn't like me to shout out a wise crack , least of all to a stranger. "Why did you call him grandpa?" "Because he is. That's my grandpa Sam." I'm not sure Angelo believed me. He had trouble conceiving of a college student coming from a family where a grandfather was a ticket taker. Maybe that image did not fit easily into the European model. In any case, we went in and enjoyed the movies as well as our post-viewing analyses. We would subsequently take in other Italian imports at the same theater. Comedies with Alberto Sordi like *Mafioso* were our favorites. We cracked up when Sordi brings his blonde wife to his Siciian village for a family feast. She brings a gift for the family patriarch, a pair of gloves, only to discover that he had lost an arm in a farming accident. Then, after finishing her plate, she takes out a cigarette and draws the stares of all those at the table. "Is it wrong to have a smoke after finishing a meal?" She asks. "Finishing a meal? This is only the first course!" Sordi exclaims as female relatives emerge from the kitchen holding steaming, bowls overflowing with pasta.

I don't think that Grandpa Sam took our tickets any other time we visited the Ascot, and maybe that made the one occasion seem like an illusion. Sam Simonson came to the U.S. in 1898 to avoid a lengthy military commitment in Austria. His parents weren't influential or wealthy enough to arrange for a deferment so they decided to leave the country as others before had done. Sam stood 5'9", on the tall side for that generation. He was a young man with fine features and black, wavy hair, and naturally erect posture. Although he would spend his life in semi-skilled labor, he gave the impression of being a distinguished gentleman. He could easily have passed for a banker, administrator, or entrepreneur as long as you did not engage him in a lengthy conversation which would reveal that his interests were strictly plebian – a card game, a few laughs, and a bottle of schnapps. Appearance and bearing were very important to Bessie Schein, a short, serious, attractive young woman who was raised in England. The Schein family had its roots in Germany, but had migrated to London in the mid nineteenth century where Bessie spent her first 14 years before embarking for the U.S. The English sense of propriety left its impression on Bessie, and Samuel Simonson projected what Bessie valued in a man. It might be a stretch to say that Bessie was in love. It was just that Sam Simonson was the kind of man with whom she could envision spending her life. She would be proud to walk down the street with such a fine-looking gentleman. Her family and friends would surely find him most acceptable. He would dress up well. He would reflect well on her taste and judgement. Sam was flattered by the attentions of Bessie. She obviously had a high opinion of him and definite plans for their future. With someone so determined, might it not be likely that they would realize all that she imagined and have a fine future together? He certainly knew that he could do worse. Was he in love? Maybe, but what was meant by love anyway? In any case, love might not have been much of a consideration. After all, they were barely a generation away from the days when arranged marriages were common, and in villages throughout

Eastern Europe they were still the rule. Before it became apparent that they were ill-suited for each other, they were wed.

"Ma, you don't have to do that. Go to the doctor. If he won't pay, we will." Vivian fielded calls regularly from Bessie who had a seemingly endless string of complaints to make about Sam. "No, wear your jewelry. Doctors won't charge you less because you dress like you're poor." At some point, Vivian would usually lift the phone off its table and take it with her into the closet nearby to gain the only degree of privacy possible in our one bedroom apartment, but we could still make out her counseling Bessie on how to react to Sam's irrational demands. "It doesn't matter how much he yells. You have to do what's best for you, especially when it comes to your health. Of course, I know he's impossible. I lived with him for twenty years, remember?" Yes, Vivian knew from first-hand experience, and it was no doubt a factor in her early marriage. She couldn't wait to get out of that apartment. At times it appeared that she was about to lose her temper with Bessie, but somehow she managed to control herself when she spoke with her. She could easily sympathize with anyone who felt trapped in that kind of relationship. The amateur counseling sessions provided Bessie with an outlet for her frustrations, but they didn't improve the situation in the Simonson household. And Sam's rages and suspicions only grew worse with age.

But this was not the Grandpa Sam we knew. Our Grandpa Sam was a cheerful, joking character. He would enter our third floor apartment in the Bronx in a suit and tie, starched shirt, and highly-shined, black, cap toe shoes (all mandated by Grandma) with a smile on his face. He was always glad to see the grandkids. He couldn't wait to remind us of past jokes and good times. After greeting us and kidding around a bit, he would ask us to play "Hinky Dinky" on the phonograph. This referred to a Yiddish classic by

Mickey Katz and His Kosher Jammers played to the tune of "Mademoiselle from Armentieres." We had a 78 rpm copy that he never tired of hearing. He continually ribbed Grandma Bessie who did not appreciate his sense of humor, although one might think that it would be a welcome break from the kind of behavior she regularly related to Vivian on the phone. Grandma had, on occasion, cared for Donnie and me when mom was ill, and we didn't like the fact that meals didn't taste quite the same when Grandma prepared them. It wasn't that Vivian was a great cook, but we were just used to the way she prepared dishes. Maybe it was just the whiff of Vivian's hand lotion or perfume we received when she served our dinner that made it seem familiar and acceptable. Kids are funny that way. In any case, Bessie was standing in for Vivian one evening. She had just provided us with our first course when I leaned over to my brother and commented in a stage whisper, "Grandma makes lousy soup." The fact that it was one of Campbell's standard, canned varieties mattered not. The remark got back to Grandpa, and he repeated it verbatim at dinner for years afterward, accompanied by a cackling laugh. It never occurred to us that there might be an undercurrent of anger in Sam's jibes. It never seemed to be the case, but how can we reconcile the bitterness in the Simonson home with the joviality at our apartment?

At the Tuxedo, Sam was the kindly old gent who showed up every day to tear tickets. At home, he fumed that enemies at work harbored grudges against him and were secretly trying to poison him. And while such perceptions were clearly delusional, he had others that were likely well-founded. I refer to Uncle Stanley, the uncle I never met. Bessie wasn't married to Sam for more than a year or two by the time she realized her mistake. Sam could be dressed up, but he had not the desire or ability to rise to the expectations she held for him. He would not be a professional man, a pillar of the community, a figure her children could hold in high esteem. He would never even take the time to become a citizen. Sam would spend his time playing pinochle, listening to Mickey Katz, and throwing back an occasional glass of slivovitz. But there was a doctor Bessie had met at an American Jewish Congress meeting who embodied all that she imagined a life partner to be. He was intelligent and respectful. He was interested in her thoughts and feelings. He treated her with deference. By all accounts, it was a mutual attraction. Unfortunately she and he had already selected their partners, and children had been conceived. Divorces were not as blithely entertained in those days. They were widely viewed as scandalous, and neither Bessie nor the doctor wanted that. But they didn't want to part either. They would meet when they could arrange it. It was easier for the doctor, but Bessie learned that she could escape from Sam when she really wanted. The affair lasted over a year. It was filled with passionate embraces, wishful thinking, promises, and lies. And in the end Uncle Stanley was conceived. Sam knew. He had to know, didn't he? Stanley was blonde with fair skin. The dentist was blonde and fair skinned. Others might not know, but Sam knew.

5

"Again?! And this time the Navy?" Art had just been drafted for the third time. Vivian was surprised too. "They said you were too old already." "That was last time. Now I'm not too old anymore." This was serious. He owed his job to the fact that the previous foreman was serving in the Army. Now what happens if he's drafted? Will his job be waiting when he came back? If he came back? What about

Viv and Harry? How would they manage? A real mess. He'd have to talk to the boss. He shoved the notice in his pocket, lit the first Philip Morris of the day, and headed for the train.

That's another thing, trudging uphill eight blocks every morning and back again at night to catch the IRT every day. He was going to buy Ida and Aaron's '39 Plymouth, but what's the sense in that if he's going to get drafted? Viv didn't drive. He should probably teach her but with whose car? Passing Montefiore Hospital, he began to limp. "Goddamn back's never been the same since that truck hit me," he thought. "Doctors. The guy told me I'd have problems later, but did he do anything to help? And look at that poor guy." Art glanced at a familiar neighborhood character, a middle-aged man, arms clasped behind his back, besieged by sudden jerks and shrugs, almost leaping off the pavement at times. As Art approached, a quarter the man had been clasping clattered to the ground. Art stopped and tried to retrieve it for him, but was abruptly shoved aside by the sufferer who unsuccessfully attempted to do it himself, thwarted by his own seizures. "What the hell, go ahead, *putz*, have fun."

He tossed the cigarette aside, picked up a copy of *The Daily News* at the newsstand, and climbed the steps to the el. Pain started shooting down his left leg again. "How the hell could I have passed that physical? Not too particular during a World War I guess. What was that old routine? A guy tells the doc, 'My right leg is longer than my left.' 'No problem, where you're going there's no level ground.' 'But doc, I'm blind as a bat.' 'Don't worry, we'll put you right up front. You won't miss a thing.' The 4 train rumbled into the station, and Art stepped inside. He stopped in the doorway to hold the door open for a woman with two kids, one in a stroller, who looked like she might not make it through before the door started closing. Flopping into a seat in a back car, he opened the paper to the sports page to see how the Dodgers were doing. Galan had three hits. Not bad. Yeah, Art lived in the Bronx, but the Bums were his team. He couldn't root for a team like the Yanks who were rich enough to just buy up all the best players.

More commuters crowded in with each stop. Art knew he'd soon surrender his seat. As he finished perusing the box scores, an elderly nun in full habit and rimless eyeglasses appeared before him. Art rose and gave her the seat. Now he was a straphanger, managing to make his way through the tabloid with practiced skill, muscle memory directing his one free hand. The doors opened and more riders poured in, each occupied with his own thoughts, glancing no more than briefly at their neighbor before adopting the required uniform persona of apathy. Now it was getting hot. Art felt sweat running down his back. "Crap, I'll need a shower before I even get out of this train," he mused. Someone opened the door and stepped through to the next car. "Leave it open for the breeze," the guy in the last seat shouted. Art put the paper away now that there was no room for it. A blind man in dark glasses, hat in hand, snaked his way through the car with practiced skill, asking for contributions. He collected a few coins from those who felt charitable and had enough room to reach into their pockets to retrieve some change. Art noticed one guy pressed closely next to a tall attractive woman who was holding on to a pole in the center of the car. The guy banged up against her with every jolt of the train. The woman looked increasingly annoyed. "Cheap thrills are gonna get that guy a smack in the mouth pretty soon," Art thought. He began absent-mindedly reading the ads posted above each window. "The Miss Rheingold contest again. They all look alike, but someone told me one was Jewish." Just then the train lurched abruptly into the 125th Street station. Art was forced to take a sudden step to his right to maintain balance, and he landed hard on the foot of the man next to him. A shout of "Jew bastard!" and a shove in return, the man glares at him, he lands in the lap of a young woman. Art springs up and takes a swing, hitting the guy in the side of his head. Now there is shouting all around. Several men step between the two and help restore order. "Too hot for this shit, calm down." Art couldn't even see the other guy now though he kept peering in his direction, but he could hear him, "Fuckin' sheeny." When he finally caught a glimpse of him, he was near the end of the car backed up against a door, muttering to himself, trying to straighten out his dented, gray fedora. Art straightened his clothes and regained his grip on the strap. Someone handed him his crumpled newspaper.

When the train finally pulled into the 23rd street station, Art jumped out and headed for the staircase. A cool breeze swept over his sweaty body as he climbed to the street. He felt inside his jacket pocket to confirm that his draft notice was still there. "Why you following me?" The voice came from directly behind. Art turned to confront an irate, bedraggled, distracted, black man. "Why you following me?!" "I'm not. How can I be following you if you're in back of me?" The man sneered and stared closely at Art, pressing closer. "Which way are you going?" asked Art, heart pounding. The man pointed south. "Well, I'm going that way." He didn't intend to, but Art quickly took off heading north. "Jesus Christ, I gotta get a car."

6

We got our first TV in 1951, a 12-inch Dumont in a fine wooden console. It was immediately granted a place of honor – a central location in the main room of our third-floor walkup. Proudly perched on the parquet floors, catching the eye of anyone who ventured into the living room/master bedroom, it was easy to believe that this device was about to alter American life as we knew it. Our daily schedule was quickly altered to accommodate TV viewing. Even the overnight test patterns were fascinating to us. Suddenly Grandma Bessie was a more frequent visitor. She needed to watch Kate Smith at 4 pm. Old Mrs. Sarabian from the ground floor made a trip up to our apartment for the first time ever in order to watch Queen Elizabeth's coronation. The Dumont was a prized possession that received prompt attention at the first sign of trouble. Bert the electrician was a frequent figure in our household, hunched over his massive toolkit, peering into the guts of our television, tinkering with tubes and connections, attempting to restore our horizontal and vertical hold. Bert never said much, but he had our complete respect, because he had the knowledge and power to revive our Dumont. All other matters took a backseat; we needed a wizard to bring us Milton Berle once again, and Bert was it.

None of this escaped Art. TV was the key to the future. No better opportunity could present itself now that the hat factory foremanship was in the rear view mirror. Art was a genial guy. He liked people, liked to speak with them, hear their hopes/plans/ideas. He had a knack for communicating with folks of different backgrounds in their own language. In high school, he had become friendly with Negro classmates Johnny Rankin and Fred Flood, fellow sprinters on the track team, and spent time with their families. Coming in contact with many Puerto Ricans in the city, he rapidly picked up vernacular Spanish. Art was a born salesman, and who could move TV's better? So it was that Art got together with Les Altman, a friend from the hat factory, and they decided to pool their savings and open a TV shop, a little store front on University

Avenue. Sure, they'd have to compete against the big boys – Sears & Roebuck and Davega, but they had the personal touch, and were located right in the neighborhood. They were willing to work hard and take losses in the short term, if necessary. But with TV booming, success was inevitable, wasn't it? They were sure they could make it work.

The first sign that it was working came when Art came home with a second TV for our bedroom – not a grand piece of furniture like the Dumont, but a little, portable, 10-inch, RCA, black, plastic box that sat on top of our dresser. Now my younger brother Donnie and I could watch Heckle & Jeckle and Mighty Mouse while bouncing around on one of our beds. We had suddenly become an affluent two-TV household.

The luxurious Dumont was used for family viewing and it was where guests would be invited to watch with us. One night, we were watching wrestling from Capital Arena in Washington, D.C. when Juan Soto, the deliveryman for Art & Les, stopped by. He was invited to sit down and watch TV with us. Me and Donnie were excited, because our favorite antiheroes, the bleached blond Graham Brothers (who were not really brothers), were telling the ringside announcer, Ray Morgan, what they were going to do to their next opponents. "Doctor" Jerry Graham was announcing, "Ray, we're going to pulverize them. We're going to hit them so hard, they'll starve to death before they stop bouncing." The good doctor was referring to Red and Lou Bastein, two other storyline brothers who reminded us of a couple of popular, obnoxious classmates at school. Ray Morgan reminded the good doctor that Lou Bastein was a strapping 250 pounder. "If he was in shape he'd weigh 145," Graham retorted. The fans in the arena hooted, howled, and booed. Some waved wrestling programs and tossed debris at the villains. Others brandished beer bottles and hat pins as weapons. The good doctor was pressing Ray to concur with his disparaging assessment of the Basteins. "When we're through with those two geeks, they'll never show their faces around here again. Am I right or wrong, Ray?" Ray, not wanting to take sides with the heavies but still hoping to move matters along, replied with a desultory "Yeah, yeah, yeah" while nodding his bewigged noggin up and down.

"The kids get all excited about these wrestlers," Art told Juan, as he handed him a glass of the iced coffee Vivian had prepared for the evening. "Oh, yeah, my kids like that too. You know when Argentina Rocca jumps in the air with those high kicks, they go wild." Just then we discovered that the Graham Brothers opponents for the evening were none other than the aforementioned Rocca and his sidekick Miguel Perez. They bounced into the ring, jumping and pumping their fists to acknowledge the cheering of the crowd. "There, that's them!" Juan exclaimed. "My brother took everyone to the Garden to see them last month." "Really?" asked Art. "Oh yeah, he got a discount on the tickets cause he works there part-time."

Ordinarily, me and Donnie would have continued to cheer on the Grahams as they strutted around the ring in their sequin capes, drawing the ire of the angry fans. But we had heard what Juan said, and we didn't want to embarrass Art. So we watched the TV mayhem for a few minutes in relative silence before retreating to the bedroom to listen to the radio. We probably didn't need to do that, because it wasn't long before Art and Juan were ignoring the wrestling, and talking business instead. Just as well, we figured, because Alan Freed was taking requests on WINS-AM, and anyway, better safe than sorry.

Unfortunately, our two-TV affluence was not built on solid ground. It didn't take long before A&L Television realized it was at a distinct disadvantage in the competitive world of commercial electronics.

Art and Les did not begin the enterprise with a great amount of capital. This meant that they could not afford to struggle very long financially while building the business. Walk-in, neighborhood traffic would not keep them afloat for long, and they did not have the ability to advertise in the newspapers or on TV. While they were becoming aware of the likely consequences of this situation, disaster struck.

While taking delivery of new stock, Art's back gave way. It happened as he was trying to move one of those heavy console TV's by himself. Instead of grabbing the green hand truck that stood by the desk at the front of the store, he decided he could maneuver it himself by walking it across the linoleum floor. Art alternately maintained that he either stubbed his foot in a torn piece of linoleum in the flooring, or that his foot slipped on a wet spot. Either way, he lost his balance, and in trying to avoid dropping the TV, he wrenched his back. In great pain, he discovered he couldn't quite straighten up. It turned out he had suffered a slipped disc. He tried to treat it himself with hot baths and painkillers, but it didn't work. He would walk from the subway to the shop each morning, listing noticeably to the left, and sit at the desk in front waiting for customers to show up or the phone to ring.

The pain and the declining fortunes of the business led Art to become something he ordinarily never was – pessimistic. It was a feeling that was new to him, and he didn't know what to do about it. Les, a burly bear of a man, was doggedly determined to stick with it. He was sure that things would turn around if they could just continue to meet their monthly expenses. He also kept telling Art that he shouldn't have been hauling TV's around by himself, that he should have waited for him to come in at noon to move the heavy stuff. Needless to say, Art was not in any mood to hear about how he had screwed up, so arguments ensued. The partnership was fraying along with Art's spinal tissue. Art made one more effort to avoid a trip to the hospital. He visited a chiropractor.

This turned out to be another misstep. Barry Peeler came recommended. He had supposedly cured Uncle Saul's neuralgia as well as his wife's asthma. Also, he was such a nice man. He always wanted to hear about your personal problems as well as your physical ailments, and he was so sympathetic. It was Barry's female patients who appreciated his empathy most. Some signed up for swim lessons that he gave on the side, and it was rumored that many of these lessons were followed by private sessions where Barry offered more intimate services in which his tongue, rather than his hand, was the most therapeutic instrument. Art didn't care about any of that as long as Peeler wasn't screwing around with Saul's wife Tillie. He just wanted his pain alleviated, and if Barry could do that, to hell with the rest.

Peeler was a wide-eyed, soft-spoken, dark-haired man in his late 40's. The hair on his head was curly but thinning. The loss of hair on his head was compensated by copious, black tufts that sprouted from his ears and covered his arms and hands. He affected a manner that resembled an overly-subservient head waiter as he ushered Art into the examination room. He had a soothing voice but frequently mumbled his words as if he lacked the confidence to make any clear assertions. "Back problems can be tricky, Mr. Feldman. It is a back problem, right?"

"That's why I'm here."

Peeler's hands probed the small of Art's back. "Now let me know if there's any pain."

"There's pain."

"Oh, I know. Let me know if there's too much pain. Then I'll stop." Art asked himself "What's too much?" Peeler probed and manipulated while relating the details of a recent trip he took to Europe.

"Twelve countries in ten days, and it only cost me $150."

"How's that possible?"

"Oh, it was run by a religious group. Not for profit."

"How can they stay in business?"

"Well, they cut corners a little. Only vegetarian meals. And you had to attend meetings where they talked about their religion."

"They were trying to convert you."

"Yes, but you don't have to listen. It's worth it, don't you think? And I met a lot of interesting people. One of them was a cousin of Arthur Godfrey. I asked her where he learned to play the ukulele."

At this point, Art realized that the conversation was not going to do much to distract him from the physical discomfort he was undergoing so he called a halt. "Oh, is it too painful? We can take a break. Would you like some Sanka? It's very relaxing."

"I got to get to work. It's getting late."

"OK, well, see how you feel the rest of the day, and call me if you'd like another session. The second one is half price, and if you want a third one…"

"Right."

"And, you know, I really like that sweater. It's very attractive. If you decide to get rid of it, let me know." As Art dressed, Peeler took a call, "No, I packed lunch, but you know what? I forgot my apple. Did you bring an extra orange or banana?"

By the time Art saw a medical doctor, surgery was the only logical option. The disc was in pieces when they removed it, and Art always blamed Peeler and his manipulations. "When they sat me up after the operation, I gave a yell they must've heard all around the hospital." Supposedly, there was going to be a follow-up procedure that was never done, and Art decided to just cut his losses. So what if he leaned a little to the left? He had bills to pay.

7

The TV shop was now in the rearview mirror. Even Les came to believe that it was a losing proposition. It was Les who suggested that they try selling. "Selling what?" Art asked.

"Si is selling pots and pans."

"Hauling around all that crap all the time? You can hear him coming a block away with all that banging in his trunk."

"Yeah, well he's making money."

"What kind of money? I met him at Yankee Stadium sitting in the bleachers with his kid in the 50-cent seats."

"You were there too."

"And he's in the same boat. That's my point."

"How about Hackley? He's selling crucifixes."

"You kidding me? Crucifixes? Ha! Where does Hackley get his merchandise? Do his kids make them in wood shop?"

"I shit you not, he's selling crucifixes, Bibles, and those little statues you put on the dashboard to keep you safe in the car – Saint Christophers or whatever."

"You know there was a nun who had one of those on the dashboard and had a crash, ended up in the hospital. A nurse asked her what good was the saint on the dashboard if she got in an accident anyway. The nun tells her 'If I didn't have it, I would've been killed.'"

"That sounds about right."

Art and Les got themselves invited to sales meeting of the Worldview Encyclopedia Company, a new outfit that had started doing business in the past six months. Art and Les were prospective recruits. Several of the salesmen already on board were either friends, acquaintances, or past associates. This included Itchy Green, an old high school classmate of Art's; Hy Rosenfield, Les's partner in a previous business venture; George Costa, who had worked in the hat factory with Art; and Whitey Connor, Art's closest friend whose high school girlfriend had been Vivian's best friend. They were meeting in the Cuban Casino, a small nightclub on 52nd Street in Manhattan. The company had the conference room reserved. A buffet featured pigs in a blanket, and there was an open bar.

When Art and Les arrived, it was apparent that the drinking was already underway. "Hey, look who's here, what the hell!" It was Itchy, rising from his seat, three-olive martini in hand. Les clapped him on the back, "Holy shit, they let you in here, you little *goniff*?"

"Plant your keester here, Les, I want to set you straight about something. Remember that tip you gave me about the horse at Belmont? He was a dog. Finished out of the running. I lost a bundle." Hy Rosenfeld drifted over, drink in hand. "Hey, Green, how the hell did you get named Itchy?" Les volunteered an answer. "You ever see him with the same dame twice, Hy? The man's got an itch he can never scratch." Green wasn't amused. "It's schmucks like you that can't pronounce my real name. It's Itche with an e. My great grandfather in Poland was the holy Rabbi Itche Greenfield who you *putzes* never heard of I'm sure." Hy was impressed, "Rabbi Itchy! Where do you get this stuff?" Les offered, "Sure I heard of the guy. My grandpa went to his shul. He said the place was covered in poison ivy."

Meanwhile Art had drifted over to George who had been working at Worldview for a couple of months. "George, you're looking sharp." Actually, George might have been sharp when he left his apartment, but his hand-painted tie was now pulled off to one side, his collar was open, his suit jacket was rumpled, and his light brown hair was disheveled. "Artie, Artie, look at you. What are you doin' here? I heard you were movin' TV's."

"That's history. But, hey tell me what's this racket about? You making a living?"

"Sure, we are. We wouldn't be here otherwise. You know me. If I'm not pulling in cash, I'm moving on. Let me tell ya, it's a pretty easy setup. Pretty damn easy." Art settled down next to George with a scotch and soda. "The leads we get are good. People expecting us when we knock on their door, see?" "How about the product?"

"The best, top notch, it sells itself."

"I heard that before."

"No, no kidding. It's a nice set of books."

At this point, Worldview's regional manager, Irv Mandel, entered and called the meeting to order. His son, Mike, pushed in a book cart with a complete, 12-volume set of encyclopedias. Art and Les heard Irv sing the praises of the publication. Irv asserted that Worldview was every bit as good as Britannica. "Don't take my word for it. Ask Mike here. You know Mike is a City College grad. Mike, what do you say?" Mike cited a review from *Publishers Weekly*, named a few colleges nobody heard of that had already ordered sets for their libraries, and said the publishers were up for a reference book award. "There you have it. You're selling a quality product. You can be proud to be associated with Worldview, and we want only the finest sales associates to represent us. "Should I get my tuxedo out of moth balls to make my sales calls?" Les whispered to Art." "Whitey, you tell them. Is there anything you couldn't find in these books? Anything a customer asked for?" Irv shouted. "Not a thing. You can find everything in the index." "Right, and just look at these pictures and charts. Beautiful work." Mike opened a couple of volumes, and Irv had the new prospects inspect them. "A product like this practically sells itself."`

While they were gathered around, Irv started touting the money to be made. "Itchy, you were the top earner last week. What'd you pull in, $600?"

"Yeah, but Hackley beat me." Hy looked around, "Where is Hackley anyway?" George started laughing, "Hackley won't show. He's takin' the money and run." Irv announced, "Hackley is no longer with us." Costa leaned next to Art and explained, "He wrote up a bunch of vacant lots. When we followed up on the leads there was no such address, no buildings there." Art chuckled to himself, a smirk on his face.

"But here's the best part, men. We have leased a fleet of brand new 1956 Chevrolets. Every salesman will be driving a new Bel Air."

"No Corvettes?" The shout came from the back of the room. Attendees laughed to see Sy Lieberman standing in the doorway. He was met with laughter and back-pounding. Sy the *shtarker* was here. Now the crew was complete. Mandel took this moment to break the news that there would be no salaries. Salesmen would work strictly on commission. Ordinarily, this might have been a deal breaker, but hey, the new Chevy, Costa said it's an easy pitch, and Si is here. Art and Les were sold.

8

Antisemitism waxed and waned in Romania over the centuries, as it did in most of Europe. Stephen the Great (1457-1517) and Vasile Lupu (1595-1661) were tolerant of the Jewish communities which had existed in what is now Romanian territory since the second century. Jews were allowed to take part in commercial activity, and individual Jews such as Isaac ben Benjamin Shor (chancellor to Stephen the Great) and Isaiah ben Joseph (counselor to Alexandru II Mircea) were able to rise to positions of prominence and influence. More common, however, were incidents like the blood libel of 1710 when Jews in Moldavia were accused of the ritual murder of a Christian child; the massacres of Jews during the Russo-Turkish War of 1768-1774; and the pogroms during the Wallachian Uprising of 1821.

With the ascension to power of Ion Bratianu (1821-1891), antisemitism received official sanction. Jews were forbidden to settle in the countryside while urban Jews could be considered vagrants subject to expulsion. The Treaty of Berlin (1878) ending the Russo-Turkish War mandated citizenship for Jews in Romania, and the Bratianu government grudgingly complied. Jewish leaders Moses Gaster (1856-1939) and Elias Schwarzfeld (1855-1915) tried to leverage this opening, hoping to achieve a general civic emancipation for Romanian Jews. Their efforts resulted only in their expulsion seven years later. An 1893 piece of legislation deprived Jewish children of a public school education, and five years later Jews were banned from secondary schools and universities. Romania had Liberal and Conservative political parties, but both were anti-Semitic.

Ironically, one aspect of Jewish life in Romania thrived in the late nineteenth century – Yiddish theater. Playwright Abraham Goldfaden (1840-1908) founded the first Yiddish theater company in the city of Jassy in 1876. Israel Feldman, an itinerant roofer, was employed to help build sets. His wife Zina sewed many of the costumes. Their son Yussel grew up among actors, singers, and directors. Israel's ancestors had lived in Romania for over 200 years, migrating south from Poland following the Chmielnicki massacres of 1648-'55. The lives these ancestors led were centered around the synagogues and study houses. Their daily routines were regulated by the dictates of religious stricture. While Israel still considered himself an observant Jew, his work had taken him as far as Bucharest, and he had met people who had traveled to Warsaw and Paris. He knew there were places where opportunities were greater, even if he was not in position to take advantage of them. If Jews had been permitted to work within Romania's organized guild system, things might have been different. But that was like imagining there would be an eventual end to the periodic pogroms and massacres. Experience had taught him otherwise.

Israel had heard that the Yiddish theater was looking for someone with carpentry skills. This bit of information reached him through Isaac Mandelbaum, a local grocer whose son worked for Goldfaden as a bookkeeper. Israel was no carpenter, but he knew his way around a hammer and saw and he was given the job. A short while later, Zina, whose family members were all tailors, became the company's seamstress. Young Yussel liked having his father around more often, and he especially enjoyed hearing all the stories told by the Yiddish actors and singers. Many of them had been to Paris and London.

Several of Yussel's boyhood friends were members of The General Association of Native Israelites, an organization that lobbied aggressively for assimilation. In 1897, however, Yussel watched as the group's congress was attacked by anti-Semitic gangs. His friend, Abraham Sorkin, suffered broken ribs. Riots ensued in Bucharest. Yussel had seen and heard enough. In the fall of 1900, he scraped together what funds he could, said his farewells to family, and set off for western Europe. He traveled by train as far as Krakow, then joined groups of fellow Jews who made their way on foot to Hamburg. From there, the Elbe River showed him a route to England. By 1902, he had made his way to the U.S.

Yussel officially became Joseph when he passed through immigration proceedings at Ellis Island. Fortunately, Yussel was in good health and passed the physical examination without any difficulty. Yussel pitied those he observed who were not so fortunate. He could easily sympathize with those facing the possibility of being sent back after having endured such an arduous journey. He was also thankful that his family name remained somewhat intact. He had heard stories about how immigration officials in America had mangled the names of many immigrants because they couldn't understand or pronounce names in foreign languages. Yussel saw some of these officials laughing and joking about something. He imagined that they were ridiculing some would-be immigrant, his appearance, his poverty, his language. One of his fellow immigrants who spoke good English told Yussel that one of the officials was saying that trying to pronounce some of these names could dislocate your jaw. Apparently, Feldman didn't present such a problem, and Yussel survived with his family name intact. Years later, Yussel was able to laugh at the story about a Jewish immigrant passing through Ellis Island who was asked his name by an immigrant official for what seemed like the 100th time. Frustrated, he replied in Yiddish *shoyn fargesn* meaning "forgot already." Hearing this reply, the official bestowed upon him the Irish moniker "Sean Ferguson" and that became his legal American name for the rest of his life.

He may have become Joseph to officials, but he was still Yussel among his relatives on Manhattan's lower east side where he took up residence. He worked at a series of odd jobs – sweeping out a grocery store, helping a pushcart peddler, carrying blocks of ice – until he saved enough money to buy his own sewing machine and shearing scissors. Then he did piece work on his own in his room while working in sweatshops on Delancey and Eldridge Streets for years until he could afford to move to the Bronx. During brief lunch breaks he ate meager meals he had packed himself – salami and bread, leftover borscht from a meal at a neighbor's house, potato and onion pierogis purchased at a local market. He spoke with them about local restaurants where one could really feast while celebrating special occasions: Katz's Delicatessen on Houston Street for kosher corned beef and pastrami and Ratner's Dairy Restaurant on Pitt Street where one could chow down on cheese blintzes, onion rolls, and potato pancakes. Yussel also began to improve his English by speaking with other workers who had been in America longer, and in his oral transactions with his supervisors. He worked twelve-hour days, six days a week. There was little time remaining for anything but work, but he still managed to occasionally attend a lecture or a labor organizer's meeting. All the while he put away money, savings from his salary. He had plans, hopes, and dreams.

One of his co-workers, Adam Rappaport, had a sister in Romania who was interested in coming to America. He showed Yussel her picture. Yussel liked what he saw. "Why don't you write her a letter to introduce yourself?"

"What are you, a marriage broker? Do you collect a fee?" They laughed. "Look, you're a young man, a good worker. I like you. I wouldn't show my sister's picture to just anybody. Don't you want to settle down with a fine woman, and raise a family? What have you got to lose?" Yussel was interested but he couldn't see himself writing a letter to a stranger. So Adam got his sister to write first. About a month letter, Yussel was surprised to receive her letter. It was in pretty good Yiddish. It was polite and self-deprecating. And she sent another even prettier photo with her name written at the bottom – Chana Rappaport.

"Greetings, Mr. Yussel Feldman. I am happy to meet you. My brother tells me you are a good friend to him in America. I know only a little about American life from what Adam tells me. I haven't traveled, and I don't have a high education. But I would like to see America for myself someday. Until now, I have been thinking about moving to Palestine. My late father, of Blessed Memory, was a member of the Yishuv Eretz Israel. They helped many Jews from Romania move to Palestine so they could find a safe life. My father even gave me a Hebrew name. My mother was called Scheine Rivka, but she started using the Hebrew name Rivka alone to show that we are a Zionist family. But I think maybe America could be a good place to live too. Could you tell me about yourself and your plans in America to give me an idea of what it could be like living there? If you have a photo to send me too that would be very nice. I am looking forward to hearing from you. I am sending you one of me with this letter. I hope you like it. Best regards, Chana Rappaport."

Yussel was impressed. He noted that Chana lived not far from his parent's home in Jassy. He wrote and asked his parents if they might be able to learn more about Chana and her family. When Adam asked Yussel if he had received Chana's letter, Yussel answered in the affirmative, and told him he had written his parents. "Well, that sounds good, but why didn't you ask me if you had questions? Didn't you think I'd tell you the truth?"

"When you make a big purchase, you want all opinions. No offense, Adam, but you being her brother, well...a mother and father sometimes see different things. You understand." Yussel tapped Adam on his chest and smiled. Adam laughed. "Well, anyway, it seems like things are moving along." And they were, rather quickly.

Yussel's parents paid a visit to Chana's home, and were welcomed by Chana and her mother. They learned that Chana's father had passed on a couple of years before from a lung ailment leaving Chana and two younger brothers. The Feldmans were well-received. The home was small but neatly maintained. Israel asked about a couple of photos on the wall. Rivka explained that the one on the left was of her late husband Meir taken shortly before they were married, and the other was of Lippe Karpel, physician and founder of Romania's Zionist organization. The photo of Meir depicted a dark bearded man with a hooked nose frowning into the camera, perhaps because of the strong sunshine. His head was bare except for a skull cap which covered close-cropped, dark hair. He wore knee-high boots that were soiled with mud, and his right hand was clenched around what appeared to be reins attached presumably to a horse. "That photograph of my husband was taken on a farm in

Dancu. That's a village east of here. Meir was a bookkeeper, but he knew that he must learn skills that would make him useful in Palestine. So he offered to help a farmer plough his fields. Oh, that was hard work for him. He came home so sweaty and dirty. I didn't think he would last at first. You can see how tired he looks there. But he stayed with it. He would always say, 'When I get tired, I rest. I don't quit.' And he never did. He became a pretty good farmer, I think. Too bad he never got a chance to use what he learned in the Holy Land."

"Did all that work make him ill?" Israel asked.

"No, the illness came from his bookkeeping work. Isn't that funny? They hired a new man who was always coughing. How could they do that? I told Meir to stay away from him, but he had to work with him. Sure enough, the disease spread quickly. Many people in the company caught it. Poor man, he didn't last very long. Three or four months and it was all over. We had doctors and we prayed but nothing helped. That was two and a half years ago. And what do you think? The man who started it all is still working there. Still coughing too. Sometimes I think there is no justice in this world, you know what I mean?" Zina noticed that Chana seemed uncomfortable when her mother spoke about her father's illness.

"That must have been very hard on you and the children," she said.

"Yes, may you never know such sorrow. But at least Meir didn't die in debt. He always paid his own way. Meir's brother helps us out. And we have a garden. I sell vegetables at the market. And I always cook extra to sell to the factory workers at lunch time. I have a lot of regular customers."

"One in particular," Chana added.

"Oh, now you be quiet." Rivka explained later that she was seeing a gentleman at a local tannery, and that it might lead to marriage. "Who knows?"

"Why not?" said Zina. "You're still young and attractive."

"You're very kind," replied Rivka.

Israel was favorably impressed by what he saw and how he and Zina were treated. Rivka served them currant wine with egg cookies and tea from the family samovar, and insisted on sending them home with a pot of her homemade cholent. Zina didn't want to take the pot but Rivka insisted. "You can return it the next time you visit."

"No, you must come see us. I will return it then. I will cook a nice fat goose." Chana was quiet but graciously answered any questions posed to her. Occasionally Rivka would ask Chana to tell the guests about her skills, how she helped prepare Sabbath meals for the family and made some of her own clothes. Chana seemed a bit embarrassed but dutifully complied with her mother's requests. When Israel and Zina returned home, they discussed their impressions. Zina thought Chana too quiet. "We couldn't find out much about her."

"She's shy. It's only natural."

"But why does she want to go to America?" "Why did Yussel want to go? What is there here for young Jews?"

"Do you think she will be good for Yussel?

"Why not?"

"Oh, I don't know. It's just such a big decision and Yussel is so young."

"He's 23, the same age I was when we were married."

"That's so, isn't it?" Israel nodded.

"And I was 21. But we didn't ask how old Chana is."

"She's young, she's young. Did she look like an old maid to you?" In fact, Chana was just 19. Zina's doubts did not prevent them from communicating to Yussel their overall positive impressions. Yussel had the reply he was hoping for, and from that point on Yussel was determined to bring Chana over to join him in New York.

Rivka had some misgivings after the Feldmans' visit when she learned that Israel was connected to the theatrical community. She associated the profession with impiety and unbecoming, ostentatious forms behavior. She had to admit, however, that she didn't detect any such signs in Israel, maybe because he wasn't one of the performers onstage. Israel had made favorable references to religious practices and had expressed regret that he and Zina would be unable to see the children stand beneath the *chupa*, and this was to his credit. In addition, he seemed like a pleasant, hardworking man. However, Rivka did have reservations about Chana's willingness to consider forsaking her Palestine plans so easily. "I'm not forgetting about Palestine, mama. I haven't made up my mind yet. It's just that I want to find out more about America, so I can really decide for myself. Besides, wouldn't it be nice to be close to Adam again?"

"You need to find out more about Yussel too, don't you?" Chana blushed a bit.

"Of course, mama. That's the most important thing." None of the doubts Zina later expressed to Israel were apparent to Rivka during their visit. In fact, Rivka was left with the belief that Zina was entirely agreeable to the match. Rivka decided to suspend judgement for the moment. She found it difficult to openly disagree with a daughter who was so sensible and self-possessed as Chana. She wasn't sure that really wanted to in any case, because Chana was so often correct in her assessment of such matters anyway.

It wasn't long before Yussel's letter arrived.

"Miss Chana Rappaport, Hello from New York. I enjoyed your letter very much and thank you for taking the time to tell me about yourself and your family. Adam speaks to me about you very often, and it is always good things that he tells me. I also want to thank your mother, Rivka, for welcoming my parents into her home. They had a very nice time, and have only good things to say. I can tell you something about life here in New York. There are many Jews like us from all over Europe, and many Jewish shops and restaurants. In that way, it isn't too different from home. But life isn't all easy. It takes hard work to get ahead here, and that means long days of work and not too much rest. But we are young, and we can plan for a better life in the future. There is a lot of opportunity for those who are willing to work and save. And families here can see a better future for their children. I am sending you a photo that your brother Adam took of me with a camera he borrowed from a friend. I don't think it's the best picture but it will give you some idea of how I look. I look taller in real life, and my hair is neater. The wind was blowing that day. I hope to hear from you again soon. Yussel Feldman."

Accordingly, the following year Chana joined Yussel. Her official name was now Claire. Yussel opened his own small shop, and began to raise a family. The sign over his door proclaimed it to be the establishment of Joseph Feldman, Custom Tailor. On opening day he fired up the old samovar that had accompanied him from

Romania, and offered a glass of tea to everyone who stepped across the threshold.

Joseph knew the advantages of advertising, and he would have flyers printed up offering discounts on custom-made suits and slacks. He enlisted his sons to distribute them throughout the neighborhood. Artie was especially energetic in his endeavors, and did not shy away from passing out the material right in front of competitors' businesses. One tailor on Fox Street would grab his broom whenever he saw Art coming, rush out to the street, and chase him away shouting, "Get outta here Little Yussel!" Artie liked being identified with his father, the custom tailor, and he wasn't deterred. He would show up again and again, especially since he was small and usually able to give out quite a few flyers before he was even noticed. Later on he learned that the man who chased him with a broom was Mendel Sheiner, a tailor known throughout the neighborhood for making special arrangements with women who could not afford to pay him in cash. He would visit them at night when their husbands weren't around to collect what was owed him.

Art always figured that he was his mother's favorite. This was because Chana would always call him by his Hebrew name, Avram. All the other children she would call by their English names. Sometimes she would go through all her other son's names before she got to Artie, who she intended to summon in the first place. It would sound like, "Solly, Saul, Davey,....AVRAM!" Even Art's brothers agreed that Chana liked Art best. Maybe it had to do with the way he saved little Davey from getting hit by that truck, but it probably went back further than that since by that time she was already calling the brothers by their English names. All except Artie. He would always be Avram.

There was one memory that lingered from Artie's childhood dwarfing all the others. It was the day he came home from the hospital, and the neighborhood threw him a block party. "Who's that? What's all the fuss?" asked Mrs. Rosen the *yenta*, eyeing the crowd with balloons and homemade signs.

"You don't know? It's Yussel the tailor's boy. He's a hero," Burton the beadle informed her. Sol pushed Artie down the street in a wheelchair as the crowd clapped and cheered. "Look at that," Burton said.

"What?" asked Mrs. Rosen.

"That's Ben Bloom."

"Who's Ben Bloom?"

"Ben Bloom, who writes for *The Forverts*. The kid's gonna be in the newspaper." As Artie sat back, his left leg in a cast up to his hip, somewhat abashed, smiling, accepting the plaudits, some little girl came up and dropped a fistful of dandelions in his lap. They were loose and soon scattered, but a few remained with him till the end of the day.

Funny, Art remembers the party, the tables full of food – *kishka* and *kasha varnishkes*, his favorites - the friends and neighbors who praised him and wished him well, but he couldn't recall running into the street to push his brother Davey out of the path of that truck. That was a complete blank. He knew he did it, because everyone told him so. He sure knew the consequences – all that time in the hospital, the many weeks before he could walk again. But not remembering the whole thing made him feel strange. Nothing like that had ever happened to him before. It was like the story of his life was interrupted and then started again. One thing he learned, though. If good stuff was happening, like the party, don't think about it too much. Just go with it. Artie was greeted by many people that day. Some he knew, others looked familiar but he didn't really know them, and still others were complete strangers. But they all shook his hand, patted him on the shoulder, and wished him well. Artie looked over the gathering and was impressed by the size of the crowd. So many people and he was the center of attention. He could understand family and friends turning out, but why so many people he didn't know? He couldn't know that among those interested strangers was someone he would come to know very well. Attracted by the commotion, little Vivian Simonson from Hoe Avenue had wandered over. She had a hard time peering over and around all the people, so she never actually found out what it was about. But she liked that everyone seemed so friendly and welcoming, and she especially liked the colored balloons.

9

Chana knew that when she left for America, she would be saying goodbye to her mother and two younger brothers for a very long time. She didn't know it would be forever. There were occasional letters that arrived from Jassy, updating Chana on life back in Romania, and fewer ones in return from Chana who was ever busy birthing and raising seven children. Chana's brother Itzhak, 12 years old when she left, entered the military during WWI. "Why would he do that?" Chana wondered. She wrote to her mother asking why, but she never received a clear answer. Did he want to go? Was he forced? Did he want to prove that Jews were loyal Romanians? That Jews could be strong fighters too? She never found out. In 1918 she learned that he did not survive the war. What had his life been like in the army? How exactly did he die? She wanted to return to comfort her mother, but she had six children by then and little financial means. Besides, what good would it really do? There would need to be another emotional leave taking, and the long trip back.

Rivka's letters became less frequent after that. Chana imagined her mother as an old woman now. Maybe she was slowing down. Could she be ill? Maybe that's why she didn't write as often. Moshe, Chana's youngest brother, took his lead from his sister. He had always wanted to go to Palestine. Whenever Rivka mentioned him in her letters, she indicated that his Zionist ideals were intact. But for some reason Moshe stayed in Romania. Chana received one letter from him in 1920 in which he said that he was working as a jeweler's apprentice and planning to get married. Then no further news until 1938 when she received a letter from Moshe telling her of Rivka's death. Chana wrote back asking for details. No reply. Then WWII was on. The next time Chana heard from Moshe in 1945 he was living in the Soviet Union with his wife and two children. He had fled eastward in the previous year when Soviet troops invaded.

Chana's older brother Adam provided some comfort. He lived nearby and would visit regularly. When Itzhak and Rivka died, they mourned together. But Adam had lost contact with the family in Romania long ago. He didn't keep in touch. He had no information to offer Chana. He couldn't fill in any gaps. Even worse, from Chana's point of view, he didn't seem to care very much. He had rid himself of the old world, and didn't want to think about it anymore. Good riddance to all that as far as he was concerned. He had rushed to become a real American, learning English quickly. It even seemed to Chana that he was in a hurry to shed his religion as well, as if being Jewish made him less American. When Adam married a year after Chana arrived in New York, he chose an Irish girl. Oh, she was nice enough, but still, who would have thought? Adam and a *shikse*. And what about their children? Would they be raised as Jews? That turned out not to be an issue. Adam's wife Molly suffered two miscarriages after which there were no further pregnancies.

Despite her misgivings about Adam's behavior, Chana's was pleased that her children were crazy about their uncle, and Adam, childless, saw himself almost as a second father to them. Adam always brought joy into the house as soon as he crossed the threshold. "How's my favorite sister and her favorite husband? Look at this one! Can this be my little nephew, so big already? Where's my gorgeous niece?" Always ready with a present or two or some flowers or a bottle of schnapps. Always enjoying himself at the top of his voice. Chana would place her hands over her ears as if to muffle the raucous arrival, but there was a smile on her lips. Yussel would open the bottle of slivovitz, and after a couple of drinks Adam would really get rolling. He liked to joke that Molly didn't have the capacity to fully appreciate Jewish cooking. Molly would protest, insisting that she loved Chana's cooking. Chana would let Molly know that she rejected her brother's instigation: "No, no, a *meshugganah*." But the one time that Molly came down with the runs after a meal of borscht and *kishke*, Adam announced in triumph, "See? What did I tell ya? Eats like a bird and shits like a horse!" Chana hit him over the head with a dish towel while Yussel roared. For weeks she had to discipline the boys who ran around the apartment repeating Uncle Adam's latest gem.

Household duties kept Chana occupied from morning till night. There was little time to reflect on matters other than family and daily life. How many hours did she spend patching clothes, emptying pants pockets of bottle caps, chalk, and string before doing the wash, deciding whose hand-me-downs would go to which child next? How often did she have to enforce household discipline? That time she found a pocket knife in Saul's jacket? The threat to tell Yussel was a convenient weapon, but it almost always came down to Chana making it clear that they were not raising any hoodlums in this family. Sometimes though, as she watched Yussel go out into the business world every day, interact with the public, become proficient in English, and come home with stories to tell about his customers, she wondered at times how things might have been different had she followed another path. True, it wasn't as if she was completely isolated. She had many friends and neighbors with whom she shared a similar existence. In fact, if anything, there were times when she wished that she was not forced to share so much with her fellow apartment dwellers on Intervale Avenue. Everyone had big families, and their activities were no secret to anyone on the street. Conversations and arguments echoed through the halls and alleyways all times of the day and night. Rarely did her sons' friends knock on the door when they came to visit. No, one would hear their shouts bellowing up from the street below, "Hey, Artie, come on down. We got a game going in the schoolyard!"

It was the boys who occupied most of Chana's time. They were the ones always coming home with shredded clothing and bruised knees. Oh, they weren't bad boys, just a little wild like all the rest. Their school reports were OK, what she could understand of them. She tried visiting the school once or twice because the children wanted her to, but the teachers didn't speak Yiddish, and she could do little but smile and nod her head at whatever it was they were trying to communicate to her. They weren't angry, so she assumed everything was OK. The girls were less trouble, maybe because Yussel kept them on such a short leash. He liked to show off his daughters, especially blonde-haired Rita. Most of the men valued sons more, but Yussel favored his girls. Maybe if Chana had never gotten around to birthing sons, Yussel wouldn't have been entirely satisfied with his daughters alone. Maybe then Yussel would have suffered a loss of face. But as it turned out, there was no problem. The three girls were followed by four straight boys. Now Yussel had his beautiful daughters and his sturdy sons to perpetuate his name and say kaddish for him.

Chana recalled when her first son Solomon was born. Yussel and Adam were gathered with the rabbi, the mohel, friends and neighbors for the ceremonial bris, or circumcision. While waiting for the rabbi to begin the ritual, Adam and other neighborhood kibitzers couldn't help but remark on baby Sol's alert appearance and active, grasping hands. "Look at those little fingers, so long for a newborn," said Adam. "You know what that means."

"What?" asked Yussel, anticipating a humorous response.

"A born pickpocket!" That got the crowd going as shouts and shoves accompanied the laughter. Molly's admonishment did nothing to rein in Adam who went on to assert that he never had any need for this kind of procedure when he arrived on the scene.

"What are you, a *goy*?" asked an attendee.

"No, I was born *fermoheled*!"

"Sure he was! He's the *moshiach* come to lead us to the Holy land! Didn't you know?" shouted a voice from the back of the room. The rabbi labored in vain to regain control of the situation. Chana thought someone would certainly need to blow the shofar now if they wanted to ever get this ceremony under way.

Decorum eventually prevailed, and the deed was done. Baby Solomon was given a piece of gauze dipped in wine to suck on after the circumcision was completed, and it quickly ended his crying. "He appreciates good kosher wine, God bless him."

"He's a fine boy, Yussel, he'll do you proud;"

"A nice head of hair for such a little fellow" were heard as Yussel accepted congratulations all around. Someone had apparently already had too much to drink and was heard to shout "Next year in Jerusalem!"

"Listen to him," Adam remarked, "he thinks it's Passover already. Hey, Shmuel, idiot, it's not even Tu Bishvat yet!" And so the oldest boy's bris was concluded. Three more were to follow in the coming years. Chana now had daughters Rita, Ida, and Fran to help her welcome guests and serve refreshments. True, they probably spent more time darting in and out of the apartment and playing with neighbors' daughters than they did actually hosting the event, but their presence made Chana feel good, even if she had to constantly remind them that this was an important occasion that required they be on their best behavior.

The Great Depression hit the Feldmans hard, as one would expect. The services of a custom tailor were not a priority for folks trying to figure out where their next meal was coming from. The five Feldman children who were still living at home worked part-time jobs after school whenever they could find them. Still it was hard to make ends meet. Yussel decided that the family's financial survival required that one of the children contribute a regular salary. Chana demurred at first. "It's not right to make them sacrifice their education, Yussel."

"Right and wrong have nothing to do with it when it's a matter of keeping a roof over your head." It was always difficult for Chana to argue with Yussel. She had accepted the fact that he would be the one to make the most consequential decisions from the beginning. But she could make him see certain facts. "We can't make Saul work. It would be bad for his health. He just got over the grippe, and you know what the doctor said about his lungs being weak." Yussel acknowledged the truth of those remarks. "And Fran is a scatter brain. Who would hire her? Besides she will graduate in a few months. Maybe she'll marry after that and be out of the house." Chana was eliminating Yussel's options pretty quickly.

"Yes, yes, and of course Davey's too young. So that means Arthur will have to leave school and get a fulltime job," asserted Yussel. Chana knew it would come down to Avram. "Little Yussel" had been her husband's go-to guy from the time he could walk, spreading the word about the family's tailor shop by leafletting the neighborhood, helping out in the store after school, always working part time jobs. Fast and efficient, he got the job done. Avram the worker. That's how Yussel saw him. But to Chana he was something special. There was some connection there she didn't have with the others. Oh, she loved them all, and they were good children. But the way Avram looked at her was different. She couldn't say exactly what it was, but it was there, no mistake. And now he would have to make the sacrifice and leave school.

Sacrifices were not unexpected. Chana knew there were always necessary adjustments to be made throughout life. You tried to make the right choice, but you always discovered that you needed to give up something along the way. All the children found jobs, married, and raised families of their own. But how would things have been different if they all could have gone to college? As it turned out, only David went, and look how well he did. He became a civil engineer and very well-to-do. David was also the only boy to serve in the military, and because of his education he was a surveyor. He didn't have to kill anyone or be killed himself, God forbid. This is what was wonderful about America, Chana thought. Thank God he returned from the war safe and sound. But how come he married Ellie Goldfarb, the one everybody talked about on the street? He could choose anybody and he chooses her? They say opposites attract. Is that it? He so quiet and smart, she so loud and *prust*. Ah, well, she has a good heart. If Davey likes her, that's what counts. And they're raising some nice kids. May they all live and be well.

Insulated from the old age-old troubles in Europe, Chana thought little about the plight of Jews until the approach of WWII. Yussel followed events more closely, reading the Yiddish papers, but Chana listened to his nightly commentary at the dinner table with only half an ear. Usually, she was preoccupied with the more practical matters over which she exercised some control. That was until Hitler began his march across Europe. They had seen and heard of pogroms in the past, but this was a threat on a much larger scale. "He must be stopped or we face catastrophe," Yussel declared. Chana was especially alarmed by reports of what was happening in Romania. "Thank God my mother didn't live to see what's happening there." She was referring to the rise of Ion Antonescu whose rabid antisemitism exceeded even Hitler's in many respects. When news of the massacre at Iassy by Antonescu's Iron Guard became known, Chana was grief stricken. How many of those killed were old relatives or neighbors of those she had known? How could something like this happen? What was the world coming to?

Yussel clung to his faith in socialism. He felt somewhat vindicated when Antonescu was captured by the Soviet army at the end of the war and executed. "Your brother Moshe did the right thing going to Russia. Stalin is no saint but the working man has a chance there." Shortly before his death, Yussel had soured on life in Russia. David had traveled to Europe after he retired and met one of Moshe's sons in Russia. When he returned, he told his father that consumer goods were in short supply there and services poorly provided. Moshe's son related a popular anecdote about someone who he had ordered a car and was asked if he wanted a standard shift or automatic. "Automatic," he said.

"Do you want it in white or black?"

"White."

"You pay now and delivery will be in two years."

"Is that morning or afternoon?"

"What's the difference?"

"I have a plumber scheduled in the morning."

Yussel smiled and shook his head. The point was well-taken. The Soviet Union was no worker's paradise. Far from it. And the revolution had not ended antisemitism. Look at all the Jews who had helped the revolution succeed only to be purged by Stalin. Still, he could not help but think that things would have been different if Trotsky had taken control as he rightfully should have. Yussel had attended Trotsky's 1917 speech in Greenwich Village shortly before the Bolsheviks seized power. There was a brilliant man, a real thinker, a speaker who could command an audience, a man of action - not a glorified bookkeeper and thug like Stalin. He had the vision and the plan that could have succeeded in building socialism everywhere, Yussel believed. Why didn't enough Americans see the truth of the situation? It didn't matter to Yussel. He was right to support Eugene Debs in his presidential campaigns. So Stalin won. Trostky was killed. The ideal still lived. Let them laugh when he stuck with Norman Thomas and the Socialist Party when so many voted for FDR. All that was good about the New Deal was stolen from the socialists. Yussel lived to collect his Social Security and benefit from Medicare, socialism in action as he thought of it.

10

Art didn't know that much of his selling with Worldview would take him out of town, but that was turning out to be the case. His Bel Air was racking up the miles: Virginia, North Carolina, Tennessee, Florida. Who was writing all these leads out of town, and why in the South? It turned out that Worldview executives had identified southern, rural blacks as prime customers. The Civil Rights Movement was in its infancy, but there was a general sentiment that change was coming. Black families were very interested in providing educational opportunities for their children, and an affordable encyclopedia was something they wanted to have in their home. So, here was this New York Jew driving into the Deep South, New York plates on his new car, asking local rednecks where Elmer Jackson lived.

"Elmer? Elmer Jackson? Hey, Doobie, get out here! Do we know any Elmer Jackson?" A slack-jawed, gum chewing, round-shouldered, Gomer Pyle lookalike slouched his way out from under a jacked up jalopy in the back of the Texaco station.

"Elmer? You mean that spook Nappy who lives out in Nigger Town?"

"That must be the one."

"Who wants to know?"

"This here gent. Now what do you want to be botherin' Ol Nappy for? He minds his own business. You don't mean to tell me he's expectin' some stranger to pay him a visit." Doobie scoped out Art's car as the manager lectured. "Now we don't look kindly on outsiders comin' on down here uninvited to bother our local folks."

"Hey, looky here Abner! This here stranger's from New York."

"Is that so? You come here all the way from New York? Well, you know, Nappy comes by here regular. We can tell him you lookin' for him. You got a business card or somethin'?" Art wrote his name and hotel number on the back of a Worldview business card, and passed it to Abner who squinted at the handwriting. "Feldman? Ain't that a Jew name? Don't it sound that way to you, Doobie?"

"Sure does to me."

"Now you're a New York Jew comin' down here askin' 'bout niggers? Goddamn, what are you tryin' to do, cause trouble? We don't need no troublemakers from New York down here."

Art headed back to his car. "Hey, you need some gas or oil. We can help you out with that. Don't mind takin' some Jew money, do we Doobie? Ha, ha!"

"Sure don't. Hey, Abner, you know what a Jew is? Nothin' but a nigger turned inside out!" After that Art made it a point to get directions from a post office or bank. The personnel there might have harbored similar sentiments, but perhaps they were more inhibited by virtue of the official capacities in which they served. In any case, he usually received the information he requested without being verbally abused. Once he succeeded in making contact with potential customers, he was pleased to discover that despite the often ramshackle conditions in which they lived, a fair share of them placed orders for the encyclopedia. The fact that business was good made the long trips worthwhile.

11

Art never really thought that the images of clownish, racist oafs that were often depicted in novels or on the silver screen were necessarily accurate, but some of the experiences he was now having made him think again. Of course, hateful episodes did not predominate. He encountered many southerners who appeared fair and welcoming. He even met some southern Jews.

He had never given much thought to the notion that there was a substantial Jewish population south of the Mason Dixon Line. But when he stopped by a department store in Knoxville one day to shop for a few gifts, he met the manager, Reuben Arnstein, grandson of one of the founders of the city's Jewish community. Art was looking at some scarves, trying to pick out one for Vivian when a tall, slim, well-dressed, young woman with large brown eyes sidled over. "Can I help you?" Art explained that he was looking for a gift for his wife. "What kind of a woman is she, I mean, does she like bold colors and designs? Then she might like our new sunny Italian line." She showed Art some samples from the rack, holding them up against her long neck. Art allowed that they were attractive, and was thinking that she was as well.

A short, smiling blonde appeared behind the counter and asked if she could assist the customer. "It's OK Beverly, I'm not busy." It turned out that Art was being helped by Joan Arnstein, Assistant Manager and Reuben's daughter. When Art told her he was a salesman from New York, Joan said that he ought to meet her father and invited him to dinner. The offer was readily accepted.

Art was impressed by the wood-panneled Victorian home on toney Hanes Avenue. He was even more taken with Reuben Arnstein and his daughter. Reuben, a leading retailer in the city, was also a civic leader and benefactor, occupying seats on numerous boards and charities. He was pleased to recount how his grandfather, on his way to Birmingham to peddle agricultural supplies in 1878, decided instead to set up business in Knoxville. "Were there any Jews here?" Art asked.

"A very small community." Art asked if his family faced any prejudice. "Oh, sure, some. But attitudes change a bit once you're successful. They might still dislike you or distrust you, but they get used to dealing with you. And some might even learn to like you."

Just then, Reuben's wife Elaine entered from the kitchen directing one of the servants who was holding a large platter of beef brisket with stewed carrots. Art's wide eyes and smile did not go unnoticed by Reuben. "A traditional *shabbos* meal, Art, with a southern touch – a shot or two of I.W. Harper in the gravy, right Elaine?" Elaine laughed out loud.

"Don't believe him. A little local red wine is all. With bourbon, Reuben would be under the table by the end of dinner."

"Hardly," Reuben retorted, "Alcohol doesn't affect me."

"Oh no?" Elaine said, "How about the time you had that two-day hangover from a slice of rum cake?" Art recognized the dialogue from a Jackie Gleason Honeymooners episode, and he felt comfortable in a home where the family members felt free to joke with each other in front of a guest. Joan smiled cautiously during the conversation, interested to see how Art would take everything. Art wasn't too busy to notice her interest.

12

Art's time on the road wore on Vivian. Harry was twenty years old, and working in a Manhattan brokerage firm. When work was finished, he stayed in Manhattan to unwind. He came home to our Bronx apartment to sleep, and he would help out financially, if necessary, but he wasn't a regular presence in the family. He didn't personify the "man of the house" image required by 1950's culture, especially in the absence of the actual husband and father. But maybe Vivian didn't want that anyway. She had fought hard for her independence, first from Sam Simonson's petty tyrannies. Marriage was the escape route. But the life of a housewife and motherhood presented unanticipated complications.

Vivian was good at establishing regular household routines. On Saturday morning she dropped off the laundry at a full-service laundromat that would have it ready for pickup later in the day. Then she headed for Jerome Avenue to do the food shopping. Me and Donnie would follow along. We would notice some kids heading for the shul on DeKalb Avenue to attend junior congregation, and be glad that we weren't among them. I already had started Hebrew School there weekdays which effectively extended the regular school day another couple of hours. If I had to spend Saturday mornings there too, what would be left of the weekend? When would I have time to scan the newspaper's sport pages to find out which college football teams were playing, watch or listen to the games, and meticulously write down the halftime and final scores on notebook paper? These documents I stored in 8X11 envelopes along with New York Yankee baseball scorecards, ticket stubs, and Golden Glove boxing programs that Art brought home after a night out with the boys. Donnie needed time to create his pencil-illustrated comic books on his drawing tablets, and scan AM radio for regional top 40 rock and roll stations in Long Island and Connecticut.

On Jerome Avenue, Vivian would dart in and out of stores, steadily loading up the shopping cart she was trailing behind her with paper bags containing cold cuts and canned goods from Moishe's supermarket, flounder from Edna's Fish Market, chopped meat from Jake the butcher, and pastries from Butternut Bakery. If we were lucky, we might grab a potato knish at Klotz Deli or even a combination plate lunch at the Jade Garden Chinese Restaurant. During our trek, we would take note of the double feature playing at the Tuxedo Theatre. Maybe next Saturday we could be released from shopping duty and take in the show preceded by 10 or 12 Warner Brothers cartoons and the Movietone newsreel. Maybe we would even have enough money remaining from our allowance to buy some bonbons and a butter popcorn.

As Saturday wore on, the tone would change. Vivian would tire of settling childish disputes, laying down the law regarding household chores, and looking forward to another evening alone. The Melmac dinner dishes (Art sold these for a while) weren't placed on the table in the foyer; they were slammed down. Vivian's face became flushed, her teeth clenched, her jaw rigid. We hurriedly finished dinner and retreated to our bedroom. We could hear Vivian's muttering as she cleared the table. Dishes, cups, and silverware clattered into the kitchen sink. We'd lose ourselves in our baseball card collection or put some 78's on the record player. Frequently we'd imitate some of the professional wrestling matches we watched on TV. One of us would be Dr. Jerry Graham, the other Skull Murphy as we grappled on the bed. So it was one Saturday night when Vivian stormed into the room after our exertions had succeeded in bending one of the bed frames. The leather belt, which always hung ominously from the dumbwaiter handle in the kitchen, was in her hand. "Goddamnit to hell! You're tearing the place apart!" Whack! One lash smacked off the mattress and sent us cowering under the bed. "You're ripping my heart out! I can't take it anymore!" One or two more ineffectual slashes with the belt, and she retreated to the kitchen. We would emerge from beneath the bed, and more quietly renew our activities. One of us was supposed to take our turn drying the dishes, but Vivian probably didn't want to see any more of us tonight. After slamming the dishes away in the cupboard herself, Vivian sat at the table grimly staring over a cup of tea.

13

"Come on, Feldman." Joan took Art by the arm and led him toward his car. They were going to head toward a bar near the University of Tennessee they had been frequenting recently. It wasn't likely that Joan would run into any of her family's business associates there. The meetings had started when Joan asked Art to talk to her about New York. She'd never been there. It was a good excuse. Art was in his element expounding on his hometown, how it had everything you might be interested in, and it was open 24 hours/day. But they both knew it was an excuse.

Joan might not have been to New York, but she'd been around. She'd graduated from the University of Virginia with a degree in

Business six years earlier. At Virginia she spent more time involved in college politics than she did studying. She quickly went through several boyfriends who were attracted by her looks and freewheeling attitude but repelled by her refusal to defer to them in matters both political and social. The boys were elated to discover that Joan had few reservations about rapidly converting a social relationship to a sexual one. They did not even need to concern themselves with the issue of birth control. Joan had already taken precautions. Gradually, they came to realize, however, that this wasn't your usual seduction. Joan didn't even pretend to have been swept off her feet. It was more like a mutual transaction. They both knew what they wanted and they took it. Not much romance involved. When one of the boys presented her with flowers or candy, Joan smiled. She found it quaint. The boy didn't know how to take it. Joan's behavior didn't correspond to past high school experiences. It was a bit unsettling to some. It was puzzling or irritating to others. Some even became angry. The sex kept them coming back eagerly for a while. There wasn't much that Joan wouldn't try. If she heard about it or read about it, she was interested. Sometimes the boy would come to feel that he was in over his head. In trying to satisfy one of Joan's particular appetites he might find himself engaging in behavior that left him cold or even repelled him. He began to feel something was wrong. Here he was presented with a situation that any red-blooded American boy would welcome with open arms. He was offered all the sex he could handle, even more. Why wasn't he responding as he imagined he would? What was wrong with him? Usually, at this point, he backed off. Sometimes a boy felt Joan's independence and assertiveness to be a threat. It represented a perverse challenge to the established order. It undercut everything he was raised to believe in. It might also be seen as a personal insult. Apparently, she thought he wasn't man enough to fulfill the masculine role. She was taking the lead;

he was forced to follow along or move on. Before he knew it, he struck out. More than once Joan came away from such encounters with a few bruises which she lied about later.

Joan didn't have a large circle of friends at school. She wasn't into sororities, tennis or the ski club. The few friends she did have would occasionally counsel her to be more careful about her personal life. They heard the rumors. They put some stock in them, knowing what a risk taker she could be. Joan would express appreciation for their concern but assured them that they need not fear for her safety. She knew how to take care of herself. But did she? She never took any particular precautions. An occasional boyfriend would begin to feel protective of her after a few weeks of dating, but about that same time things usually began to unravel. Joan did not reciprocate such loyalty. It wasn't that she didn't appreciate the sentiment, but she wasn't ready to commit to an exclusive relationship. It conflicted with her desire for sexual adventure. Someone new loomed on the horizon and she was off.

Alcohol became something of a problem. College was swimming in it. Underage drinking rules were easily circumvented, and Joan joined those who imbibed readily. No, she wasn't an alcoholic. It wasn't an addiction, just a lubricant. It made it easier for her to act on her strongest impulses. It erased any lingering inhibitions. Sometimes, though, it moved things along even faster than she wanted like the time when she found herself copulating with a boy in a back bedroom at a party. Joan had always been careful to restrict such activity to surroundings that were under her control. Now she could hear music and laughter in the next room. Before she knew it they had company. Afterwards she couldn't recall if there were two or three others, but it was frightening to think about. Strangely, she couldn't remember if she was frightened at the time it was happening. And the fact that she couldn't was somewhat scary to her as well. She did cut back on her drinking after that.

Occasionally, Joan found a partner who provided her with all the sexual activity she desired as frequently as she desired it. But usually she found something lacking elsewhere. He was not intellectually interesting, not curious enough about issues of the day, or he had no sense of humor. This would not cause Joan to break off the relationship. She wasn't looking for a marriage partner, and she was perfectly capable of compartmentalizing different aspects of her life. But she began to hold such a boy in lower esteem than others she imagined were more well-rounded. She liked boys who could put the sex aside after it was over. She didn't want someone who cared if she fell in love with him. Most boys didn't want that anyway, right? That's something she liked about them. She liked to keep company with a boy she was sleeping with if he could be cool about it. She didn't want to hold hands or put her head on his shoulder. Ideally, she wanted him to be by her side at Civil Rights rallies and Save the Children Federation benefits. She wanted him to be a leader or at least an active participant in causes she cared about. Sometimes that was too much to expect and she settled for less. As long as he didn't bother her after the sex was over, she might accept the situation until something better came along.

After leaving school, she found herself with a more meager supply of potential lovers who were less likely to let her take charge of the affair. Back home, she had appearances to keep up for her family's sake. As a result, she needed to be more circumspect in her behavior. Some of the men she found most appealing, like Art, were already married.

Art was hard pressed to keep up with Joan's drinking, but he felt obligated to keep pace. Joan's eyes would glaze over, but there was no other indication that she'd had too much to drink. The conversation, however, drifted from business opportunities in New York to immediate needs and wants. Then one drunken afternoon she flatly stated, "I need a lot of sex." Art didn't have a verbal reply handy, but he didn't need one. Next thing he knew, they were headed out the door, on the way to Joan's apartment. On the way out, the bartender, who felt a sense of responsibility for his regulars, said, "Take good care of her."

Joan wanted to swing by the store so she could pick up her car. "I'm going to need it in the morning."

"Do you think you can drive?"

"Are you kidding? Alcohol has no effect on me." They both laughed. But Joan's driving that early evening was no joke. Art hoped her weaving would not cause an accident. Should he make her pull over and get out of the car? Then again, was he in any shape to drive either? Fortunately, they made it to Joan's apartment unscathed. She went through the motions of inviting him to have dinner with her. When he accepted, it was obvious that she had only enough food at home for one. Art imagined that they would jump into bed right away, but they were both reluctant to make the move. Joan decided she had to make some business calls. Art lit a cigarette, and wondered how the evening would turn out.

After Joan got off the phone, he found himself telling her inexplicably about being hit by a truck as a kid and his sister's diabetes. He wasn't used to drinking so much. It seemed to have dampened his ardor at least temporarily and made him nostalgic. Then Art did something that should have put an end to the whole drunken escapade. "I promised to call Vivian tonight. Can I use your phone?" Of course he could. He checked in with her, and heard that everything and everyone was fine. When he hung up, it was apparent that Joan was subdued. He got up to leave, and was halfway down the stairs when Joan called him back. "You can sleep here. You had too much to drink." It was true, and it decided matters for him. He climbed back up, she took him by the arm, and they went to bed. Joan undressed and Art followed suit. It was back on. Art shoved everything but his libido on to the back burner. He allowed himself to experiment, something he dared not do with Vivian. He indulged his imagination. Joan welcomed it. It was nothing new to her. Art became a bit alarmed by the intensity of Joan's exertions as she thrust her sweaty body energetically about. At one point, he feared she might be going into convulsions when, teeth clenched, her eyes rolled upward and her breathing became uneven. He wanted to tell her to calm down, but ended up just going with the flow. Joan took charge, moving energetically and deliberately from one position to another. After a while it seemed all mechanical to Art. He continued to be aroused by the obvious pleasure Joan was experiencing as she thrust herself at him from so many different vantage points, but it occurred to him that there was no real personal connection here. He could have been someone else, anyone for that matter. Eventually, they collapsed side by side and slept for a couple of hours. Art rose early and dressed. Joan barely moved and mumbled something unintelligible. Driving away, Art wasn't sure what he thought at first. Fact is, it wasn't about thinking at all. It was just about feeling. In the past he'd had difficulty separating sex and emotion, but this was different. It was clear to him that the episode was purely a physical exercise for Joan. Now, hung over and exhausted, he began to regret the whole thing. "What am I, sixteen for Chrissake? I don't need to learn anything from her. How the hell could I think this was a good idea?" He placed a Philip Morris between his lips and reached for the cigarette lighter. "Feldman, you're a stupid son of a bitch. With my luck, I'll come down with the clap too."

He spoke to Joan a couple of times on the phone before leaving the area but never saw her again. She was up for another session but could sense his reluctance. He couldn't say that he wasn't just a bit tempted, but it wasn't really a close call for him. The whole episode was too far outside his normal existence to hold much meaning. It didn't seem quite real. One thing for sure, it was no real remedy for the loneliness of being on the road so much. In the end, Art thought it best to just forget the whole thing, and he fervently hoped it would never come to light.

14

"Who is that?" Apartment superintendent Louise O'Donnell was in the back courtyard of our apartment building, staring up at the top few floors, peering through a tangle of wash lines attached to fire escapes. She was trying to identify the source of the screaming threats she was hearing. Louise asked the question of her mother-in-law, white-haired Mrs. Oakley who occupied a ground floor flat.

"Sounds like Mrs. Aaronson, doesn't it?" offered the elderly woman.

"No, she's on the first floor." The screaming dissipated, being replaced by sporadic outbursts, sudden thumps and bangs.

"Isn't that awful?" The question was shouted from the roof where Mrs. Sullivan and Mrs. Garrity were perched, keeping eagle eyes on the neighborhood stretched out below them, ready to challenge young hooligans who might scrawl obscenities in chalk on the blacktop, or jump up and down officiously on car fenders. Louise glanced upward. Both women shook their heads in silent dismay. "Disgraceful,"commented Mrs. Garrity in a stage whisper that somehow made its way intelligibly down five floors to Louise's ears.

"Charlie!" Louise called for the handyman who occupied a tiny room in the basement amid tenants' baby carriages and bicycles. A former merchant seaman with a drinking problem, Charlie's duties included regularly chasing kids out of the front court and off the stoop, hauling trash cans full of ash from the incinerator out to the curb, and managing minor apartment repairs. He silently presented himself, head with its shock of unruly black hair, upraised, awaiting his instructions. "Who's making all that racket up there?"

"That? Oh, that's Feldman." Louise peered skeptically over to her mother-in-law.

"Vivian? Impossible." Mrs. Oakley knew Vivian Feldman to be a proper lady, always neatly groomed and fashionably turned out, a cool but polite smile on her face. The chaotic noise that was now subsiding didn't square with the woman Louise saw last week either when Vivian asked if it would be alright if the rent payment could be postponed till the 15th. "Not a problem," Louise had answered, after all, the Feldmans were long-term, reliable tenants who caused her no difficulties. "No, no," Louise agreed, "probably just a loud television."

Just then a late model Buick pulled up to the curb, and Pete O'Donnell stumbled out of the driver's seat. Pete worked the early shift at the Sunoco station on Mosholu Parkway. Sometimes he immediately headed for one of the Irish bars on 204th Street. Today was one of the days when he came home to drink. It was obvious, however, that he had already started. Rail thin, florid complexion, sparse brown hair, greasy company uniform, he walked stiffly by Louise without so much as a greeting. Checking his wristwatch, he stated, "Mmmm, 5 o'clock, the girls'll be home from school soon." Louise knew they had been home for a couple of hours already. She quickly said her goodbyes to Mrs. Oakley, reminded Charlie that the courtyard needed sweeping, and followed her husband in to the apartment to see about dinner.

15

We were old enough to be left on our own, or so Vivian thought. But the three-room apartment was a bit confining for brothers aged 10 and 7. In particular, the three beds, one for each brother occupying the single bedroom, didn't leave much room for running the bases, executing pass patterns, or slashing to the basket. So it was one summer afternoon that Donnie whipped a basketball in my direction, and sent it flying through the bedroom's rear window. After ascertaining that the crashing noise apparently did not attract any of the neighbors' attention, our main concern was in cleaning up and/or somehow concealing the situation from Vivian. I could at least clear some of the larger glass shards off the window ledge, couldn't I? With this end in mind, I extended my right hand through the shattered window, and succeeded in painlessly opening a gash in my forearm. Bad became worse. What to do? Just then we heard knocking at the door. Louise, the building superintendent, was investigating the situation.

After quickly surveying the scene of the crime, Louise wrapped my arm in a towel, left Donnie with her mother-in-law, and bundled me off to the emergency room. The doc asked me who they should call. Art was out of town, and Vivian was out shopping or banking or something. That left grandma. "Your grandma? Isn't she a little old to handle this?"

"She's not that old."

As I waited for Grandma Bessie to make the subway trip, I watched the basin water in which my arm was sitting turn increasingly red. By the time a doctor turned his attention to me, I had a sick feeling in the pit of my stomach. He didn't seem to notice. Instead, he focused his cheerful confidence on the wound. "Oh, this is not so bad. No major blood vessels or nerves involved. We'll take care of this in no time." And it wasn't long before the doc was asking proudly, "Know how many stitches you got?" I couldn't guess. "Seventeen!" Which was about a dozen too many, according to our family doctor, Caleb Brownstein, who had to remove them a couple of weeks later. He shook his head in dismay as he pulled out the stitches, struggling to untangle the crowded mess without reopening the cut. He was unsuccessful, and had to close it again with a butterfly bandage that left a noticeable, V-shaped scar. This proved useful when Donnie and I were in our teens, and we imagined ourselves belonging to a street gang named the Vorkians. My scar identified me as a founding member.

When Grandma Bessie finally arrived, the medical drama was over. I was glad she was there, nevertheless, and surprised to notice the hint of a smile on her usually expressionless visage. That unusual occurrence is what sticks with me most about this incident. "They told me what you said, that your grandma wasn't so old."

16

When Art came home from a sales trip, he arrived bearing gifts: a few 45 rpm rock 'n roll records for Donnie, and sport scorecard or autographed baseball for me. One time he brought back a rather exotic item: a box turtle that had washed onto the roadway after a rainstorm. We kept it in a cardboard box set out on our fire escape, and took it downstairs with us when we went out to play. One day, sitting on our apartment building front stoop, Donnie had the turtle sitting in his lap. A woman waiting for a bus kept staring at it. When it craned its neck out of its shell, she gave a start. "My goodness, I thought it was a stuffed toy!" The turtle's incongruent residence in the Bronx did not last very long. Its cardboard container fell apart during a heavy night time shower. In the morning, we spotted it lying on the concrete three stories below. He (she?) was still alive, but the shell was badly cracked. Despite (because of?) our ministrations, it expired in a couple of days.

Vivian would be relieved once Art set foot inside the door. He was back, safe and sound. She wouldn't need to shoulder all household duties alone. If it had been a good trip, she would let herself be swept up in Art's exuberance and good humor. He would take her in his arms, swing her around, and plant a kiss or two on her lips. She would be laughing.

On summer Sundays, Art would drive the family out to Jones Beach on Long Island. He would settle beneath a rented, mulit-colored, beach umbrella, protecting his fair, freckled skin from the sun's rays, occasionally emerging to take a plunge into waves, then dog paddle around until the next wave broke on him. The Atlantic Ocean was not the ideal place to learn how to swim, and none of us three boys learned as children. At Jones Beach, we would wade into chest-high water between crashing waves, choose one to body surf on, then ride it as far as we could into shore. If our timing was wrong, of course, we would be tossed around beneath the surf, scraped up on gravel and shells, reappear coughing up mouths of saltwater, struggling not to be pulled back out by the undertow. Vivian would pack a lunch for us – Wonder Bread sandwiches wrapped in wax paper with an apple or orange for dessert. Sometimes we were given permission to buy a snack from one of the vendors that trudged through the hot sand with his offering. Our favorite was the Eskimo Pie man: "Eskimos pies sweet as honey, here is where you pay your money." Before leaving in the late afternoon, we would try to wash all the sand off our exposed parts, but we could still feel all the grit trapped inside our swimsuits as we rode home in the car. We didn't mind it much. It had been a good day, even if we ended up with sunburned shoulders that night. A little Noxzema helped cool them down.

Art was easy-going by nature with the kids. Always ready with a joke, and he didn't mind being the butt of one either. When he was home for dinner, he would wolf down Vivian's offerings with gusto. Donnie and me would comment on how fast he could eat, even though his mouth was so small. Art would open his mouth as wide as possible to demonstrate it was more than adequate to the task at hand while we would laugh. Art would enjoy watching with us the outlandish displays of bravado presented by professional wrestlers on weekly telecasts. One day, Art brought home a reel-to-reel tape recorder, and we used it to produce our own version of professional wrestling interviews. Donnie was the announcer interviewing Art, playing the villain as I booed, hissed, and heckled in the background. Donnie: "You know Sailor Art Thomas is a big, strong guy."

Art: "First, I'll break his arms, then I'll break his legs. You can have an ambulance there, and I'll shove that hulking body of his…."

Me: " Boo, boo!"

Art: "Shutup, you rat bastards!" We replayed the tape for friends, and they never believed that was our dad.

Some Sundays we would drive to New Jersey to visit Art's parents and siblings. All his brothers and sisters except Saul lived in the Paterson/Fair Lawn area. Saul lived in the Bronx, near us. Grandpa Joe had retired, and he and Grandma Claire rented an apartment near their children. Grandpa Joe had suffered a minor heart attack that had convinced him to retire. He would be glued to the TV, watching Meet the Press or Face the Nation while his sons noisily traded stories and jokes in the living room. The daughters and daughters-in-law gathered in the kitchen, preparing snacks. Vivian had a fixed half-smile pasted on her face, speaking only when spoken to. She looked on disapprovingly whenever Ida or Fran erupted in a raucous laugh. Grandma Claire, slowed by various ailments, usually stayed in the bedroom where the grandchildren dutifully paid their respects, kissed her on the cheek, and received a quarter in return. Ida had to go to the bank every Friday before the Sunday visits to make sure Grandma had an ample supply of quarters handy.

Sometimes at home we would wrestle around with Art on the hideaway bed/couch that stood in the living room. It would fold out into the bed that Art and Vivian slept on at night. One evening, Donnie got Art into a reverse leg lock, tugging away as he writhed in mock pain. But at some point, the clowning stopped. Art had a puzzled, semi-amused expression on his face. Donnie had released his hold on Art's leg, but it remained bent and cramped. "Hey, what is this?" We looked on, amused. After a few seconds, Art managed to straighten his leg and he shook it. "A cramp, just a cramp." Funny that it was a cramp without any of the usual pain.

17

Sam and Bessie would visit us frequently. Bessie would engage Vivian in quiet conversation while Sam would see what his grandkids were up to in their bedroom. Sam had given Donnie his old TV set. Donnie had discarded the TV itself, and used the wooden console and speakers to amplify the rock music he played on his small record player. On one of Sam's visits, he gave a puzzled look at Donnie's creation. Donnie asked if he liked it. "Oh, it's a beauty. What is it?"

"It's a hi-fi." Sam had no idea what that meant.

"Chai-fop!" he replied.

"Can you give me another TV?" Donnie asked.

"I gave you one."

"Yeah but I want to make another one."

"Ha-ha!" Sam couldn't believe it. The attempt to make sense of all this seemed to tire out Sam, and he proceeded to stretch himself out on one of the beds to nap. He didn't care to remove his shoes, loosen his starched shirt collar, or remove his tie. The shiny black cap toes pointed straight up at the ceiling as he lay there on his back, eyes closed, a serene expression on his clean-shaven face. His posture was rigid, but he slept. Donnie proceeded to blast Chuck Berry, Gene Vincent, and Jerry Lee Lewis from his jerry-rigged hi-fi, but it did not disturb Sam's repose. He appeared to be enjoying the sleep of the just.

It wasn't only the creative electronics of his grandson that bewildered Sam. He had a hard time understanding popular culture too. One Sunday evening, we were gathered around the TV when Ed Sullivan's Toast of the Town Show began. Ed marched on stage to stiffly welcome the audience and viewing public in his characteristic wooden, lock-jawed fashion. Sam stared at him, as if seeing this well-known toastmaster for the first time. Who was this *golem* masquerading as an entertainer, and what possibly can his talent be? He wasn't singing or dancing, and it looked like he couldn't even talk. What is he doing on television? Do people really like to watch this? Is someone paying him good money to do whatever it is he's doing?

Sam's idea of an entertainer was Eddie Cantor, born Isadore Itzkowitz, the eye-rolling, frenetic song-and-dance man who would prance across the stage clapping his hands, belting out a tune. He could really put a song across, make the audience feel it, get excited about it. That was an entertainer. But this Ed Sullivan? He's supposed to be a toastmaster? You can't even understand him. You want to know who's a toastmaster? Georgie Jessel. If you can't sing like Eddie Cantor, then at least you should be able to talk with energy like Georgie Jessel, tell a good story, make people laugh. Sam fashioned himself something of an entertainment connoisseur. He used to steal away to the Yiddish Theater on Second Avenue whenever he had the chance. There he would watch the great Molly Picon and her husband Jacob Kalich live on stage. Those were performers! Boris Thomashefsky and his wife Bessie – those were actors. They should be on television, not this character Sullivan. Sam couldn't understand how he could even earn a living. "How much does he make?" Sam asked.

Vivian answered, "Ed Sullivan? Oh, he's very popular. He's probably a millionaire."

"What does he do?"

"He introduces people."

"Who does he introduce?"

"Everyone who's famous. He had Eddie Cantor on his show last year."

"Eddie Cantor? He doesn't need to be introduced. Everybody knows who he is. This Sullivan puts the audience to sleep." Sam peered closer at the screen, but he still had no clue what it was that Ed Sullivan did. "What am I seeing? I don't know." He gave a laugh, shook his head in bewilderment, and gave up. "What's for dinner, *mamaliga*?"

"Whitey asked me to tell you he'd be at the Cuban Casino." Art was surprised at Les's comment. They had just knocked off another work day, following up on some local leads together.

"What's he doing there? It's Christmas Eve, isn't it?"

"Well, you know he's got problems."

"Don't we all." Things hadn't been going well at Worldview recently. Commissions had been reduced – temporarily, it was said - and the number of leads were down. But the sales crew suspected Mandel and son were dipping into the company till, maybe getting ready to cut and run.

"Ain't it the truth? But you better go over and see him. He needs some advice." Les dropped Art off.

Art spotted Whitey over at the bar right away, and judging from the lopsided grin he received as a welcome, his friend was already three sheets to the wind. "What are you doin' here? I thought you were going home."

"Sit down, sit down. It's early. Hey, bartend, get this man a scotch and soda. J&B, only the finest."

"What's up?"

"Nothin', nothin', just unwinding. You know how it is."

"Hey, Whitey, Marge'll be expecting you. It's holiday."

"Yeah, yeah, later. Hey, remember when you and me took the girls to that Giants game? We didn't have tickets, so you fixed it up with whatshisname?"

"Rico."

"Rico, yeah, Rico. He was working at the gate back then. And you fixed it up with him. And Marge, she didn't know, so she kept lookin' around for the tickets like we were goin' to give one to her. And you said, just give him your finger. And she thought you wanted her to flip him the bird or somethin'. Ha!"

'Yeah, Ol' Rico. He was something else."

"What happened to him after he got canned?"

"They were going to press charges for embezzlement, but they let him go. Wasn't worth their trouble."

"That's the question, Art, is it worth the trouble?"

"What?"

"All this. Everything. Is it really worth the trouble?"

"Hey, Whitey, how about we.."

"No, no, I'm serious. This sales game is bullshit. You know that. I can sell, you know I can sell. They didn't want to let me go at Melmac. I was their best seller. Am I right or wrong?"

"Right."

"So all of a sudden, I'm the weak link?"

"Who said that?"

"That little prick Mandel Junior."

"He don't know his ass from his elbow."

"Right! And he comes to me sayin' I gotta get MY act together. You believe that shit?"

"Forget about it. He don't know nothing. It doesn't matter. His old man is just keeping him around so he has a job. He couldn't find one anywhere else. Forget about it."

Whitey lit a Lucky Strike, and offered Art one. "Art, you ever get lonely on the road?"

"Don't we all?"

"Yeah, but I did something about it, and Marge found out."

"She blow up?"

"No, that's just it. You know how she is. She keeps it all inside. You can't really tell what she's thinking."

"You want me to speak to her?"

"I don't know"

"Or Viv. She can give her a call."

"Think she would?"

"Sure, they were pretty close."

"Maybe that would be good." Whitey ordered another Canadian Club and water. "Art, you ever run into this kind of situation?"

"With Vivian? Yeah. Sure. But we got a system."

"A system?"

"Yeah, We go to dinner at a real nice place, a little candlelight, a little wine, a little dancing --- she goes Tuesdays, I go Fridays."

"Ha-ha, I shoulda seen that one comin'."

"No, seriously, me and Viv, we sleep in separate beds, we eat separate, take separate vacations. We're doing everything we can to keep our marriage together." That got a laugh out of Whitey.

"Hey, remember when Hackley's old lady surprised him at the door in a negligee?"

"Oh, yeah, the only trouble was, she was just coming home."

Art was relieved that the tone of the evening had improved. He looked at his watch. "Hey, Whitey, it's 9:30. Time to go home and trim the tree, huh?"

"Tree? Crap, that's what I was going to do tonight."

"Sure, you got all the tinsel and angels and stuff?"

"Tinsel? I don't have the tree." So Art paid the tab, took Whitey by the arm, and steered him toward the door. As Whitey wrapped his arm around Art for support, he felt the corset Art had worn ever since his back surgery. "Art, how long you been wearin' a girdle?"

"Ever since Viv found it in my glove compartment." They stumbled around the neighborhood, finally locating a tree dealer still open on Central Park West. Art helped Whitey pick one out. I never knew they let you take a tree on the subway, but that's the way they got it up to Whitey's apartment on Sedgwick Avenue in the Bronx.

Marge was waiting at the head of the staircase, one hand on her hip, watching as Art and Whitey labored up the flight with the tree on their shoulders. Art said she didn't seem angry. Viv wasn't either when Art explained why he was so late.

But Whitey Connor wasn't the only one having problems with Worldview. The paychecks weren't regular. One week the leads were great, you were selling, and the money was pouring in. Other weeks, you couldn't find a buyer no matter what you did, and the check was practically nonexistent. It was hard to plan a life when working purely on commission. Similarly, it was difficult to know how Vivian was going to respond when the money was short. Sometimes she was supportive. But there were other times too.

There was one week when Donnie was acting up in school, and Grandma Bessie was constantly on the phone complaining about Sam's stupidities. Vivian felt the walls of the apartment closing in. She had no healthy outlet for her frustrations. She found it hard to make friends. Others would start to share their problems with her, but she couldn't reciprocate. She had no job, no recreational activities to escape the frustrations at home.

She hadn't been feeling well lately. Her periods were irregular, and she was getting hot flashes. She went to see a gynecologist, and he told her she might need surgery. Art didn't know all this when he returned from a less than successful sales trip, but when he received a cold greeting from Vivian, he knew a storm was coming. The pots were banging on the stove as dinner was prepared.

"I can't live this way anymore. I'm telling you I'm sick of it!" Vivian's foot was stamping on the floor. "How much do you think I can take? No one can live like this! I won't stand for it!" Doors were slamming. Mrs. Greenwald from downstairs was banging on her ceiling with a broom. Then it was quiet.

Harry wasn't home. Me and Donnie stayed in the bedroom. It turned out that the last door slam we heard was Art leaving through the front door. He didn't know where he was going. He didn't even intend to leave, but how much can one man take? Didn't he try his best, give it his all? He wasn't like so many other guys who took their paycheck and headed for the bar or the racetrack. He came home every night he was in town and took care of his family. What does she expect? She wants to live on Fifth

Avenue? Let her find someone else to put up with this crap. Lots of luck with that. He had enough. He galloped down the stairs, missing the last step of the flight and nearly twisting his ankle. He stalked up the street. Al Wallach, a neighbor, nodded a greeting and looked like he wanted to talk, but Art walked right by. He lit a cigarette and headed the long way around the park passing a couple of bars on 204th Street. The air was befouled by smoke emitted from trash incinerators of surrounding apartment buildings. Art coughed but thought it appropriate. "There goes the marriage up in smoke." He thought about getting a drink, but he had never found alcohol helpful when he was feeling down. It had always been something to help him celebrate. Should he be celebrating his escape, his freedom? No, he didn't feel like celebrating. Maybe he could call Whitey and talk, but he didn't really feel like talking either. What was there to say? The anger, the hurt couldn't be put into words right now. If he opened his mouth, he felt like he would just scream. He was finished with the whole thing. He had to get away to think it all out. But where was he going to go? He had maybe forty bucks in his wallet.

There was no dinner that night. Donnie had snuck into the kitchen and returned with a pack of Twinkies which we shared. Vivian took a few phone calls, but we didn't know who she was talking to because it sounded like she was speaking in a whisper. Besides Donnie was playing around with the radio again, trying to bring in out-of-town stations on the AM dial. Harry got home around 10. Vivian met him as soon as he stepped inside. "Go get your father. He's at the bus station. Bring him home."

"The bus station?" Harry repeated. It didn't immediately register with him. What was Art doing at the bus station? He never rode the bus.

"Yes, Port Authority. Get down there before he takes off for somewhere," Vivian responded. Art had left the car parked on the street. Either he was completely distracted, or he intended to quit his job and didn't want to be charged with stealing the car. He had taken the subway to the Port Authority Bus Terminal. One of the calls Vivian had received was from Art. He wanted to tell her where he had stashed some extra cash and to remind her that the electric bill was overdue for payment. Vivian realized that this was a signal that he was cooling off, that he didn't really want to leave. Maybe it also served as a reminder that her temper had taken them both to a place where they didn't want to be. What would she do without Art? His sales trips on the road were bad enough. How could she possibly put up with the kids and the household by herself fulltime? She never directly confronted the damage wrought by her rages. Did she ever recognize that it was a serious problem? Why wouldn't Sam's example serve as a cautionary tale? Didn't she realize that it needed to be dealt with somehow, that unless she did so we would have more scenes like this? Did she ever consider seeking help? None of us had ever heard her express regret after one of her tantrums. She never seemed sorry. Was it that the explosions were too monumental to even address? Was it that the only way Vivian could carry on was to act as if these rages had not occurred? This is how it seemed. After regaining her composure, the events were never referred to. It was if they had never occurred at all. Was this Vivian's way of making them go away? If she did not acknowledge them, then they had to be aberrations. They did not represent the real Vivian. They did not count. But did her inability to deal with these contradictions amount to mental instability? Was she clinically ill? If so, how best to coexist with such a person on a daily basis? There was always a period of calm, but it was not likely to last very long. Daily existence entails frustrations. Eruptions were always on the horizon. What happens then? A replay of this night?

More doors slamming, more attempts to escape, more fracturing of the family? We couldn't assume that such blowups would always end with reconciliation. Art was approaching the breaking point. Would he be gone for good one of these days? We were learning that many times history repeats itself. Would Harry, already reluctant to spend much time at home, look to flee the conflict through an early marriage as Vivian had done? What could Donnie and I do to deal with the situation in the coming years?

Harry didn't have a driver's license so he followed Art's route, taking the subway to the bus station. He knew that, as the eldest, he was the logical choice for this task, but he didn't relish it. He resented the fact that, no matter how much he tried to establish an independent existence for himself, it always came back to something like this. "I put up with all of this when I was a kid. Why do I have to be caught in the middle of it as an adult? Why can't they solve their own problems?" he thought. He tried to forget about the purpose of his errand during the subway ride. He looked around at the other passengers and tried to imagine who they were and why they were there. Where were they going? They had to be traveling for a more pleasant reason than he. He tried to find someone he found attractive. Would that person return his glance? What would he do if they did? He wasn't successful in forgetting the coming confrontation for very long. What would he say to Art? Would Art resist coming back home? What would he do if Art refused? He tried to think of something to say, something that would be appropriate and convincing. After some deliberation, after mentally composing then rejecting several options, he came up with what he thought was a good approach: "Pop, you can't leave. We all need you at home. Mom needs you. She didn't mean what she said. You know how she is." Yeah, that sounded good. That might do the job.

When he got there, he began to survey the premises. He didn't see Art at first. He walked up and down the station, looking in all directions. There were families dining on sandwiches they had just removed from brown paper bags. There was a thin man dressed in a dirty trench coat sorting through a trash can and a sad woman standing by waiting to see if he found a makeshift meal for them. There was a dark-eyed woman in a bright turquoise skirt slit up the side and spiked heels with bright eyes whose gaze followed Harry as he roamed the premises. There was a sailor with his feet propped up on his duffle bag, cap pushed down over his forehead, sleeping. There was a bus driver banging a vending machine that had just eaten his quarter without dispensing the Snickers bar he had selected. There was a line at the entrance to the women's rest room where one woman was complaining about the fact that one of the toilets was backed up and the place stunk. There was a tired looking janitor trying to mop the floor and while collecting all the discarded newspapers. Finally, Harry spotted Art seated on a bench, a paper cup of coffee in his hand. He looked somewhat surprised to see Harry there. "Mom asked me to come get you." Art looked down at his shoes. He didn't say anything. Harry thought he looked confused and ashamed. After a moment Art got up.

"Are you hungry? Would you like to get a hamburger?" Art asked. Harry shook his head no. Art drained the dregs from his coffee cup, crumpled it, and tossed it in the direction of the trash can. It bounced off the rim and fell to the floor. Art shook his head in disgust, and they headed back to the subway entrance. Art didn't say much on the ride home, and none of what he said had to do with Vivian. And we never found out where he had planned to go.

Art's younger brother Saul was the only one of his brothers and sisters who stayed in New York. His first wife Tillie suffered from a congenital heart condition, and she died while still in her thirties. After that, Saul got an apartment in our building, and he was a regular presence at our family functions. Genial, bald on top except for a few wisps of hair, Saul remained rail thin while his brothers put on weight once the Depression was history. He worked as a projectionist in a movie theater, chain-smoking Chesterfields as images of Victor Mature and Rita Hayworth flitted across the screen. He never got home before 2 a.m. or so. He would then turn on his TV and watch the city's culture maven Joe Franklin interview local entertainers and would-be celebrities while he built a sandwich for himself from whatever leftovers he could find in his refrigerator. Frequently, Saul would select a few slices of liverwurst garnished with a wedge of Bermuda onion and a brown-edged leaf or two of iceberg lettuce, placing it all on a couple of slices of Arnold's white bread smeared with Gulden's spicy brown mustard. He would wash it down with a bottle of Yoo-hoo chocolate drink. Saul always felt that liverwurst went well with Joe Franklin's cornball telecasts. Joe started out chasing Al Jolson and Eddie Cantor around the city, trying to sell them his jokes. He gradually advanced from groupie and hanger-on to broadcaster and telecaster. There was no doubt that he was passionate about local entertainment history, much of which he committed to memory. His office was a veritable storehouse of Broadway memorabilia. Nothing that occurred in the city's entertainment scene was too insignificant for Joe Franklin to collect and memorialize. It was all important to him. His intense interest on all things show business bordered on the psychopathic. He cared about little else. He dressed haphazardly in random jackets and ties that rarely matched and were always out of style.

He combed his hair in the same manner for decades, probably with the same comb. Throwing it back off his face was sufficient.

Joe would always fawn over even the most obscure singers and dancers who he managed to recruit for his low budget program. His manner was one of quiet persistence. His guests appreciated his interest, but they often became disconcerted by Joe's inability to discuss anything other than who was performing where and who in past decades had performed there as well. Joe would digress only slightly from his usual formula by searching his prodigious memory to locate a litany of old recordings and concerts that he would improbably relate to the guest occupying the seat before him. The recitation would serve to advertise to the miniscule audience watching that Joe Franklin was indeed the premiere archivist of the New York entertainment scene. Saul would always smile when Joe Franklin ended each interview by asking where his guest was appearing. When he received a reply, Joe would always say, "I'll be there." One time Saul recalled, the guest answered, "You haven't been there yet." Joe, taken aback by such a bold response, reassured the guest that this time he was really coming. Saul was willing to bet that Joe never showed up that time either.

Saul's late hours didn't prevent him from meeting his second wife Edna, a stolid, pleasant woman. Someone was always trying to fix Saul up with a nice lady they knew, and Saul was usually agreeable. He didn't like being alone, and he didn't mind meeting anyone that a friend or co-worker recommended. What was the worst that could happen? A wasted evening wasn't so bad when there was a chance to meet someone who might make him happy. Edna was the sister of a co-worker's wife. She was forty years old and had not been married before. For some, that might set off alarm bells. She hadn't met anyone she wanted to marry by age forty? Why hadn't someone grabbed her up by then? Was there something wrong with her? Saul didn't jump to any conclusions. He wanted to see for himself, and he was glad he did. As it turned out, it wasn't exactly love at first sight, but they hit it off pretty well right from the start. Art and Vivian liked Edna too. She had a ready smile, was agreeable and obviously taken with Saul. One date led to another, and before they knew it, they were planning a life together. Once remarried, Saul took a larger apartment on nearby Pelham Parkway, and the new married couple visited often.

One evening, sitting around our dinner table, Vivian and Edna were talking about Uncle Sol's son Gilbert who had just taken a job as a social worker after graduating City College. "Good for him," Art said, "but it's going to be hard to feed a family on a social worker's pay." Edna lamented that public service jobs always paid such low salaries.

"It is nice having a college graduate in the family," Vivian offered.

"But that don't pay the rent," Art countered.

"It isn't always about money," Vivian asserted.

"Could've fooled me," Saul chuckled, and Art laughed with him.

"If that's all there is to it, would you take a job pushing a broom if it paid you a good salary?" Vivian asked. Art and Sol looked at each other for a split second before answering

"Yeah!"

Edna could be heard above the general laughter insisting, "No you wouldn't, no you wouldn't." Maybe the question should have included whether Edna and Vivian would have been OK with a husband who worked a menial job. The truth was that both Art and Saul were intelligent men who had never had the opportunity to explore their academic potential. Family responsibilities and the Great Depression deprived them of that. In Saul's case, health problems had posed an additional obstacle. Whatever job they worked, however, they applied themselves diligently, tried to make the best of it, and took pride in their accomplishments. Does that mean that they would have demonstrated those same qualities as janitors? Probably, but it's doubtful that they would have found such repetitive, stultifying work satisfying for very long. And what about the wives? Would they have been satisfied being married to low-end workers, or would they have cringed when they had to answer the question, "What does your husband do for a living"? Would a healthy salary have compensated for any social embarrassment they might have suffered? It's questionable. Saul terminated any such serious investigation of what was intended as a humorous jibe to begin with by relating the sad tale of a friend's brother-in-law. "The poor guy was a night watchman. He ended up losing his job to a lock."

Saul was the one uncle who was most familiar with Donnie and I. He took a casual interest in what we were up to although the usual generational differences often prevented him from fully appreciating our pastimes. Saul was visiting one afternoon when Donnie was blasting a Chuck Berry 45 on his home-made stereo. He strolled into our bedroom just as one of Chuck's extended, repetitive, proto-head banging, guitar riffs was in full swing. Donnie pointed toward the speaker nodding his head in appreciation. Saul stood leaning in the doorway, Chesterfield in hand, hint of a smile on his face, shaking his head in gentle dismay. "That's not music, that's not music." Surely, to Saul such cacophony was little more than noise. But it said a lot about Saul that he did not angrily condemn what he could not appreciate. His attitude was one of bemusement. It seemed that he kind of liked the fact that we had found something that we enjoyed even if he couldn't participate in the enjoyment. He would stand firm in maintaining the line he believed existed between what was and what wasn't art, but he was tolerant of those who had a different understanding of the issue. Yes, Saul was a good guy.

21

Harry was the worker. For as long as I can remember, he had a job somewhere doing something. At first, he was the delivery boy for Hirsch's Grocery. He'd pile housewives' produce orders into an old, dilapidated baby carriage and wheel them around to neighborhood apartment houses. Most other delivery boys rode a bicycle with a large, metal basket in front for the delivery order, but Hirsch didn't want to invest in one so he used a baby carriage someone had apparently discarded. Besides, the carriage could hold more orders. It occurred to Harry that he would look a lot better riding a bike than pushing a baby carriage. But even if Hirsch had a bike Harry couldn't use it because he didn't know how to ride a bike. Neither could me and Donnie. When Harry arrived at the correct address, he would carry the order up the stairs to the designated apartment, and more often than not, receive a couple of deposit bottles as tips. If he was fortunate, the building had an elevator and the tip would be a few coins.

When Harry got back with his soda pop bottles, he'd plant his rear end on a peach crate out in front of the store and wait for Old Man Hirsch to send him out again on some more orders. While waiting, he'd clean his nails with a pen knife and listen to Hirsch's short, squat wife badger her husband. "Hoisch, get the boy to sweep out the back room. The ants are driving me crazy." "Hoisch, when are the cantaloupes coming? We promised Birnbaum, remember?" "Hoisch, it's time for lunch. Go, I'll watch the store."

Other times, Harry would run errands for Jimmy the Chinese laundry man or Tony the hatter. Once he graduated high school, he got a job as an IBM keypunch operator in Manhattan, and he discovered a different life. Even though he was obligated to contribute financially to the household, he'd have some cash left to play with. After work, he and his co-workers would head for the Latin Quarter or the Stork Club, and we didn't see him much except when he came home to sleep. Before me and Donnie went to sleep, we'd load up Harry's sheet and pillow case with wooden blocks and books. He'd wake us up later when he'd toss the junk out onto the floor, and we'd know that that our mission had been accomplished.

Me, I was the student. Art would proudly sign my stellar report cards at the bottom with his confident flourish. He stood with his hands on my shoulders as Hebrew School teacher Mr. Rosenberg presented me with a silver mezuzah pendant emblematic of receiving top grades. Art liked to repeat something I told him once, "I got brains I haven't used yet." Maybe I'd go to college like his younger brother David and amount to something.

Donnie was the fighter, the tough guy. From the time he was in first grade, he'd be getting into fights. I'd be called out of my fourth grade class by Donnie's teacher to hear about how my brother was causing trouble, and told to report this to my parents. The problem was, Donnie could never accept any slights, any teasing. He couldn't ever turn the other cheek. In fact, he could never even get to the point of thinking about it. Striking out at his tormenter was a reflex act for him.

Alfie Hupman was one of the neighborhood tormentors, a kid whose mission in life seemed to be getting under your skin. He appeared to get a rise out of seeing someone lose their temper. He's find some way to get you going: curses, taunts, insults, whatever got the job done. Then he'd dance around just out of your reach and get you to chase him. He was quick, and could usually stay just out of your reach. If you did corner him, he was a good fighter. You were in for a battle.

One day, we were hanging out with Ed Mitzner, a friend of mine, in front of his apartment building when Alfie appeared. He immediately took up a position behind Ed, and started playing hide-and-seek with Donnie, tossing insults, then disappearing behind Ed's back. After the third taunt, Donnie had the game figured out, and he nailed Alfie in the face with his fist. The fight was on, and both Donnie and Alfie tumbled into the shrubbery which decorated the outside of the apartment building, pummeling each other. The noise prompted Ed's mother to open the window of her ground floor apartment and stick her head out. When she saw the two boys grappling with each other on the ground, she chuckled and seemed relieved. "Oh, it sounded like someone was dragging some cardboard outside the window. I thought maybe it was my produce order." Then she disappeared back inside her home. By this time Alfie was trying to secure Donnie in a headlock while Donnie was gouging Alfie's eye with his right thumb. When Ed and I managed to separate the two, Donnie seemed none the worse for wear, but red-faced and breathing hard. Alfie was bleeding from a cut beneath his eyelid, and didn't seem anxious to continue. He would be waiting for another opportunity to revenge himself and Donnie knew it.

During the winter, snowball fighting was a favorite pastime. Cars passing up and down Gun Hill Road were a favorite target. Donnie was especially adept at nailing them no matter how fast they were going. One afternoon, he and his friend Curtis were engaging in this sport, both peppering a sedan with snowballs as it cruised to a stoplight. Now, ordinarily a car that was not moving was no longer a fair target, but Donnie and Curtis felt they were in a zone. They couldn't miss, and they kept tossing snowball after snowball at the motionless car relentlessly. The driver became irate at the ceaseless barrage. He pulled his vehicle over to the curb and got out. At this point, most kids would turn and run, but not Donnie. He continued to pelt the driver who was advancing upon him with snowballs. Curtis, following Donnie's example, did the same. The enemy was almost upon them, and they desperately sought to halt his advance. Only when the man was within arm's length did Donnie try to flee, but by then it was too late. The man seized Donnie by the collar while Curtis ran away. After undergoing a vigorous shaking by the cold, wet, and the red-faced adult, accompanied by numerous threats, Donnie told the man who he was and where he lived. Vivian soon received another unwelcome visitor reporting on yet another misdeed by her youngest son, and for Donnie, there was more hell to pay.

Donnie and Curtis were quite a pair. Even though the snowball affair ended with both being punished by their parents, they continued to find new ways to get themselves into trouble. It occurred to Donnie that it might be fun to mimic a neighborhood man who was afflicted with a disease that caused his muscles to jerk uncontrollably as he tried to walk. Everyone in the neighborhood had encountered the man at one time or another. For some reason, he usually clasped his hands behind his back. In one of his hands he held some change, usually a quarter. Occasionally, someone would try to assist the man when he stumbled or dropped his quarter, but the man did not welcome any assistance and would frequently shove the would-be Good Samaritan out of the way. We never could determine whether the man was antisocial or mentally impaired. He either would not or could not engage in a conversation. Donnie and Curtis came upon the man one day. Donnie took a nickel out of his pocket, held it behind his back and began to jerk his shoulder up and down as he walked around. The man, noticing the mockery, became enraged. His jerking was exacerbated. Donnie increased his jerking accordingly while Curtis laughed. The man pointed at Donnie and shouted "You!" Donnie, who continued jerking and dropped his nickel, explained, "I got it too!" Then Donnie and Curtis ran away laughing. This escapade was the only one about which Donnie later on expressed some regret.

Vivian was sensitive to the fact that Donnie was getting a reputation as a roughneck. She was certainly aware of his struggles in school. His grades weren't very good, and then there were the reports of occasional fights with classmates. But she wasn't about to accept the fact that he was some neighborhood terror, and woe to anyone who suggested as much.

Beverly Rubin was a fiery redhead with bulging eyes and a mouth no one wanted to fall into. One day, Art brought Grandma Claire over to our apartment for a visit. He introduced Claire to Beverly who happened to be leaving the front entrance to the building as Art and Claire were entering. Claire, who never had a harsh word for anyone, took the measure of Beverly and commented in Yiddish, "She must have a very nice personality." Beverly had a redheaded son who appeared helpless in the face of her household dominance. She told Robert what to do, when to do it, and how to get it done – all at the top of her voice. Robert, who was a year younger than Donnie, was severely lacking in confidence and coordination. Any street game he tried to play, he approached with foreboding. He knew in advance he would not only lose but also be unable to make a decent showing.

One day, however, he had managed to get himself included in a game of King and Queen, a simplified version of handball played against the side of a brick apartment building. Not having played very often, Robert was not knowledgeable concerning the game's rules. He did not know that players could hold onto possession of the ball by repeatedly bouncing it off the pavement and brick wall until they had set up a shot that would give an opponent maximum difficulty. Of course, Robert was the kind of kid that other kids enjoyed giving difficulty, because they knew he couldn't take it. So, when Donnie set up his shot by bouncing the ball so close to the wall that it would be virtually impossible to return it without scraping your knuckles against the brick, and then sent it on to Robert, the outcome was assured. Robert whiffed on it, then had to watch as we all laughed derisively.

But this humiliation did not end like all the others Robert had endured. This time, Robert's accumulated frustration erupted. Teeth clenched, face flushed, teary eyed, Robert gave a guttural growl and grabbed Donnie's T-shirt by the neck. His convulsive grip stretched and tore it down to the waist. Donnie reacted as he always did, punching Robert in the side of his neck. They fell to the pavement, and Donnie kicked Robert off him. Robert's rage subsided, and he got to his feet crying, and ran back to his apartment.

The neighborhood soon heard from Beverly Ruben. She stormed up to our apartment, and when Vivian opened the door, we could all hear the yelling echo throughout the hallway. "Donnie is a mad dog! Everybody knows it! He should be locked up! Look what he did to my Robert! Robert doesn't know how to defend himself!"

Vivian couldn't match Beverly in decibel power, but could be clearly heard: "My son is not a dog, and you better not use that kind of language around me. Robert needs to learn how to defend himself against you and the other boys."

We didn't see much of Robert again after that. Several years later, we noticed he had grown his hair long, and seemed to be turning on, tuning in, and dropping out. This was not what anyone had foreseen for Robert, least of all his mother. Beverly and Vivian, once on friendly terms, remained distinctly cool to each other from then on.

Beverly, however, continued to keep her critical eye on neighborhood activities. In warm weather, she would seat herself in a folding chair on the sidewalk and grimly survey the landscape. She had a small terrier that would seat itself in the Rubens' first-floor window and bark at all the kids who were noisily playing on the streets below. Donnie used to rile up the dog by barking back and tossing stones its way. One day, Beverly had the dog's leash tied to her folding chair when Donnie walked past with Marvin Shapiro, a neighbor and friend whose gay tendencies were an open secret . The dog leaped at Donnie, turning the chair sideways and nearly sending Beverly crashing to the sidewalk. Beverly righted herself and struggled to get control of the dog. "Get outta here!" she shouted at Donnie who was laughing as he walked down the street. "And you too, sissy Mary!" Marvin didn't laugh.

Marvin Shapiro was terrible at any sport involving a ball – football, baseball, basketball, you name it. He wore large, heavy eyeglasses, and spent a good deal of time walking his dark-haired, docile dog ironically named Terror. Despite his scholarly appearance, he wasn't much of a student either. His great passion was cars. He would spend his money on small model cars, assemble these replicas of 1950's classic autos, paint them, and customize them with continental kits and fender skirts. He acquired this interest from his older brother Alex who was a vocational school graduate and employed in an auto body shop.

Molly Shapiro, Marvin's mother was a swarthy woman of melancholy temperament. Her husband had deserted the family years back, and no one was sure of his whereabouts. Marvin told people his father was dead. We knew this wasn't true, because the Shapiros had been quite close with Art and Vivian at one time, and they would have known if he was deceased. The Tom Shapiro they remembered was a rotund, fun-loving man comically nicknamed Skinny. Alex resembled his father physically, but it was questionable whether he shared his sense of humor. Alex would attempt to regale us with jokes we weren't sure were funny. One time he told us of a man who went to a doctor complaining that his dick was too small. The doctor prescribed a special ointment, and told him to return in a week. When the man came back his shlong was so long it was wrapped several times around his waist. He had to unwind it to show it to the amazed doctor. "You think this is something?" said the man. "They're bringing my balls over by Mac truck." Another time Alex asked us to count how many fingers he was showing us, and he proceeded to open and close both fists in rapid succession innumerable times. We would blankly look at each other, wondering what response Alex had in mind. Alex thought this was hysterical.

Alex spent little time at the Shapiro apartment. He had a job and he would disappear in a hurry whenever Molly began venting her frustrations on her kids. Marvin, younger and still in school, had nowhere to escape except the streets. He would go walk Terror and hope that not too many neighbors had heard Molly's hoarse voice berating him for some actual or imaginary offense. Marvin was my age but we were usually placed in different classes at school. The school tracked students according to academic performance. I was placed in classes with good students, and Marvin found himself in classes with struggling ones. Unfortunately, these classes also were likely to include misfits who were fond of bullying kids like Marvin who were not athletic and did not display the requisite amount of macho characteristics. Marvin attempted to remedy this by attempting to appear tough. He would disrespect his teachers, and he took up smoking. Outside of school he started carrying a pack of L&M's which was rolled up in the sleeve of his tee shirt. Jeans and a red vest completed his outfit. He also affected an interest in girls. At the time we didn't know if this was real or just an act, even though Marvin was routinely taunted as being a "homo."

Perhaps we should have known after an incident that occurred in our apartment when we were eleven. We were in the bathroom, and 8-year-old Donnie was assuring us that he knew how babies were made. "The man puts his penis in the woman's vagina."

"But he has to have a hard-on," added Marvin. "You know what that is? Here." And Marvin indicated his own stiff dick, the outlines of which could be clearly discerned beneath his pants. I'm sure Donnie got the point, but neither of us reacted. We just moved on.

We all still hung out together for another couple of years, lounging on the front steps of the apartment complex until chased off by Charlie the building superintendent's helper; listening to rock on a transistor radio; playing punchball and touch football in a side street, using parked cars and manhole covers as bases. There were a few memorable occasions. One time I heaved the football as far as I could, and it fell right into Marvin's arms. He didn't even have to reach for it. For the only time we could recall, Marvin scored a touchdown. He was a sport hero for one brief moment. Kids pounded him on the back and yelled in celebration. Marvin discovered what it felt like to be one of the boys.

Then there was the time we were listening to Peter Tripp's countdown of the week's top hits on WMGM-AM radio one summer night. It was late summer and already getting dark when the Peter Tripp announced number 6, Jerry Lee Lewis's "Whole Lotta Shakin' Going On." When we heard that pumping piano begin to play, we dialed the volume all the way up and began to run down the street, tossing in the air our jackets along with tin cans, cardboard boxes, and any other street debris we came across — evidence, I suppose, that there might be something to our parents' contention that rock 'n roll caused juvenile delinquency. Jerry Lee had yet to announce his marriage to his 13-year-old cousin, an act that had serious consequences for his singing career. Of course, it wouldn't have made any difference to us even if the media had a field day with it. Reporters cornered country rocker Carl Perkins whose tune "Blue Suede Shoes" was a big crossover hit. "Are you married to a 13-year-old too?" they asked.

"Nope, divorced" he replied.

My friendship with Marvin ended abruptly. Our junior high school held a dance at the end of ninth grade just before students graduated and departed for their respective high schools. Neither Marvin, me nor our friend Harold Bierman had dates, so we decided to go stag together. The day of the dance both Marvin and Harold called me to announce that they had both arranged dates for themselves at the last minute. That left me alone to attend by myself. Irate at what I considered an inexcusable betrayal, I stayed home rather than attend and be scorned as a loser who couldn't get a girl to go with him to the dance. Three losers going together is not so bad. You have company, and besides there are probably quite a few others in the same situation. But one guy going all by himself? That would take a lot of nerve and self-confidence, both of which are usually in short supply when you are 14 years old. So I didn't go. I remember my home room teacher, Mrs. Church, asking me about my absence from the dance the next school day. I don't remember replying. I just wanted to forget about the whole thing.

The next time I saw Marvin in the street I refused to speak to him or even acknowledge his presence. He came over and told me how easy it would have been for me to get a date for the dance. There were lots of girls I knew who would have gone with me. This made matters even worse. Here was Marvin Shapiro - a likely "homo" – giving me advice on how to get girls. It didn't matter that he might be right. His patronizing me was insufferable. I walked away. I saw Marvin the next day again. He came over and tried to put the whole matter behind us. He patted me on the shoulder in a gesture intended to mean "let bygones be bygones" but I would have none of it. We went our separate ways after that, attending different high schools. Later on I felt bad about it. Marvin didn't have many friends, and the whole dance incident seemed much less important as time passed.

A few years later, after I left the Bronx, Donnie ran into Marvin. He was in an Army uniform. "Did you join or were you drafted?" Donnie asked.

"Yeah, I joined, I joined," Marvin replied sarcastically.

"What do you do there?" Donnie asked.

"Oh, fun things like crawling through mud." That was the last encounter either of us ever had with Marvin. I wonder sometimes if he ended up in Vietnam, and if he made it back.

23

In our family's collection of memorabilia are contained several identical greeting cards congratulating Art and Vivian on the births of Donnie and me. The cards were from family friends, and they depicted rows of newborn infants bundled up in their hospital cribs. One infant is sitting up, looking around in amazement, and declaring, "What, no girls?!" Those cards reminded us of a cartoon we saw in a popular magazine of the day. The diapered infants were crawling out of the hospital nursery in a long line. An alarmed doctor, peering around the corner, is holding back a couple of his colleagues and declaring, "It's a break!" Were they the same infants portrayed in the cards? Were they breaking out to look for some girls? In any case, the Feldman household consisted of all male children. We three boys had no sisters. Vivian was without a daughter. How life might have been different had there been a female presence among the siblings is something we will never know. But there is no doubt that things would not have been exactly the same. Once Donnie became aware of the anatomical difference between males and females, he sympathetically fashioned a penis for Vivian out of his modeling clay. Vivian found it amusing, but rather than be converted into an honorary male, I think she would have liked to have enjoyed the company of a daughter. It's questionable whether Art and Vivian wanted a third kid, just as it's doubtful that they wanted their first one as early as he turned up. But if they had decided on a third, couldn't it have been a daughter?

Donnie was a bit premature in his arrival, weighing barely five pounds. As a kid, he was asthmatic, but unlike the stereotype, he was not fragile. He stoically withstood all the scratch tests and injections that went along with allergy tests and treatments. Doctors remarked on his unusual fortitude, and that kind of strength became his trademark. He could take it, and he could dish it out. This became apparent in school where he could not be cowed or bullied. As a result, he ended up fighting kids others sought to avoid. There might have been initial pride in how tough Donnie seemed to be, but at some point it had to be acknowledged that there was a problem. Donnie wasn't learning much in school. His annual promotions to the next grade were often in doubt. Then there was also the reputation he was gaining in the neighborhood as a troublemaker, if not a terror.

Donnie was becoming a lot for Vivian to handle, especially with Art so often on the road. She would complain to Art, but he tended to privately dismiss her concerns. So he was a fighter. Is that so bad? He doesn't take any crap. That's how you have to be sometimes in this world, right? Yes, sometimes, perhaps, but all the time? And what happens when he begins to get a reputation in the neighborhood? What if friends and neighbors begin to wonder what's going on with the Feldmans? How can they raise a kid who's ready to hit you in the mouth at the drop of a hat? How can Vivian

Feldman, always so proper and self-possessed, have a son like that running loose in the neighborhood? Who's she kidding? Something wrong must be going on in that household to produce a kid like that. Vivian hit Art with all this when he returned from a road trip. "You got to do something about it. He doesn't pay attention to anything I say. I scream myself hoarse. He's unmanageable. I can't take it anymore, I'm telling you." It was time for the man of the house to do his thing. Art couldn't avoid it any longer. The belt hanging on the dumbwaiter door was no longer adequate for the job.

Donnie had heard the threats before. "Your father will hear about this." "Wait until your father gets home." But Art was the guy who participated in our jokes and games, and brought home rock and roll records. This time it was different. Art confronted Donnie. "What are you doing? Why are you causing so many problems for your mother?" Donnie couldn't answer, because he found himself immediately ducking a right hand swat. Art didn't seem to have his heart in this whole thing, but he was frustrated by the fact that Donnie was too quick. "You're going to have to learn how to behave." Donnie continued to bob and weave, ducking behind furniture. Art smacked the back of a chair, and pushed aside a table. Vivian stayed in the kitchen, listening to all of it. "I don't want to hear any more reports like this, understand?" Art was ending this exercise in futility, hoping Vivian would be satisfied with the effort. Donnie scampered out from behind the couch, and retreated to our bedroom. He didn't say anything, but he seemed a bit shocked that Art had turned on him like that. Sure, he got into trouble often, but it's not like he planned it. It seemed to him that Vivian was always yelling about something. That was nothing new. It was natural that Art would take her side, but he had never tried to hit him. Why would he do that now? At least he had managed to escape. Mingled with shock and puzzlement, there was a bit of pride about that.

24

What we knew about sex we learned mostly in the streets. This amounted to rumors, largely misunderstood interpretations of voyeurs, and poorly related experiences of older brothers. Sure, parents would usually make an effort to provide some information when they thought the time had come, but the effort was generally ineffectual. I knew the time had come for me. I had been having some exciting sensations about girls ever since I held hands with Lois Roth during a fifth grade dance lesson. In sixth grade, there was blonde, beautiful Eleanor Posner. Every guy was crazy about her, and I took my chance to sit next to her when the opportunity presented itself. My semi-pubescent hormones simply overrode my natural shyness, but they didn't help me to figure out what to do once I was seated face-to-face with Eleanor. So I merely declared my attraction to her by claiming a spot next to her, then, after a minute or two, thinking of nothing in particular to say, retreated to my assigned seat. A dubious victory, perhaps, but one small step for adolescence nonetheless. It was in the seventh grade, however, when puberty arrived in force. I woke up one morning to discover that my underpants were uncomfortably coated with a dried yellow substance. I changed into a fresh pair and stuck the soiled one in the laundry. Not long after, Vivian gave me a library book that discussed what happens when boys become men. I found it more scary than educational. Many of the details didn't register with me, but I did receive the impression that the physiological changes occurring within me would result in a loss of control. A powerful urge would change the way I behaved, like it or not. In the section that covered what parents might do to help their son in this situation, it even mentioned possibly obtaining a prostitute for him. This seemed incredible to me. I couldn't imagine Art or Vivian doing something like that. They didn't do it for Harry, did they? I had never heard of any parent doing anything like that for their son. But what if they did? I didn't want that. I wouldn't let them. The book's author couldn't be serious, but it didn't seem to be a joke. Maybe he was just mentioning all possible options in that situation, no matter how far-fetched. But did that mean that there were some places where they did things like that? Who knows, maybe there were. I was just glad this wasn't one of them as far as I knew. But that was the problem. I didn't know much about this whole thing.

When Art got back from his sales trip, Vivian had him sit down with me to have a talk. This was very awkward. I guess it is for most every father and son, and definitely so in our case. Art didn't have the kind of relationship with his sons that would make this scenario seem natural. But, then again, how many fathers did? Art was busy trying to make a living most of the time, usually out of town, and when he was home, he was more of a buddy than a mentor. This situation called for an abrupt role change. Now Art had to be someone like the ideal father we would see on TV shows, the one who instinctively knew just the right thing to say in delicate situations - Robert Young in "Father Knows Best" for instance. But in that kind of a show someone was writing the script, and it reflected an image of an America that just didn't exist. It was an imaginary place where all family members were genteel and well-dressed, and all children well-scrubbed and respectful. Hell, Robert Young came to the dinner table in a jacket and tie, and the woman of the house did the vacuuming in what looked like an evening gown. This definitely was not the reality we knew in the Bronx. Our household bore a closer resemblance to Jackie Gleason's in "The Honeymooners." Yes, we had upgraded from an ice box to a refrigerator and we owned more than a few sticks of furniture, but we had real conflicts with hard feelings, and we regularly made fools of ourselves. Troubles were never resolved in a matter of minutes with a few well-delivered platitudes. They lingered and we had to struggle with them the way real folks do.

Anyway, we had the talk, and unfortunately it wasn't much more informative than the book. Art talked off the cuff, tossing out ideas and impressions he had on the subject in an informal manner. Sex felt great. It was maybe the best sensation in the world, but you have to know how to handle it . That was the crux of the matter. But I never really found out how to go about that. At least Art mentioned masturbation, although I wasn't quite sure he was referring to it at that moment. He said something about some guys "putting it on a pillow and yelling come, come." I got the general gist of the matter but the image seemed bizarre. Why would a guy be in that kind of agony if sex felt so good? Art asked me if I had any questions. I said I didn't, but actually I had too many to even know where to start. Plus it didn't seem natural to bring them up with him, so the session ended right about there. I had to give Art credit. He made the effort, and what he tried to communicate was based on real life experience. So maybe father didn't know best, but how many fathers really did? If we were living in the TV show, the subject wouldn't have ever been raised. I wouldn't have gotten any more guidance than what was offered in that book.

I probably ended up learning more about sex by reading erotic fiction than in any other way. Harry had copies of Henry Miller's paperbacks. *Sexus*, proved especially incendiary, and I dove into it without Harry knowing. It was definitely educational. Also fantastic. I couldn't relate the wild sexual activity the author described to the everyday life I experienced and the people I knew, but it was definitely eye-opening and stimulating. It presented a range of possibilities that I hadn't even imagined. For one thing, I never thought that women could be as excited about sex as much as men. Then I started wondering whether I could really trust what I was reading. It wasn't like this was a scientific account. On the other hand, someone said that you could learn more about real life from a novel than from any scientific volume. In any case, I reasoned, even if an author was only imagining things like this, they could probably be done. Maybe they even were being done. I didn't really see myself ever participating in the kind of sexual gymnastics that the author described, but who knew what the future might hold? At least I was no longer completely ignorant of the wide and varied sexual landscape that lay before me. Then I started thinking about Harry. Did Art have a talk with him too when he came of age? And if so, did he tell him what he told me? I wasn't going to ask Harry. He was ten years older than me and more like an uncle than a brother. And not all that close an uncle either.

25

Harry the worker always had a job, some money, and an active social life. A decade older than me, thirteen years older than Donnie, he was almost from an older generation. He liked Lauren Bacall and Eartha Kitt, and listened to Vic Damone and Kay Starr. He denigrated Buddy Holly and Gene Vincent, and mocked us for listening to them. He didn't like professional wrestling, and hated Laurel and Hardy. Who hated Laurel and Hardy, for chrissake? Harry also had little appreciation for sports. He wasn't any good at them either. When he became frustrated with our antics, he would threaten to smack us across the room. Smack? We would laugh in derision.

But Harry had it covered on the social front. He hung with some semi-hoodlums in high school, wore jeans and penny loafers, and chain smoked Lucky Strikes. And he would go through one girlfriend after another. Our family photo albums were packed with pictures of Harry and Eileen, Harry and Diane, Harry and Naomi. At 21, It looked like he was going to get married to Helen, a personable, bright, attractive, young lady. We all liked her. But something happened, and it was over. Next thing we knew, he was dating Deliah, a girl who lived across the street. She looked OK, and was pleasant, but kind of dull, and her mother Sandra was known as Old Stoneface. She never cracked a smile, never seemed to take joy in anything. Before we knew it they were engaged.

Old Stoneface was a problem, though. She didn't seem to take to Harry very well. But then again, she didn't seem to take to anybody. Harry had a sarcastic sense of humor and would dredge up every mother-in-law joke he could remember to characterize Deliah's mother. And this was before the wedding. Perhaps Sandra Bolek was depressed, but back in the 1950's we weren't quick to apply psychopathological labels to misanthropic behavior. She was antisocial. She felt she was unappreciated, a victim. She imagined she was ill. She was a problem for anyone who had to deal with her except maybe her husband Ira who appeared to take everything in stride. Maybe that was because Ira was largely unaware of his wife's problems and grievances, or maybe he thought everyone's wife had similar complaints. We really couldn't tell, because Ira faced every situation and individual with a pleasant, relaxed smile and said very little.

Despite potential pitfalls, the engagement took place, and everything seemed on track. Sandra even seemed semi-normal for a while. She approached me and Donnie in the street, and invited us in to her apartment for ice cream. Maybe she wasn't such a bad old bat after all. Then it happened. Sandra declared that the engagement was off. Had she heard what Harry was saying about her? Did she decide that the match was socially and economically unacceptable? Ira Bolek was a property owner (he owned a parking lot), and the Boleks lived in an upscale apartment building. (Even though it was directly across the street, it had a bigger lobby and an elevator.) Art was a traveling salesman, and everyone knew all about those kind of people.

We never found out exactly what Sandra's objections were, but they probably had something to do with Vivian, because one day she accosted Grandma Bessie to complain: "Do you know how your daughter treats me?" Did it bother Sandra that Vivian carried herself as if she was the one who lived in a building with an elevator? That Vivian was treated with greater respect and deference in the neighborhood? That a neutral observer would choose Vivian as the one who most likely belonged to a higher social class? In any case, Grandma Bessie must have been taken aback by this strange encounter. What did she know or care about Sandra's imaginary grievances? She listened silently, nodding her head, looking questioningly and uncomprehendingly at Sandra, and went on her way, not really knowing what to make of it all.

Now it was up to Art to salvage the wedding. On one fair evening, he marched across the street, intent on exercising his diplomatic skills. He would have liked to tell Sandra where to get off, but the moment called for tact and sensitivity. It was beyond Art's ability to genuinely sympathize with Sandra's paranoia, but it was well within his skill set to sell Sandra on the desirability of maintaining this match. "Let me go set her straight," he told Vivian. "If the kids want to get married, they should. She's just going to have to step aside."

"She's not happy unless she's causing trouble," Vivian replied.

"It's not going to work this time," Art maintained.

Sandra welcomed Art into her apartment stoically, Ira at her side. "She looks like she's ready to face the firing squad," Art thought. Sandra motioned Art to a seat on the sofa which was wrapped in a thick plastic cover, but offered him no refreshments. "Thank you, Sandra, how are you?" Art asked.

"How can I be?"

"Well, our kids are getting ready for a big moment. We should all be happy for them, right?" Sandra closed her eyes and tossed her head a bit. "I mean why don't we see if we can do what's best for them?"

"And what is best for them? Should Deliah attach herself to someone who will eat her heart out?"

"She always seems happy to me when I see her."

"A mother can tell when her daughter is miserable." Art looked at Ira who was shifting uncomfortably in his seat. "Do you know that Harry told her he was looking for a job half way across the country? That he was going to drag her to Pennsylvania or Colorado or somewhere? Is that the way to start a marriage? By breaking up a happy family? How is a grandmother going to see her grandchildren when they're living thousands of miles away?"

It occurred to Art that responding directly to Sandra's delusions would be fruitless. "Happy family?" Art saw Deliah taking every opportunity to escape from the grim landscape Sandra had created.

"I heard that you were going to get a nice apartment for them in your building."

"Yes, and I had to twist a few arms, let me tell you. I had to go hat in hand to that landlord, the beast, because he wanted to keep the apartment for his own daughter. I had to humble myself before him, practically kiss his feet."

"That I'd like to see," Art thought. "I heard it's a beautiful place," Art said.

"Oh, it's very nice," Ira broke his silence. "It's a regular palace. It's right above our apartment. Hardwood floors, parquet yet," Sandra added. Now Sandra was in here element. "A garbage disposal and he said he'd put in a dishwasher. Why should Deliah have to slave over the sink, washing dishes like a drudge?"

"Sounds wonderful," Art lied. He could imagine how much Harry would love living so close to his in-laws.

"But do you think Harry appreciates it? Sandra asked."

"I'm sure he does."

"I can't tell. He never says anything to me. Never a word. Now shouldn't a son-in-law show some consideration?"

"That doesn't sound like Harry."

"Oh, I know, he's always with the jokes and the laughing, but when it comes to showing respect and appreciation..." Sandra shrugged her shoulders.

Art knew that he needed to exert great effort at this point to avoid blowing it all up. "I tell you what, Sandra, I'll speak to Harry about it."

"Is he well?"

"Harry?"

"Yes, I mean with those dark bags under his eyes. I've never seen that in a boy of his age. And he seems to be going bald too." Art glanced at Ira whose dome was largely bereft of hair.

"He's fine, Sandra." She closed her eyes and raised her brows. "Oh, would I like to..," Art said to himself.

"Well, if you think so. I'm just looking out for my daughter's best interests. I wouldn't want her to attach herself to someone with liver or kidney problems. You understand. This is a step that cannot be taken lightly."

"Right, well, I'll talk to Harry, and I'm sure we can get things straightened out." Art rose and headed to the door.

"Come again," Ira said.

"Don't bet on it," Art thought.

"What did she say?" asked Vivian when Art returned.

"Nothing that bears repeating. She's *meshuggeneh*."

"There's something wrong with her."

"I had to sit and listen to her bullshit."

"But it's settled?"

"For now."

"What's going to be with her?"

"I don't know, but I'm sure we'll find out.

So the wedding took place. Harry and Deliah slow-danced to Santo and Johnny's "Sleep Walk," collected the checks that were passed to them in clean, white envelopes, and smiled politely to each guest who wished them well. We all dined on roast chicken and brisket, drank sweet red wine, and had a slice of the three-tiered wedding cake with a miniature, plastic bride and groom on top. Grandpa Sam kept laughing and asking when they were serving the *petchah*, and Grandma Bessie kept telling him to be quiet. Donnie ran around finishing abandoned cocktails, and fell asleep at the table.

Harry and Deliah honeymooned in Miami Beach for a week. Deliah languished by the pool, paged through the latest issues of *Colliers* and *Look* magazines, and returned with a deep tan. Harry took her to Joe's Stone Crab, the greyhound races, and Jai-Alai. Deliah even returned with an extra few bucks when Harry let her place a few bets and she actually a couple of winners. "Beginner's luck," Harry said. He seemed happy.

Upon their return, Harry turned the key to open the door of their new apartment. He was surprised to find it unlocked. He and Deliah walked in to find Sandra on her hands and knees scrubbing the kitchen linoleum. "What are you doing, ma?" Deliah asked.

"I'm working!" Sandra barely lifted her head before returning to the task at hand, grinding the scrub brush into the flooring, slowly advancing across the kitchen, leaving a trail of soapsuds.

"Ma, there's no need..." Sandra's head shot up.

"There's no need?! There's no need?!! Someone's got to do it!" Deliah looked despairingly at Harry before taking her travel bag into the bedroom.

"Ma, get up," Harry said. Sandra stared at him. Harry took her by the elbow and lifted. She got to her feet, scrub brush in hand.

"Go downstairs. We're tired. Deliah needs to rest."

"But who's going to...?"

"We'll finish up."

"You don't understand. Mrs. Cohen told me she saw a roach last week. A roach, do you hear me. Do you know what that means?"

"Yes, I've heard of them."

"Don't be sarcastic with me, Harry Feldman. You know, if you let one of those disgusting bugs in, the whole building is finished. Finished, I tell you!"

"Yes, of course."

"And the way that you two left this place without a thought to go galavanting all over Miami, you'd think there was nothing to be concerned about. But how do you know if the previous tenant took proper care? Well, I can tell you they didn't. You could have asked me, and I would have told you. Not everyone is as careful as I am." Harry led her toward the door. "You left it to me to see that the apartment wasn't overrun with vermin. And I saw crumbs, I tell you. You know what that means. Where there's crumbs, there's roaches. Where is Deliah? Deliah, there were crumbs!"

"We'll take of it." Harry ushered her out. He picked up the wash bucket, and dumped it in the sink. "You can come out. She's gone."

The sound woke me up. Art was home from a sales trip, getting ready for a meeting. Still half asleep, I'd heard him run his bath, talking to Vivian through the closed bathroom door about not wanting breakfast. But now there was this choking, coughing and retching followed by the toilet flushing. "Maybe you should stay home today."

"No, I'll be OK." I'll pour you some coffee to take with you," Vivian yelled.

"Yeah, that's all I need."

"Get something to eat later. You shouldn't work all day on an empty stomach."

"After this heartburn clears up."

But it wasn't clearing up even though Art had taken the Ipecac. Because of the commotion, Vivian hadn't awakened me as early as usual. I was going to be late for school if I walked, so Art was going to drive me. The Chevy was parked a couple of blocks west in the only street spot Art could find when he got home the previous night. We didn't talk much as we walked. Usually there would be a few comments about the Yankees or Dodgers, or Art would ask "How you doing with the girls?" This time he only asked about what time I need to be in class. And Art looked so pale. I wanted to ask him if he thought I should go out for the cross country team. Vivian said I was already too skinny. She was afraid I would lose weight. She didn't seem to realize that being skinny was an advantage when it came to distance running. But Art didn't look like he wanted to talk much.

Even though it was obvious he didn't feel good, he handled the Chevy as smoothly as ever, spinning the steering wheel around with one hand. He opened the fly window to get a morning breeze. We zipped around a bus that was slowly leaving its stop and headed downhill toward the high school. After a few blocks we heard loud barking, and became aware of a stray dog chasing the car. Art glanced in the side view mirror about the same time we heard a loud bang, and the bark turned into a howl. Brakes squealed, and I saw the dog shoot by us on the right at a tremendous rate of speed. "What happened?" I asked.

Art shook his head. "The guy in back of us hit him." I turned my head to see the driver behind us examining his front bumper as we pulled away. A couple of car horns sounded from vehicles that were being delayed as a result. We reached my school, and I thanked Art for the ride as I got out of the car. He nodded his head, popped out a cigarette from a pack he kept in his jacket pocket, and headed for the Bronx River Parkway.

When he got to the sales meeting, he sat down next to Whitey Connor. "No doughnuts?"

"Not even a bagel."

"Shoulda brought my own."

Whitey noticed his friend's pallor. "Hey Art, you feeling OK?"

"I think Fishface sold my wife some bad herring."

"Gotta stay away from that stuff. It'll kill you. I got some Tums if you want." Art popped a couple in his mouth but it didn't help. During Mandel's presentation he broke into a cold sweat.

When I got home from school, Art was in bed, his face as white as the sheet. Vivian told me to wait downstairs to help Dr. Brownstein with the cardiograph machine he was bringing. It was only 4:30 pm, but it was already mostly dark. While I was waiting, it began to snow – big fluffy flakes that stuck on the pavement as they landed. By the time the doc arrived, a couple of inches covered the ground. Doctor Brownstein was our family doctor, a short pudgy man with a serious demeanor. He was expecting me, and I climbed the three flights with him, the green metal box in my arms.

I stayed in the bedroom with Donnie while the doc did his exam and Vivian watched. Next thing we knew the ambulance siren was wailing, a couple of men were knocking on our door, and they were carrying Art out. Some neighbors in the building peeked out through partially-open front doors and spoke softly to each other about what they saw. "Who is it?"

"It's Feldman from upstairs."

"Oy, such a nice man."

"What's the matter with him?"

"Who knows? But it's not good. They don't carry you out like that if you're doing well."

"Feet first, that's how we all go in the end." Mrs. Moran in 2D crossed herself. Some people passing by on the street stopped to watch, some concerned, some just attracted by the ambulance with the flashing lights, some feeling relieved that it wasn't them or someone they knew. Art didn't pay attention to any of them. He was scared, and just hoping that he would come through this OK. He didn't like being made a spectacle like this. "Did they really have to send an ambulance?" he thought. "The pain isn't so bad. I could have walked the two blocks to the hospital myself anytime." He was suddenly seized with the urge to vomit again. One of the ambulance attendants handed Art a plastic bucket. "Oh, I hate when this happens," he said." He looked like he was about to heave as well. Art regurgitated into the bucket and thought, "Man, are you in the wrong business." As the vehicle pulled into the hospital emergency entrance, Art began to feel a little bit more at ease. He thought that he'd read somewhere that most deaths occurred before the patient reached the hospital. Despite the seriousness of the situation, this scenario reminded him about a guy who was being carried into a hospital. Someone asked him how long he was going to be there. He answered, "If everything goes alright, a couple of weeks. If not, about an hour and a half." Art would spend the next two weeks in the hospital recovering from a heart attack.

27

With Art not working, the paychecks stopped. Vivian knew she would have to visit Mr. Kaplan again. The Kaplans owned the candy store on the corner, and Mr. Kaplan was a kind, elderly gent – quiet, serious, thinning white hair, pale, a large hearing aid in his left ear, he squinted through his eyeglasses and sat in a folding chair clad in a white apron, occasionally rising to issue change for customers who wanted to use the bubble gum, sunflower seed or pistachio nut dispensers. He had helped out Vivian before.

Mrs. Kaplan was another story. Short, gray hair and complexion, scrawny, wrinkled, bent, looking impossibly old, she spent her day chasing kids away from the merchandise. She guaranteed that as soon as a pair of grubby fingers picked up a magazine or a Clark Bar, they must immediately pay for it or put it back where they got it from. "This is no library" was her mantra to anyone who dared to open any piece of literature on the premises.

Although Mr. and Mrs. Kaplan were the owners of the dingy, disordered establishment, the heart and soul of the operation was their 45-year-old son Louis who was a local legend. No one in our section of the Bronx could create an egg cream like Louis. He didn't need to consult a recipe. He knew instinctively, the exact amount of chocolate syrup, milk, and seltzer to pour into the funnel-shaped paper cups that were then placed into their metal holders and pushed across the counter to each customer lucky enough to be in possession of 15 cents. Louis was also a master of the malted, the ingredients of which he whipped up in a large metal canister that attached to a mixer. But Louis did not want to be there. He was a dutiful son, the Kaplan's only child, loyal and dependable. But he chafed beneath the burden his parents placed upon him. His frustration was reflected in his appearance. Mostly bald, a reddish brown fringe of hair encircled his head. Louis was never seen to smile. Diligent but dour, he served up whatever the customers ordered at the soda fountain.

"Hi Louis, how's things?" a genial regular would ask. Louis would merely mutter

"How's things, how's things?" never looking up from the task at hand. He had no patience for neighborhood schnorrers.

"I vant you should give me a two-cents plain. Put a *bissel* syrup in it to give it flavor," Old Man Schwartz would say, trying to obtain a 5-cent chocolate soda for 2 cents.

Louis would slam down his wash rag and demand, "You want a cup of seltzer or a chocolate soda? You can't have both." Targets of Louis's intemperance would merely shrug. They couldn't be surprised, having witnessed Louis's muted tantrums before, but they were puzzled by his continuous refusal to engage socially with his longtime customers and neighbors. This did not, however, persuade anyone to switch their allegiance to another establishment. The egg creams were just too good.

The Kaplans appeared to live their entire existence within the walls of their dim store. Most folks in the neighborhood never recalled ever seeing any of them outside of it. The only time Donnie and me ever saw Louis leave its confines was the time we were playing ball on the street with Billy Sullivan. Billy stumbled backward through the candy store doorway trying to catch a long throw and crashed into a lightbulb display, sending several 60-watt globes crashing to the floor. Much to our amazement, Louis emerged from behind the soda fountain counter, sprinted out of the front door, tossed his wash rag at Billy, and ran him off the block. A couple of weeks later, Billy ambled into the store to get himself an orange soda after a heated punch ball game, and Louis threw him out, shouting, "You! Get out of here. Last week I chased you to Jerome Avenue!" Actually, Louis hadn't covered more than 10 yards in pursuit of the miscreant, but the image of the middle-aged, sedentary soda jerk sprinting half a mile to Jerome Avenue amused us for months.

Fortunately, Vivian wasn't going to deal with Louis Kaplan. Benjamin Kaplan was the legal proprietor. He held the purse strings, and he held them tightly. When Louis's wardrobe was becoming threadbare, he would say to his mother, "Mama, I need a new pair of pants." Mrs. Kaplan would tell Mr. Kaplan, and Louis would usually get his money. Vivian, however, would not need to go through channels. She was talking to the head man. But that didn't mean that the other Kaplans wouldn't offer their opinion. "Mrs. Feldman wants another loan?" asked Louis. Mr. Kaplan nodded.

"*Nu*, the husband is sick," Mrs. Kaplan offered.

"She always pays back," Mr. Kaplan asserted. Neither wife nor son contested this statement.

"If she needs, she needs," said Mrs. Kaplan. Vivian's prospects looked good.

28

Once Art was back on his feet, his first order of business was meeting with the principal of Donnie's school. Donnie's problems had only increased when he reached junior high school – failing grades and more fights. He had been "left back" and now was repeating seventh grade. Being held over did not improve the situation, far from it. It had no chastening effect on Donnie. He was placed in classes among other troubled students who, for various reasons, did not take to standard education. Because they found the classroom to be a place where they repeatedly failed to achieve, they often rebelled against the fact they were required to spend six hours five days a week listening to teachers tell them how stupid they were. Of course there were some teachers who were more insightful and creative, who occasionally succeeded in motivating a few students to improve their situation. Unfortunately, Eugene Templeton was not one of them.

Mr. Templeton was the Wood Shop teacher who presided over one of Donnie's last classes at our local junior high school. He had a reputation as being incompetent when I had attended the school, although I never had the misfortune of being placed in his class. Templeton had been attempting to educate students for the previous five years. In that time, he had been transferred in and out of three different schools. In none of those locations was he able to establish a working relationship with any of his students, nor did he display the ability to manage a classroom in a manner that anyone would describe as orderly. He wasn't particularly skilled at getting along with his teaching colleagues either. Despite the fact that his classes were always among the most chaotic in the school, Templeton insisted on crossing picket lines during a teacher strike in order to report to class every day. This resulted in several unpleasant confrontations. "You want to go to work, you scab?" yelled one Physical Education teacher. "You should be thanking God that you don't have to face your classes for a few days, you idiot!" shouted the school librarian. Needless to say, Templeton's inexplicable strikebreaking behavior effectively alienated him from many of his teaching colleagues.

On the first day of class in September, Donnie was stunned to hear Mr. Templeton announce, "I urinate at 6 am every morning. I do not urinate again until 3 pm. If I can do it, you can do it." This represented the teacher's misguided effort to impress upon his charges that he did not take kindly to students who regularly ask for a hall pass in order to leave class. Donnie wasn't the only student who was taken aback by Mr. Templeton's clumsy introduction. The entire class was immediately placed on notice that this was not your ordinary teacher. The students suspected that something was wrong here. Their suspicions were to be reinforced quickly and continuously in subsequent sessions. During the second class, Templeton stated that he was building a house and might offer some part-time work to a few of his students, because he relied upon the assistance of many "small-minded big backs" to do the heavy work. It wasn't long before many of Templeton's students retaliated against what they viewed as their teacher's disrespect. These were students who did not need much reason to act up under ordinary circumstances. With a teacher like Templeton, disruption was guaranteed.

Ervin Hunter, a tall thin Negro led the charge. He had been held back in elementary school, and suspended for misbehavior several times. It was Ervin who tossed a rotten egg at Templeton when he turned his back. The egg had been baking on the classroom's radiator for several days, and the odor was nauseating. "Who did that?" Templeton asked, as if the offending party was likely to raise his hand. The class broke into loud laughter, and the party was on. In subsequent days, Templeton arrived in class to discover that the lock on his door was glued shut; that his eyeglasses were missing (they had been placed right above his head on a ledge over the classroom's chalkboard); that the clock in the room had been set an hour ahead, leading him to dismiss class early; and that his chair had been partially dismantled causing it to collapse beneath his weight. After students tampered with the classroom clock for a second time, Templeton remarked, "I suspect tomfoolery."

"Who's Tom Fooley?" asked one student.

"Ain't no Tom Fooley in this class," yelled another.

"Tom Foley? He's in Metal Shop down the hall," shouted a third amid the general cacophony. One day someone had hurled a chalkboard eraser at him, and Templeton exploded in rage. Incorrectly, but understandably, identifying Ervin Hunter as the offender, he sent for the assistant principal who removed Ervin from the room. Irate at being blamed in error for this particular incident, Ervin unleashed a string of threats as he was being led away. Templeton, apparently unfazed, responded by taunting his student, "You're still failing, Ervin. Don't worry, you're still failing."

Donnie, as one might guess, was no innocent bystander in Templeton's class. He took part in several of the disruptions. But these incidents were not responsible for his final break with the school. Instead, it was a fight in the school hallway that resulted in his exit. Donnie was battling another disruptive student when the principal intervened physically, securing Donnie in what professional wrestlers referred to as a head scissors, Donnie's head firmly squeezed between Hiram Trabant's ample legs. Donnie was livid at the fact that a grown man had bullied him like that. Vivian had recently received a letter from Trabant informing her that Donnie "could and would be held back again" if things did not change.

So it was that Art, with Donnie in tow, headed for a meeting with the school principal. Art didn't know what to make of Donnie anymore. This was an old story. He understood the fights. Donnie didn't take any crap. But couldn't he pull it together enough to get himself promoted? He didn't know anybody whose kid couldn't make it out of seventh grade. "When we get there, let me do the talking. Don't get into any arguments with the principal." Donnie nodded.

When they arrived, they discovered that Trabant was not available. They were going to meet with Assistant Principal Robert McLaughlin, a dapper little man who had a reputation for being able to smooth things over, mediate differences, and reach consensus. He welcomed Art and Donnie into his office. "I'm sorry that the principal will not be here today. He was called to an important meeting at the district office, but I'm glad to meet with you instead." Art explained that he had been looking forward to asking the principal why he found it necessary to physically attack his son. "Yes, I understand. It was an unfortunate incident, but Donald was out of control. Why don't we see if we can come to some agreement on a plan to avoid similar problems in the future?" Art was willing to listen. He looked over at Donnie. Here was the son who most resembled him physically, who reminded him most of himself as a youngster, but whose head and face bore bumps and scars that he would probably never get rid of. Donnie was ready too. He needed a way out.

McLaughlin proposed transferring Donnie to a newer junior high school in another neighborhood. Practically speaking, this would enable him to get rid of a habitual troublemaker while at the same time giving Donnie a chance for a fresh start. "New surroundings might be the answer to the problem. Donald can make new friends and get away from some students with whom he has had long term problems." Donnie liked the sound of the last few words. He was getting tired of feeling the need to engage in continual combat with a growing list of enemies.

Art was concerned about the situation Donnie might face in the new school. "Is he going to be placed in the worst classes with the same kind of kids he met here?" McLaughlin explained that students are placed in academic tracks, not grouped according to their disciplinary records. "Yeah, but doesn't that come down to pretty much the same thing? The kids who get bad grades are the same ones who end up getting in trouble. Look, my son is no genius, but he's not a stupid kid. Can't he be put in a decent class with normal kids?" McLaughlin said he would see what he could do.

Art gave credit to McLaughlin for resolution of the situation. Donnie was transferred and placed in a mid-level academic class. He did not distinguish himself scholastically, but was able to make at least some friends whose self-worth was not tied to violent combat. Donnie liked the newer surroundings, as if the freshness of the establishment had wiped his slate clean. As the months passed, however, he did find himself gravitating toward some of the same sort of characters he befriended before at his old school. For various reasons, none of them were able to concentrate on school work, so they congregated with classmates who had similar challenges. Some of them looked for trouble, but others tried to avoid it. Donnie was trying to become one of the avoiders. At the end of the school year he was relieved to learn that he had been promoted to eighth grade.

Several years later, I came upon Eugene Templeton yet again. It was Parents' Night at my old high school, and I was accompanying a friend who decided to return for a visit. His younger brother was now a student at the school, and his parents were unable to attend the event. He was going to see if teachers would accept an older brother as a substitute for a parent. As we entered the school vestibule, there I spied Eugene Templeton, grayer in both complexion and hair color than I remembered him. He also now sported a partially gray goatee and wore thick eyeglasses, but there was no mistaking him. Here he was on the faculty of yet another school. He was speaking with someone who had been a colleague of his at a place where he had previously taught. "Are you still teaching?" Templeton asked him.

"No, Gene, I left teaching a few years back. I'm a librarian at Hunter College now."

"Well, they still got me, they still got me," Templeton lamented, as if he was permanently relegated to purgatory. I couldn't help reflecting on the fact that I was sure the school didn't want to have him, and that he had no business being there. From his sad remark, it was obvious that he was no more effective as a teacher now than he had been in past years, and that attempting to run a classroom was as much of an ordeal for him as ever. Why would he voluntarily submit himself to such misery day after day, year after year? Surely, there was something else he could have discovered by this time that would have proved more rewarding.

29

Harry got settled in at his new apartment across the street, and Deliah became pregnant in short order. Before the end of the year, he was the father of a son. In a way, Harry had been something like a surrogate father for me and Donnie while Art was on the road. But Harry had always been able to maintain a comfortable distance for himself, working in Manhattan, establishing a social life with others who were looking to become upwardly mobile. Now he came home directly from work to help care for the new arrival and support Deliah who was new to motherhood and could not count on Sandra for competent assistance.

Donnie and I would occasionally jaywalk across the street to pop in on Harry and his new family. Young Eddie, clad in his onesie, would be in his playpen having pulled himself erect, his sturdy little legs sunk knee deep in layers of stuffed animals and plastic toys, trying to peer out at us, emitting regular yelps and shrieks. Harry, red-faced, wiping a sweaty forehead with a handkerchief, welcomed us. "Hi, hi, come on in, sit down."

"We just came by to see how Eddie is doing," I said.

"Oh, he's doing great. He's got more toys than Macy's and Gimbels combined. He's gonna learn to climb before he can walk just to free himself from that mound of crap. Heh-heh-heh. You want some soda? Delilah, my brothers are here. Bring a couple of Cokes! Let's see if she can manage that without breaking something, heh-heh."

Eddie kept throwing a plastic baseball against the side of the playpen until he finally succeeded in tossing it out onto the floor. Donnie bent down to retrieve it. "Don't give it back to him. He'll just keep on throwing it out," Harry said. Eddie began to yell for the ball. Deliah entered from the kitchen in a housecoat, her hair in disarray, carrying two plastic cups of Coke for us. "Aren't you dressed yet? We're going shopping, remember?"

"Yeah, but mom said she wanted to drop by first. I think maybe she has something for Eddie."

"Where are we gonna put it? He's already up to his neck in junk. What did she get him, an erector set? Lionel trains?"

"She didn't say what it was."

"Get dressed. Maybe we can get out of here before she shows up."

"Well, she should be here pretty soon." Deliah wandered into her bedroom.

"If that witch shows her face here one more time this week, I'm leaving." Eddie's screams became louder.

"Give him the damn ball. I think my eardrum was just shattered, heh-heh." Donnie tossed it back into the playpen.

"How's pop?" Harry asked.

"He's OK," I answered.

"He didn't look so hot when I saw him last week. You know the doctor said he should stop climbing stairs." Deliah re-entered half dressed, holding a blue skirt against her body.

"How does this look?"

"Fine, fine, let's get going. Wait, that pattern doesn't go with the blouse."

"But the blue matches the off-white."

"It's not the color, it's the pattern. It clashes, too busy." Eddie started coughing and sneezing. "Get the kid out of the playpen, and wipe his nose. I'll pick out the skirt."

At this point, we headed for the door. When we opened it to leave, Sandra was standing there. "Oh, hello, where's your brother?" She wasn't bringing a new toy, but she had some paperwork in her hand. "Harry, Harry, I have something important for you!" Harry and Deliah both appeared, each with a skirt in hand. Eddie started screaming at the sound of Sandra's voice. "Here it is, Harry. Ira got the application straight from the Grand Master."

"What is this?"

"It's the application." Harry looked puzzled. "The APP-LI-CATION! For membership in the lodge. You must remember. Ira told you he would use his influence to get you admitted even though you haven't met personally with the membership committee to present your credentials and that is always mandatory for a new member."

"Uhh, I don't have time right now. Deliah, pick the kid up. Maybe he'll shut up." Deliah lifted Eddie from the playpen.

"Harry, Ira went out on a limb for you. You know that the enrollment period is over in less than two weeks. You must give this your prompt attention."

"Yeah, OK, mom, give it to me."

"So, I'll tell Ira that you will fill this out right away." Harry took the form and laid it on the dining room table. "Oh, and very important, the initiation protocol is on the back of the form. Ira wrote it out for you personally. You need to memorize it. You have to know it by heart without any mistakes, Ira said." Harry nodded and explained to Sandra that he and Delilah were on their way out. "I see. Are you going to wear that skirt, Deliah? It looks so drab. Why don't you go get something more colorful?" Sandra then turned to me and Donnie who were still standing in the doorway. ""You boys would like some ice cream, wouldn't you? I have some Breyers in my freezer downstairs." And she led us out toward her apartment.

"Your mother is certifiable." Deliah picked up the application.

"The Grand Master gave this to dad in person? He's wanted to meet him for years, but never got the chance. Those higher-ups only associate with other muckety mucks."

"If he wanted to meet him all he had to do was take the subway down to Yankee Stadium. He scalps tickets there every weekend."

30

Catholic classmates of ours were excused from afternoon public school class time every week to receive religious instruction. At times, we were envious of them, especially when they were able to miss some math drills. Even worse, though, was the fact that Jewish kids, with an eye towards their eventual bar mitzvah, didn't enjoy the same privilege. They had to receive religious instruction after public school concluded for the day by attending Hebrew school. This meant a dreaded, prolonged school day. It was like an undeserved punishment. After public school let out at 3:00 pm, we needed to trek to Hebrew school for another hour or two. While other kids were out playing in the street or watching cartoons on TV, we were toiling over Hebrew-language prayers and rituals presided over by often poorly trained and ill-tempered, taskmasters.

Rabbi Appelman, a middle-aged, clean shaven clergyman with curly red hair that protruded beneath his knitted skullcap, presided over the educational establishment. He had a distracted demeanor, as if the religious training of young Jewish boys was a regrettable but necessary detour along the path to salvation. The rabbi could often be seen in the lobby and hallways habitually chewing on bits of paper (in absence of a traditional beard?) that he would occasionally unroll then reinsert in his mouth. A classmate of mine said that the paper was actually a miniature Torah scroll, and that by chewing on it he was really performing a type of silent prayer. Others argued that it couldn't be, because chewing on the Torah would be sacrilegious. Whatever the significance of this unusual practice, it was clear that Rabbi Appelman wasn't much of a disciplinarian. When your Hebrew school teacher would give up trying to manage you, and sent you to the principal, the rabbi would sit you down for a brief, calm discussion then send you back to class. No corporal punishment. Not even a phone call home. Conversely, whenever a student excelled in some respect, the rabbi would invite you into his office to select a reward from his closet which was chock full of goodies. One year, I obtained a new baseball bat for collecting the most money for the school's "Trees for Israel" campaign. It really wasn't that difficult. All I had to do was knock on all the doors in my heavily-Jewish apartment building, and I was able to collect a steady flow of coins plus the occasional dollar bill. Even most of our gentile neighbors contributed once I showed them the official collection can, so they knew it was legit. I guess most folks prefer to see a bunch of trees growing somewhere where there used to be a desert.

A few of the Hebrew school teachers were skilled veterans, experienced in controlling restless, tired, and bored young boys who would much rather be somewhere else. Some would adopt an entertaining persona, play a role that succeeded, at least partly, in engaging the attention of the students. Others ran a restrictive class, letting rigid routines do the disciplinary work for them, leaving virtually no room for students to engage in disruptive behavior.

Then there were the inexperienced newcomers who were clearly in over their head. Such was the case with Eliezer Silberstein, a 27-year-old, first time instructor who didn't seem to have any idea how to control his class. Almost anytime between the hours of 4 and 6 pm, one could hear explosive shouting coming from Silberstein's classroom, followed usually by foot stamping, and an occasional thud against the thin metal partition walls that separated the classrooms. This was amusing to students in surrounding classes, but not much fun for Rabbi Appelman nor for any student who was actually interested in learning anything.

I became aware of this when I was placed in Silberstein's class during my second year of Hebrew school. Students could sense Silberstein's unease and lack of confidence. A dark-haired, dark-complexioned, fierce-looking, small man, Silberstein's eyes darted around constantly as if searching for trouble he was sure of finding.

When any student uttered a word or displayed a facial expression of which he did not approve, he pounced, intent on attempting in vain to impose a level discipline one might expect to find in a maximum security prison. The natural result of such an approach was a classroom that lacked even a modicum of order.

Unlike most other instructors, Silberstein addressed students by their last name. When he caught Warren Goldberg talking to me during class, he shouted, "Goldberg, move two chairs away from Feldman!" Warren, complying literally with the teacher's instruction, stood up and pushed two chairs away from me. Laughter erupted from our classmates as Silberstein slammed a book down on his desk.

"Hey, that's no way to treat the holy siddur," yelled Seymour Traybitcher, a perpetual ne'er-do-well, possessed of a voice that resembled a foghorn. Shouts of "Kiss the siddur" and "Apologize to God" echoed through the room.

"You told me to move two chairs," Warren explained.

"That's what you said, we heard ya," yelled Seymour.

"Shut your stupid, screaming mouth!" shouted Silberstein, advancing on Traybitcher. Seymour got to his feet, Silberstein grabbed him by the shirt and shoved him toward the door, bouncing him off a wall in the process. Traybitcher, who probably outweighed the teacher by twenty pounds and could not have been bounced off a wall by Silberstein unless he complied, kept bouncing himself from one end of the classroom to the other like some demented whirling dervish, reeling and shouting as if in pain at the thrashing he was undergoing. Silberstein attempted in vain several times to grab him as he spun by. In the course of his journey around the room, Seymour grabbed on to chairs, books, and desks as if trying to steady himself, sending several objects crashing to the floor. Mr. Silberstein finally succeeded in seizing Seymour by the shirt, and Traybitcher allowed himself to be led toward the door. He looked back and winked at us as he exited our learning laboratory.

Seymour was used to being tossed out of class, but this time was different. This time he did not return. We learned that he had finally been expelled, and that he was receiving private lessons to prepare for his bar mitzvah.

31

When we saw Seymour back at our junior high school, he was challenging guys to punch him in the stomach as hard as they could to demonstrate his strength and imperviousness to physical pain. We asked him what happened after he was expelled from Hebrew school. "Huh? Oh yeah, they got me going to this other guy, the one with the blind kid. You know, Teachermutter." It turned out that he was receiving private confirmation lessons from Rabbi Abraham Perlmutter. Rabbi Perlmutter had a small, storefront congregation a couple of blocks north of our Hebrew school, and he welcomed new students who had been rejected elsewhere. Sometimes new students came to Rabbi Perlmutter because they could not hack it at conventional Hebrew school – Seymour's situation. Other times, a family might decide belatedly that they wanted to have their son bar mitzvahed, and it was too late to enroll him in the standard three-year Hebrew school course. This had been the case with Harry who had also been a student of Rabbi Perlmutter. Seymour had neither the time nor inclination to elaborate on his new bar mitzvah preparations. He didn't want to be late meeting up with his buddy Bobby Stone. Bobby had a giant spool of string that he was going to hold while Seymour unwound it by running in and out of the kids who were climbing the school staircase, hopelessly entangling them all in the process.

Rabbi Perlmutter was often seen as a rabbi of last resort, and he was well suited to the role. A tall man with a dark beard, he was calm and patient, a scholar who devoted most overnight hours to Talmudic study. He was the image of a traditional holy man. He lived simply, in poverty, largely scornful of worldly influences. He led a spiritual existence, doing his best to adhere to all religious strictures found in scripture. In Europe, he might have been considered a wonder rabbi. In 1960's Bronx, he was an anachronism, but he played an important role nonetheless. He ensured that no student, outcast though he may be, would be denied the opportunity to stand before the Torah and become a man in the eyes of the Jewish community. There was no reason in Rabbi Perlmutter's eyes that would justify denying a young Jewish boy confirmation. It was too important.

The rabbi was married and had a son. His wife, Vered, kept house and worked as a matron at the local YMHA. His son, Ezra, was born without eyes and was mute. We did not know the precise nature of his disability, or to what extent (if any) his intellectual ability was affected, but it looked like he wasn't receiving any special schooling. Ezra used to prance erratically around Rabbi Perlmutter's apartment, frequently thrusting his fingers into his empty eye sockets, emitting humming sounds. The rabbi would place an arm on his shoulder and speak to him softly, sometimes direct him toward accomplishment of a given task. But most of the time, the rabbi let Ezra be Ezra, and students receiving instruction from the rabbi grew accustomed to having Ezra around even though they did not interact with him.

When it came time for Donnie to prepare for his bar mitzvah, it didn't make sense that he be sent to a class where it was easy to fall in with the Seymour Traybitchers of the world. Art and Vivian had seen Donnie go through enough of that in public school. Instead, he too would become a private student of Rabbi Perlmutter.

32

Shortly after Donnie started lessons with Rabbi Perlmutter, we awoke one morning once again to chaos and commotion in the living room. Art was still in bed, clutching his chest in pain. Vivian was rushing around in her robe. She had already called for an ambulance. "They'll be here in a few minutes. What can I do?"

Art responded haltingly. "Call Whitey...Tell him I won't be in today." Vivian nodded then walked to the front door and opened it, listening for the sirens. Art rolled onto his side, eyes closed, teeth clenched, clutching his left shoulder. Me and Donnie got out of bed, and began to dress. "Are we going to school today?" Donnie asked.

Next thing we knew, there were men with a stretcher in the apartment. They examined Art, strapped him into the stretcher, and carried him out down the stairs into the waiting ambulance. Once more they would make the short three-block trip to Montefiore Hospital. This coronary, however, was more serious. During the three weeks Art spent in the hospital, doctors advised him to avoid climbing stairs in the future. His heart was no longer strong enough for such strenuous activity, they told him. It was decided that we would move to an apartment building with an elevator.

When we visited Art one afternoon, we found him sitting comfortably in bed, squeezing a small rubber ball in his left hand. "They found some weakness in my arm, and said I should exercise it," he explained to Vivian. She told him that Deliah was expecting again, and that Harry had found them a larger apartment in a different neighborhood. "Maybe Eddie will have a little sister," Art opined.

"Feldmans don't make girls anymore," Vivian joked. They both agreed that it was good that Harry was getting away from Sandra's constant meddling. Harry's new apartment was close by Donnie's new junior high school, and Donnie would sometimes stop in after school to visit.

During Art's hospital stay his brother Saul and his sister Rita from Jersey visited, as did Whitey Connor and Les Altman. Art enjoyed the company. "Hey, when are you gonna end this vacation," Les asked.

"As soon as Mandel gets him that new convertible with power steering, right Art?" Whitey offered. Les told Art that Si Lieberman wanted to visit, "But he can't take hospitals."

"He can't take hospitals? Whattaya mean?"

"All the tubes and needles and stuff, they make him sick."

"That big *shtarke*? I can't believe it."

"It's true," added Whitey, "when we went to see George after he had his appendix out, Si smelled the ether or something and he turned green. He had to sit down. I thought he was going to pass out."

"Hey Art, I got something for you." Les pulled a pint of J&B scotch from his jacket pocket.

"What are you bringing that in here for?"

"What, would you rather have a fruit tray? Stick it in the drawer, it's good for what ails ya, whatever it is. Puts lead in ya pencil and hair on ya chest. Get ya back on your feet in no time. Don't let the nurses get their hands on it, though. I heard they're a bunch of *shikers* here." Les shoved it under a pair of pajamas in the bureau.

"Hey, and don't worry about anything at work. Hackley's coverin' for ya," Whitey joked, "he wrote up a couple dozen orders and put your name on them – all parking lots and whore houses!" They laughed their way out. They were concerned, but it was easier to joke about the situation. They had been hesitant to pay the visit, but now they were glad they came. Art was easy to visit. He didn't need much cheering up to begin with. Just seeing some familiar faces, and hearing the good-natured banter put him in a fine mood.

Rita's visit was a lot calmer. She was the older sister, and had taken care of Art when he was little. She was glad to see Art looking well. They talked about life in Jersey. Fran wasn't taking care of her diabetes. She had burned herself on the stove the other day – didn't feel a thing. Rita admitted to being a bit bored now that her kids were grown and out of the house. "You should do some volunteer work," Art suggested, and Rita agreed. But Rita didn't talk about one very important thing. She didn't think it was the right time to mention it. Art didn't find out until he left the hospital that Grandma Claire had died in her sleep a week earlier.

Vivian obtained a lease on an apartment a couple of blocks east of our old building. It had an elevator. As soon as Art was released from the hospital, we moved in. It was a nice place, but the only thing I didn't like about was the fact that there was a cemetery across the street. During our first ride up in the elevator, we observed an unusual framed notice attached to the wall of the conveyance. A photo of a middle-aged couple that was captioned with the statement "Building Superintendents Franklin and Marjorie Santoni Welcome You to Putnam Arms." I had travelled up and down many elevators in the Bronx, but had never received such a formal welcome. And "Putnam Arms"? Nobody had ever heard the building called by that name. In fact, it was extremely rare that apartment buildings in our neighborhood had any name at all. They were just known by their address numbers. Was the landlord trying to make us think we were living on Manhattan's Upper East Side? At least there was no fear that we would be forking over money as if we were living in some such toney neighborhood. This building was under rent control as our previous one had been. In the posted photograph Frank Santoni looked as if he had been dragged before the camera against his will. "Looks like a mugshot," Art commented. Actually, there was something vaguely menacing about his grim visage. He had dead eyes. There was no smile, not even a grin, just a flat stare. His graying hair was slicked straight back, flat to his skull. There were several knots on his forehead and a scar on one cheek. It did look like a face one might come across on a wanted poster. Vivian peered more closely at the image, as if she had seen it somewhere before. "Don't get too close. He'll give you the evil eye," Art joked. Marjorie's photo depicted a bleached blonde, heavy-set woman with several chins and what appeared to be a pair of blackened eyes. Her complexion was almost as yellow as her hair.

Overabundant flesh hung down on both sides of the broad, fixed smile she was offering the photographer. At least it looked like a smile. It was hard to tell, because she had one of those mouths that had become naturally down turned with age. When she smiled, it merely became transformed into a rather straight line across her face. You could tell that she was smiling, though, because the wrinkles around her cheeks and eyes lifted a bit. It seemed strange that despite her obesity, those long wrinkles marked both sides of her face, traveling down her cheeks like dry riverbeds.

"Putnam Arms, huh?" Art said as we stepped into our new flat. It had a large, dark foyer off the main entrance which would serve as a TV room.

"Oh, it's not so bad," said Vivian. "Pretty nice, really. More room than our old place." Me and Donnie would share the only bedroom with Art and Vivian again sleeping on the trundle bed in the living room. The windows in the front of the apartment looked out on the street below with that large cemetery clearly visible to the north. On the east was a small parking lot owned by Ira Bolek. He had purchased it as an investment, although there was usually sufficient parking in the area. We would see him there occasionally shoveling out the snow that had accumulated after winter storms. "Too cheap to hire a boy to do the job," Vivian had commented. There was a large L-shaped bathroom, and for the first time, a room that was air-conditioned. The large living room was equipped with a window unit, another concession to Art's ailing heart. A folding door separated the living room from the foyer, and was only closed when the air conditioning was running.

There was a fire escape outside the kitchen window, and we were visited regularly by a squirrel that made frequent trips up from the street to peer in at the new tenants. Donnie got in the habit of feeding him peanut butter whenever Vivian would announce his arrival. This ensured his continual return, although try as he might, Donnie never succeeded in getting the rodent to eat from his hand.

"Just as well," said Vivian, "he might have rabies."

"Rabies?" replied Donnie, "He's not a dog."

"Squirrels have them too."

"They do? Maybe you're thinking of bats."

"I don't think bats have rabies. They just fly around and get stuck in your hair."

"And then they lay eggs and make you crazy, right?"

"Where did you hear that?"

"Alvin Preston said so at school."

"Isn't he the one who eats glue? Don't listen to anything he tells you."

A couple of days later, we were awakened by shouting coming from the courtyard in front of the building. A loud, hoarse croak communicated a dire threat. "Get outta here, you fuckin' jailbird! You think you can come around here to get my money? Over my dead body!" Looking down from my bedroom window, I could see Marjorie Santoni, her sagging body clad in a faded, flowered sundress, berating a young man in a sleeveless t-shirt and tight jeans who had his tattooed arms raised to protect his head from blows being rained down on it by the handbag Marjorie wielded.

Marjorie's flabby upper arms shook back and forth with each exertion. "Don't come around here no more! You're no son of mine, hear me?" The boy skulked away, a scowl on his face, muttering an unintelligible oath. Frank appeared and grabbed Marjorie by the wrist. A very short but leanly-muscled man dressed in a black work pants and shirt with rolled up sleeves, he said nothing, his face absolutely expressionless. Marjorie grudgingly let herself be led away from the courtyard, repeatedly looking back at her son. "The stinkin' bastard, he thinks I'll support that slut wife of his? After what she said about me.? Not in this lifetime." Then she and Frank disappeared into the building.

34

Donnie's bar mitzvah was not an event of great pageantry. It was bereft of pomp and circumstance. It was not attended by community luminaries. But it was an event of great consequence. All the New York and New Jersey Feldmans were present, as were Sam and Bessie Simonson. Harry and Deliah brought little Eddie, but Sandra and Ira were not there. In fact, Sandra had returned her invitation unopened without explanation. Even though we had come to expect somewhat bizarre behavior from Sandra, this was a new turn of events. In the past there had always been some indication, some inkling of why Sandra was acting as she did, unreasonable as it was. Vivian asked Art what they should do. Art was in favor of forgetting the whole thing. No one would care if Sandra and Ira didn't attend. Vivian decided she would call Sandra. Perhaps the whole thing was a mistake that could be easily corrected. Sandra wasn't in the mood for conversation when Vivian phoned. She merely told Vivian to "Ask your mother" and hung up. Vivian didn't take well to being cut off like that, but she did call Bessie, probably because she could not imagine what role her mother could possibly have played in this scenario. Vivian wasn't even sure that Bessie and Sandra had ever exchanged words. As it turned out, Bessie had no idea what this was about. She couldn't recall ever speaking to Sandra. Then she remembered. Sandra had stopped her on the street to complain about Vivian mistreating her. "I didn't know what she was talking about. I couldn't answer her. There's something wrong with that woman." So that was apparently it. Bessie hadn't demonstrated enough sympathy with Sandra's complaints. She had just stood there and listened. Sandra thought that she could detect a bit of animosity. In reality, Bessie was trying her best to make heads or tails out of the whole encounter. "What is this woman talking about?" she thought. Sandra equated her clear lack of empathy with enmity. Bessie must be siding with Vivian. Of course, Vivian was her daughter. Like mother, like daughter. In fact, reasoned Sandra, Bessie was more responsible for this disgraceful state of affairs than Vivian. She was older and should set the right example. It was becoming obvious to Sandra that it was Bessie all along who had set Vivian against her. How else could she stand there when Sandra had clearly displayed the facts for her and not react? Any idiot could have seen how Vivian had wronged her. It was the quiet ones you needed to keep an eye on. Bessie was the trouble maker. There was no getting around it. And if they thought that Sandra was going to attend this affair and demean herself by sharing a room with Bessie Simonson, they had another think coming! They probably even planned to seat Sandra right next to Bessie on the dais so they could rub her face in it, humiliate her. But Sandra was wise to their scheme. She wouldn't give them the satisfaction of attending! So Sandra and Ira did not grace us with their presence. What Ira thought of the whole situation is unknown. Deliah shrugged it off. She was accustomed to her mother behaving irrationally.

Seated on well-worn benches, we looked around at the dark walls decorated with copper plaques memorializing departed congregants and their family members, each one illuminated by a small, dim light bulb; the small tabernacle; and the little congregation of regular attendees. One of them, a dapper 70-year-old in a brown suit, plaid shirt, and embroidered skullcap walked over to shake our hands. He introduced himself as Herman Lemel. "So pleased to meet the boy's family. *Mazel tov, mazel tov*. How are you? An auspicious occasion, no? Don't be nervous. I'll tell you when to come up to the *bimah*. You will all do fine. The boy will make you proud."

Aunt Ida arrived, she rushed excitedly to the front of the room to congratulate Art. Ignoring the gesticulations of Mr. Lemel, she thrust her red face into ours, hugged everyone, pinched some cheeks, and proclaimed, "Wonderful! *Mazel tov*" repeatedly, as a large, prominent vein on the side of her throat throbbed enthusiastically. "Look at Donneleh all dressed up, a real *mensch*. Harry, having adopted the more urbane cultural practices of his upscale Manhattan colleagues, rolled his eyes and shook his head at such a naked, emotional display. Rabbi Perlmutter glanced over at the disturbance, but did not pause in his methodical recitation of the *Shabbos* service. He would diligently observe all requisite practices. He did not announce when the congregation was to stand or sit. The regulars already knew. The others could follow Mr. Lemel's lead. Mr. Lemel would nod, raise his eyebrow, and occasionally gesticulate with a hand to indicate the correct procedure, but he would not utter a word to interrupt the rabbi. On the rare occasion when a man would enter the sanctuary with a bare head, Mr. Lemel would rush over to offer a yarmulke. As chief beadle and usher, he was always ready to ensure that propriety would govern on the Sabbath.

A few minutes after the beginning of the service, Daniel Darrow arrived. Daniel was a few years older than I, but he was a neighborhood fixture who knew and conversed with everyone regardless of whether they were receptive. He wrapped his head in his prayer shawl and swayed as he recited the traditionally prescribed blessing for donning the *tallit*, then reached over and patted Donnie on the shoulder and smiled before wiping off the bench with his handkerchief and seating himself. Daniel was always pleased to see a neighborhood youth make good, especially someone like Donnie who had had his share of difficulties. Daniel saw himself as a gentle mentor or an honorary uncle. He looked about approvingly at the comforting manifestations of *yiddishkeit*. Even Daniel, however, was a bit anxious. His main concern was that he not be assigned to the children's table at the reception, as had happened at the last bar mitzvah celebration he attended. As it turned out, he would have nothing to worry about. We had assigned him a spot with the rabbi since he was the most religious guy we knew. If Rabbi Perlmutter would be puzzled by Daniel's presence and his disquisitions, he would have the forbearance to accept everything without complaint. Besides, Daniel would spend a good deal of time out of his seat, circulating throughout the room, dispensing good wishes and making discreet inquiries. Daniels was both a self-appointed goodwill ambassador and a source of reliable information which he gleaned as he made his rounds.

Donnie looked stoic, but a glimmer of a smile flickered whenever someone offered congratulations. He felt odd in a suit and tie, but accepted such attire as part of a temporary ordeal. His yarmulke was perched precariously atop his thick hair which was rebelliously styled in the fashion of his rock music idols. Donnie had refused to employ any kind of pin to fasten the skullcap to his hair because he thought it looked bad. "I'm no faggot," he had stated. There had been a scene the day before when Donnie had returned from the barber with almost as much hair on his head as when he left. And if this hadn't angered Vivian enough, he also sported what could only be described as sideburns in training. Vivian associated such grooming practices with delinquency, and she would have none of it. Screaming imprecations, she sent Donnie back to the barber with clear instructions to have all signs of such degeneracy removed. Donnie returned an hour later with somewhat less hair, and smoothly shaved cheeks. "It's alright," he said as he retreated to the bathroom mirror with his comb to demonstrate how he could still tease his mini-pompadour into a Presley-like cascade down onto his forehead.

Now Mr. Lemel was beckoning in our direction. It was time for Art to come to the Torah for the *Kohen Aliyah*. Grandpa Joseph should have done the honors but he had declined. He would remain seated with Aunt Ida's family, looking stoically but approvingly upon the proceedings. He regretted that Claire had not lived to see her favorite son have his last boy bar mitzvahed. Ida was entrusted to deliver Joseph's cash gift at the reception. Art had attended a yeshiva for a while as a young boy, but he had pretty much forgotten how to read Hebrew by now, so he had to pronounce it in English transliteration. He practiced a bit the night before, and there was a lot of kidding when he had to stop briefly once or twice before completing the blessing. "Was that a dramatic pause?" joked Uncle Saul.

"It's traditional, just building up to the bar mitzvah boy's performance," added Uncle David.

"Oh, leave him alone. He's doing a good job," interjected David's wife, Ellie, "isn't he?" she asked Vivian. Vivian merely answered with a fixed smile and a brief nod. She didn't feel comfortable with this kind of semi-raucous, Feldman banter, and disliked brassy Ellie in particular. "Why was Ellie offering her two cents? Who asked for her opinion?" thought Vivian. Art believed that Vivian's animosity was rooted in jealousy. Why should someone like Ellie end up married to a wealthy engineer when she had to struggle along to make ends meet?

In any case, Art wasn't worried about his son performing well. As he had already told Donnie a few times, if you get stuck, the rabbi will bail you out, and nobody will even notice. In our family, there were no Hebrew scholars anymore. So Art ascended the *bimah*, which in this little shul was not much of an ascent, and pronounced his prayers, even remembering to touch the edge of his prayer shawl to the Torah passage and kiss it, then hold the Torah scroll open as the reader continued his chants. At this point Art looked over to Donnie and winked. Donnie was slouched over in his chair up on the bimah, awaiting his turn. When Art descended the *bimah*, he couldn't decide whether to walk down the two steps facing forward or to do it backwards, as many Orthodox Jews do because they never turn their back on the Torah. In the end, he descended in a sideways manner, betraying his confusion on the theological question. Uncle Saul laughed quietly at the sight and kidded Art about it afterwards. "You probably started a new trend. Maybe it will be the beginning of a new branch of Judaism, the Sideways Jews. They don't face east when they pray, but they don't face west either. They face either north or south."

"Hey, I got the prayer done right," Art countered. "And no dramatic pauses either." Saul smiled and patted Art on the back.

There was no small concern about how Donnie would do, given his dismal academic record so far, but there was one aspect of the question that wasn't being considered. Chanting the *haftorah* was a musical task, and Donnie liked music. True, this ancient Hebrew document didn't have a great deal in common with Gene Vincent's "Be-Bop-a-Lu-La," but it was a series of tunes, and Donnie could definitely carry a tune. I had watched him listening to Rabbi Perlmutter's chanting of the *haftorah* on the 78 rpm record he was given, and he picked it up pretty quickly.

Sure enough, when it came Donnie's turn, he stepped up, settled in, and sailed through. Nary a mistake, he needed no real prompting. When he got near the end, the Feldmans began glancing at each other in proud approval. Aunt Ida looked like she wanted to clap but realized it was inappropriate. After it was over, Donnie accepted the verbal congratulations, the handshakes, and the claps on the back. Years later, he would say that it was the *"mazel tovs"* and handshakes from anonymous members of the congregation that he would remember and value most. You expect it from relatives who are partial and may feel obligated. But here were a series of people he did not know, appreciating him, and welcoming him as a new congregation member. This was something new and different. He felt that he had really achieved something. He hadn't experienced that in a long time, if ever. Even though he was now considered a legitimate congregation member, however, he would never set foot in the shul again. This was par for the course for almost all of the bar mitzvah boys tutored by Rabbi Perlmutter. They were just trying to get through the obligatory ceremony. They didn't intend to devote themselves to a regular religious life, and the rabbi realized it.

As we filed out onto the street, we saw Daniel Darrow, hands on hips, involved in a theological discussion with Herman Lemel. "So, do you think this congregation will ever consider allowing the women to sit with the men? You know some of the synagogues are doing that now."

"No, no," answered Lemel, "this is an Orthodox congregation, you see. We don't do that here."

"But why not consider it? I mean what's the reason for the separation anyway?"

"If the men sit with the women, you understand, they can't concentrate on the praying. You know what I mean, don't you?"

"Oh, sure, sure. I was just wondering if you might consider changing in these modern times."

Lemel put his hand on Daniel's shoulder and turned him toward the front door. "Don't you worry about it, son, there's a bar mitzvah to celebrate now."

The kind of question Daniel was raising would prove moot. Rabbi Perlmutter's congregation would be gone within the next decade. All the regular attendees were elderly men, and it wasn't very long before it became difficult to form a minyan. Lemel would get on the phone to try to recruit the one or two men they needed to make the requisite ten so they could conduct a service. If that didn't work, he might grab a pedestrian who was passing by on the street, as long as he was Jewish. In the end, even these tactics didn't work. They had to cancel the afternoon service and merge it with the evening one. A few more deaths and they couldn't even manage morning and evening services. It was time to close the shul. The Torah scrolls were donated to a congregation in Honduras that was in need. Lemel and a few others joined a synagogue on Mosholu Parkway about a mile away, but that meant they had to violate the proscription against riding vehicles on the Sabbath. They could have joined a congregation that was closer but they insisted that the presiding rabbi should be a truly holy man, someone like their longtime spiritual leader. Rabbi Perlmutter was reluctant to join another synagogue. He probably could have signed on as an assistant rabbi or ritual director somewhere, but he just couldn't make himself agree to such an arrangement. Instead, he made his religious devotions in his home where he could continue to *daven* in the manner to which he was accustomed. Surely God would understand. He would hear and accept his prayers.

35

Art had rented out the K&B Restaurant ballroom for Donnie's bar mitzvah reception. It must have cost him a month's wages. Donnie didn't need to swipe leftover drinks from dining tables. Although only 13 years old, he was now a man in the eyes of Judaism. This night, he could drink as many glasses of traditional Manischewitz concord grape wine that he wanted. A bottle was provided at each table. But you know what? After one obligatory glass, Donnie wasn't interested. Was it because the challenge of doing something forbidden was missing? Perhaps, but it turned out he didn't even like the sweet syrupy stuff that was provided. The man tending the open bar wasn't about to serve a thirteen-year-old hard liquor, and since Donnie was the center of attention he couldn't very well go about finishing others' leftovers.

One thing he did like was collecting all the gift envelopes from the guests, because he knew each one contained a check made out to him. And each check could be cashed, and that cash could buy a more powerful AM radio; a bigger, better Hi-Fi record player; and lots of rock 'n roll records. Maybe he didn't know that Art would need to use a part of the take to help pay for the hall rental, but it would still leave Donnie more money than he had ever had in his possession before. Many folks would say that the money should be used to build a college fund, but the City University of New York was tuition free for those qualified students. So if Donnie managed to turn himself into a good student, lack of money would not be an obstacle.

One of the biggest checks was delivered by Grandpa Sam Simonson. This came as quite a shock to Vivian who had spent countless hours consoling her mother over Sam's skinflint ways. "Mom must have finally gotten to him," Vivian opined. Or maybe it was the slivovitz Sam was swigging from a flask he kept in his jacket pocket. But I think Sam had a soft spot for Donnie. Nobody else could have made him laugh after trashing Sam's TV in order to create an echo chamber for his record player.

Grandpa Joe shook Donnie's hand and motioned to Aunt Ida to hand over the envelope. "Good job" is all he said. Grandpa Joe always seemed a little removed from what was going on around him these days. Maybe he missed Grandma Claire, or maybe he was thinking about all that had happened to him since he was bar mitzvahed in Romania. In any case, Joe would refuse to play the traditional role of family elder who would rise to say the blessing over the challah before cutting the first slice to open the banquet. For many years it was thought that Joe didn't want to be the center of attention. He was just an immigrant tailor with an imperfect command of English. But since The death of Grandma Claire, he had clarified the situation. "I just don't believe in all that stuff." Tradition be damned, Joe didn't believe in saying prayers to someone he did not believe existed. God? Where was God when

Romanian Jews were robbed, beaten, and killed whenever their Gentile neighbors needed a scapegoat? Where was God when the remnants of his family were incinerated during WWII? No, Joe cast his lot with the Socialists. At least they had a plan to achieve justice in this world.

Art was taking the last few bites of his roast chicken when Uncle Saul walked over. "Look who's here." Art looked over in the direction Saul was indicating and spotted Ben Schwartz advancing, hand extended. Ben hadn't been invited, but that had never discouraged him in the past. He was known for being anywhere where anything was going on. Once obese, Ben had taken up walking a few years back, and lost weight. He put his ramblings to good use, visiting every meeting or celebration that came to his attention, especially if food was being served. His last surprise appearance had occurred at the local YMHA a few weeks back. Saul was present when Ben crashed a handball tournament banquet. Ben had not played a single game of handball in his life, but he knew everyone, and was sure they would not consider it a proper celebration without his presence. When tournament organizer Jack Rothko handed veteran handballer Irv Isserlis his 1,000 match handball pin, he announced that the next presentation would be to Ben Schwartz for his 1,000 hour steam bath pin. Ben laughed with the others, and he did not let such pointed humor deter him from attacking the ample buffet with relish. "He cleared it like a hurdler," Rothko commented.

Now Ben was pumping Art's hand, his curly reddish brown hair framing the broad smile of a *schnorrer*. "Mazel tov, Art, three boys bar mitzvahed and such a swell affair." Ben eyed the pickled herring and bagels.

"Thanks, Ben. So nice of you to drop by."

"Don't mention it. I was in the neighborhood. Much *naches* to you and yours."

"Try the chopped liver, Ben," interjected Saul, "I'm sure it's up to your standards."

"Go ahead," said Art, "enjoy."

Ben made a beeline to the buffet and dug in, greeting others as he made his selections and gently but firmly elbowing out of the way anyone who tried to come between him and the food. He emerged from the crowd surrounding the buffet table holding a plate piled high with three kinds of salad, two varieties of kugel, a pair of gefilte fish patties, and two bagels, one of which he bit into. As he passed Art and Saul he gave them the high sign. "I think the herring is gone but this looks absolutely delicious."

A recording of Hava Nagila had begun playing, and dancers had formed a circle to perform the Hora. But the shouting and laughing that ensued seemed much more raucous and unrestrained than usual. "Who the hell is that?" Harry asked me. Occupying the center of the circle was none other than Seymour Traybitcher doing some demented version of the Kazatsky, arms crossed, kicking his legs out wildly, bouncing up and down. Seymour's exaggerated gyrations caused the dancers to stop dancing and start clapping their hands. Laughter transitioned to general pandemonium. Next Seymour broke out of the circle, and reeled toward the buffet table where he grabbed a bottle of wine and started guzzling. After Art confirmed that Traybitcher hadn't been invited, he told the building staff to get rid of him. By this time Seymour had grabbed a fistful of cake which had not yet been served. As a couple of ballroom employees led him to the door, he yelled "Next year in Jerusalem!" and stepped into a trash can from which he was unable to extricate his foot. While he was being dragged out the door, trash can and all, Seymour grabbed hold of the drapes in the vestibule causing one section to crash to the floor. He wrapped some of the fabric around himself as he was shoved out the door and paraded down the street, shouting admonitions and curses to the multitudes like a bizarre Old Testament prophet prematurely bedecked in his shroud.

This turned out to be the last insane clown show by Seymour Traybitcher. Maybe he got tired of playing the fool. The laughs were gratifying, and it was nice being the center of attention, but it was a dead end after all. Sooner or later you run out of ideas. It was hard to keep from repeating yourself. He also began to wonder if they were laughing with him or at him. Maybe it had begun to look like he himself was the joke. Besides, his celebrity wasn't making much of an impression on the girls. Sure, they laughed with the others, but none of them wanted to go out with him. Maybe he'd be better off using some of his other talents. He was strong. He was tough. He had other options. So it was that Seymour Traybitcher became "Tray." He started wearing a black motorcycle jacket bedecked with chains. He wore combat boots, grew his blonde hair longer and combed it into a ducktail. He affected a sneer. Gone were the laughs. Now he was respected by the delinquents, attractive to their girlfriends, and feared by the general population. But some of us didn't consider this an improvement.

36

Art was given local leads to follow until he felt fully recovered. When he returned from work a couple of weeks after the bar mitzvah, Vivian told him that Aunt Ida had called. Fran had died from a heart attack. She was just 52. "You should call her back now," said Vivian.

"After supper." Art went to the bathroom to wash his hands. "Jeez, she was only in her early 50's, Art thought. I knew she was sick, but to die so young? Why didn't she listen when we told her she needed to take better care of herself?"

"She was very upset," Vivian related. "It's her sister. They were close. I could hardly hear what she was saying."

"Alright, I'll call her back now." Art dialed the number and pulled the red ball from his pocket to squeeze on as he talked. This time it served more to distract him from the difficult task at hand than as a therapy tool for his curiously weakened hand.

"I heard the news, Ida."

"Sidney found her dead in the morning, Artie. She was already gone. They couldn't do anything. I had to tell pa the news."

"How did he take it?"

"It's not right. A child going first. Thank God ma didn't live to see this."

"Is he OK?"

"He didn't say anything. Just went to his room and closed the door. He won't let me in."

"I'll be over, Ida."

"No, no, not tonight. It's a long drive. You get your rest. It's OK, Sol's here and David's on the way. I'll call you in the morning."

After he hung up, Art called Saul, and they drove to Jersey. The Epstein Funeral Home had already picked up the body. Fran's husband Sidney was roaming about the apartment rooms aimlessly. Their 16-year old son Marvin was seeking solace in the food that was already arriving. He was pleased to receive the fruit basket Art and Saul had brought. The family did not regularly attend synagogue, but they were nominal members of Congregation Beth El, and the rabbi was coming over to express his sympathy and prepare for funeral services.

Sid was explaining his grief to Uncle Sol who was trying to comfort him. "A heart attack. A heart attack? Sol, she had diabetes. God in heaven, where did the heart attack come from?"

"I know, Sid, it's difficult."

"How many times did I tell her to take care of herself? You know it, Sol. I was after her day and night. But did she listen?"

"She looked after others first."

"She was laying there so peaceful. Like always in the morning. I thought she was sleeping. I told her it was time to get up, to make the Sanka – you know caffeine didn't agree with us. She didn't move. How could I know?"

"You couldn't."

"Sol, I'm seven years older. I should have gone first. It's not right." Sol patted him on the back. Aunt Ida took Sol's place by Sid's side. Sol shrugged his shoulders and walked over to Aunt Rita who was arranging more food trays on the dining room table.

Ida wanted to know the friends and neighbors who should be notified. "I can't think of anybody."

Marvin overheard the question. "Mrs. Serrano from across the street would want to know."

Sid suddenly noticed that his son had started on the new egg salad tray that had just arrived. "Get out of the food, do you hear?!" Marvin skulked away.

Shortly thereafter Rabbi Elton Sunstein came through the front door with a stack of hard, wooden benches appropriate for sitting *shivah*. A thin, gray man in a black, silk skullcap, he was greeted by Ida who gathered Sid and her siblings about her for the pre-funeral interview. The rabbi was not personally acquainted with the deceased or her husband, and he needed information in order to officiate at the service. "I know this is a difficult time, but tell me if you can, what kind of woman was Mrs. Lichtman?"

Sid said, "She was a saint, rabbi, an absolute saint." The rabbi nodded.

"She lived for her family, her husband and son. She was always there in times of need," added Ida. The rabbi began taking notes.

"She never thought of herself even when I told her…" Sid started to say when Marvin began to choke over a chicken leg. His coughing fit interrupted the proceedings. Rita wrapped her arm around Marvin's ample back and guided him, red-faced and teary-eyed, away from the table. He still held a half-eaten drumstick in his fist as the slowly circled the room.

"He's broken up about losing his mother, and only by eating her favorite foods can he console himself," Ida suggested. Sol gave his sister a deadpan look. "As good an explanation as any," he considered. Sid added,

"As terrible as it is for all of us, we know the sun will come up tomorrow, and Marvin needs to realize that there will be food. We're not going to starve."

After it was determined that Marvin was out of danger, the rabbi suggested that Aunt Fran be eulogized as a woman of valor, referencing Proverbs 31:10-31: "A wife of noble character who can find?" This was a popular fallback position for clergymen who had no personal knowledge of a woman to call upon, and it resonated with those present as Rabbi Sunstein hoped. Certainly Sid felt that his wife had discharged her domestic duties faithfully, and to him this was noble. Fran's siblings were also pleased that their sister would be memorialized properly, and the rabbi was invited to partake of the available refreshments. "Thank you, just a bite. I have another call to make," stated the rabbi.

"Not another funeral, God forbid," Sid inquired.

"No, thank God, a troubled colleague who needs my counsel. He's questioning whether he can continue to serve his congregation, given the depressing state of the world. I told him I'd stop in."

"So much sorrow, but we all have to keep going, don't we?"

"Exactly the message I was planning to convey, although in different words.

"Sure, you can quote scripture to back you up."

Before Art left, Saul took him aside. "You remember that chiropractor I sent you to, Peeler?"

"I wish I could forget. He messed up my back more than it was to begin with."

"I still feel sorry about that."

"Forget about it."

"Anyway, you know how they renovated the theater where I work, and they have three screens now?"

"I hadn't heard."

"Well, they did. And guess who got caught trying to watch his third movie for the price of a single admission."

"You're kidding."

"They threw him out and told him not to come back."

"They should've run him in, the freeloader."

"He gave them some cock-and-bull story about getting confused and not knowing which theater was showing the picture he'd come to see."

"And they bought it?"

"He was bowing and scraping so hard they took pity on him."

"He's pitiful alright. Pathetic when you come right down to it."

"Hey, are you going to let him know when you're getting ready to throw away that sweater?"

"Get outta here."

"Just asking because I like it too, and I got priority being your brother and all." Art gave him a playful shove and they headed for the door.

37

Harry was happier living at a distance from his in-laws. It was a healthier situation for the whole family. They could go about their business without interference from Sandra. Harry was certainly willing, however, to allow Delilah to maintain a proper relationship with her parents. They were entitled to see the grandkids – Eddie and newborn Susan. The problem was that Delilah didn't drive and had no desire to do so. Since Sandra considered public transportation beneath her, it meant a visit was contingent upon the ability of Harry or Ira to drive her.

Harry was working fulltime for a Manhattan firm as a systems analyst. Ira Bolek was retired. Let Ira do the driving, Harry reasoned, and that's the way it usually worked out. Ira would drive Sandra over for a visit. One day, however, Sandra wasn't feeling well. She had a headache, and didn't feel up to traveling. Could Harry bring the family over for a Sunday visit? It turns out Harry's car was in the shop for service. He wouldn't pick it up until Monday. "Well, Ira could come get you," Sandra offered.

So it was that Ira drove over in his massive, gray Chrysler New Yorker, and Harry's family piled in. Harry sat up front with Ira, while Delilah juggled the kids on and off her lap in the back. "I wasn't sure Ira knew his way back home," Harry joked. Truthfully, Harry was never a great driver, but Ira made him look good. Ira held the steering wheel with what resembled a white-knuckle death grip as he attempted to pilot his vehicle, his hands held curiously at 12 and 6 o'clock. "It was a consolation that at least we had a lot of steel surrounding us," Harry stated. Ira's right brow was lowered over his eye, his left brow raised, as he peered through the windshield as if his destination would reveal itself to him through the mist on the horizon.

Harry knew that Ira was a challenged driver, but this was the first time he had been a passenger in Ira's car, and he was becoming more concerned by the minute. Delilah, on the other hand, saw nothing amiss. She chattered on about Eddie's teething, and Susan's colic as Ira turned on to the Cross Bronx Expressway. "He was one of those guys who slow up on the approach ramp," Harry observed. "Three cars in back of us cut around us, because there was no way they were going to be able to merge into traffic while traveling 30 mph. Two of them honked their horns. One guy looked back and gave a middle finger salute." Ira barely noticed. "Sunday drivers," he dismissingly commented. A line of cars moved over to the middle line, obligingly giving Ira room to enter the highway. Now he had problems staying in one lane. This was exacerbated by the fact that he adjusted his rear view mirror several times and fiddled with the heater causing him to take his eye off the road. "I don't know how he got a license. He must have paid off the examiner," Harry said.

It couldn't be said that Ira was a distracted driver, though. If anything, he concentrated too much. It was as if the intensity of his gaze on the road, which allowed for no athletic relaxation, detracted from the natural driving process. Cognitively, he focused on the trees, or perhaps only a single tree, but did not notice the forest. Harry became so concerned for the family's safety that at first he didn't realize that Ira might, in fact, not know how to get back to his own home. Suddenly it occurred to him. What are we doing on the Cross Bronx Expressway? It was taking us the wrong way. The joke Harry had made was coming true.

"Pop, wouldn't it be better if we just take the streets?"

"What? Oh, no. Exit 5 leaves us right where we want to go."

"Exit 5? We just passed it."

Ira turned his head and saw Exit 5 passing by. Immediately, he slammed on the brake, shifted the car into reverse, and began backing up. "I was speechless for once on my life," Harry said. Deliah merely looked back through the rear windshield and gave encouraging directions as stunned drivers behind them swerved away amid a chorus of squealing brakes and sounding horns. Undaunted, Ira continued to back up until he was able to leave the highway via Exit 5. "You think he moved over on to the shoulder? No, he stayed right on the highway. I'm thankful to be alive, but where's a cop when you need him? If there's a God, someone took down Ira's license number and reported him," stated Harry. As Harry had predicted, Ira was wrong about Exit 5. It left them off somewhere in the South Bronx, nowhere near the Bolek residence. "I could have sworn that this is the exit I took last time," Ira mused.

"Did you get lost that time too," Harry said to himself.

"Let me ask this young man, Ira said. Pulling to the curb, Ira asked for directions from a disheveled character in a rumpled blue suit. "Could you please tell me if that is Jerome Avenue up ahead?"

"Jerome who?"

"Jerome Avenue. You know, the shopping district?"

"I don't know no Jerome whoever."

"Pop, I think he's drunk," said Harry.

"Well, you can be drunk and still know where Jerome Avenue is."

"I think if you make the next left, we'll be headed in the right direction." Ira decided to follow Harry's suggestion.

"Imagine a postman drunk on the job like that," stated Ira disapprovingly.

"A postman?"

"Sure, didn't you notice the blue uniform?"

"Pop, not everyone in a blue suit works for the post office."

Before Ira could reply, Deliah confirmed that Harry's instructions had been correct. "Look, dad, that's Yankee Stadium up ahead. We're headed in the right direction."

"So, Exit 5 was correct, wasn't it?" Ira asserted.

Harry just ran his hand through his hair and shook his head. "Yeah, if you don't mind traveling 12 miles out of the way," he thought.

38

Exercising his hand with a rubber ball wasn't working. Not only wasn't Art regaining strength in his left hand, it was getting weaker. "Maybe I'm overdoing it. Too much exercise?"

"That could be it," Vivian replied hopefully, "too much exercise makes you weaker." But now his left leg felt weaker too, or was it his imagination? "Let's go to Brownstein and have him give you a physical," Vivian suggested.

'What does he know?"

"He's a doctor. He knows, or he can refer you to someone who does."

"I'm sick of seeing doctors. They got a real racket going, sending you around from one to the other. Everyone gets a piece of the action, and the patient just plays along. What choice does he have?"

It was the tube of Pepsodent that finally got Art to Brownstein's office. He went to brush his teeth one morning, and couldn't open it. When he couldn't exert enough pressure on the cap with his left hand, he shifted it around and tried to open it with his right. That didn't work either, because he couldn't hold the tube firmly enough in his left hand. "Goddammit!" Art flung the tube into the sink. "What the hell's going on here?"

Brownstein gave Art a thorough examination. He told him that he either had a thyroid problem or a nervous system disorder, and wanted to refer him to a neurologist. Art didn't want to see any more Bronx doctors. "I'm tired of these quacks. Remember that hack who told Sy Lieberman he had multiple sclerosis when it turned out he had the flu? And I'm not going to any chiropractors anymore either. I want to see someone who knows something. I want real answers." Vivian didn't know what to tell him. But Whitey Connor had an idea.

Art was having a beer with Whitey after work. "Art, you should go to the Mayo Clinic. They know what they're doing over there. My brother-in-law was given the runaround for months until he went there. They figured out he had an aneurism. He had surgery and now he's fine."

"Your brother-in-law, huh? Didn't I meet him a couple of years ago at your place? Red-haired guy with a moustache?"

"Oh, no, that's Ernie, my cousin. That guy's never been sick a day in his life. But he was 4F during the war — flat feet."

"So I never met your brother-in-law?"

"I think you probably did. Remember when we had that bowling tournament, the guys from the Bronx vs. the Brooklynites? He was the guy who missed a perfect game by a couple of frames. A helluva bowler. He had that huge hook. It looked like every ball was in the gutter, but it always found the pocket. Don't know how he does it."

"I remember him. Short, hairy guy with long arms. Almost bowled 300, but acted like it was no big deal."

"That's him. But his arms aren't really that long. It just looks like it the way he bowls."

"And he went to the Mayo Clinic?"

"Yeah, he was getting this pain in his belly all the time. He thought it was a pulled muscle from bowling or something. Nobody could find anything wrong until he went there. They said if he hadn't gotten it taken care of it could have killed him down the line."

"The Mayo Clinic. That's in Washington, isn't it?"

"No, Minnesota. You're thinking of Walter Reed."

"For a healthy guy you seem to know a lot about hospitals. Minnesota, huh?"

"Yeah, Ronnie's brother lives in Chicago. He went to stay with him for a while, made an appointment, and drove there. Took him about 5 hours. And they told him what's what. They know their stuff."

"Five hours from Chicago? Shit, it would take a couple of days driving from here. And I can't use the company car for that."

"So get a plane ticket." Art had never flown, but maybe it was time.

Art had a sneaking suspicion that Brownstein actually knew what was wrong with him but didn't want to tell him. "Why would he keep it from us?" asked Vivian.

"Some doctors think the patient can't take bad news."

"Oh, Brownstein's not like that. He's known us a long time. He knows we want to know the truth."

"Maybe you're right." It had even occurred to Art that Vivian might know the truth but wouldn't say, but he dismissed it as unlikely. "She couldn't hide it from me. I'd see it in her eyes," he thought. Whatever the case, he was intent on getting the facts from the Mayo docs. Not knowing was driving him crazy.

39

Art had never been on a plane, and he would not have chosen this occasion to make his maiden flight. For Vivian this was her second plane ride. Art had driven the family, minus Harry, down to Miami Beach the year before for a week's vacation. At week's end, Vivian and the kids had flown back to New York while Art stayed on to work. Vivian thought back on those days as she boarded the plane.

It has been a leisurely, carefree week. We all drove down from New York in Art's company car, stopping overnight in Virginia, crossing the Potomac in a ferry as we continued south. Donnie had a field day tuning in all the different AM stations on the car radio, listening to local rock songs and top 40 countdowns. After two days, we checked into Morgan's Hotel Rooms, a small, family-run outfit just two short blocks from the ocean. Les Altman and his wife were already settled in, having arrived a day earlier. Art and Les would be busy running down leads during the day while we would live at the waterfront. All Vivian had to do each day was pack a lunch to take with us to the beach. She would read or knit under an umbrella, occasionally venturing waist-deep into the surf to cool off. No neighbors complaining about Donnie, no bad school reports to deal with, no money problems at the moment, she could unwind. The only "crisis" she had to deal with was an invasion of man-of-war jellyfish sailing in on the surf seemingly in battalion formation. Me and Donnie started popping them with rocks we found on the beach. Vivian made us stop, because she believed that it was dangerous. The exploding jellyfish might release a poisonous fluid, she thought.

Sunset ended our beach day. We'd meet Art and head for a local restaurant. Seafood, Italian, Chinese – we hit them all. On the way home, we picked up bagels and cream cheese for breakfast. After Al Morgan came around in person to collect the soiled towels, Vivian would play cards with Carol Altman while Donnie and me, our sunburns coated with Noxzema, caught up with Dick Van Dyke and Candid Camera on TV.

The flight home was a novelty for us. But it was a trip back to the familiar surroundings of home. We looked forward to it after a week by the seashore. We were tanned and rested. Even Vivian looked at life in the Bronx in a new light, because she was less stressed. She felt more capable of dealing with whatever the future held. But she didn't count on a health crisis. No one ever does.

Vivian accepted the extra pillow offered by the stewardess and placed it in the small of her back. Maybe that would ease the stiffness. She wanted to kick off her shoes but didn't think it proper. Looking around, she didn't see anyone else who had done so. She noticed one small woman who was crowded into a small corner of her seat by the grossly obese passenger crammed into the seat beside her. "They should have made him pay for two seats," she thought. Just then the woman seated in front of her reclined her seat, leaving Vivian what seemed like a mere three inches in which to work her crossword puzzle. She looked around as if to locate someone who might sympathize with her situation. She saw a woman who had it worse – her infant suddenly began writhing and crying in discomfort of some kind. A child in the back answered with shrieks of its own. "Great," Vivian thought, "now I'll probably come down with a migraine." She wished this was the return flight, that everything was already over, that they knew the verdict. At least then she might be relieved of the continual tension that accompanied her, and she might be better able to cope with life's normal discomforts. She looked over at Art. He was engaged in a conversation with the gentleman on his right who sported a neatly-trimmed moustache and a three-piece suit. He was traveling to see his son in St. Paul.

"My son got us tickets to see the Twins on Friday night."

"That's great," said Art, "that Killebrew is a monster. I was listening to a game on the radio in my car. The Yanks were up 3-2 in the ninth. Killebrew came up with a man on base, two outs. The Yanks brought in their top reliever to save the win."

"Don't tell me…"

"You got it. The radio announcer says, 'He's into the windup, the pitch comes in, the pitch goes out, Twins win 4-3, see you tomorrow.' Just like that. I swear." Lots of laughter from the gentleman.

"That's hammerin Harmon. He's ended a lot of games like that."

"You ever been to a ballgame in New York?" Art asked.

"Oh yes, the Polo Grounds the last season that the Giants played there. What a strange park. Those short distances down the foul lines. Lots of history though, like when Willie Mays patrolled centerfield."

"You know the Mets are playing there now."

"The Mets! What a crop of losers! Don't tell me you're a Mets fan."

"I am now. I was a Dodger fan before they moved to California. Funny, I always hated the Yankees and that included Casey Stengel. Now I love him with his doubletalk. He's a real entertainer."

"Like when they lost again the other day, and he asked 'Does anyone here know how to play this game?'"

"Yeah, and he told the press that the secret to being a good manager was keeping the guys who hate you away from the ones who are still undecided." More laughter.

"It's great that Art can be so relaxed. You'd think we were going on a vacation," mused Vivian. During a lull in the conversation, she asked Art for a cigarette. She didn't smoke often, but really felt like one now.

40

I remembered reading a collection of Jack London stories when I was about 12, and I was struck by their rawness, tales of suffering and survival. The one they taught in English class was "To Build a Fire" about a guy who freezes to death because of a mistake he makes in an unforgiving environment. He was warned not to venture out alone on such a cold day, but didn't take heed. He accidentally plunged into water that had not yet frozen over, then sealed his doom by starting a fire to dry himself underneath a snow-laden tree. The snow dropped down and put out the fire. What stuck with me most though was the way he tried to run for safety on frozen legs. He was able to do it at first, running even though he couldn't feel the ground beneath him. But as the freezing process advanced, eventually he broke down and death won out. As terrible as it was to die, freezing seemed relatively painless, just like falling asleep.

My favorite London story was "Love of Life," a brutal tale of elementary survival in the Arctic where a man is abandoned by his companion and eventually reduced to dragging his bleeding carcass over a bleak landscape as a sick wolf trails behind, waiting for his prey to weaken enough so he can pounce. Not only was the starkness of the story memorable, but there was the excerpt from a poem by Hamlin Garland: "But this out of all will remain/They have lived and have tossed/So much of the game will be gain/Though the gold of the dice has been lost." At first reading, it pertained clearly to the characters in the story, gold prospectors who risked everything for the chance at fortune. But later I came to see that it could apply to a wider set of life experiences.

I was walking to school one morning when I saw "Tray," formerly known as Seymour Traybitcher, give his old friend and past partner in crime Bobby Stone a hard shove against the chain link fence surrounding the schoolyard, then strut away in disgust. I walked up to Bobby who was straightening his hair and clothes, and asked him what was up. "He's crazy." This was not an original or revealing observation.

"But you were always friends."

Bobby told me that Seymour had gone completely off the rails. "He punched out an old lady who lived near him on Clermont Avenue. She was always catching him doing stuff, and was on his case all the time, reporting things to the cops. I never thought he would do that though. They say she's going to need surgery." I asked Bobby how he found out about this. "That's just it. He came to me, and told me about it, laughing like it was nothing. Maybe he expected me to laugh too, but what's funny about that? It's not like we are friends anymore, and now after this, there's no chance."

"Why did he shove you?"

"I just told him he's gonna end up getting himself arrested if he keeps hanging around with Frankie Bayless and those guys from Van Cortland Park. It's the truth, but he don't care about nothin' no more."

The thing is Bobby was Seymour's last normal pal. Bobby could move on. He was a decent student. Even when he was busy joining in Seymour's games, he still usually did his schoolwork. He had lots of other friends too. But Seymour? Sure, he was gaining a lot of credibility with a gang of lowlifes, but were those guys really his friends? And where was that going to get him?

41

While we were waiting for Art and Vivian to get back from Minnesota, I decided to take a walk around the old neighborhood. There was a rumor that the Kaplan's candy store was going to close. Someone said that the Health Department was forcing them out of business. Others maintained that Louis had gotten another job, and was finally going to move out of his parents' apartment. Whatever the case, everything looked pretty much the same when I stopped in. A couple of kids were feeding nickels into the pistachio nut dispenser, catching handfuls as they poured out; Mr. Kaplan was stacking packs of baseball cards with their sheets of stale bubble gum on the shelves; Mrs. Kaplan, plastic apron draped over her scrawny neck, was asleep in her chair; and perched on the center stool at the soda fountain was none other than Daniel Darrow, naturally morose in appearance, but unfailingly cheerful in demeanor.

"Oh, hi, how are you? I haven't seen you in a while. How's your family? Your brothers?" I assured Daniel that we were all pretty much the same. I didn't mention Art's health problem. "That's good, that's good. Same here." Louis interrupted to ask Daniel if he wanted two cokes. Daniel answered,

"Just one."

"Your girlfriend's not coming?" Daniel saw me looking questioningly at him.

"Oh, he's talking about Tamar. You know, Herman Lemel's daughter."

It took me a minute to place Herman Lemel. "The guy at Rabbi Perlmutter's?" Daniel nodded. "I didn't even know he had a daughter."

"Oh yeah, she's a really nice girl. Very smart too. She started Hunter College last year when she was only 17."

"And you've been dating her?"

"Well. We've been seeing each other, but I'm afraid she may be getting the wrong idea."

"What idea?"

"It's just that she thinks we're a serious couple."

"And you're not?"

"No, not really. Well, we're a couple, kind of. Or at least we were starting to be, but we were never what you'd call serious."

"You should settle down. Be good for you," Louis interjected, as he handed me the egg cream I ordered, and wiped the counter down with a wet rag.

Daniel began to explain in a subdued voice. "I think Tamar has picked up some strange ideas at college. I mean she's a very nice girl, but she's behaving badly." Daniel had visited the Lemels one day last week. He expected a family dinner, but arrived to discover that the parents were gone. Tamar had cooked chicken soup, and it was going to be an intimate dinner.

"And you weren't dressed for it?" Daniel, who always wore a suit, didn't appreciate the attempt at a joke. "OK, sorry, go on."

"We started to eat, but she was wearing this robe, and she had it half open. And she kept waving her legs at me."

"Waving her legs?"

"I mean she was opening and closing them, crossing them one way and another. It really caught my attention." Daniel paused. Louis was listening in and shaking his head in disapproval.

Then we heard a familiar sound. A hand bell clanging followed by the cry, "I cash clothes, I cash clothes!" It was Abie the rag man making his rounds.

"Louis, tell him to come in," said Mrs. Kaplan, suddenly awake. "I have some things for him." This allowed Daniel to continue his tale unimpeded.

"The next thing I knew, she had her hand on my knee. I nearly choked on a parsnip."

"What happened next?"

"She was smiling at me, but not her usual smile. I mean, I could tell what she wanted. It was pretty clear."

"Did you give it to her?"

"How could I? What would Herman say? I kept seeing him walking in on us."

"But you wanted to."

"That's another thing. I'm not sure I did. I always thought I would. Who wouldn't? Of course, I wouldn't do such a thing just like that. But it was like I was frozen. It was probably the shock."

So Daniel didn't react. He finished his soup. Tamar, took the hint and closed her robe. "I could tell she was disappointed. I felt like I had failed her. She was blushing too. I mean, she wasn't embarrassed before when she should have been, right? Go figure." I suggested that maybe he had saved her from herself.

"I tried to tell myself that, but now I'm just thinking maybe there's something wrong with me. I mean, she's an attractive girl. Why didn't I react? Anybody would have. Naturally, I wouldn't have done anything. It wouldn't have been right. But I didn't feel anything."

I felt sorry for Daniel. I never saw him so down in the mouth. But at least his dejection didn't prevent him from engaging Abie in a conversation about the quality of clothes he was collecting these days, whether he was interested in children's wear, and if paint stains were a disqualifying factor." "Lemme look at it," Abie replied, and Daniel told him to come by his apartment later.

Mrs. Kaplan returned from the back of the store with a bundle of old clothes. "Ma, you're not giving him my burgundy slacks, are you?" Louis asked.

"*Oy vay*, you don't wear them anymore. Besides they're too small. I let out the waist three times already." Louis turned his back in frustration and walked away.

I don't know. I didn't think there was anything wrong with Daniel. He was just a little old-fashioned, but one of the nicest guys in the neighborhood. The thing with Tamar? He was probably just caught off guard – shocked like he said. Yeah, it was probably just the shock.

42

My high school friend, Angelo Morano, was fluent in Italian. It was his parents' first language. I had been studying French for a few years, and had been required to memorize epic poems in class. Angelo thought it would be fun to confuse our schoolmates by loudly conversing in foreign tongues, him spouting Italian and me reciting verses from *Le Chanson de Roland*. So there we were talking incomprehensibly past each other in rival romance languages when Sam D'Argonne, the elderly chairman of the school's Foreign Language Department, stopped to take in our act in the hallway. Rather than comment on our Franco-Italian gibberish, he led us into his office, and told us he needed a couple of students to work in the office. "And you two linguistic scholars are, no doubt, the precise answer to my particular problem." So began our formal relationship with Sam D'Argonne, originally Samuel Sheinman, an 80-year-old WWI veteran who stayed on to study in France after the war, and proudly received a decoration from the Academie Francaise which he still displayed on his suit jacket.

Sam was a tall, heavyset gentleman with a shock of gray, unruly hair and a large, gray, walrus moustache. He dressed impeccably in a style that had been popular twenty years previously. Whatever suit he selected on any given day, the jacket would always display the emblem of recognition by the French Academy. Ironically, Sam's gruff, and at times crude, manner with us was at variance with his scholarly bearing. This aspect of his personality invariably surfaced when we brought Sam his packet of daily mail from the school office. One day, he was conversing with Italian teacher John Scarpelli while sorting through the stack of envelopes we had delivered to him. "Chuck this," Sam directed, as he handed us one item. "Chuck this," tossing us another. "Chuck the whole fucking thing," he decided.

"Sam, Sam, you'll corrupt the boys' morals," said John.

"They wouldn't be working for me unless their fucking morals were corrupted already," Sam responded. We laughed to ourselves, proud to be associated with such a distinguished individual who felt comfortable enough with us to treat us as colleagues with whom he could speak most informally.

Sam let us see ourselves as worldly adventurers, smoking our cigarettes in the school restroom, mixing scholarly references with obscenities in our daily discourse, and working for Sam D'Argonne, the very image of the dissolute academician. Sam took little interest in the regular routine of his office staff. His attention was directed toward weightier matters, no doubt. As a result we were able to frequently indulge in the sort of sophomoric pranks that betrayed our pseudo-sophistication. We would gather all the misprinted mimeographed sheets and shove them into John Scarpelli's print order before having them delivered to him, or we would create impossibly complicated fake exam questions and ask one of the teachers to try to explain them to us. Sam didn't notice or care, but he did continue to joke with us, take a benevolent interest in our academic progress, and provide us a haven from the usual school grind, a place where we could forget for a brief time the tests and competitiveness – both scholarly and social – that inevitably accompanied high school life.

Sam was my teacher for fourth year French that year, and he led us through several literary classics, engaged us in critical conversation, and had us commit to memory some cogent passages – all from the seat at his desk. I suspected that his health was failing a bit. He walked more slowly, his gaze seemed more distracted, and his eye bags sagged lower. Still, his class was always interesting. He displayed a broad knowledge of French literature and history, and delivered it in an amusing manner. In addition, he liked his students and wanted them to succeed. Sam retired at the end of the school year, but he returned occasionally the next year as a substitute teacher. I guess he was attached to the place. Maybe he didn't feel like himself unless he was teaching in some capacity. We would see him in the hallway during change of classes dressed in one of his old three-piece suits, toting his briefcase, wearily but genially making his way slowly to class. We never looked in on the classes he was teaching that day. It might have been sad to see Sam trying to impose order on some of the students he was charged with educating as a substitute. What would those kids know about the distinguished Sam D'Argonne and his triumphs at the Academie Francaise? They wouldn't understand or appreciate such achievement. All they would see was an infirmed, old man who was set before them in place of their regular teacher. He would be easy pickings for anyone who wanted to act up and create havoc. On the other hand, maybe Sam possessed some kind of magic that enabled him to charm any class and seduce them into participating in intellectual investigation. Unlikely, but we never found out for sure.

One day he stopped Angelo and asked him, "It's Tuesday, isn't it?"

"No, it's Thursday," Angelo corrected him. Sam nodded and started to move on. Angelo asked him if he'd met Mrs. Franks, the new head of the department who had replaced him. "Yeah, I met the skank," he said with a smirk, and shuffled on. Angelo had used the put down before in describing the less-than-attractive woman who now occupied Sam's old office, and I bet Sam had overheard it, and was now throwing the term back at him. Sam, fading and confused at times, still knew what was going on with his boys, and still valued his ability to shock. Sadness, however, was the lasting impression of this final encounter. Here was a man who had been dignified, authoritative, had stature. Now he resembled an old ghost. Before, when he tossed out obscenities, he did it as an administrator demonstrating that he too could be one of the common people. Now when he spoke crudely, there was a note of desperation, as if he was trying vainly to be one of the boys. The situation provided me with a better understanding of why some people never want to retire. They are in danger of becoming nobody. They are powerless, without influence. When someone no longer occupies the position to which they have been long accustomed, they are no longer relevant. It helps explain why some folks are willing to embarrass themselves in their old age by accepting almost any kind of position as long as they are not tossed aside like a useless relic. They would rather throw away their longstanding values and principles as long as they can still occupy center stage. At least Sam didn't stoop to that level.

I don't know how long Sam continued to work as a substitute teacher or with what success. I learned later, however, that Angelo, kept in touch with him for a while, and looked upon him as a mentor. I was pleased to hear this. Sam deserved to know that he had had a beneficial influence upon students with whom he had interacted over the years, and that he was not forgotten.

The tests were complete. Art and Vivian were sitting in the doctor's office waiting for the results. Art found himself strangely calm. In fact, he'd been quite calm throughout the whole process. They had told him there would be little to no pain involved, and they were right. "I guess the pain comes now," he thought. He couldn't say that he was optimistic, but for some reason he wasn't particularly worried. "Who knows? The news could be good. And if it's not, there's nothing I can do about it. I wish to hell we could get it over with, though."

With Vivian it was different. When Art looked over at her, she had that fixed smile on her face. Very composed, as she always was in public. She was steeling herself for whatever was coming. At least that's what the façade told everyone. An attractive, capable figure, perhaps even imperturbable. But her private rages indicated otherwise. She had more than enough to deal with already. How could she handle a serious health crisis too?

"You want some coffee? I saw a machine in the hallway," Art asked Vivian. Vivian turned to consider the question when the doctor entered. Art started to rise from his chair. "What is he, a judge? What am I doing?" he thought, catching himself. Art hadn't met this doctor before. At least, he didn't think so. The doc carried a folder thick with test results. He introduced himself, and began to explain what they had found. "Your nerve conduction study..." Art knew he had that test, but what was the doctor saying about it? He was having trouble listening to this. Why don't we just get to the verdict? The doctor continued, "..no abnormalities." Art knew this was good. But did that mean he was going to be OK? "Your EMG, however, indicated..." continued the doctor. "However," thought Art, "there had to be a however. Here it comes." Art heard a string of phrases.

He heard "lower motor neuron involvement" and "spontaneous electrical activity. " He glanced at Vivian. She seemed to be hanging on the doctor's every word, a Kleenex clutched in her fist. "No, this is not good," Art thought. "Why doesn't he finish? I got the message already." The doctor continued to speak of what was ruled out, what was found, what this meant in all probability. A ray of morning sunlight was slicing through the window blind and striking the metal frame of the doctor's eyeglasses. Art focused on the play of light, the colors, the shapes. The doctor moved his head, and the reflected light momentarily blinded Art. He moved his head aside and looked at Vivian. She was nodding at the doctor, holding the tissue to her mouth like she did when she forgot to insert her dental bridge. Suddenly Vivian grasped Art's wrist. She looked at him and her eyes were wet. "It's alright," he told her. "It will be alright."

44

Art and Vivian returned from the Mayo Clinic with the answer they had sought. The doctors had pulled no punches. Art had ALS, and was given 2-5 years to live. There would be various therapies made available to keep the patient as comfortable as possible and avoid complications, but there was no cure. There wasn't even a hope of remission. The disease would advance relentlessly, following its own timetable. ALS was amyotrophic lateral sclerosis, popularly referred to as Lou Gehrig Disease after the New York Yankee great who was famously afflicted. He lived for two years following his diagnosis. Not much had changed in the three decades since. During a day celebrating Gehrig and his career at Yankee Stadium, the ballplayer declared that he considered himself "the luckiest man on the face of this earth." Art didn't feel lucky, but neither he nor Vivian seemed any different, and we didn't feel that there was going to be any change in our daily lives. He had some weakness in his left arm and leg, but nothing that was immediately noticeable, nothing that was going to handicap him right away. He seemed the same as when he had left on his trip. So life went on.

Worldview let Art work locally. He wouldn't need to embark on tiring road trips. Art worked purely on commission. He received no salary. Everything was off the books. But he had decided at the start to voluntarily pay into social security. He had been building his account in earlier jobs, and wanted to continue to do so. This was beginning to look like a very wise decision. Art was driving through Harlem one day, following up on a few leads, when he decided to stop for lunch in a cafeteria. While carrying his tray toward an unoccupied table, he spotted a familiar bald-headed figure crouched, pencil in hand, over a racing form. "Well if it isn't Professor Benedict Hackley." Hackley raised his head.

"Art, Art Feldman, as I live and breathe!" Hackley kicked out the chair opposite his, inviting Art to sit down. "How long has it been, 20 years?" Art asked.

"You haven't changed a bit."

"You mean I looked like this 20 years ago?" Hackley quipped.

"What are you up to?" Art inquired.

"Business, my friend, always business." Art thought it ironic that he had known Hackley longer than any of his current associates, but had not run into him personally for all these years. He had been hearing about Hackley's escapades from everyone, and he had no trouble believing them, but somehow their paths have never crossed until now.

Hackley had been a classmate of Art's at James Monroe High School. Before dropping out, he'd earned a reputation as a guy to go to if you needed anything – cigarettes (he sold them individually), beer, fireworks. Hackley always had a connection. He served in the Army during the war, and Art always figured he'd find a spot on some officer's staff, supplying the brass with all the items they needed to live a life of luxury while in the field. Instead, he ended up in the infantry, and spent three years up to his ass in mud. Go figure. When he was discharged, he picked up where he left off wheeling and dealing in anything that might pay him a living. Nothing illegal as far as Art knew, although he wouldn't put it past him. But if there was an easier way of making a buck, something that required less effort than actually knocking on doors and delivering a sales pitch, Hackley would find it.

Art noticed that, despite what Art had said in his greeting, Hackley had aged a lot. He looked a good 15 years older than Art – mostly bald, and what hair remained was graying, deep creases around his eyes, and he seemed to be missing teeth. But he was dressed well – striped seersucker suit, blue shirt, red tie, shined shoes. If there was anything youthful about him, it was his eyes. They were always active, his glance sharp, taking in all that went on around him. Soon after Art sat down, the waiter, a large black man with a small moustache, walked over. "Here you are, Mr. Hackley." And he deposited a tube of denture cream on the table.

"Thanks, Jimmy." Hackley took an upper plate out of his pocket. "It pays to come to a place where they know you," Hackley said.

"Now that's what I call personal service," Art acknowledged.

"Jimmy's a good man. He can take care of you whatever the situation. Last winter I was here, it was so fuckin' cold my car's door lock froze up. Remember that Jimmy?"

"Sure do."

"I couldn't get into the goddamn car. Frozen shut. I was working on it for a good half hour. The door wouldn't budge. " Am I right or wrong, Jim?"

"Ah, that's right."

"So what does Jimmy do? He goes into the kitchen and comes out with a roll of paper towels. Now I'm thinking what the hell am I gonna do with that? Wipe my ass?" Hackley and Jimmy both start laughing. "So what does Jimmy do? He unrolls all of the towels, and it was a big roll. We got piles of paper all over the fuckin' sidewalk there. Finally he's got an empty roll, you know, just the cardboard tube. And he gets down on one knee, puts the cardboard tube to the door lock, and he breathes into it. I shit you not. I'm tellin' you, he's one hot son of a bitch, because after 4 or 5 breaths that door opens like it was summertime. Now that's real talent, my friend. And ever since then, I carry a roll of paper towels around in my trunk."

"So what happens next winter when your trunk lock freezes up?" Art asked. Jimmy cracked up. "A wise guy, huh? You hear that Jimmy?"

"He's right. Better keep one in your glove compartment too," Jimmy said.

"It won't fit in the fuckin' glove compartment," Hackley replied.

"You know what you can do? Use a toilet paper roll instead. It's smaller," Art suggested.

"Yeah, can you see me driving around with a roll of toilet paper in my glove compartment? People will think I'm fuckin' nuts. Am I right, Jim?" Jimmy just smiled, shook his head, and headed back to the kitchen. "Jimmy's a good man. Used to be a boxer. Had a lot of matches at St. Nick's back in the '30's and '40's. A helluva middleweight back in those days. He's put on a few pounds since then, of course. But if you need a tip on any of the local fighters he's the man to go to. I made a few bucks on info he passed along to me, I tell ya," Hackley rambled on. "Anyway, what brings you to my neck of the woods? I heard you were working in in Mississippi or some place with the Worldview racket."

Art explained his health situation in general terms. "That stinks," Hackley responded. "So now you're back knocking on doors in Harlem and Hell's Kitchen."

"It's a living," Art stated.

"Sure, sure, but there are easier ways," Hackley offered.

"And you're the expert on easier ways."

"You know me."

"That's the problem."

"No, no, don't tell me you're going to bring up all those lies they tell about me," Hackley protested.

"You're a legend, my friend."

Hackley smirked. "Don't believe half of what you hear. Look, we're all about the same thing – putting food on the table, right?" Art nodded in acknowledgement. "You got to spot the opportunities."

"And the opportunities are at the racetrack?"

"If you see the right angle. I'm not talking about making sucker bets and losing a bundle. I'm talking about covering all bases so that you can't lose." Hackley went on to describe a scheme where he touted "winners" to bettors in return for a share of the take.

"And what happens when the suckers find out you're touting different horses in the same race to different bettors?"

"That's where you come in, Art. You cover half the bettors reducing my risk by 50%, and in return you collect half of my fee. We can cover more territory – Aqueduct, Belmont, Yonkers. We can rotate locations. Nobody sees the same face around all the time. We'd clean up. Before you say no, consider. No doors slammed in your face, no doing battle with Manhattan traffic, no depending on Mandel & Son to give you good leads."

"I'll admit it has some advantages, Hack."

"You bet your ass it does. Now you consider it. Don't answer right now. Sleep on it and get back to me. You know I always liked you, Art. You're a straight shooter, and I'm trying to do you a good turn. You deserve it, especially with what you're dealing with now."

"Call, for you, Mr. Hack." Jimmy dragged the phone over from the counter along with his order of corned beef hash and eggs. Art started in on his coffee and English muffin.

"Yeah, John, what? They delivered the Bibles? How do they look? Make sure they're all genuine leatherette covering with the gilt edging on the pages. We don't deal in cheap crap....Alright...OK...That's right...And remember, watch your language. These are Bibles, for chrissake. You're bringing them the fuckin' word of God, understand? OK, see you tonight." Hackley explained to Art, "My nephew. He's working his way through college. A good kid."

Jimmy returned to retrieve the phone. "Jimmy, I want to introduce you to my friend here, Art Feldman. Art, Jimmy Rollins. Jimmy, I been meaning to ask, how's your grandson doing?"

"Oh, he's just fine."

"He's a real sharp kid. That was a great graduation party you threw him. Who was that guy, that singer?"

"Lonnie Brown?"

"Yeah, yeah, Lonnie. He was tremendous. Art, you'd have sworn this guy was Big Joe Turner the way he belted out Corrine, Corrina and Shake, Rattle, and Roll. A real talent."

"I didn't know you could dance like that," said Jimmy.

"Ha-ha, me and the missus used to cut the rug pretty good back in the day. But let me ask you something Jimmy, How's your grandson doing in school?"

"Pretty good."

"That's good to hear. Kids should get a good education so they don't have to end up beating the pavement for a living like yours truly. You know, my friend Art here deals in encyclopedias. You ever think about getting a set?

"I don't know."

"It would really help out the kid. It's like having your own library in the house. He could look up everything, every subject. He'd be an honor student. Get into a great college. You ought to think about it."

"I will."

"You let me know, and I'll hook you up with Art. He'll treat you right. Give you a great deal on a set."

Hackley had finished his meal and was about to close up shop. "Stop by my office here anytime, Art. And give my regards to the boys. Tell them Ol' Hackley is doing good. Hey how's Whitey doing? You and him still tight?"

"Whitey's OK, but he's still a little pissed at you."

"Pissed at me, why?"

"He's the guy they sent out to the imaginary addresses you wrote on those fake leads."

"Really? My apologies to Whitey, but those SOB's had it coming. You heard about the way they screwed the sales crew, didn't you? Shorted us on commissions, reneged on bonuses. They had it coming. Sorry Whitey got caught in the middle. You tell him to come by. I'll buy him breakfast. And you think about what I told you, Art. Don't forget. It's a good deal. Easy money. I wouldn't steer you wrong."

Art left the cafeteria and headed back to his car. He started to reach for the keys in his left pants pocket then remembered that he had started to keep them on the right side after having to fumble for them the other day with his weakening left hand. "Guys like Hackley, they go on forever," Art thought. Nothing fazes him. Half a dozen guys after him for shit he pulled on them in the past. Creditors trying to track him down. No teeth, no problem. If Whitey got ahold of him, he'd need a lower plate too." He had to laugh. "You got to admire a guy who lets it all roll off his back. And he's always got another iron in the fire." But Art wasn't going to join Hackley at the racetrack. What did he need that kind of *tsouris* for? He had enough difficulty just trying to keep on as it was. He didn't need to get in trouble with the law too. Maybe he'd see about keeping an empty paper towel roll in the car just for the winter, though. It could come in handy. You can never tell.

45

During the next few months, Art continued to make his rounds. Worldview was working a new scheme. They offered a free volume of the encyclopedia to prospective customers. Then they sent a salesman to deliver it. Art was tasked with turning a free book giveaway into a sale for the complete set, and he did pretty well. He got his share of sales. Being out and about was therapeutic for Art. Sure the left arm was pretty weak. He tooled around in his Chevy steering only with his right, but it didn't seem to affect his driving. You didn't need more than one arm to control the car. It had power steering. "All that stuff about keeping two hands on the wheel – one at 10 o'clock, the other at 2 o'clock. That's fine for teaching beginners. I've steered with a couple of fingers at 5 o'clock for years," thought Art. True, he was walking with a limp now too, but lots of people his age had a touch of arthritis. It was hardly noticeable, he thought. He was still making his appointments. He was getting around fine under his own power. He wasn't in pain, didn't have to take any pills. No problem. His heart felt fine. His cardiologist said he had passed his last checkup with flying colors. Lots of people had it worse off. At least he wasn't in a wheelchair, didn't even need a crutch or a cane. And how about those paraplegics? How much worse would it be if he was in their condition? There was even one guy panhandling on 59th Street who couldn't move anything but his head. He sat in a wheelchair with a cardboard sign propped up next to him, asking for money. Art had contributed a few bucks to him now and then. Once, he'd given him something in December, and the guy told him, "Thanks, if I don't see you again before Christmas, have a good holiday." Art appreciated the thanks, but the way the guy had said it, so flippant, it bothered him a bit. It was like the guy was working a regular job, like he punched a time clock at 59th Street and covered his regular shift. There must be a better way for guys like him to be taken care of. Maybe the guy liked not relying on the government. He could be a little proud that he was still providing for himself. You couldn't blame him for that. Anyway, at least Art could still hold down a regular job. He was a long way from having to rely on charity.

Art didn't think of the long term prognosis anymore. What mattered was what was happening here and now. And right now, he was doing OK. Yeah, he started wearing loafers now, and he always hated those things, but he didn't need to do battle with shoelaces anymore. Why keep bothering Vivian every time he needed to get dressed? Some adjustments were necessary. Everybody makes them when they get older. "I'm not going to be like Fran, ignoring her diabetes until it was too late." Art ignored the fact that diabetes was, to some extent, a manageable disease, ALS not so much.

Then one day as he was delivering his free book to a would-be customer, Art limped past a Chinese laundry storefront. It had one of those windows that was blacked out halfway up. You could see yourself in it, almost like it was a mirror. Art's attention was directed to his left arm. It was dangling loose, lifeless-looking, straight down from his shoulder, the hand flapping loose below the jacket sleeve. As if it wasn't so much a part of his body, but rather a useless appendage that had somehow been tacked on to his torso without rhyme or reason. Art stopped in his tracks and stared. He rotated his body a bit left then right, watching the result in the window. "No, no, this isn't good. Can't go around like this. I'll scare the hell out of the customers." Art then took his left arm in his right hand, and tucked his left hand into his jacket pocket. He looked into the window to check out the result. "Yeah, that's better. It could be a war injury or something." Still, it shook him. He took out a cigarette, lit it, and began to walk. He walked past the address, circled the block, once, twice, then headed back to his car to finish his smoke. "What's going to be? What's going to be?" He finished his cigarette and stubbed it out in the ashtray. He checked his wristwatch. Only five minutes late. "No, I won't let things get too bad. I'll end it if I have to." But how? He didn't own a gun. He wasn't about to jump off a roof. Maybe he could collect enough drugs to get the job done. Wait, the car, that was it. He could drive into a tree or off a cliff. A car accident, they happen all the time. People would just say that he shouldn't have been driving in such a condition. He had just found the solution, and it calmed him. He could still be in control of this thing even when it got really bad. Time to get to work. He took the free book in hand, stood up, locked the car, and headed back to his appointment.

"You see, Mrs. Pacheco, this is an offer that can really benefit all your children."

"Yes, but I only want the one book. It's free, right?"

"Yes, it is, but this one book only has words beginning with the letter P. How much good would that do your children when they're doing their homework? Not every word they want to look up begins with a P, right? But here, let me show you the kind of information you can find, and the beautiful pictures. This is the article on Puerto Rico." Mrs. Pacheco took the volume from Art and examined the pages. "What city are you from, Mrs. Pacheco?"

"Ponce."

"Ponce? Ah, *Ciudad Senorial*!" Mrs. Pacheco smiled. "We are in luck, Mrs. Pacheco. Ponce begins with a P, so we have an article here on Ponce too." Except Art had spoken too soon. There was no article on Ponce, only a sentence or two identifying it as Puerto Rico's second largest city. Quickly recovering, Art read the identifying information then returned to the map of Puerto Rico located in the article on the island. "Can you show me where Ponce is on this map?" Mrs. Pacheco indicated the location. "Right on the Caribbean Sea. Did you spend a lot of time on the beach when you lived there?"

Mrs. Pacheco warmed to the question, and she began to tell Art about her childhood and how they used to pack a lunch and go to *El Malecon*. Art realized that this was a good sign. He knew that customers like Mrs. Pacheco enjoyed the fact that someone was paying attention to them and listening to them. Art seemed interested in what she was telling him, even though he had heard much of his many times before. In fact, he was interested in making customers feel comfortable enough to open up about their life. It made Art feel good to know that he had the skill to bring this forth. And look how pretty Mrs. Pacheco looked now, talking about her early years in Ponce, her features animated, her eyes lit up. Now she was asking Art questions.

"You visited Puerto Rico?" No, Art admitted he had never been there. "You don't know *fruta estrella*? Here they call it star fruit." Art knew star fruit. "We would pick it from the trees. Very fresh and delicious."

There was a knock on the door. It was her friend and neighbor, Mrs. Diaz who wanted to know if Mrs. Pacheco wanted to go food shopping with her. Noticing Art, she smiled and waved. She didn't know Art personally, but she had seen him in the neighborhood, and she knew other families that had spoken with him. She even knew a couple who had purchased a set of encyclopedias from him. She asked Mrs. Pacheco if she needed anything from Santiago's Bodega. Yes, could she please get a bunch of plantains for her? Mrs. Pacheco excused herself for the interruption. "That's OK, I have to stop by Santiago's myself for cigarettes.."

"Oh, I'm sorry, I should have asked if you wanted Mrs. Diaz to get them for you."

"I'm sure Mrs. Diaz has a lot to do today."

"Do you know Mrs. Diaz?"

"I've seen her in the neighborhood. Her cousin was one of my customers." Now the conversation shifted to Mr. Santiago's Bodega, and why his prices were much higher than those at the Safeway, but how he carried products you couldn't get at the supermarket. "And he's a nice man. He can help you out sometimes if you need to borrow money, or if you want to wire money to your family in Puerto Rico," Mrs. Pacheco added.

"He's the man to know in the neighborhood," Art replied.

Mrs. Pacheco started telling Art about Mr. Santiago's two sons – Alberto who was a star baseball player at Stuyvesant High School where you need to be very smart to get in, and how the other boy, Carlos, worked in the Manhattan Borough President's office even though he was only 14 years old. "He talks so good, and he helps out on Election Day, getting everyone to vote, telling who is the right one to vote for. He says he's going to be president one day." Art told her how he knew Mr. Santiago when he operated a food truck, selling empanadillas and rellenos to factory workers in the garment district. "It's nice to see him doing so well now with his own store. He's a good man." Gradually, Art steered the conversation back to the matter at hand. "So, do you think you would like to make a down payment on the encyclopedia? I can get it delivered for you next week. If you don't like the books, you can return them in the first 30 days at no cost. Nothing to lose, really."

"I think so, but I have to speak to my husband."

"Sure, sure, and tell him I would be glad to come talk to him about it." Mrs. Pacheco nodded.

Art felt good about things when he left Mrs. Pacheco's apartment. He had a good chance of making a sale, and more important, he still had it. He could still connect with people, get them to believe that he had something worthwhile to offer, that he was offering them something that could improve their lives. He felt a renewed hop in his step as he entered Santiago's Bodega. Santiago was waiting on a customer, but waved hello. Once free, Santiago walked over. "*Que pasa, mi amigo*?" Santiago accompanied his greeting by laying a pack of Philip Morris on the counter.

"*Bien como estas tu*? You know what? Let me have a few Parodis too." Santiago pulled a box from beneath the counter.

"You made a sale, Art?"

"Looks like it."

"Looks like it means Parodi; sale completed means Dutch Master."

"You got it."

"Hey, I ever tell you about my uncle? He put the Parodis in rum. Let them soak in there. Then he dried them out before he smoked them. And he inhaled them too. The man had iron lungs. Lived to 98."

"They don't make 'em like that anymore."

"You said it. Hey, you're not double-parked are you? Cause the cops are giving tickets this week. They come by regular." Art told him he had a spot by the curb. "Good. Hey, who's your customer?"

"Mrs. Pacheco in 1324 down the street."

"Mrs. Pacheco? Oh, a very nice woman. But her husband, not so good."

"What's with her husband?" "He's a hustler. Runs the numbers racket around here. Into a lot of illegal stuff. Doesn't like to work a regular job. Likes the easy way, you know."

"Sounds like maybe I don't have a sale."

"Maybe you do. He likes to get things for the kids. Not a bad father in some ways."

Then Santiago asked Art if he was having trouble with his arm, and told him about a woman he knew who might be able to help him. "She's not a doctor, but she helped a lot of people with her treatments." Art told him that he'd been to the Mayo Clinic.

"They can't do much. If they can't help, nobody can."

"No, no, don't think like that, my friend. The *espiritista* knows more than the doctor sometimes. Science isn't everything, Art. You need to have the right spirit. I can tell you many stories." Art lit up a Parodi and listened politely, but this was bringing him down. He was feeling good after his meeting with Mrs. Pacheco, but this talk about Spanish witch doctors was making him depressed. Santiago had noticed he wasn't right. Art didn't want to be reminded of his illness. He didn't want others to see it. He liked Santiago, and realized that the man thought he was helping, but he didn't want to hear this kind of talk. He had already accepted the Mayo Clinic verdict, filed it away, and was trying to get on with what was left of his life.

Art thanked Santiago for his concern, but said he had to get going. "OK, my friend, I know. Business doesn't wait. Take care. *Vaya con dios.*" Art walked back to his car. A couple of kids who were leaning against it while they smoked moved off as Art approached. As Art pulled away from the curb, he spotted a well-dressed man in a phone booth with a pad and pencil taking notes, and he wondered if that was Mr. Pacheco.

46

Harry had left his job at IBM for a position in the city housing administration. He'd been offered the position in appreciation for his work with the campaign committee that helped elect John V. Lindsay mayor of New York. Harry had started with IBM as a punch card operator, and worked his way up to job as a systems analyst. He'd taken some night courses offered by Rutgers University, and somewhere along the way had begun to pass himself off as a graduate of the institution. No one ever checked. Anyway, you didn't need to be a college graduate to get a political appointment. The question was whether it was wise to leave a secure job with a technology giant like IBM in return for a position that depended on a politician hoping to maintain his tenuous grip on power.

Harry was now a manager in the city housing administration. He liked everything about it. He was a great admirer of the new mayor John V. Lindsay, a young and handsome former congressman of Manhattan's silk stocking district. Lindsay was what some called a liberal Republican. As far as Art and Vivian were concerned, there was no such thing. Having come up during the Depression, they were died–in-the-wool Roosevelt Democrats. Art's political leanings were even to the left of FDR. He was going to vote for Henry Wallace in 1948, but at the last minute pulled the lever for Truman, thereby contributing to HST's upset victory over Dewey. In this instance, Art took Voltaire's advice: *Il meglio e l'inimco del ben*, or "Don't let the perfect be the enemy of the good."

Anyway, Harry loved everything about Lindsay - his dashing demeanor, reformist image, and affluent lifestyle. Harry always believed Manhattan was where it was at. Everything worthwhile was there — swank nightclubs and restaurants, the bright lights, the celebrities, the movers and shakers. When he was there, he could forget the grubby, lower middle class surroundings of the Bronx. No *yentas* on beach chairs sitting in front of rent controlled apartments; no penny-pinching candy store owners sneering at you as you perused the magazines, no smoked herring salesmen standing in front of stinking barrels of kosher pickles and sour tomatoes, no mustard-smeared delicatessen owners wiping off formica tables with wet rags between taking orders for hot pastrami and corned beef sandwiches. Now me and Donnie could agree with him about the *yentas*, but we regularly stopped into the local appetizing store presided over by a man known popularly as "Fish Face" for a sour tomato or garlic dills after lunch, and we absolutely feasted on hot pastrami and corned beef club sandwiches (usually preceded by a couple of hot dogs with mustard and sauerkraut). We never could understand how Harry couldn't appreciate these treasures of Bronx life.

Since Harry scoffed at our affection for these treasures in the down-and-dirty Bronx milieu, we scorned his new-found status as a member of the Manhattan elite. We didn't stop to consider that it might be a good thing if someone could reform New York politics which was rife with the kind of corruption found in most big cities. We automatically took the side of the machine politicians and union bosses who were Lindsay's enemies. When the Transport Workers Union went on strike because Lindsay refused to accede to their demands as previous mayors had done, we championed the TWU cause just to see Harry's blood pressure rise. The TWU was led by crusty old "Red Mike" Quill, a former Communist who spoke with a pronounced Irish brogue that he had no interest in losing. Quill lambasted Mayor "Linsley" and boldly asserted that some real bargaining might take place if someone would take away the mayor's comb so he could concentrate on the issues at hand. Some observers pretended to see in this remark a sign that the bald-headed Quill was envious of the thickly-maned Lindsay, but me and Donnie laughingly took Quill's criticism at face value, much to Harry's frustration. When all of New York's trains and buses were tied up by the strike, Mayor Lindsay advised commuters to stay home from work rather than get themselves trapped in a nightmare traffic jam. In contrast, Mike Quill counseled New Yorkers to go to work: "Mayor Linsley wants you to stay home and lose your paycheck. I say go to work. By all means, go to work." Since me and Donnie didn't have to go to work, we found the image of hundreds of thousands of commuters trapped in the midst of a paralyzed transport system hysterical, simply because the situation could all be laid at the doorstep of Harry's idol, John V. Lindsay, for failing to deal effectively with the union.. Eventually, the strike was settled in the union's favor. It was chastening for Lindsay, and the first of several lessons he was to learn. Even Harry had to see that he was not the shining knight riding in on a white stallion who was going to clean up old New York. When Mike Quill died shortly after conclusion of the strike, we told Harry that Lindsay was responsible.

Harry had his job though, and his upscale Manhattan lifestyle. Sure, he still came home to his Bronx apartment with a wife and two kids, but all day long and into the evening he lived the life of a Manhattan operative. His friends were other ambitious social climbers. They all held in disdain the people who reminded them of their humble origins. They had risen above the squalor and were now basking in the sunshine. Harry even harbored some resentment over the fact that we grew up on the poorer side Gun Hill Road where the apartment buildings lacked elevators and well-appointed, spacious lobbies. Maybe he was also humiliated by Vivian's occasional reliance on the Kaplans to get her through till Art's next payday. When he married into the Bolek family, he was able to cross the divide and leave what he characterized as his "poor upbringing" behind him. Of course, he had to deal with Old Stoneface and her wimp husband, but it may have seemed worth it to him.

Harry, however, was having a problem with Deliah. He never did have much respect for her. He knew she was not an intellectual giant when he married her, but now that he was mixing with the Manhattan crowd, he found her lack of knowledge and curiosity embarrassing. She knew nothing about politics. Harry would tell her how to vote every Election Day. "I have two votes," he would boast.

Deliah's interests were entirely conventional. She liked to sleep late and watch soap operas on TV. She didn't know how to drive and had no interest in learning. She couldn't speak intelligently about any subject of interest to Manhattan's smart set. She had graduated high school with a commercial degree that taught her how to be an efficient secretary, but she didn't work either. As a result, she didn't meet people who might broaden her horizons, pique her interest in world affairs, or at least provide her with different perspectives. It didn't bother her though. She was comfortable being a housewife. She took care of Eddie and Susan uncomplainingly. She was pleasant. She never looked for trouble. She usually thought the best about others. She regularly cooked dinner, although she wasn't very good at it. One Thanksgiving Harry and Deliah hosted the family get together. The turkey was half raw, and the stuffing was inedible. She had experimented with new ingredients she had seen published in *Good Housekeeping*, but Vivian said she couldn't imagine that reputable magazine recommending quite the concoction that her daughter-in-law had produced. The only other time we ate dinner at Harry's, me, Donnie and Art spent half the night throwing up Deliah's salmon croquettes. It was little consolation to us that she meant well.

Harry would bring the family over to see us on the weekend. He started coming more often now that Art was ailing. Art liked to play with Eddie, giving him a playful little boot in his posterior whenever he bent over to pick up a toy. Eddie would look around to see who had done that. After a short while, he realized it was always grandpa, and would laughingly run at him for a hug. One Sunday, Harry came over with some interesting news. He had been in his office the other day and a clerk stopped in to drop off his mail. Harry looked up and who did he see? None other than Louis Kaplan. "Harry?" Louis had asked. Harry acknowledged that he was indeed

Harry Feldman, former childhood customer of the Kaplan candy store, son of Vivian Feldman, former supplicant of the Kaplans' largesse. Imagine Louis Kaplan, now a humble clerk working a menial job in city government. Harry told the tale in a manner that indicated the worm had indeed turned. The little boy who had been chased away from the magazine display in Kaplan's candy store would now be composing performance evaluations for the old proprietor. And that's also how we learned that the Kaplan candy store was no more.

I wondered that I hadn't learned about that earlier. I had run into Daniel Darrow a couple of times, but he hadn't said anything about it. He had told me that he had broken up with Lemel's daughter, but that didn't seem surprising given their conflicting natures. Daniel asked about Donnie and Harry. I told them both were fine, and didn't think anything of it initially. Later, I started to wonder why Daniel had asked about Harry by name. I had never known Daniel to exchange two words with Harry. I wasn't even sure the two had ever actually met. But then again, Daniel knew about everybody in the neighborhood as well as anybody who had ever been in the neighborhood. It would be natural for him to ask about someone he knew to be the older brother of a friend. Still, he had never specifically mentioned Harry before. To satisfy my curiosity, I resolved to check further into any possible Daniel/Harry connection. A couple of weeks later, I spied Daniel walking about a block ahead of me, and I hurried to catch up with him. After exchanging pleasantries, I asked him if he had seen Harry lately.

"Actually, I have. I ran into him at Carmine's Inn last week. Why do you ask?"

"Oh, no special reason. We haven't seen much of him lately. I was just wondering if anyone had." Carmine's Inn. My friend Angelo had mentioned Carmine's before. He called it that fuckin' place on Fordham Road where the queers hung out.

47

Donnie seemed to be doing better. After transferring to a new junior high school, he didn't get into any more fights. He didn't become a great student, but at least he did well enough so that he wasn't in any danger of being held back. He was promoted at the end of each year, and he advanced to high school without further delays. But he seemed to associate with some unusual characters.

I hung out with Angelo Mancini, Mike Cavelli, and a bunch of their friends I met in high school. Sometimes I would get Donnie to join us. We would play touch football and softball, set off fireworks in the summer, ride around with someone who had a car, and talk about girls we knew. But who were Donnie's friends? We would never see any. But we would hear him talk about some. There was some guy named Billadino who hung out around Mosholu Parkway and looked for fights. Donnie said he would plant himself in the path of those whose looks he didn't like and ask them if they wanted a piece of him. When they walked around him, avoiding a physical confrontation, he'd say with disdain, "I knew you'd do that." Donnie said his real name was Bill Dino, but they just call him Billadino. Tito Tracy was his friend. Tito was thin, dark, alienated, antisocial, and on edge. He was a confirmed insomniac. Instead of sleeping, he'd roam around nights with Billadino, smoking, and putting down all the kids who were good students, popular, thought they were cool. Then there was Murray Kamenstine, a manic joker who lived for laughs, often lapsing into hysterics over incidents that few others found funny. When Kamenstine really got going, he couldn't stop his hysteria, and someone had to call the squad to transport him to a hospital. And there was Joe Carnowitz who lived to eat. He was obese and lazy, sardonic, sarcastic and often the butt of Kamenstine's jokes. According to Carnowitz, if you ate all night, you didn't need to sleep. He laid around watching TV and listening to rock music. But don't get on him too much. He'd let you have it. Larry Sawyer was a short, quiet, thoughtful guy. "You know that guy with the long brown hair greased back who we saw walking on 210th Street that time? That's him," Donnie said. Larry was a loner and tough. They all were tough. They had their own pickup football team, and couldn't be beaten. They formed their own street gang that others wouldn't dare to challenge. But who were these strange people? How come no one else ever saw them around? One day Donnie pointed out a figure walking through the neighborhood cemetery off in the distance. He looked tall and dark. He appeared to be wearing jeans and a light-colored shirt. "That's Billadino," Donnie said.

"Oh, where's he going?" I asked. Donnie didn't answer.

Angelo was the only other person who heard about these characters. He would sometimes ask Donnie what was going on with Kamenstine. Donnie would tell him about Kamenstine convulsing in laughter over the scholarly but nerdy meteorologist who delivered the weather forecast in his boring, idiosyncratic manner on local channel 4 every night. "Fuckin' Kamenstine," quipped Angelo. "Did they call the squad?" Donnie nodded, and Angelo guffawed, shaking his head in disbelief.

 Maybe it was because of Art's illness and watching him get weaker, knowing there was nothing to be done, and realizing the ultimate outcome, but a feeling of sadness seemed to pervade the apartment. The sadness didn't come from Art, though. He carried on as always – no sign of depression or anger. Maybe it also had to do with Donnie's situation. True, he wasn't getting into fights all the time. He'd made it to high school. But his grades were still poor. He could never deal with schoolwork. For some unknown reason, he was unable to internalize anything that did not have to do with rock music or professional wrestling. He lacked direction, and didn't seem to be going anywhere. He wasn't involved in anything positive. I began going to college. The City of University of New York was still tuition free. If you were a high school graduate who managed a B average in an academic course of study, you would probably be admitted. Although I was attending a four-year college, I was still living at home, still sharing a bedroom with Donnie. I was beginning to separate myself intellectually, however, by becoming involved with my studies. There was no more hanging around the streets after school or during vacations. During summers, I worked at department stores as a stock boy, cashier, and sign printer. Now that Harry was working for the city, he promised me a future summer spot in some city agency. I was beginning to make a life for myself. But when I came home at night it was to the same cramped, gloomy bedroom with Donnie rambling on about Billadino and Kamenstine.

To complicate the situation, we began to have trouble sleeping. We wouldn't get to enjoy descending into seven or eight hours of oblivion. We began to worry about the consequences of long term sleep deprivation. That made it even harder to sleep. Art and Vivian were both annoyed by our pathological wakefulness and concerned that something might be wrong. I was working at S. Klein's in Yonkers as a cashier that summer of. I'd get home about 11:30 after taking the bus back to the Bronx. Everyone was already in bed. Not wanting to disturb the household, and desiring to grab a bit of privacy, I'd wheel the TV stand into the bathroom, throw a few towels on the floor to use as pad and pillow, and watch Johnny Carson until 1 am. If I was lucky, Donnie would be asleep when I finally turned in for the night.

If I wasn't fortunate, Donnie would still be awake, and I'd have to listen to the latest news about Billadino & Co. These tales were becoming progressively more bizarre. Billadino scorned any human emotion as weakness. This included sexual urges. To put an end to these, he had emasculated himself. It was better that way. What did he need that crap for? Kamenstine cracked up laughing so often he was locked up in Bellevue, but he escaped. They couldn't keep him in there anyway. Laughing didn't mean you were crazy, did it? Tito didn't sleep all summer. Carnowitz was probably right. If you ate an extra meal or two during the night, you didn't need to sleep. We should try that. Carnowitz weighed over 400 pounds now. So what? Eating was his thing. He did what he wanted, and nobody was going to bother him. I'd heard enough. I'd take a meprobamate that Dr. Brownstein had prescribed and try to get to sleep. While waiting for it to take effect, I'd pretend I was sleeping.

48

Art and Vivian never had their own bedroom. Changing apartments after Art's heart attacks didn't gain them one. They still slept in the living room on a trundle bed. The one improvement was air conditioning. Just like the elevator was considered a necessity to enable Art to avoid stairs when possible, a/c would minimize heat stress. The air conditioner was a window unit that was placed in the living room. A folding door was affixed to the doorway separating the living room from the large foyer in the front of the apartment where the TV was kept. When the door was closed, the a/c could adequately cool the room. Art and Vivian never closed the folding door for privacy, only when the a/c was running .

I discovered the awkward ramifications of this arrangement one morning when I awoke one morning and walked from the bedroom into the foyer. The folding door was open, and I could clearly see Art hurriedly rolling off of Vivian. I guess it's always shocking to see their parents in the act, but in another sense, it was good to see that Art and Vivian's relationship was still loving in that way. And it was nice that Art still felt strong enough for that kind of activity. Vivian had commented a few times that women didn't really go for that kind of stuff. They just wanted to be cuddled. If that reflected her actual feelings on the matter, it was still apparent that she was receptive enough to Art's advances. Needless to say, I didn't linger at the doorway, but from what I remembered seeing, Vivian seemed very welcoming and cooperative. Art and Vivian never mentioned the incident and neither did I. We all behaved as if it had never happened.

It didn't seem possible that anything good could come out of Art's ailments, but it had to be admitted that the household was less turbulent. There were no more arguments over money. Art and Vivian seemed closer. Vivian's temper still erupted occasionally, but Art was not the target. It was usually Donnie. Vivian would buy him a new radio, and Donnie would break it in a matter of days by tinkering with it in an attempt to bring in more distant stations. Vivian would buy Donnie a new record player, and Donnie would break it by slowing down the turntable mechanically so that the records sounded better to him. He was never satisfied with the original product even if it was something he had selected himself and eagerly anticipated purchasing. Our bedroom closet was filled with electronic components from devices broken by Donnie. He loved high fidelity but scorned newer technologies like stereophonic sound. He knew what he wanted from radios and record players, but he didn't have the skill to achieve it. And he didn't have the discipline or patience to learn how to accomplish it. Even if he did, he probably wouldn't be satisfied very long with the finished product no matter how it turned out. This would become a dismal pattern that would be repeated time and again in the future. Donnie would insist on tinkering with the 1960's equipment with which he was fascinated as a youth. What was it he was trying to achieve? With his radios, he was attempting to bring in AM stations all over the country. Local radio outlets featured rock musicians who were not very popular nationally, but may have recorded songs that Donnie really liked. He would spend his nights slowly and painstakingly scanning the AM dial trying to find new, out-of-town stations. Many of these were excruciatingly difficult to uncover, because their frequencies were often interfered with by more powerful transmitters in our own area. With patience that he rarely exhibited elsewhere, Donnie would search the dial all night, noting where he thought he'd heard a new station. Then, night after night he would tune in to listen again and search for new stations. He would pay close attention to the weather. Clear nights were best. He noted sunset times, because many of the stations he honed in on were not accessible during daylight hours. He raged against neighbors who used electrical equipment that interfered with his radio reception, and vowed to take some action against them. He could tell that they were doing it on purpose just to annoy him. He took note of architectural structures that might conceivably interfere with incoming signals to his radio, and tried to adjust his antenna to circumvent such problems. At times, he tried moving his radio and speakers to a different location in the apartment to see if that would improve reception, but there were only so many possibilities in a one-bedroom apartment. Plus Vivian wasn't about to have Donnie's contraption permanently residing in her living room or kitchen, so he usually ended up back where he started.

With his old record player there was only so much anyone could do even if you were exceptionally skilled. Donnie would attach larger, more expensive speakers, ones that accentuated the bass range of the recording. He would play with the turntable speed, usually slowing it so that individual notes of a tune might be extended and accentuated. But exactly what elusive sound was he trying to capture? These weren't intricate orchestral recordings. It wasn't like Fabian was going to sound great even on the finest equipment. The improvements he managed to make by trial and error would provide him with only temporary satisfaction. Inevitably, he would discover that the sound wasn't precise enough, or that the speed of the turntable was not slow enough. Further adjustments would be necessary. He would tinker further, encountering problems he knew not how to solve, and end up breaking the record player. The broken device would end up stored in a closet. He wouldn't dispose of it altogether, because he might want to hook up a speaker from a broken radio or record player to a newly obtained phonograph, or perhaps use some copper wiring to fashion a radio antenna that would bring in more distant stations. He would try to purchase new vintage radios or turntables, but as time went on, these became increasingly difficult to locate. When he did find one, the cycle would repeat itself. Donnie had no interest in newer electronic devices. He dismissed cassette and CD players, loudly berating all those who appreciated them. He would not welcome the advent of the internet either. This only served to alienate him further from the rest of the population.

Donnie did possess some natural talent in art and music. He was a skilled cartoonist from a young age, and he could cite and sing on key entire catalogs of popular musical artists. But he lacked the diligence necessary to develop and apply any of these skills. Later on Donnie commented that he could never concentrate on anything in school. When it came to reading, he could pronounce most of the words and knew what many of them meant individually, but he could not absorb and comprehend whole passages. This meant that the whole range of written material regarding radios and phonographs was inaccessible to Donnie. How might things have been different if his reading ability could have been improved? For some reason, the educators in his life never identified this problem. This made it impossible to seek out therapies for dealing with it. It is unlikely that Donnie's reading problems could explain all of his psychological and social challenges, his distinct preference for a solitary existence, his increasing tendency to insist that others were intentionally thwarting or harming him.. We couldn't understand why Donnie seemed unable to latch on to something that would enable him to begin to create some kind of life for himself in the outside world. He couldn't spend the rest of his life in this apartment, could he? All of this drove Vivian to distraction, and her temper would flare. When this occurred, most people would flee the scene, but Donnie would shout out his resentment and angrily retreat to his bedroom.

49

Vivian got a call from Bessie. Sam had finally agreed to have the surgery on his hernia that their doctor had prescribed years ago. Sam was a difficult man to manage under normal circumstances. Now Bessie had to accompany him to the hospital, and see that he behaved himself in surroundings that were likely to set him off. Sam would inevitably think that he was being taken advantage of, taken for a sucker, and overcharged. He might think that the medical staff was plotting against him, planning to do him harm. How was Bessie going to get through this? Would she be able to keep Sam calm, and prevent her impossible marriage from being put on display for all to see? There was little love lost between the two of them. Sam had not forgotten Bessie's past betrayal, and he was constantly worried that she would let the doctor and hospital cheat him out of money. Bessie was frustrated at having to put up with Sam's ravings, but she didn't see any other viable options. This was the life she found herself living, and she didn't see any other opening up before her. At least she could pour her heart out to Vivian. If her daughter didn't exactly welcome hearing all this on a regular basis, she was willing to listen to it and that was some consolation.

"Bessie, did you pack my pajamas? They're not going to get me into one of those hospital gowns. Bessie, did you hear me?"

"Yes, yes, they're packed." Bessie was almost finished preparing Sam's overnight bag.

"And remember, don't wear any jewelry when we go. You know the doctors are all thieves. They'll take advantage."

Bessie thought to herself, "Here we go again. God in heaven!"

"A plain, simple dress, nothing fancy."

"I know, I know!"

"I don't know why I agreed to this. A mistake, a mistake!" Bessie looked around for anything else she might have forgotten. "Damn doctors! If you're healthy, they can't make a living! They'll find something else, you'll see."

"Will you stop it? Just stop it!"

"They'll invent some new diseases. You'll see."

"A hernia's not a new disease."

"Did you call the theater? Tell them I won't be in for a day or two?"

"I told them you'll be out for a week at least." "A week? They'll let me go. I won't have a job when I get out."

"They said it's OK. They'll see you when you feel better." Bessie thought, "These are the same people he swears are trying to poison him because he knows company secrets."

"I feel fine. This whole thing is ridiculous! A little discomfort and they can't wait to get you in a hospital bed. Next stop the grave."

Bessie gazed skyward. "Give me the strength."

The wind was howling down Burnside Avenue as Bessie and Sam made their way tentatively downhill toward the el. Snow was in the forecast. Vivian had told Bessie to take a taxi. She would pay, but Sam wouldn't hear of it. He took the train to work every day, and he'll take the train today. A man rose from his seat in the car to allow Bessie and Sam to sit together, and Bessie thanked him. Sam looked about the car worriedly, his mouth partially open, his tongue trembling, as if he was about to say something but thought better of it. Ordinarily, he would scan the ads on the walls of the train car for discount offers but now he was too distracted to take notice of them.

Once they made their way to Bronx Lebanon Hospital, Bessie had to answer the plethora of questions thrown at them while simultaneously helping attendants guide Sam through the check in process. Sam was upset with all the strangers trying to attend to him. "Bessie, where's the doctor?"

"He's on his way."

"He said he'd be here, didn't he?"

"He will." "Just like a little kid," she thought. She tried to get Sam involved in conversation about something other than his impending surgery. She gave him a magazine to read. But nothing distracted him from his fears. He was incapable of understanding what precisely was happening. He was on a gurney in a waiting area, but thought he might already be in his room.

"Why don't they open the curtains? It's too dark in here. I want a private room, remember, you tell them that." Bessie wondered if they might transfer him to a mental hospital. She would be hard pressed to make an argument against it. It was three hours before they wheeled Sam into his room. It was semi-private, but the curtain was pulled completely around the other patient's bed, so maybe Sam wouldn't notice right away that he wasn't alone. At this point, Sam became quieter, and Bessie thanked the Lord. He had Bessie adjust the bed so that he was sitting at a comfortable angle, and he lapsed into relative silence.

One of the nurses entered to offer a brief greeting. "Hello, Mr. Simonson, I'm Jackie the duty nurse this morning. We'll have breakfast for you in a moment." Sam nodded and smiled.

"Thank you, thank you very much."

"At least he's still capable of keeping up appearances," Bessie thought.

"Are you Mrs. Simonson? You can stay as long as you like."

"I'll stay until Doctor Chase gets here."

"He usually makes his rounds around noon." Sam laid his head back, crossed his hands, and closed his eyes. Bessie looked at him and took a deep breath. As Sam began dozing, he imagined himself stretched out on the bedroom in Vivian's apartment in his suit, starched shirt, bowtie, polished leather shoes, listening to his grandkids play Mickey Katz and His Kosher Jammers singing "Herring Boats are Coming with Bagels and Lox."

Vivian received a phone call from Bessie the next morning reporting that the surgery had gone off as scheduled. The doctor said it was successful and that Sam would be able to go home in a few days. Meanwhile, the snow that had been forecast arrived in force. Gale force winds made it difficult to estimate how quickly it was piling up because the snow appeared to be falling sideways. Meteorologists predicted at least a foot would cover most parts of the city before the storm tapered off. Cars were stranded in the streets, and shelves in supermarkets had been emptied by frantic shoppers. City officials advised all but emergency workers to stay put at home.

That evening Vivian received another call from Bessie. She and Sam were home. That morning Sam had awakened in his hospital bed, decided he needed a shave, yanked the IV out of his arm, and walked to the bathroom to look for his razor. Hospital officials had found him, ushered him back to bed, and reinserted the IV. In the afternoon, when Bessie had arrived, Sam was demanding that they go home. She enlisted the aid of the nurse to keep Sam in his bed, but he kept insisting on leaving. He said the nurses had attacked him, and he showed her bruises to prove it. They were planning to do him in. He was sure of it. There was no calming him down. Bessie was afraid they might transfer him to Bellevue. Hearing this, Vivian thought to herself that it might be a good idea. In the end, Sam could not be deterred. Against doctor's orders, he had checked himself out of the hospital. The staff that had been dealing with him directly must have been greatly relieved.

Bessie had packed Sam's belongings into three shopping bags and they set out for the train. Sam wouldn't hear of taking a taxi. Stumbling through snowdrifts that were knee-deep at times, climbing the hill up Grand Avenue, they finally arrived at their apartment soaking wet and exhausted. Bessie didn't know how they had managed to survive the ordeal. The man in the train token booth had looked at the elderly couple strangely, as if he couldn't believe that they were traveling in the middle of a blizzard. The train car was practically empty so at least they had no trouble getting seats. Once they were back in the stormy streets, Sam kept wandering off in the wrong direction, and Bessie had had to hurry as best she could to grab him before he got away. She had stopped several times on route to rest, and was sure each time that she would be unable to take another step. Sam didn't notice or care whenever Bessie stopped. She would yell after him, but he continued to trudge forward in whatever direction he believed was appropriate. Perhaps he couldn't hear her through the howling wind. Bessie had to gather her bags and try to catch up with him. The shopping bags became wet as the snow fell and Bessie dragged them through the drifts. Passing cars and busses splashed slush upon them and they began to degrade. One, then another, fell apart completely. Each time this happened, Bessie, left holding the handles, tried to cram the torn bag's contents into the remaining one(s). After the second bag was gone, there was no more room in the sole remaining one so she started stuffing Sam's belongings into her coat pockets. Several items had to be left in the snow because there was no place to put them. Bessie knew for sure that a pajama bottom, a plastic drinking cup, and a pair of hospital slippers were among them. It was becoming a march for survival. If they did not make it, one would be able to follow the trail of Sam's belongings to locate their remains. By the time she was able to discern their apartment building through the whiteout, she felt faint. The good news was that they were finally safe, if not completely sound, at home. The bad news they discovered several days later at Sam's follow-up exam: Sam was again ruptured.

50

Art was still able to drive his car, but he was trying to minimize the number of times trips he had to make, the number of times he had to get in and out of the vehicle. It was actually this getting in and out that was the biggest problem for him. His left leg was getting weaker, and he had only one good arm to help him bear the weight when he was swinging himself into the driver's seat. Once behind the wheel, he was the same old Art Feldman, capable and confident. Power steering enabled him to maneuver the car as well as ever, and there was no problem accelerating and braking with his right leg. He thanked God that he didn't have to try to manage a clutch. It was never discussed whether there were any actual rules and regulations about how healthy you needed to be in order to keep driving, and whether Art was beginning to violate any of them. One thing was sure though. If Art had to take a driving test again, he would have passed it with flying colors.

There was one New York City regulation that was starting to be a problem, however – alternate side of the street parking. On certain days you couldn't park your car on one side of the street between the hours of 11 am and 2 pm. This meant that you were unable leave your vehicle parked in one spot for more than a day or so without being in violation. The city had this rule in effect so that they could send out their street-cleaning trucks on a regular schedule. If you hadn't moved your car by the time the trucks came by, you would be ticketed and maybe even towed. If you were towed, you had to make a pretty long trip to the impound lot and pay a hefty fine in order to retrieve you vehicle.

So it was that one morning that Art asked me to go out and move the car from one side of the street to the other. It was parked only a block away, and it shouldn't have taken more than a few minutes to accomplish the task. Now here is where we come up against those pesky rules and regulations once again. I did not have a regular driver's license yet. I was only in possession of what they called a learner's permit. I had passed my written exam, which tested my understanding on rules of the road, and was allowed to practice driving when a licensed driver was in the car with me. Art had been letting me pick up Sam and Bessie when they wanted to come and visit, and we had gone out on other practice sessions in the general neighborhood. Obviously, he thought I was skilled enough to move the car to another parking spot by myself. It's just that I hadn't yet taken, much less passed, my actual driver's test.

I was a little nervous getting behind the wheel for the first time alone, but I was confident that I was up to the task at hand. Parallel parking wasn't something I had completely mastered yet, but I could fit the car into a spot if it was big enough. I got into the car, started it up, and pulled away from the curb. As I headed down the street, I was feeling very adult and competent. It was a real rush. I noticed one or two possible parking spots, but they looked kind of tight. Besides, I was in no hurry to rush things. I was enjoying my time behind the wheel by myself. I decided to circle the block to see if there was a larger spot further on up the street. That would also give me a little more driving time. As I approached the corner, the traffic light began to change from green to red, and I was faced with the question of whether I should stop or go on through the intersection. It was a close call, and I wasn't experienced enough to follow my instincts in situations like this. At this point, I saw that there was a policeman standing on the corner. Not only was this an alarming sight to someone who was driving without a regulation license, but it was puzzling as well. There was never a policeman stationed on this corner before, as far as I could remember. Why was he there? It wasn't time for school to be dismissed, and they used crossing guards to oversee that anyway, not real policemen. As this was all going through my mind, I quickly decided that I'd better stop the car. I did so abruptly, lurching to a stop and squealing the brakes a bit in the process. This did not fail to draw the attention of the policeman. He peered into the car and became suspicious. Apparently, he thought I looked a little young, because he walked over and asked me what I was doing. I told him the truth, that I was moving the car to another spot because of the alternate side of the street parking rules. Then he asked me for my license. He had me there. I showed him my learner's permit, and he accurately identified it as not being a license. I knew I was in big trouble. I imagined that he could have issued me a citation, barred me from taking the driver's test, suspended me from driving for years, or even run me in. Either it wasn't worth the trouble to him, or he took pity on me, because what he did was point on up the street at one of those small-sized parking spots I had driven past and told me to back the car into it. The odds against me driving in reverse and actually fitting the car into the spot he indicated at that time had to be great, but luck was with me. I succeeded on the first try, and he let me off with a warning for which I was very grateful.

I told Art what had happened, and he seemed amused. At least the car got moved to a legal spot, if not exactly in the way he envisioned. Plus I had an interesting story to relate to Angelo when he picked me up on the way to classes the next morning.

51

Art figured it was time he got back in touch with Mrs. Pacheco, so he headed back to Spanish Harlem. Managing to climb the stairs to the Pacheco apartment, he knocked on the door. A man about Art's size, with a black moustache and dark wavy hair opened the door and peered at him. "We don't want any."

"Is Mrs. Pacheco here? She's expecting me."

"Mrs. Pacheco is busy today. Housework, you know. And whatever you're selling we don't need it."

"Are you Mr. Pacheco? Maybe your wife spoke to you about me."

"My wife don't talk to me about every..." Just then Mrs. Pacheco arrived on the scene.

"Oh, Mr. Feldman, come in." Mr. Pacheco slowly stepped aside and let Art enter. Mrs. Pacheco explained to her husband that this was the man with the books they were interested in. "*LIbros para el nino.*" Her husband reluctantly waved Art inside with an air of disgusted resignation.

Mrs. Pacheco invited Art to take a seat on the couch, and she sat facing him in an armchair. Art was hoping that Mr. Pacheco would join them, but he quickly grabbed his jacket and made a move toward the door. "Luis, what about the books?"

"*Esta no es una biblioteca.*"

"But it's good for the boys. They will be better students. You know we want that for them."

"You talk to the man. I got rounds to make."

Mrs. Pacheco turned to Art somewhat apologetically. "He wants to do right by the boys. It's just he's not patient. He can't sit and listen to all the details. It makes him crazy. Maybe we can work it out. He doesn't mind spending the money if it's reasonable."

"Did Mrs. Diaz show you her cousin's encyclopedia set like I asked her?"

"No, I been meaning to go but I didn't have the time."

"Maybe we can go now." Mrs. Pacheco seemed agreeable, so Art phoned Mrs. Diaz to set it up. Mrs. Diaz's cousin lived only a couple of blocks away on 107th Street. Art and Mrs. Pacheco walked past a group of men playing dominoes on a card table, and a makeshift garage with several older model cars up on lifts being serviced while a few others waited their turn in the small front yard. A city bus turned a corner, graffiti scrawled on its side, and a young man ran after it, a bag of papayas tucked under his arm.

Mrs. Diaz was waiting for them in her cousin's apartment. Louisa, her cousin, had coffee and sponge cake waiting for them. The Worldview Encyclopedia was proudly displayed on a bookcase they walked past in the foyer. "My boy Jose uses it every day for his homework, and you know I don't let him out of the house before he gets the homework done." Art asked Louisa to show Mrs. Pacheco the new 1965 yearbook that had just arrived.

"And you see, Mrs. Pacheco, you don't pay extra for the yearbooks. They come free every year with the latest happenings. You just add them to your set. You can see this latest edition has an article on the death of Pedro Campos, the independence leader in Puerto Rico."

"He died? Oh my God, I didn't know. How they tortured that man. Always throwing him in jail, and for what?"

"They had a hundred thousand at his funeral," added Mrs. Diaz, nodding her head in sympathy. They all looked at the yearbook article paying tribute to the Puerto Rican independence leader, and recounted several times when they had heard him speak and how inspired they were by his message.

"If it wasn't for all the corruption, he would be president of Puerto Rico today," added Mrs. Diaz.

As they continued their discussion over refreshments, Mrs. Pacheco was persuaded to order a set from Art. She completed the necessary paperwork and gave him a check as down payment. Art thanked Mrs. Diaz and Louis as they left the apartment, and walked Mrs. Pacheco back to her front door. "Be sure to call me after you receive the set, and let me know if that everything is OK. Any errors or shipping problems, we will take care of very quickly."

"Gracias, Mr. Art. Thank you for everything."

Back in Louisa's apartment, the cousins were talking about Art. "Such a nice man, but what's wrong with him? *El esta muy enfermo*," said Louisa.

"Tal vez un derrame cerebral."

"He can recover from that if he gets therapy. I can recommend someone. Fix him up right." Mrs. Diaz replied. "He works very hard. He should take it easy. He'll live longer."

Art felt good. He'd made the sale, and everyone saw the benefit of having a set like Worldview in the house. Not only was he making a living but he was performing a public service in a way. Everyone benefits from education, especially the children. As he approached his car, he noticed that it wouldn't be necessary to chase any kids off. It was parked right where he left it, nobody lounging against it. No ticket either even though he was a little close to that fire hydrant. Hey, with the way spots were so scarce around here you couldn't be too particular. Art opened the driver side door with his key and crouched down to slide himself behind the wheel. But this time his right leg wouldn't hold his weight. He felt himself slipping to the ground. He tried to hold himself up with his right arm – his left was in a better position to do so but it was absolutely useless. Nevertheless, he reached out with it as part of a reflex action. All to no avail. He fell to the pavement right next to the car, landing on his back. Now he was really helpless. If he was laying on a bed or couch, he could roll on to his stomach and manage to get himself up. Lying flat on the ground all he could do was reach his right arm out and touch the car. He didn't have the strength to pull himself up enough to get his right leg underneath him, and his left side was no help at all. "Like a fuckin' turtle," Art thought. He began to be afraid. He was helpless. How long would he have to lie like this? He would need assistance. Who could he get? Mrs. Pacheco? Mr. Santiago down the street? While these thoughts were racing through his mind, several pedestrians walked past. They all took a look as they went by, but no one stopped to offer any help. *"Borracho,"* said one man to a woman who accompanied him, and he made a motion with his hand to indicate someone throwing back a bottle of beer. "So that's what they think, Yeah, I guess it looks that way. Is it better to be considered a drunk than a cripple?"

After a few minutes, one woman stopped. "Oh, are you alright? Can I help you?" Art explained that he needed to get up into the car. "Can you drive?' He assured her he could. "I don't know if I can lift you."

"Can you try a little? If you can't, you can't. I don't want you to hurt yourself." She began to help Art up but quickly decided it was beyond her capabilities. Art asked her if she could go to Mr. Santiago's store and see if he could help. She agreed and set off for the corner shop. Art began to feel a bit better. Someone had spoken with him, and she was able to see that he wasn't drunk. She was going to get him the help he needed. But before she could return, a burly police officer arrived on the scene. "What seems to be the problem, sir?" Art explained the situation, and the officer bent down and easily lifted Art upright into the driver's seat. Before he let Art drive off, however, he checked his driver's license and insurance coverage. Then he ascertained that alcohol was not a factor and asked several questions relating to Art's physical competence to manage the vehicle. "Sir, I have to make sure you are capable of safely handling this car on the road, that you're not a safety hazard to yourself and others around you."

"I understand, officer." In the end, Art convinced the officer that he could handle the car safely, and was allowed to set off for home. He led the officer to believe that he was getting better, that he was only temporarily indisposed, and he promised to keep the car parked until he had regained better use of his left arm and leg.

Shortly after Art drove off, Mr. Santiago walked up the block. One of his customers had told him there was a man lying in the street. There was only an empty parking spot by the time he got to the place where Art had fallen, but from the description of the man and car he had received from his customer he guessed it was Art. He wondered about how someone can get sick like this, and why him, still a young man and a nice fellow, hard-working too? What is it they say — only the good die young? Ah, but he's not dead yet, and may it not happen soon. Is there any reason why he should be the one? Santiago couldn't make sense of it. Only God knows and He's not telling.

52

Initially, Art couldn't decide whether to tell Vivian about the fall, but in the end he did. We heard about it too. He didn't stop driving immediately. I know that, because I saw him tooling around the neighborhood once or twice. Maybe it's like the tale they tell about someone getting thrown from a horse. You need to get right back on and convince yourself you can still ride. Art could still drive if he had to. At least for a little while anyway.

Now there was the question of the car. If Art wasn't going to be selling anymore, wouldn't the company take the car back? After all, Art didn't own it. He only had use of it while he was employed at Worldview. Was he working for them anymore? If he had quit or been fired we probably would have known. For the time being nothing was said about it. What we did know was that Art was spending more time around the apartment, getting up later, and spending less time outside. He began to take a folding chair out on the street in the evenings, sometimes engaging a neighbor in conversation. One time, Marjorie Santoni was sweeping the courtyard in a flowered, print house dress that hung loosely on her large, flaccid frame. She shuffled along in sandals that were so worn at the heel that her calloused soles scraped against the concrete with every step. Art said hello. Marjorie nodded and remarked about how hot it was for October. Art said it wouldn't be long before they were shoveling snow so maybe the heat wasn't so bad. Next thing he knew, Marjorie was telling him that Frank was impossible to live with. "He never says nothin' from morning till night. Can you believe it?"

"A man of few words?"

"A man of no words. What kind of man is that? Maybe he wants me to guess what he's thinkin'. Do I look like a mind reader? Even when he does talk, it's nothin' worth listening to."

Art told her he liked the photo of Frank and Marjorie that greets riders in the elevator. "It's a nice touch, welcoming tenants like that."

Marjorie snickered. "Yeah, well you know I practically had to drag him to the photographer. He wouldn't do it otherwise. And, you know, it was the landlord's idea. He said we had to do it or he'd let us go. You think Frank cared? Hell no. He'd just as soon have us thrown out into the street."

"Maybe he thought the landlord was bluffing."

"Ah, nothin' makes an impression on him except a smack in the mouth. You know, they locked him up a couple of times because he wouldn't pay no attention to them warrants and summonses. He's been some example for our son, I can tell you." Art asked how long they'd been superintendents of the building. "Oh, we been here since 1949. After Frank got out of the military, he took the job. He was in the Navy for 15 years. I told him to do another five and get a pension, but he wouldn't listen."

"He must've done more talking when he was in the military."

"Hah, I don't know. I kind of thought that's where he learned to stop talking. Just taking orders and keeping his mouth shut. One thing I know, he didn't lift his hand to the lieutenants and admirals the way he does to me. They woulda thrown him out on his ass."

Art asked her if she ever thought about leaving Frank. "A man should never get physical with a woman," Art added.

"You're damn right. I told him before if he hits me again, I'll walk out that door and he'll never see me again."

"Who could blame you?"

Marjorie told Art he had a nice family. "You raised your boys right. I can tell. They never cause no trouble."

Art thanked her but added "You know, sometimes you can never tell how a kid will turn out."

"Ain't that the truth? I gave mine everything I could. Spoiled him even, and it was never enough. He went out and started going with a bunch of car thieves, ended up in jail. How do you figure? Maybe I shoulda made him join the Navy. He might've come out deaf and dumb like Frank, but it's better than stealing cars." About that time Marjorie realized she had better finish the sweeping because it was getting close to dinner time. Art wished her a good evening. "You too. Take care." She flashed him a half-smile and went back to her broom. Then she remembered something. "Oh yeah, your wife wanted that clothes line put up outside a window? Frank says he can't do it 'cause all your windows face the front and they don't allow clothes lines except in the back." Art nodded. Marjorie had a rough life, but she was easy to talk to once she opened up. Art had met many people who had gone through similar experiences with their husbands or wives or kids. He wasn't shocked by what he heard. Everybody's got their own stories to tell. Some folks might make it appear as if they didn't have any problems. Some might think that everything is just fine all the time with them. But Art didn't believe it. Life takes its toll on everyone. Many people don't have anyone to talk to, and then the situation is even worse.

When one day Sandra Bolek decided to pull up a chair and fill Art's ear with her troubles, he found it pretty nerve-racking. Art didn't see her coming until she was almost upon him. Either he was in a distracted state of mind or Sandra was a lot faster on her feet than he had previously given her credit for. In any case, she unfolded her chair, sat down, and without so much as a greeting launched into her usual litany of complaints. The fact that she was telling all her medical troubles, mostly imagined, to a man with a legitimate terminal disease did not faze her in the slightest. Art's patience was being severely tested, but he knew her to be a disturbed woman and made allowances. Not all illnesses are immediately obvious, but in her case it became apparent after the first couple of sentences she uttered. True, she wasn't sick in the same sense as he, but mental illness can be just as bad. He resisted the urge to get up and leave. "Everything she says is bullshit, but what's the difference?" he thought, "I don't have anything better to do."

"Let me tell you, these doctors are absolutely worthless." Sandra declared. "I went to one last week and he refused to help me. As sick as I am, I dragged myself to his front door and sat in his waiting room for over two hours. Two hours! Can you believe it? I could have expired on the spot before getting into the examining room. Then when he finally decides that he has some time, do you think he would listen to me, give me a real examination? Absolutely not! He wouldn't give me ten minutes, not ten measly minutes." Sandra related this with a grim determination. She related a lengthy list of grievances that had accumulated over the years. She saw it as her duty to bear witness against these continuous burdens that had been laid upon her. She didn't look into Art's eyes at any point. She stared all around him as if she were able to see these travesties occur again as she described them. Art figured she probably made these same speeches to herself when she was alone. It wouldn't matter all that much to someone like Sandra whether she had someone to talk to or not. Occasionally, she would point a finger to drive home a point. "And do you know what he said to me after doing no more than take my pulse and listen to my chest with his ice cold stethoscope? He told me to go home and get some rest. Is that what he learned in medical school? After his nurse told me that my blood pressure was 190/105? I could have had a stroke right on the spot. She wanted to call the squad right then and there, and she probably should have, and he wants me to go home and rest? I gave him a piece of my mind, I can tell you. It probably raised my blood pressure another 50 points, but he had it coming. I hope the other patients could hear me, because they would do well to clear out of that place. The man is definitely a quack." Sandra lifted her chin a bit as she finished her pronouncement, satisfied that she had rendered a just verdict upon this miserable individual, this poor excuse for a physician. She took no visible pleasure in it, though. Her expression remained severe, the corners of her mouth turned down, her thin lips clamped shut, her eyes dark and cold. Her upper lip and cheeks were marked by vertical lines formed from the grim pressure of her longstanding facial grimace. Her dark hair, streaked with gray, was pulled tightly back and gathered in a bun, adding to her forbidding aspect. "Do you know I heard that a man dropped dead just outside that doctor's office as he was leaving?" Sandra continued. "The doctor had just given him a clean bill of health. So what do you think he did? He told his nurse to turn the body around to make it look like he was coming in! That's the kind of so-called doctors we have today." Art almost erupted into a laugh. He couldn't believe that Sandra took that old joke literally, and that she could incorporate into her demented monologue.

Art wondered about Ira. How could the man put up with this all the time? He must be completely oblivious. "Did Ira go with you to the doctor?" he asked.

"Oh, he drove me there, but I told him to wait in the car. I didn't want to involve him in this. I suspected something unpleasant might happen – I've seen other doctors like this before, you know – and I didn't want Ira to lose his temper. Why he might have even struck the man after the way he behaved toward me, and who could blame him?"

Art could not picture this. "So you've been to many doctors, Sandra?" Art knew he shouldn't lead her on this way, but he was interested to hear her reply.

"You have to. There are so few good ones it takes forever to find one who will really listen and make an effort to understand. I'm beginning to think they are all incompetent. There was one doctor – I hesitate to even call this person by that title, he doesn't deserve it – well, he wanted to send me to a psychiatrist. Can you believe it? He said it was all in my mind. All the suffering that I go through, and all the medical records I could show him, and he had the nerve to say that to me. I wanted to spit in his face! Do you know all the pain medication I have to take each day? All the sleepless nights I put up with? Ira can tell you. And this pipsqueak tells me it's all in my mind. He should have to go through what I endure. I wouldn't wish it on my worst enemy. I told him I was going to get a lawyer and sue him for slander, and I will. You wait and see." Sandra reminded Art of the one about the hypochondriac who had engraved on his tombstone, "I told you I was sick."

"Did you want the doctor to give you more pain medication?" Art asked.

"Not more medication, better medication. This stuff I take doesn't work. Anyone can see that. They're giving me fakes. What do they call them when they only look like real pills but they are really nothing at all?"

"Placebos."

"That's it! They're giving me placebos just to shut me up. They're not interested in my suffering. They don't want to help me. You know what I should do? I should go to the Mayo Clinic like you did. Maybe then I could get some satisfaction."

"Maybe that's what you should do, Sandra."

"You're darn right. Now, who was the doctor that you saw out there?"

"I could give you his name, but he was a specialist in nervous system diseases."

"That's what I have! I get a pain right down my spine that shoots to my leg. Some days it's all I can do to make it from my bed to the bathroom. And my right arm gets numb all over too. That's nerves isn't it?"

Art could only imagine how "grateful" the Mayo Clinic doctors would be if he sent Sandra to them. "Maybe you just work too hard, Sandra. If you took it easier, your health might improve."

"And who's going to scrub the floors and iron the drapes? The work won't get done by itself. These young people today, they don't know what work is. They just want to lie around and watch TV and chew gum and do crossword puzzles. They don't care. You know Mrs. Toobin in 3F? She hired some house cleaners, because her mother was coming for a visit, and she wanted to have everything look right when she got here. Well she came home early before the cleaners left and do you know what she found? They were sitting at the dining room table with their feet up eating her leftover pot roast. Not doing a lick of work! And on top of that, they were getting crumbs and stains all over the apartment. The house was dirtier when they left than it was when they got there. That's what they call cleaning today. In my mother's house you could eat off the floor." That expression always got to Art. Who the hell would want to eat off the floor?

"Well, Sandra, parents always want an easier life for their kids."

"And they got it alright. Too easy, I tell you. They don't know what work is. With all the clothes dryers and dishwashers they don't have to work. I used to wring out clothes with my own two hands, and hang them up to dry on the clothes line. My hands became crippled from it, but that's the sacrifice you must make if you want to do a job right. And I can tell you the clothes were cleaner and smelled sweeter than they do today when they come out of a clothes dryer."

Art thought he better wrap things up before Sandra started to tell him how she walked eight miles to school every day, uphill both ways. "Well, I better be getting back upstairs. Harry said he might drop over."

"Oh? Deliah didn't say they were heading this way."

"Maybe he's not bringing the family."

"That's possible, I suppose. But why would he do that? Heaven knows he leaves Deliah alone long enough during the week." Art folded his chair and made his escape.

53

Artie Feldman was fast. When he tried out for the track team at James Monroe High School, he saw himself as a quarter miler – fast but with enough stamina to go pretty much all out for one circuit around the school's cinder track. Some guys would start out like a house afire, but in that last turn they looked like they had a piano on their back. Artie would pass them easily. Yeah, he figured, this was his event. The track coach, however, had different ideas. His team was bit thin when it came to the sprint events. He saw Artie's speed and he immediately thought, "Here's my new 100 and 200 meter man." That's how Artie Feldman became a sprinter.

 The team already had a couple of good sprinters – Negro students Johnny Rankin and Fred Flood. Artie didn't see how he could compete with them, and he thought he might spend the track season mostly watching instead of competing. Besides, Artie didn't have the build of a sprinter. He was too skinny. All the real sprinters looked like football running backs. They had massive thighs that allowed them to explode out of the starting blocks. The best Artie could do was try to time the starting gun just right so he could get out to a fast start. Otherwise he had no chance. He just didn't see the sense of the coach's decision, but he was a newcomer and didn't feel he could confront the coach about it. During practice things began playing out exactly as Artie predicted. Rankin and Flood were easily the fastest sprinters in both the 100 and 200, and Artie and a couple of others were the also-rans.

As the season approached, though, Fred Flood started missing some practices. Without Fred, Artie became the team's number two sprinter more often than not. One afternoon he finished a close second to Johnny in a 200 meter practice session. "Lookin' good, Artie," Johnny said. Artie looked up and smiled. "You know, you might be pickin' up some medals if Fred can't make it to the meets." Artie asked Johnny if Fred was sick or injured. "Nah, that's not the way it is. It's just that Fred's mom needs him at home. He's got six brothers and sisters and his mom works." That explained a lot. Johnny took Artie under his wing. He showed him how to lean into the tape at the finish line, told him about the differences in the school tracks they were going to run on, and warned him about troublemakers who routinely showed up at rival schools. "Show him that scar, Fred." Fred pointed to a crease on the left side of his forehead. "Fred beat this dude who ran for Clinton, and the cat pulled a knife on him after the meet." Artie asked if the guy was still on Clinton's track team. "Nah, but he shows up at all the meets. Always lookin' for a fight. He gets thrown out of football and basketball games all the time." "If he comes at me again, I'll be ready for him," Fred added.

Artie did pick up some hardware that track season – two seconds and a third. Not a bad showing for a first-year man. When Fred was there, Artie knew he was the number three sprinter. There were no hard feelings on his part. One day Warren Berlin, one of the team's middle distance runners, told Artie that it wasn't right for Fred to just show up to run when he felt like it. "Coach oughta' kick him off the team. He don't even practice most days. You don't practice, you don't run. That's the way it should be." Artie listened but he didn't pay him any mind. The other guys probably didn't know about Fred's situation, and they had no right to talk that way about him.

After the season Johnny had Artie and Fred over his house. They lived in a small single family home on Thieriot Avenue. Johnny's mom served them blueberry muffins and lemonade. Johnny was graduating, and he had a track scholarship to Colgate University in upstate Hamilton, New York, but Fred was just a junior and Artie a sophomore. "You two guys should go out for cross country in the fall. Get you in shape for the track season."

"I get enough runnin' in the spring,' said Fred, "besides I don't even know if I'm coming back."

"What are you gonna do if you drop out, man? You gotta get the diploma." Artie thought he might go out for cross country if he could find the time. Joseph still depended on him to help out in the shop. "You two be carryin' the torch now. The coach will be dependin' on you two."

"Shoot, you go up there to that toothpaste college," said Fred, "get your degree, and come on back and be the coach your own self." They all laughed, then Johnny draped his arms around Fred and Artie's necks and they headed over to a local luncheonette where they had a radio that broadcast the Yankee games.

Fred didn't come back for his senior year. Art did but he didn't run track. The family needed him to get a job after school and bring home an extra paycheck. Art thought back to those days more often now. You don't appreciate what you have at the time – your health, your strength, your whole life in front of you. Who was it that said youth was wasted on the young? Those were good times, even if they didn't last too long.

54

Art used to wonder how far track could have taken him. Oh, he knew he wouldn't have been an Olympian like Marty Glickman who grew up in Brooklyn and ended up on the U.S. team with Jesse Owens. But maybe he could have gone to college, and how would things have been different then? Glickman's parents were Rumanian immigrants like Art's folks, and his running got him a ticket to Syracuse University. Then when his running days were over, he got a job broadcasting football games on the radio. What was the use of thinking about that though? There would have still been the Depression and the need to bring home some money to help out the family. It didn't pay to linger over "what-ifs." There were always more than enough challenges to deal with in the immediate future.

No, Art's running days were over by the time he was a senior. There was at least one consolation that year, however. It came in the form of a slim, dark-haired, brown-eyed girl who sat in front of him in math class. She seemed kind of quiet and rather studious, especially when she put on her eyeglasses in order to get a clear view of the blackboard up front. Vivian Simonson was a year younger than Art but somehow they had ended up in the same math class. Lucky for Art, but he couldn't seem to figure out at first how to start a conversation with her. That particular problem was solved for him, however, a week or so later during school assembly. Students were given a preview of the school play that was scheduled to be presented that fall, and Art thought one of the tall, thin actresses playing a Japanese schoolgirl on stage looked familiar. Yes, that was Vivian Simonson in James Monroe High School's production of The Mikado. How could such a retiring, introverted kid get up on stage in front of the whole school? She wouldn't even return his glance in math class. But here she was emoting for an audience, and she wasn't a bad actress either. Art could see how she enjoyed performing, putting herself out there. You could never tell about people. They had other sides of their personality that you would never suspect existed.

Anyway, this gave Art his opening. Next math class he blurted out, "Hey, I saw you in the play." Vivian answered with a small smile. "Yeah, you were really good."

"It's only a small part. How did you know it was me, anyway?"

"Oh, I could tell. You were the tallest one there." Art had second thoughts about that remark. Maybe he should have said "prettiest one there." Maybe she was self-conscious about being tall. Vivian didn't seem to take offense, though. After that, Vivian gave Art daily updates on the progress of the play, and led him to understand that they really needed more male actors in the dramatics club. Art considered going out for it even though he didn't have any interest in acting. He even told Vivian that he was thinking about showing up for the next club meeting.

"That would be great. We still need to cast a few male roles for the next play." It would be worth it to be able to spend more time with Vivian, but the truth was that he just didn't have the time due to his after-school job.

One day the math teacher instructed the class to take out their textbooks and turn to page 125. Funny how Art always remembered that it was page 125. Maybe it was because he had just come from Hygiene class and all the students had been weighed, measured, and had their eyesight tested. Art was told that he weighed 125 lbs. Five feet six and one half inches and 125 lbs. His eyesight was 20/20. One of his classmates had eyesight that appeared to be much better than that. When he was called upon to read the last line on the eye chart, he squinted noticeably and pronounced the words "Made in U.S.A." Even Mr. Daugherty, the Hygiene teacher, had laughed.

Now Mrs. Bowen, the math teacher directed the class to page 125 in the textbook. Ironically, it was the section on weights and measures. Vivian turned back to Art with her hands held upward in a gesture of helplessness. She did not have her textbook with her. Art realized this was an opportunity, an invitation. He grabbed his text and started for the seat next to Vivian. Not only would they share the book, Art anticipated, but they would feel each other's bodies pressing closely together. Art slid in next to her. Vivian didn't move away. As thin as they both were, most of the body pressing turned out to be knees, shoulders, and elbows but Art still found it stimulating. Art's concentration on the textbook wandered to Vivian's knee visible below her skirt. He imagined that he might place his hand on her leg and see what she would do. Instead, he decided to drape his arm over the back of the seat, lightly touching Vivian's shoulder. It seemed something natural, given that they were sharing the same book. Vivian didn't mind. Art had trouble following the lesson. In fact, it soon became the last thing on his mind. Fortunately, Mrs. Bowen didn't call on him. Suddenly, Vivian crossed her legs, giving a little tug at her hem so that her skirt wouldn't ride up too much. This maneuver occupied Art's thoughts for the rest of the class. Had she noticed him admiring her legs? Did she intend to show him more of them? If so, then why did she then lower her skirt? Was she offended that he was looking at them? Was she just showing him that she wasn't a slut? Now she was swinging her leg. Isn't that a come on? Art didn't learn much about weights and measures that afternoon.

When the bell rang, Vivian closed the book for Art and pushed it over to him. "Thanks for sharing," she said and gave Art a broad smile. Art noticed that Vivian's teeth were not looking too good, and he thought that was a shame. But he still liked her smiling at him. "Will I see you later?" she asked.

"Later?"

"At Dramatics Club."

"Oh, yeah, I'm gonna try." Another smile. He started imagining some ways that he might be able to skip work once in a while. Art was thinking that it had been a good afternoon.

55

Bessie told Vivian that she would have to finish cleaning up after dinner. "Where are you going?"

"I'm going to the AJC meeting with Mrs. Horowitz." Vivian could hear Sam banging around in the bedroom, making it clear that he did not approve of Bessie leaving the apartment. "And make sure you look after Stanley. That one in there couldn't care less about his son." And she was out the door. Stanley sat in a corner of the room playing with his baseball cards, oblivious to Sam's gathering tirade in the next room.

"American Jewish Congress meetings? Hah! Who does she think she's fooling? Like I don't know. She thinks I'm deaf, dumb, and blind? I'm wise to her tricks. She won't get away with it!" Something heavy slammed down on the bureau. Stanley jumped in his seat, but did not look up. Vivian walked over and took Stanley by the arm. "Do you want some cookies and milk?" He followed her into the kitchen. Sam appeared in the kitchen doorway. "Where does she keep the phonebook?" He began rummaging through the kitchen drawers. "Mrs. Horowitz, huh? I'll find out where she's going. Where is that book?" Stanley hopped off his seat, went to the foyer, and returned with the city phone directory. Sam grabbed it from his hands and flung away on to floor. "Not that one, dummy!" Crestfallen, Stanley slumped on to the couch in the foyer. Sam continued his frantic search in vain.

"She's going to the meeting. I heard her talking to Mrs. Horowitz about it yesterday," said Vivian.

"Hah! She lies and you swear to it." Abandoning his search, Sam took a seat at the kitchen table. "It's spite, plain and simple. That's all it is. Just because I'm not made of money and can't buy her everything she wants." He ran his hand through his thinning hair and unbuttoned his shirt collar. "Money, money, that's all she thinks about. She should have married the company executive when she had the chance or some doctor or lawyer. They would keep her in style. Why can't I have some peace and quiet? How much can someone take?" He began to fiddle with a napkin on the table, crumpling it up then smoothing it out again. "She's trying to ruin us. Spend everything and be left with no money in the bank.

We'll end up in the poorhouse. If she comes home again with another bastard, I won't be responsible for what will happen."

Vivian jumped up. "Don't talk that way in front of Stanley."

"You speak to your father that way?" Sam slapped Vivian across the mouth and stomped out of the room. Back in the bedroom, Sam began to throw objects against the wall, muttering loudly to himself. The neighbor downstairs began to bang on the ceiling with a broom handle, complaining about the noise. Sam began to stomp on the floor with his feet. "They have the nerve to complain about noise after their screaming all night long? I'll give them some noise. How do you like that? Keep banging and you'll get more!" Vivian sat at the kitchen table, her head resting on her hand. Stanley, standing, leaned against her. Vivian wrapped an arm around him. "How about we go to a movie? You can get some popcorn and we'll watch the cartoons." Stanley nodded. Suddenly Sam stomped back in. He grabbed the phone and dialed his brother Ben.

"Ben, Ben, she's started again. I can't take it anymore." Ben, Sam's older brother, was an accountant for a shipping firm in Manhattan, and not given to emotional outbursts.

"Sam, what are you working yourself up about? Calm down. It's not worth it."

"She walked out on me. Lied about going to some meeting. I know what she's up to."

"What do you know? You know nothing, as usual. It's all in your mind."

"All in my mind, is it? Hah! I suppose it was my imagination when she was carrying on with that dentist." Vivian stood up and took Stanley with her into the foyer.

"Sam, don't get carried away again. You make a mountain out of a molehill."

"Don't I have good reason? What if it was Rose? You'd be singing a different tune then."

"How do you know she didn't go to that meeting? That's what she probably did."

"If I could find that phone number of her friend I'd know for sure, but she hid the phone book from me. She knew I'd check and find out she's lying again." Sam started pulling out drawers again as he spoke. One of them slammed onto the floor.

"What are you doing there, wrecking the place?"

"Ben, if she's not home by dinner time, I'll call the police. They'll fix her wagon."

"Sam, be sensible. It's almost dinner time already. The police are not going to be interested in a wife who's ten minutes late for dinner."

Sam looked up and noticed Vivian and Stanley with their coats on, heading for the door. "Hold on, Ben, Vivian's leaving too." Sam put the phone down and rushed to the door. "Where are you going?"

"I'm taking Stanley to the movies."

"Tell me the truth. You're running away like your mother, aren't you?"

"What?"

"Everybody leaves me. How did I deserve this?"

Vivian gave Sam a tired, disgusted look. ""Don't go. I'm sorry, I shouldn't have hit you. I'll get your teeth fixed. I have the money. Only don't leave."

"We are just going to the movies." Vivian pushed past Sam and left with Stanley.

Distraught, Sam returned to the phone. "Ben, they're all gone. They all left me. What am I going to do?"

"You're going to calm down and face facts. No one wants to stay with a raving maniac. You drive everyone out of the house with your lunacy."

"What can I do?"

"You can take a shot of slivovitz and sit down. They will all be back later, and if you can behave like a normal human being, they will stay there."

"I don't know."

"Well, I do. I'm talking sense to you. Do as I say, understand?" Ben knew that when nothing else worked, slivovitz usually did the trick. Fortunately, Sam had no trouble locating the bottle. He took a shot, sat down and poured himself a second. "Now listen to me Sam. You've got to get a hold of yourself. Stop obsessing about your family. Get out of the house. There's life going on outside. You can't just work and go home to all those arguments. Why don't you come with me to the party meeting tomorrow night? Morris Hillquit is going to tell us about the cigar makers' strike. You know, there are many ways we can respond to the way the company is mistreating the workers down there in Florida. Morris will let us know the best course to take. You can help out. You did a good job last time, remember?" Ben's soothing tone and the slivovitz slowly took effect. Sam grew quieter. The crisis had passed. By the time Bessie returned home, he was lying on his back on the couch snoring.

"Look at him with his shoes up on the furniture," Bessie exclaimed to herself. With one swipe of her right arm she swept Sam's legs off the couch. He awoke and immediately sat up, rubbing his eyes. "Why don't you go to bed?" Bessie said. "You're getting dirt all over the furniture lying there like that."

"So, you finally saw fit to come home, did you?" Sam responded.

"What are you talking about? Of course I came home. Did you think I was running to away to Germany with Rabbi Wise?"

"Don't try to fool me. I wasn't born yesterday. I know what you've been up to!"

"Oh, for Pete's sake, here we go again." As Sam renewed his attacks, Bessie noticed the absence of Vivian and Stanley. "Where are the children?" Sam stopped his rant and looked around bewilderedly. "What have you done with them?"

"What have I done with them? You're the mother. You're supposed to be home watching them instead of galavanting all over the city!"

"You can't even keep an eye on them when I'm gone for a second."

Vivian and Stanley walked in while this round of mutual accusations was still in full swing. Stanley was yawning. He had fallen asleep in the theater. Vivian calmly led him by the hand to his bed, commenting to Bessie, "We were at the movies" as she passed. Turning again to Sam, Bessie asked, "Why couldn't you tell me they were at the movies?"

"How should I know where they go? No one tells me the truth in this house. You're all against me." The broom handle was banging on the ceiling downstairs again.

 "Someone's going to call the police on you one of these days," Bessie warned.

"When they come, I'll report you for plotting against me, do you hear? Plotting against me!" Bessie walked into the bedroom, shedding her coat in the process.

"I married a crazy man."

56

Sam had made promises to change his ways before, and they all had come to nothing. A leopard doesn't change its spots, after all. But this time was different for some reason. A few days after Sam's most recent eruption, Bessie told Vivian that she had made an appointment for her with Dr. Bernstein the dentist. Sam had acquiesced. Vivian wanted to get her teeth fixed, but her past experiences with Dr. Bernstein were most unpleasant. Perhaps this could be said about most everyone's encounters with dentists. They were not usually enjoyable occasions. But visits to Dr. Bernstein were usually more frightful than most.

Dr. Oswald Bernstein was the brother-in-law of a man Sam used to work with during his early days in this country. Since Bernstein was the relative of a co-worker, it was assumed that the Simonsons would get a better deal on dentistry from him, or at least more favorable treatment than if they were dealing with a stranger. They had no way of knowing that Bernstein was a poor dentist who adhered to obsolete methods. His techniques were guaranteed to cause the patient more discomfort than was ordinarily the case. In addition, he was slow. Every procedure took Bernstein at least as twice as long as it would with most other dentists. If you had a cavity, Bernstein would make you pay two visits. No matter how minor the decay, the patient would have to receive a temporary filling first then return to get the permanent one installed. This meant that Bernstein would be digging away at the patient's tooth twice as much as was necessary, causing twice as much anxiety and pain. Furthermore, Bernstein employed an old mechanical drill that slowly ground down the patient's tooth, significantly extending the amount of time that one was exposed to this most dreaded of dental experiences. Instead of getting it over relatively quickly, the patient needed to sit and listen to the drill laboring through the procedure, smell the decomposing enamel, and experience extended periods of unrelenting pain. And it definitely was going to be painful because Bernstein did not use anesthesia of any kind. He didn't like using needles, and if a dental procedure absolutely could not be done without anesthesia, Bernstein would make a referral to another dentist. Of course, patients don't like needles either, but most would opt for them if the alternative is excruciating agony. With Bernstein you didn't get the option. He would not inject. Maybe he had botched some injections and didn't care to take another chance. Perhaps injections violated some obscure moral code to which he adhered, or maybe he was an outright sadist. In any case, if you were his patient, you were not receiving any novocaine.

Sam and Bessie were not knowledgeable concerning modern dental practices. Therefore, they had no way of knowing that Bernstein was a poor dentist. Most of their contemporaries did not visit dentists unless they had a bad toothache and needed an extraction. Even then, they would sometimes handle the matter themselves. So it was that Vivian, with much trepidation, paid a visit to Dr. Bernstein's office. Bernstein operated his dentistry practice out of his home in the Bronx. He had outfitted one room of his apartment with a dentist's chair, drill, and all the necessary implements. His wife served as receptionist, bookkeeper, and dental assistant. Even before the patient was greeted by Mrs. Bernstein, however, one encountered Bernstein's beagle who barked incessantly at the approach of any visitor. It did not matter if the person was a regular patient who had been to Bernstein's apartment many times. The dog would still break into its usual routine. One would think that Bernstein would realize such behavior was forbidding, that the patient was not put at ease by such harassment. Perhaps he thought that his patients were all dog lovers who would interpret regular, familiar barking as welcoming. Such was not the case for most, however, and certainly not for Vivian who jumped every time the dog yelped. The dentist or his wife would hold the dog back from the front door, thereby clearing a small path through which the patient might enter the premises. Vivian would sidle into the apartment, still afraid that the beagle could possibly break free and attack her. Vivian had read somewhere that beagles were the stupidest of dogs, the dunces of the dog kingdom, and after her encounters with Bernstein's beast, she was sure it was true.

The usual routine repeated itself yet again this time as Vivian visited Dr. Bernstein – the beagle barking and lunging; Mrs. Bernstein attempting to smile at the arriving patient while simultaneously grimacing with the effort of holding the dog back to permit Vivian's entry; and finally Vivian's tense recline in the dentist's chair to await her sufferings. But this time it was different. As Dr. Bernstein examined Vivian's decayed teeth, he hemmed and hawed a bit, mused over his diagnosis, and at last pronounced his verdict. Vivian needed multiple extractions. The teeth could not be saved. They were too far gone. He would need to refer her to a dental surgeon.

Harold Levy was the dental surgeon Dr. Bernstein sent Vivian to. He was a friend of Bernstein's from dental school, and his office was nearby. Fortunately for Vivian, Dr. Levy availed himself of the latest in dental technology. Vivian was quickly anesthetized, and as a result the extraction of four of her teeth on the upper right side of her mouth was painless. The same could not be said, however, of her recovery. She was reduced to taking only liquid nourishment for the following week. In addition, her missing teeth on the upper right side caused her great embarrassment, and she took great pains to cover the gap with a handkerchief or facial tissue.

Art told her that it was unnecessary to hide her mouth that way, but she continued to do so. Art took her for milkshakes and malteds after school. He was late for work but didn't care. Vivian told him that she was going to get a dental bridge that would make her look good again. "You always look good to me," Art told her and she grinned at him. Predictably, the idea of a bridge sparked more clashes at home, Sam maintaining that he couldn't afford such an expense. "She looks fine. What is she a model?" Bessie went to work on him, but it was tough going. Art realized how important this was to Vivian, to her confidence and self-image, so he began to put aside some money from his weekly paycheck to help her out. After a few months, Bessie had secured enough money from Sam so that, with Art's help, Vivian was able to get her bridge. Art's generosity and dedication made a great impression on Vivian. Here was someone with admirable qualities, someone she could depend on. Plus Art knew how to show her a good time. They went to the movies, to dinner, and dancing. He took her swimming at Orchard

Beach, and they went to City Island for clams. Art helped her forget her troubles at home. Vivian grew to feel very close to him.

57

The fact that Sam had acquiesced, at least in part, to provide for Vivian's dental care did not alter the pattern of domestic strife in the Simonson household. Sam's suspicions did not abate and neither did the continuing battles. Increasingly, Vivian looked to escape. She spent as much time as she could participating in school plays and productions. When she wasn't cast as a player, she helped out with lighting or props. She saw Art whenever he was available. Still she dreaded returning home, even if it was just to sleep. A solution to the situation was difficult to see. Neither Vivian nor Art had the financial means to support an independent existence. After tossing around ideas for a few weeks, Art thought he may have hit upon a solution. "My sister Rita has a big house in Jersey. Maybe she would put you up."

"Jersey? That's a long way. How could I get to school?"

"Her husband works in the city. He could drop you off." There were several reasons why this probably wouldn't have worked. Rita and Leonard Edelman had just gotten married and weren't looking to take in borders. Also, Leonard worked in Manhattan, and it would have been well out of his way to drive Vivian to school in the Bronx. That's not even taking into consideration the fact that if Vivian were living in New Jersey she would no longer be legally eligible to attend school in the Bronx. Putting all that aside, Art decided it would be a good idea to introduce Vivian to Rita just to see if there might be any way to work this out. Besides, Art was eager to show off his beautiful girlfriend. He arranged for a visit on a Saturday.

Vivian told Bessie that she was going to Jersey to visit Art's sister. She didn't ask for permission to go, but Bessie probably would have granted it in any case. She was quietly pleased to see Vivian happy, and everything she had managed to learn about Art was favorable. He seemed like a responsible young man, a hard worker, and most important – he treated Vivian well. Sam wasn't so sure. "Who is this Art? We haven't met him, have we? He's Jewish? OK, but is he *Galitzianer* or *Litvak*? Who are his parents? Where are they from? How do they make a living?" As he was giving Bessie the third degree, Sam had decided to change a wall switch that had been out of order for weeks. Bessie told him that the building superintendent could handle it, but Sam refused. He knew that there would be no charge for the repair, but he didn't want to be coerced into paying the man a tip. He wouldn't admit this to Bessie. Instead, he declared that he was tired of waiting until the superintendent finally got around to fixing it. Bessie reminded him that they had never reported the problem to him. Sam ignored the remark and began to unscrew the switch plate.

Sam was not a skilled do-it-yourself kind of guy. He had never owned a home nor did his parents. He had neither interest nor talent in making any kind of mechanical or electrical repairs. However, his intense interest in saving money plus his impatience overrode all else. After removing the switch plate, he discovered that the electrical wire he needed to attach to the new switch his brother had bought for him was a bit short. He attempted to pull it into place without success. "This damn thing isn't long enough!"

"It was long enough to reach the old switch," Bessie replied.

"The old switch was broken."

"It worked for years before it broke." Sam tried twisting it into place with an old pliers. "Did you turn the electricity off? You might electrocute yourself."

"The switch is turned off."

"That's not enough."

"If this goddamn wire doesn't connect, I'm going to pull the damn thing out of the wall!" Sam gave the wire a violent twist with the pliers and broke off a 3-inch segment. ""Goddamn it to hell!" With that, Sam kicked his foot in frustration into the bathroom wall. His soft bedroom slippers provided scant protection for his foot. As a result, the second toe on his right foot received a traumatic injury that drove it out of its socket. A searing pain shot up Sam's leg. When he pulled off the slipper he saw his toe pointing straight upward at a right angle to his foot. He cried out as much in shock as in pain and proceeded to hop around the room on his good leg. Bessie grabbed him around the waist and guided him to the living room couch and sat him down. Then she called Sam's brother to ask if he could drive them to the hospital emergency room.

When Art and Vivian arrived at Rita's home in Patterson, they were warmly greeted. Rita gave Vivian a hug and took her by the hand. "So lovely to meet you, Vivian." Rita showed Vivian around the 3-bedroom, single family home. Vivian was impressed with the space and privacy. "You have a beautiful home." Rita prepared coffee and served sponge cake. As they were seated at the dining room table, the front doorbell rang. "Oh, that must be Ida. She said she'd try to stop by." Ida didn't wait for Rita to open the door; she opened it herself and entered, tramping into the house, loaded with shopping bags. Her dark hair was tumbling out of its restraining clips and bands. Her brown striped skirt clashed with her black print blouse. "There you are! Oh, I didn't want to miss meeting Artie's girl so I changed my beauty parlor appointment. And am I glad I did! Artie, your Vivian is a real beauty. Look at you! I'm Ida, Artie's sister like Rita here and then there's Fran too. You haven't met her yet." Vivian hardly had time to return Ida's greeting. She didn't know whether to smile or laugh. She felt like hiding somewhere until this storm blew over. "Rita, look what I picked up at the A&P. Chocolate macaroons. Do you believe it? And it isn't even Passover." Ida placed the treat on the table. "Eat, eat, they're delicious. Take it from me. They melt in your mouth." Rita got up to bring more coffee. Ida sat down next to Vivian. "So tell me, how did you meet Artie?" Art explained that they were classmates. "I bet you're a good student too. Am I right? Smart AND beautiful – a deadly combination. You better be careful, Artie." Ida laughed loudly, pointing at Art. Art looked over at Vivian. For the first time he noticed the fixed smile on her face, the one that didn't look natural to anyone that knew her. Vivian was bravely standing up to Ida's rude assault on her sensibilities, hoping that Art's other relatives were more like Rita and less like Ida.

In this regard she was to be somewhat disappointed. Oh, there was no one quite like the boisterous Ida, but all of Art's siblings with the exception of young David, were outgoing. They freely expressed their impressions, their likes and dislikes, and they did so in enthusiastic exchanges punctuated by humor and sarcasm. When the Feldmans got together there was laughter. Anyone could be the target of anyone else, but no one seemed to take offense. "Wasn't anything serious with these people?" Vivian thought. "Was everything grist for their mill?" Vivian didn't consider herself to be a prude, and sure, she liked to laugh too, but some of what the Feldmans found funny was just plain rudeness. What was that name Sol called Ida's boyfriend? Shelly Shitstain? Just because he had that unfortunate accident during a ballgame when he was sliding into second base? And that was supposed to be funny? Why couldn't they think about how he felt? You know her boyfriend must have been mortified. What if one of them was the butt of all those jokes? Can't they just be polite sometimes?

And what really bothered Vivian was how Art changed when he was with his brothers. He relished trading barbs with them. He was anxious to participate in their insults. Was this the real Art, or was the Art she knew the real one? She was worried about this. And what about Art's sisters? Fran was almost as raucous as Ida. Only Rita seemed to act properly, but she never took offense at all the others' behavior. How could she find all this acceptable? She must know it isn't right, but she acted like nothing was wrong. Sometimes she even laughed along with them. Vivian found herself trying to copy Rita's reactions, but her heart wasn't in it. What else could she do? Vivian just couldn't understand all this.

None of Art's sisters knew what was going through Vivian's mind. Their impressions of Art's girlfriend were generally favorable. After Art and Vivian left, Rita remarked that it had nice been to meet Vivian. "I can see why Art is so taken with her. She's a very attractive girl."

"But kind of quiet, don't you think?" asked Ida.

"Everyone seems quiet compared to you," quipped Fran who had arrived later.

"You're no shrinking violet yourself, Frannie." They all agreed that she made a nice impression. What was there to dislike? Vivian had accepted everything the girls had presented to her, studiously avoided taking issue with anything that was said or done, and had answered everything sent her way with what could only be interpreted as a pleasant smile.

Art was satisfied that Vivian's first introduction to the family had gone well. She seemed to have gotten along well with his sisters. In the coming weeks, Vivian would meet Art's brothers and his parents. The pattern repeated itself. They all commented on her physical attractiveness, her quiet composure, and her generally pleasant demeanor. Art couldn't have hoped for anything better. It took a while before Art saw anything different in Vivian.

Art had to work after school, the Dramatics Club only met a couple of times each week, and Vivian was never eager to return home, so she decided to find a part-time job for herself. She secured a sales position at Alice's Dress Shop on nearby Hunts Point Avenue. Vivian was a quick learner and a hard worker. The customers liked her too. Alice was impressed and raised her salary after the first month. Sam Simonson, however, was not pleased. Not only was his wife frequently gone from the house when he returned from work, but his daughter was now never around. There was no one to greet him when he got home, no hot dinner on the table, and no one to keep little Stanley out of his hair. This was too much. Whenever Bessie or Vivian showed up they got an earful from him. And when Sam started his rants there was no stopping him. He succeeded only in driving them from the house for ever longer periods. Bessie had succeeded in liberating herself from Sam's domination. He could no longer control her behavior no matter how much he tried. Vivian, however, still a minor, was not yet independent. When Sam started threatening to make her quit her job, she became scared and angry. In the relatively brief time that she had been employed, Vivian quickly came to appreciate the advantages of an independent existence. It wasn't just the money which gave her a certain degree of financial freedom. It was the sense of being confident that she could meet her own needs. She didn't have to depend on others. She was capable of standing on her own two feet. Now Sam was vowing to take all that away from her. What would happen if he insisted on her quitting? What if he showed up at the shop and made a scene? She knew he was quite capable of that. Sam was also using Stanley to try to achieve his aim. "You don't care nothing for your little brother? You leave him alone in the house all afternoon? What kind of sister are you?" Even when she came home late, Sam was waiting for her with his set of recriminations. If Bessie was there to defend her, it only ended up in another all-night verbal battle from which Vivian could not escape.

Art was used to living what many would describe as a hectic existence. School and work consumed most of his waking hours. In addition to his own after-school job, he still helped out at his father's business. What free time he could find, he spent with Vivian. When he returned home, he found an apartment bustling with activity. Four of his six siblings still lived at home. Several of them were always coming and going, grabbing a meal, changing clothes, on the way or returning from school or work. Inevitably, there were disagreements and arguments. "Who took my sweater I was planning on wearing today?" "Why isn't there any cholent left for my lunch?" "Who spilled milk all over my homework?" But more often there were supportive gestures and jokes. "You got a flat tire? Take my bike, but I'll need it this afternoon." "Your boss said what? Don't pay attention to him. Go to the assistant manager. He's a good guy." "Don't tell your teacher that the dog ate your homework. We don't have a dog, remember?" Claire Feldman did her best to keep the household running smoothly, preparing meals, doing laundry, shopping, and seeing that her children were properly fed and dressed to ward off illness.

Vivian's daily home life was very different. She was effectively alone in dealing with Sam's rages and her parents' incessant arguments. Stanley was too young to offer support. He needed help himself, and she tried to provide it when she could. Bessie would keep house and provide occasional meals, but frequently she sought to escape from Sam and family life, such as it was. Vivian followed Bessie's example. She tried her best to create a life for herself in the outside world. Her job was essential for this purpose. Sam's threat to take this away was unbearable to her. The idea that her hard won emerging independence might be destroyed in this manner made her very angry. It occurred to her that this anger was something that she might not be able to control. She wasn't sure what she might do if this anger was triggered, and she found this frightening. She wondered if this wasn't what Sam felt when he launched his tirades.

One evening Vivian returned home after her shift at the dress shop to find Bessie washing dishes. "Your dinner is on the stove, Vivian." Vivian grabbed a dinner plate and fork.

"Where's dad?"

"He went out."

"Out where?"

"Sit down and eat your dinner." Vivian took a seat at the table. Bessie called Stanley in to eat. "He didn't want to eat before you came home." Vivian thought it was unusual that Sam had gone out in the evening. He rarely did so. She asked Bessie about it again.

"Oh, don't worry yourself about it. You know him and his ravings." Vivian was losing her appetite."

"Don't tell me..."

"Now Vivian, he won't do anything. He's all talk." Vivian threw down her fork and headed for the door. "Vivian! They won't listen to him even if he goes there. They'll just think he's some crazy man!" Vivian grabbed her coat and headed out the door. "Where's Vivian going?" Stanley asked.

Vivian wasn't sure where she would go when she stormed out of the apartment. She looked at her watch and realized that Art was probably home from work, so she hurried into a phone booth inside a local candy store. Thankfully, Art was home. "Art, he's going to get me fired. He's going to cost me my job." Art agreed to meet her at the schoolyard on Hoe Avenue. Vivian was angrily pacing up and down in front of a bench when Art got there. He tried to get her to sit down but she wouldn't. Her face was flushed, her teeth clenched. "I can't take this anymore. He's going to ruin my life."

"Maybe he won't do anything."

"He won't let me live!" Art put his arm on Vivian's shoulder but she shook it off. "Goddamnit to hell! He should drop dead!" Art looked around to see if anyone was watching this. Fortunately, the few kids playing basketball were not paying attention. Art had never been unable to communicate with Vivian before. "Vivian, take it easy." Vivian was sweating although the evening air was refreshingly cool. Suddenly she turned and shoved the bench off its moorings and stormed off. "Leave me alone!" Art stood bewildered. "Why call me to meet her if she's going to run off?" he thought. He had never seen her like this. What had he got himself into?

Art didn't call contact Vivian the following week, and he didn't hear from her either. He thought about speaking to his brother Saul about the situation. Sol was older and busy most of the time, and David was too young. But then maybe one of his sisters, being women, would have better insight into Vivian's behavior. Or maybe he should talk to one of his friends at school about it. But once you started talking at school, it usually got around pretty fast, and Vivian might hear about it. In the end, Art didn't talk to anyone. He just brooded by himself. Should he make the first move? Wasn't it her place to apologize for the way she acted? While he was still trying to work this out, he found himself wandering the school hallway. He found himself outside a meeting of the Dramatics Club, peering through a pane of glass in the classroom door. There she was looking calm and collected, listening to Mrs. Van Horn, the Dramatics Club advisor, talking about the upcoming spring play. Art kept staring at Vivian until she finally noticed him. He couldn't tell anything from the glance she returned. It seemed blank, devoid of emotion. Then she rose from her seat and approached Mrs. Van Horn. She wrote Vivian a hall pass, and Vivian headed toward the door. Art stepped back and she opened the door. They walked slowly together down the hall and ducked into a stairwell. Nobody was around. Vivian spoke first, her head bowed. "I'm sorry. I don't know what got into me."

"Yeah, I didn't know how to help you."

Vivian looked up. "You're helping me now. You didn't leave me." Art took her in his arms and looked into her eyes. She laid her head on his shoulder. They were back.

In the following months, Art and Vivian became inseparable. Art was Vivian's rock. He was the only one who could make her feel grounded, calm, and somewhat optimistic about the future. With Art she could see a new life rising on the horizon. Why couldn't they be happy together? They could make a home for each other, maybe a real family. When she was in his arms, the world was alright. For Art it was just the opposite. Vivian was his escape from the world of continuous work. She excited him. When she was in his arms, his desire grew. Art had been a few dates before, but not with anyone with whom he could connect emotionally. There had been some kissing and grabbing before being pushed back in the name of propriety. With Vivian it was different. They had strong feelings for each other. It wasn't long before Vivian found herself participating in extended necking sessions in theater balconies, on dark park benches, in the grassy fields wrapped in a blanket, and in the backseats of borrowed cars. Sometimes she felt like she was going to be carried away by Art's passion. Other times she felt like everything was moving too fast. Then one night, the preliminaries were over. Art had borrowed Sol's car, Vivian was as aroused as Art, and he was prepared. He'd brought a condom. From then on, physical intimacy became a normal part of their relationship, but this began to bother Vivian. She didn't like living a hidden life. She wanted to make it all legal and legitimate. Art wasn't surprised. He understood and respected her feelings. And he felt ready to assume responsibility.

So it was that they found themselves on a bus one day heading for a Justice of the Peace in Stamford, Connecticut. Art had heard from a co-worker that it was quick and easy to get married there. Plus everything was taking place away from the prying eyes of those in New York. They would have their piece of paper. If anyone challenged their status, they could prove that they were a married couple. Vivian kept looking over at Art as they traveled north holding hands. She had a smile on her face. She was happy for the first time in a long time. She had some concerns about the future, but they were kept at bay. Today was a time for celebration, even if the party was going to be a very small one.

They couldn't afford their own apartment yet. Art had arranged for them to live with Rita's sister-in-law Lena who had a place in Washington Heights. She had an extra bedroom and was willing to let Art and Vivian stay there in return for sharing costs. The location was close by a subway line that could get them to where they had to go. Lena and her husband Laszlo had a young daughter who slept in the apartment's other bedroom. Things might be a bit crowded but they would manage. They would keep busy working and saving to get their own place. There was no reason they couldn't make this work.

When they got to Stamford, they grabbed coffee and a doughnut at Howard's Diner then found the location of the courthouse which, as Art was told, was within walking distance. Before entering, they circled back to a local florist where he bought Vivian a small bouquet. He wanted her to have flowers for the occasion. At least it would be something nice for her. The ceremony itself wouldn't seem like much without family and friends. Vivian hugged him around the neck and planted a kiss on his cheek.

Art had the marriage license, the fee, and a small gold ring he had purchased at a pawnshop. They were ready when they returned to the courthouse, entered, and met J. Kenneth Miles, the Justice of the Peace. Miles's welcoming demeanor seemed genuine and it put Art and Vivian at ease. The ceremony was simple and quick, but it accomplished its purpose. Art and Vivian were wed. Before returning on the bus, they had a celebratory dinner at Howard's. The place was filled with travelers coming and going, burdened with canvas bags and cardboard suitcases. Many were weary, impatient, and hassled by restless children. Art and Vivian weren't disappointed that the setting was far from ideal for newlyweds. They were seated at a booth covered in red leatherette and opened the stained menus. Vivian ordered a burger and fries and a chocolate milkshake. Even though it was late afternoon, Art decided to have another breakfast. He was very hungry and intrigued by the featured item, "The World Famous Breeches Buster." Vivian gasped when the waitress brought Art his mound of biscuits, home fries, and scrambled eggs covered in a river of sausage gravy. "You're not going to finish all that."

"Wanna bet?" And Art pretty much did. After all it was a special day.

On the bus ride home Vivian began to be bothered by an upset stomach. She thought it might be the dill pickles on the burger. When they reached New York, she rushed to the restroom in the bus terminal. She was pale and sweaty when she emerged. "You're the one who ate the 'Breeches Buster' and I'm the one throwing up." She gave Art a wan smile. He hoped that she wasn't getting really sick. It wasn't until three weeks later that she discovered she was pregnant.

Once it became clear that Harry was on the way, Art and Vivian realized that it was time to come out in the open about everything. They realized that many would figure that they had rushed to get married because Vivian was expecting. So what? Although not technically true, it wasn't far from it. In any case, now that a child was on the way, family and friends insisted on a real marriage ceremony. As a result, a second, more elaborate wedding occurred three months after the first.

Rabbi Edwin Adler bore no resemblance to JP Miles, but his manner was equally welcoming. Rabbi Adler was the son of the rabbi whose synagogue served the section of Manhattan's Lower East Side where Joseph and Claire Feldman first lived after Immigrating to America. Both the Feldmans and the Simonsons were receptive to the idea of celebrating their children's marriage in the old neighborhood where old fashioned *yiddishkeit* still reigned. Consequently, the wedding took place at the Stanton Street Shul with a reception at a ballroom adjacent to the venerable Ratner's Dairy Restaurant on Delancey Street. For the first time Vivian was glad to hear Ida's loud voice announcing the number of times Vivian had walked circles around Art under the *chupah*, because she was getting dizzy and might have lost count. Art's brothers kidded him about botching the traditional breaking of the glass that sealed the wedding ceremony. Legends abounded about nervous bridegrooms who rolled an ankle trying to smash it, and stumbling awkwardly on to their keester. Not only did such a mishap bode ill for the success of the marriage, but it painted a humiliating picture that could be recalled for generations. Art had no intention of becoming the butt of such a joke, but he couldn't say that he wasn't at least a bit concerned. When Rabbi Adler wrapped the glass cup in a linen napkin and placed it on the floor, Art made sure to aim slowly and carefully. There was the loud pop which meant a cleanly smashed the vessel, and the celebration was on.

Some feared that a reception at Ratner's meant a meatless dinner, but Claire had prepared her delicious borscht wIth beef, stuffed cabbage, and a tasty brisket. Art's brothers ran over to Yona Schimmel's Bakery on Houston Street and returned with one tray of potato knishes, a second of kasha knishes, and a third of sweet *lokshen* kugel. Manischewitz Concord Grape Wine flowed like water, and a good time was had by all. Sam Simonson brought a flask of his beloved slivovitz which he offered to whoever approached him. Hard feelings fell by the wayside as everyone put aside old grudges, at least temporarily, to celebrate the wedding. Art and Vivian kicked off the dancing with a foxtrot to Bing Crosby's "You Brought a New Kind of Love to Me" rendered faithfully by Murray Rosen's Merry Wanderer Band. Most of the guests did not need encouragement to join in, and many an energetic, if somewhat less than graceful, version of the hora and kazotzky were strenuously enacted. Nobody in this crowd was self-conscious. Mastery of the actual dance maneuvers was unimportant. It was the enthusiasm that counted. Vivian watched all the dancers and placed her hand over her abdomen. She didn't feel any movement yet, but she knew that her own baby would be bouncing around in there soon. Vivian was sure that her pregnancy showed even if many guests told her otherwise. Art told her that it didn't make any difference. Everyone knew that they'd been married already. And anyway whose business was it? What did they care what anyone else thought? If anybody said anything rude they were welcome to leave. And Art was right. He always had the right attitude. Things just didn't bother him. Art had joined the circle dancing the hora, and he was motioning for Vivian to join in, but Vivian waved him off. She didn't want to take part in any of the dancing because she thought it was better to be careful. You could get banged around or even tripped up by some of those big, clumsy oafs. Vivian would play it smart for the baby's sake. With all the dancing and noise she felt the room beginning to spin and she took a seat. It was good to think though that all this celebration was for her and Art, and for the baby too, of course. She looked over at Art as the evening wore down and took his hand. They surveyed the joyful scene and reflected that surely many happy days lay ahead.

59

Art spent more time watching TV these days – political shows like Meet the Press and Face the Nation on Sundays and baseball all during the week. Art had been a longtime Brooklyn Dodger fan, even though he lived in the Bronx. But he wasn't one of the faithful who followed the Bums when they moved to Los Angeles and became the darlings of southern California. To hell with them, and to hell with California. Art didn't think much of the west coast lifestyle and those that lived it. Of course, he didn't have much actual experience with it. He'd never traveled there. It was just the image that rubbed him the wrong way. He saw a cartoon once that summed it up pretty well for him: The difference between Los Angeles and New York. Two guys meet on the street and shake hands. In Los Angeles they say to each other "Have a nice day," but they are really thinking "Drop dead." In New York the two guys say, "Drop dead," but they are really thinking, "Have a nice day."

Art was left without a team to root for. The Yankees weren't his type. Too wealthy and elite. The organization could buy anyone they wanted. Besides they won too much. How could any regular person relate to that? Then, in 1962, New York got a new National League team, the Mets. They were a hapless conglomeration of has-beens and never-will-be's, and the manager was none other than the old Yankee skipper, Casey Stengel. Art didn't care so much that they were champion losers. That's only to be expected at first, since the team was formed with other organizations' cast-offs. But he had trouble at first warming to a team managed by Stengel. That was before he realized that the old curmudgeon's bizarre, confusing oratory and sense of the absurd was perfect for a team like the Mets. The "Ol' Perfessor" regaled the public with endless streams of semi-comprehensible diatribe that delighted fans and press alike. "We're losing games in ways I never knew existed." "See that young 20-year-old over there? In ten years he's got a chance to be a star. See that one over there? In ten years he's got a chance to be 30." "Don't cut my throat, you press guys, I may want to do it myself later." "The key to being a successful manager is keeping the 5 guys who hate you away from the 4 that are still undecided." And, of course, the immortal "Does anyone here know how to play this game?" Now this was a team and a manager Art could relate to.

Casey was man who had been on top of the world, managing greats like Joe DiMaggio and Mickey Mantle. By the time Mantle arrived, Stengel – a former player himself – had been piloting clubs for decades. Now he was charged with teaching Mickey the finer points of the game. Mickey, fresh out of Oklahoma and blessed with great athletic ability, asked his grizzled, old mentor if he had ever played baseball. "Yeah, I played this game. You think I was born in a dugout at the age of seventy trying to manage guys like you?" Stengel had so much talent with the Yankees that he had to turn away legitimate prospects. "We'd like to keep you around kid, but we're going to try and win a pennant."

With the Mets, winning championships was out of the question. But filling the stadium with fans was not, and it turned out that Casey's showmanship was just the ticket. This was a man who had doffed his cap one day and had a pigeon fly out. He knew how to entertain, how to keep the crowd interested. If he had a team of losers, they could at least be lovable. And Art the salesman could appreciate this. Casey had hit upon the right approach. Whether by design or mere happenstance, he was the right man at the right time. Sure, fans would prefer to support a winning team. But New York baseball fans had suffered the loss of both the Giants and the Dodgers in 1958. Now they had a National League club again, and if they were losers at least they were their losers. And their losers were unique. They had Casey who could put on a show by himself. He was the great (mis)communicator, holding in rapt attention journalists and fans alike who hung on every word of his impromptu dissertation as he expounded on the greatness that was to come from his temporarily disadvantaged ballplayers. Some might just dismiss him as an old bullshitter, but Art knew different. Here was a man who knew his business. He could entertain and inspire at the same time. He wasn't putting on an act. This is who he was in this particular circumstance. Sure, he was someone different when he went to work as a bank executive. Then he was Charles Dillon Stengel, man of finance. And he was someone different when he went home to his wife who knew him as a husband and father. But as a baseball manager, this was the baseball man who was still devoting himself to his chosen profession. He came to work every day, put on the uniform, and did his thing. Love him or hate him, this is how he played the game. And he kept playing it that way until he fell off a barstool early in 1965 and broke his hip. He didn't heal as well as he expected, and he didn't want to be pushed out to the mound in a wheelchair, so he retired. At least it was better than when the Yankees fired him because they thought he was getting too old. "I'll never make the mistake of being seventy again," bemoaned Casey.

Art knew he wouldn't see seventy, but he could still take pleasure in those who knew how to play the game right, knew how to make something good out of a tough situation. He was watching a ballgame between the Yankees and the Detroit Tigers on TV when 22-year-old Mickey Stanley stepped to the plate. Red Barber, the old Dodger broadcaster now working for the Yankees, commented, "This young man Stanley is a good young prospect, probably a little nervous about facing the great Whitey Ford for the first time." Art was listening closely. He didn't have a dog in this race, didn't like the Yankees but wasn't a Tiger fan either. He always liked the Old Redhead, though, the old Dodger broadcaster. Red was a man of few words, especially for someone who made his living by talking. Somehow, however, his quiet demeanor and down home, southern vocabulary enabled him to tell a story with a personal touch that captured the attention of many fans. "If young Stanley's folks are watching in Grand Rapids, I'm sure they are enjoying seeing their boy making his major league debut for the home town team." Whitey slipped a fastball by Stanley for strike one. "The Yankees don't have a line on this young fella yet, so they're playing him straight away." Stanley swung at the next pitch and sent a long fly ball to left center field. "Mantle is racing back to the wall. He won't get this one. It's a home run for the youngster." In the background we could hear Red's broadcast partner Mel Allen exclaim, "How about that!"

I looked over at Art, and he had tears in his eyes as he watched Stanley round the bases and receive congratulations from his teammates. I'd never seen Art cry before. He saw me watching him, but he didn't really seem embarrassed. He just sniffed and gave sort of a sheepish smile.

60

Vivian was cooking dinner when the phone rang. She picked up the receiver from the wall phone in the dining room, answering with the lilting, musical "Hello" some folks affect, a sound that bears no resemblance to their natural, conversational tone. "Just a second. I'll see." Vivian peered into the living room where Art sat in front of the television. "It's for you." The expression on her face indicated that the caller was nobody she knew. Art picked up the phone. Art's questioning "Hello" was answered by man who identified himself in a measured, polite, and tentative manner.

"Mr. Art? This here is Jimmy, Jimmy Rollins from the restaurant. Mr. Hack's friend."

"Oh, Jimmy, yes, I remember. How are you?"

"Oh, I'm fine. The reason I'm callin' is, it's about my grandson. You remember Mr. Hack told you he's a real good boy. And good in school too."

"I remember that."

"Well, I know you sell those cyclopedias, and I'd like to get the boy a set."

"Well, sure, Jimmy. Uh, the thing is, I'm not driving right now. But, you know what, I think I can come over with a friend and show you the books. And if you like them, we can get you a complete set for the boy." That was agreeable to Jimmy, and he gave Art his address. After Art hung up, Vivian asked who that was. "A friend of Hackley's. He wants to buy some books." "That must be the first time a customer ever called you." And as far as Art could remember, it was.

Art felt invigorated by the call. He got out of his chair, walked haltingly over to his box of Dutch Master cigars, unwrapped one, and lit it up. Who would have thought it? A sale after all these weeks. But he wasn't really working for Worldview anymore, at least not in a regular capacity. How was he going to arrange this? He decided he would call Whitey Connor. Let him get credit for the sale. He'd go with Whitey to Jimmy's, make the introductions, and see that everything went smoothly. He'd be a consultant. Yeah, that's the ticket: Art Feldman, consultant. Maybe that would be his new career. Then Art thought about what Vivian said. How often does a customer ever call a salesman? Maybe this was just Hackley feeling sorry for him, showing him some charity. He wouldn't want that. Then again, maybe Jimmy really wants to buy a set for the kid. And when did Hackley ever have a soft spot for anybody? Sure they knew each other a long time and got along OK, but Hackley wasn't any social worker. He always looked out for himself first and foremost. Yeah, Hackley was just doing me a good turn for old time sake, and helping out Jimmy at the same time. Nothing wrong with that.

It wasn't surprising that Whitey had other ideas. Riding down to Harlem, it was clear that he approached this opportunity as he would most any other potential sales deal. "I appreciate you cutting me in on this, Art. The extra commission check will look good with the bills I got coming due. You just make the intros and I'll hit him with the free book, the super-saver shtick, and the rest."

"There's no need. He's ready to buy."

"The whole set? Just like that?"

"That's right. He's crazy about that grandson he's raising. Wants him to have all the advantages."

"Yeah, well. maybe, but you know the coloreds. They get these hot ideas but then don't follow through. I'll make sure I get the John Handcock on the contract before I leave." Art started thinking about the way they spoke about customers – the coloreds, the C's, the Puerto Ricans, the PR's. It had never meant much to him one way or the other. Hell, if he was a customer, he'd just be a JW, a Jew. Was this kind of racial and ethnic shorthand any different than calling the Irish "micks" and the Italians "wops"? Then there was the way the *goyim* referred to Jews as kikes or sheenies. He wondered if Whitey saw him that way sometimes. And then there was the way that all his fellow Jews referred to coloreds – *shvartses*. "I'm cleaning out my back room. I'm almost finished, but I got to get a *schvartse* in to do the heavy work." Like they were dumb pack horses.

"Turn left here on Cathedral Parkway," Art directed, "Hackley said it's right around here."

"If we're relying on Hackley's information, we'll probably end up in Jersey." Whitey would never come around to seeing Hackley as anything but a louse. As they were cruising down Central Park North, Art noticed a familiar figure. "Look at that guy." He directed Whitey's attention to a man in a wheelchair.

"Who's that? asked Whitey, squinting through the smoke wafting into his eyes from the Camel cigarette between his lips.

"That guy who's always panhandling on 59th Street. You know, the one with paralyzed arms and legs."

"Oh, that guy? He's a con man."

"No, I spoke to him a few times. You could see he's in a bad way."

"He's a fake, I'm tellin' ya. Ed Heller seen him walking around with his wheelchair under his arm, for chrissake."

"I don't believe it."

"Believe it. Think about this. How does the guy get to 59th Street or Central Park if he can't move? It's a racket."

"No, I'm sure the guy can't move."

"He can't move? Alright, then he probably works with that guy I heard about who has a whole crew of cripples. He sets them out on the streets all around the city every morning. They beg money all day, and the boss takes his cut from all of them. It's another con." Art still couldn't quite believe it, but it sounded possible. There were worse things going on every day in the city.

After circling the block a couple of times, they found a parking spot that was technically too close to a fire hydrant. Whitey began hauling a stack of promotional material out of his trunk, ready for a full sales pitch. Art knew it wouldn't be necessary but didn't want to argue about it. Jimmy was waiting for them when they knocked on his door. "Well, come on in Mr. Art." Jimmy was wearing the same blue cap he sported at the restaurant and the same relaxed smile. Art introduced Whitey then saw Jimmy's grandson look up from the TV as they entered. Art would have guessed the boy to be about ten or so, but he knew Jimmy had thrown that graduation party for him when he graduated elementary school the previous year. In fact, the boy was thirteen and had started seventh grade at nearby Wadleigh Junior High School on 114th Street.

Whitey quickly unpacked his sample books, pamphlets, and flyers, and began to launch into his sales pitch. Jimmy invited Whitey to have a seat on the couch, but Whitey believed that his performance benefitted from an aggressive posture that depended upon his ability to think and act on his feet. Jimmy said little, looking on with a fixed, placid smile, muscular arms crossed, seated in a folding chair, as Whitey went through his paces. "Mr. Rollins, this publication has been honored with numerous awards. You couldn't possibly purchase a better set of encyclopedias for your home. As you can see from this report, Worldview outperforms every other educational set in its category, and you won't believe how easily and affordably this collection of books can be yours. Let me show you the quality of this sample volume." Art had taken a seat in an easy chair. He had heard the spiel Whitey was delivering countless times. Jimmy's grandson noticed that Art wasn't paying any more attention to Whitey than he was, and he held up a copy of a book. Art tried to read the title, but couldn't make it out. Once the boy saw Art was interested, he walked over and showed him the copy of *Tom Sawyer*. "I liked this one last year. My teacher said it's a classic." Art asked him what he liked about it. "The boy, Tom, is very smart and brave. He knows his way around. He can get what he needs done." The boy asked if Art would like to see some of his other books, and Art let the boy lead him into his bedroom where he had copies of books by Jules Verne, Jack London, Robert Louis Stevenson, H.G. Wells, and John Steinbeck, even a copy of *The Diary of Anne Frank*. "I didn't read all of these yet, but I will."

Art pointed to the Jack London volume. "My boy likes this one."

"I bet you can probably get a lot of books for your boy."

"Some he gets from the library."

"Yeah, I go there too. Look." The boy showed Art a certificate the local library branch had given to him. It read, "This is to certify that Lester Rollins has successfully completed the summer reading program for 1966 by reading and reporting on twenty books included in the school reading list."

"That's something, alright. Your grandpa must be proud."

They could hear Whitey droning on in the living room. "Not only do you receive the complete 20-volume set but each year you will be mailed a yearbook that compiles all the new information from the previous year, so your encyclopedia never gets out of date." Lester showed Art a couple of paperbacks. "Do you like poetry? My teacher gave me these." They were volumes by Langston Hughes and Countee Cullen.

"I don't read much poetry myself, but it's a good thing to know."

"I like this one." Lester opened the Hughes book to "Let America Be America Again." Art perused it. It reminded him of his own father's complaints about, and hopes for, a more just nation. "Oh, yes/I say it plain/America never was America to me/And yet I swear this oath/America will be!"

"Do you like it?" Lester asked.

"It makes a lot of sense." Lester asked Art about how many children he had, and how old they were, and where they went to school. Art learned that Lester was the son of Jimmy's daughter Ella who wasn't living at home right now, and that Jimmy's wife Cora was busy most days cleaning office buildings. As Lester filled him in on these details, Art noticed that Whitey was no longer talking books in the next room. He could hear Jimmy telling Whitey about a fight he had with Indio Barretta back in 1944.

"Wasn't he that skinny welterweight from Mexico with the wild hair?" Whitey asked. "No, suh, he was a middleweight, always movin', bobbin' and weavin'. High energy type."

"Yeah, that's the one. He had some fights on TV in the '50's didn't he?"

"I believe so."

"And you fought him?"

"Twice. Both split decisions went to him. I hit him a few good ones, but the boy was hard to knock down."

"Split decisions are always tough. It means you could've won both of them, depending on whose adding up the points."

"You right about that." When Art returned with Lester, Jimmy was showing Whitey a recent photo taken in a local tavern featuring Jimmy and half a dozen other ex-fighters from the '40's and '50's.

"Isn't that Archie Jackson? Hell, I saw him fight in the Golden Gloves, musta been fifteen years ago."

"Probably longer than that."

"He won them that year, didn't he? I used to go to all the Golden Gloves every year." When Whitey saw Art re-emerge, he drew him over to the collection of old pictures on Jimmy's credenza. "Did you see the photos Jimmy's got here? He fought a lot of great contenders. Remember those fights at St. Nick's we used to go to? Hell, half the guys we watched are here." Jimmy told Whitey that Archie Jackson's nephew was the basketball coach at Bronx Community College, how Indio Barretta still helps train young boxers at the local Y, and how some of the old fighters meet for breakfast once a month at the automat. "Archie, he still gets up at 5:30 most mornings and does some roadwork runnin' around Central Park."

"Just like he was still fighting?" Whitey asked.

"Yessuh, he likes to keep in shape."

"You look like you could still go a few rounds yourself, Jimmy," said Art.

"No, that's all in the past for me now. Got some good memories though."

When Whitey left Jimmy's place he had a purchase order and cash deposit in his pocket, but he wasn't talking business. "Can you believe that picture? All those guys he fought? He must've been on some of those cards at St. Nick when we were there, don't you think?" As Whitey got in his car, he noticed Art tossing something into the back seat. "What's that?"

"A book Jimmy's grandson gave me."

Whitey glanced at the title. "1984?"

"He told me he didn't understand it, but thought maybe one of my kids would like it."

"Nice boy. You think Jimmy will make him a boxer?"

"No, I think they have other plans."

61

That was the last time Art went on a business call. He really couldn't walk much anymore, and was largely confined to life in the apartment. He was able to haltingly make his way from room to room if he had to. He couldn't use any devices that might help him walk, like a crutch or walker, because his arms weren't strong enough. Vivian was becoming increasingly concerned about possible falls. For this reason, he was sometimes seated in a newly-acquired wheelchair and pushed from room to room. Donnie was enlisted to help Art get around. Because Donnie's solitary existence made him most available for such duty, he also attended to many of Art's personal needs. Donnie didn't complain, but Harry and I sometimes wondered about the effect of witnessing so closely Art's inexorable physical decline may have had on him.

Thanksgiving, 1966 wasn't quite as joyous as in previous years, but we were all gathered to celebrate the holiday as usual. Vivian had the turkey roasting when the mishap occurred. Vivian was in the habit of storing old paper grocery bags in a compartment adjacent to the oven. We used them to dispose of trash. In retrospect, one would have to admit that this was not the best place to keep flammable material. This was pointed out to us dramatically when the collection of bags burst into flames which shot out into the kitchen. While we all watched in surprise, Art quickly grabbed a plastic bucket from under the sink, filled it with water and doused the flames. How he managed to move so quickly and maneuver the bucket with only one good arm is still puzzling. Maybe it was a case of pure adrenaline overruling apparent incapacity. In any case, he demonstrated to himself and the rest of us that he was still capable of responding to emergencies. It was a brief moment of triumph over adversity. Art had not yet been relegated to complete impotence. Of course, we would never come to think that his physical limitations would render him insignificant in our lives, but here was a clear indication that Art was still a force, still who he had always been, even if just for this moment.

Unfortunately, it was only a few hours later when this feeling of victory quickly evaporated. The turkey was done to a golden turn and placed on the dining room table. We were all eager to partake of the feast. Art was watching little Eddie build a tower with his blocks, and talking to Harry about how quickly the boy was growing up when Vivian announced dinner was ready. "Wash up, it's time to eat." Art turned to see the serving platter already stacked with sliced breast meat and browned drumsticks and wings. Apparently having assumed that Art was no longer equal to wielding a carving knife, Vivian had coopted Art's traditional role. "What the hell! What is this?" Art angrily confronted Vivian.

"I just thought..." Vivian started to explain, but Art would not be mollified. He got up and limped off into the bathroom, slamming the door for good measure. Vivian was at a loss. Harry tried to comfort her. "You couldn't know he'd feel that way." After an awkward moment, we went slowly about the motion of filling our plates with food. Not long after, Art returned to join us at the table, taking his rightful place at the head. No one spoke of the incident anymore, but it threw a pall over the remainder of the meal.

A couple of months went by and Art was no longer walking at all. He had fallen in the apartment several times. Fortunately, he didn't suffer any serious injuries, but he was now relegated to the wheelchair full time. Harry had stopped by with the kids for a visit. Art was sitting in his wheelchair when Eddie ran by, excited about some game he was playing. Art, in a playful mood, told Eddie, "Better slow down or I'll give you a kick in the behind."

Eddie looked up and replied, "You can't get out of that chair."

Stunned by his grandson's response, Art chuckled a bit then looked around at the rest of us with a quizzical expression on his face. "How did he know that?" Yes, the new generation was growing up, and Art realized that his grandkids would never remember him as a healthy, active grandfather.

Art was declining, but Harry was rising. The eldest son had always been something of a puzzle to Art. He wasn't the rambunctious, aggressive, athletic son so often depicted in macho literature and film of the day. He wasn't any good at sports. He was only a mediocre student, but he wasn't a troublemaker. He has always worked at a job, brought his paycheck home, contributed to the household, and babysat his younger brothers. And he had a lot of girlfriends as a teenager, so that laid to rest any thoughts Art might have had about Harry's sexual orientation. So what if he wanted to be an interior decorator? Kids have strange ideas when they're in high school. How could he become one anyway? He didn't know anything about it. Who did, living in the Bronx? Just a crazy idea.

Now Harry was flying high, a political appointee, a responsible official in a city department, serving at the pleasure of the mayor. Harry always held a grudge about the way he was raised. Nothing personal against Art, but why did we have to live in one of the less attractive apartment buildings in the neighborhood? The one across the street where his future in-laws lived had an elevator and a nicer lobby. Everyone knew it was for the better class of Bronx residents. Even the building down the block was tonier, and the one across the street to the west had better quality brick. Harry felt stigmatized. He was of the poorer classes. No, he never went hungry, never was in danger of being thrown into the street, but he felt somehow slighted, inferior in the eyes of his contemporaries because of his humble origins. Things were different now. He had risen above the slovenliness. He associated with a better class of people. He was one of the movers and shakers. He was bringing home some serious change too. Only Harry wasn't one to sock it away somewhere. If he had it, he went with it. What was the purpose of having money if you didn't spend it? You had to use money to show that you had now arrived. Harry seemed to follow the example set by Jackie Gleason's Ralph Kramden in *The Honeymooners*. When Ralph became briefly wealthy by discovering a suitcase full of cash in his bus, he didn't keep it a secret. He didn't quietly invest it. He had it, and he went with it. If you found out he had it, you could have some too. Harry was far from rich, but now at least he had some expendable income. He could afford a new car, better clothes and furniture. One day Harry discovered that Little Eddie had damaged the family's new coffee table by beating on it with his wooden toys. I guess the repressed interior decorator in Harry emerged, because he told folks that the table was constructed of "distressed wood." He wasn't really lying. Eddie had distressed it pretty good.

There was only one problem bedeviling Harry's *nouveau riche* existence – Delia. She wasn't fit for public display in the new arena in which Harry operated. She was a simple, young woman without ambition. Of course, it wasn't required that she have ambition. She was merely required to support Harry's appropriately. But she wasn't equipped to do that either. She didn't know how to hold an intelligent conversation. She wasn't informed, and she didn't care to be. She just wanted to sleep late, watch her soap operas, and provide for her family as best she could. When she opened her mouth in company, it was embarrassing to Harry. How was it possible for her to have a more pronounced Bronx accent than Harry? They grew up across the street from each other. Were there ethnographic boundaries stretching across the middle of the street that dictated such differences in one's speech patterns? No, it had to be that Delia just didn't care. She didn't care that she was demonstrating her ignorance publicly in front of people who mattered in this society. She didn't care that the nonsense she spouted wasn't even pronounced correctly. Maybe Delia had been brow beaten into a sense of dull submission by her mother. Living with Sandra must have been a stultifying experience. You learned to shut off your mind and accept defeat early in life. Do whatever you were told to get Sandra to shut up. Any intellectual curiosity you might have had was provided no outlet. If Ira had been a factor, maybe it could have been otherwise. But Ira was a benign, almost invisible, presence.

Now Harry was stuck with this albatross. He would introduce Delia then try to get rid of her before she could say something that humiliated him. Worse, at times he publicly humiliated her himself. He would brag about the fact that he was a man with two votes. "She knows nothing about politics. I just tell her who to vote for and she does it." Of course, there is the question of whether Delia was capable of being humiliated. No one could ever be sure if she felt insulted when Harry would go on one of his rants about how inept she was. She would never argue with him. She openly admitted to a lack of interest in anything that was considered substantial by the rest of society. She was interested only in her TV shows, and lying in the sun to get tan. Tan for what? She was hardly ever interested in going anywhere and being seen, maybe because she dreaded being drawn into conversations where you were expected to know something about a subject. Or did she really dread anything? It was difficult to know, because she generally affected a blank expression. What was concealed beneath? It was hard to know. Maybe nothing was concealed. Maybe there was just a void. She conceded that she was not much of a cook. Nor did she have much interest in what they called Home Economics. She cooked and cleaned but ignored anything that smacked of study concerning how best to run a household. Her approach to family affairs was strictly practical. "See this fork?" Harry would announce, holding up a stainless steel implement with impossibly twisted tines. "It's the one Delia uses to clear the garbage disposal." Delia liked to serve Harry breakfast and go back to bed. What was there really to do anyway? The kids were small and slept in the morning too if you let them. Delia reminded Harry of an old Fats Domino song, *Sick and Tired*: "I get up in the morning, give you something to eat/Before I go to work I even brush your teeth/Come back in the evening, you're still in bed/Got a rag tied around your head."

It was clear Harry was not satisfied with this situation. He spent more and more time away from home. The evenings were occupied with his other political appointee friends, frequenting fashionable night spots in Manhattan, talking about their promising futures. But there weren't really any outward clashes taking place between Harry and Delia, at least none that we could see. They seemed to accept things the way they were.

63

Donnie's high school career never really got going. He tried to get into a school that specialized in art, but even though he was a talented sketcher, he didn't have the discipline to compile a real portfolio of his work, and he was rejected. Another rejection. It didn't surprise him but it sure didn't do much for his confidence. Since he couldn't be admitted to the school of his choice, he had to select which neighborhood school he'd like to attend. Actually, he would have been fine with not attending any of them, but that was not an option. The deciding factor for Donnie turned out to be which school had the fewest students who harbored grudges against him and were waiting to kick his ass when he showed up. Donnie had fought so many different neighborhood kids over the years that this was a serious consideration for him. It wasn't like

Donnie was bringing much scholastic capital with him from his misadventures in elementary and junior high school. The only things he liked to do were draw cartoons and listen to rock music. These were not, in and of themselves, intellectual pursuits. Now if he had learned to play a musical instrument or read musical notation, maybe that could have led to something. But he never was interested in that either. Why not? No opportunity? Lack of exposure? Laziness? All of the above? Who knows? Some kids blamed their folks for not introducing them to subjects and pursuits that the kids later realized were great passions in their lives. Donnie wasn't that way. Hey, Art used to buy him records he liked to listen to. Was Art to be blamed for not being a music lover himself? Should Art and Vivian have forced Donnie to take music lessons? Would that have opened up new vistas for him? More likely, it would have been just another discipline beneath which Donnie would have chafed and rebelled. Even though Donnie liked to listen to music, he had no curiosity about how music was made. His comments were restricted to "good drum here" or "listen to that horn." Beyond that he wasn't interested.

In the end Donnie elected to go to DeWitt Clinton High School, an all-boys institution. There were too many old enemies attending the other schools. Needless to say, this wasn't the best reason to attend a school. There was nothing positive that attracted Donnie at Clinton. He didn't look forward to attending. He didn't expect to do well there. It was just the lesser of several evils. He would just bide his time there, make a few friends whose main interests were also in escaping the place, and drift along. Who knows what might happen? In time, it would all be behind him.

I was plugging along in college and still living at home, although I spent all day on campus, coming home mainly to sleep. Donnie and me still shared a bedroom, and at night he would still occasionally talk about his bizarre friends, Billadino & Company. Summers I worked in department stores. Summer 1966 I worked at Corvette's in Yonkers, New York in the sign printing department. My boss was a guy named Ted Frakers, a frustrated industrial designer. He supervised a staff of two: me and a guy who who carried mannequins around all day that Ted dressed for window displays. John Acosta, who was Ted's assistant, had a brother Bill who had been the sign printer before me. Ted had liked Bill, and never stopped running down John because he wasn't as sharp, in Ted's opinion. Ted's favorite insult for John was "pus nose" as in "Pus nose, bring that stool over here," and "It's time for your break, pus nose." Yeah, Ted was a real prince.

Autumn 1966 I left my summer job and returned to college for my senior year. By this time, Donnie, going nowhere fast, finally convinced Art and Vivian to let him drop out of high school and get a job. He dropped out and got a job in the same department store I had just left. This was one disaster I could clearly foresee, and I told Donnie to find a different job. Donnie, however, was just glad to get out of high school, and he didn't know much about job-hunting. Besides, he didn't have much of a resume, and was satisfied to have something fall into his lap. Needless to say, Donnie became Ted's next "pus nose." He lugged the mannequins around, and because they had yet to fill the sign printing position I had vacated, he printed signs too. One day he took an order from the manager of the women's department for a sign advertising ladies' pantyhose. When the manager came to pick up the sign, he found that it didn't mention panty hose. Instead it read: "Sale on Ladies Over-the-Knee Party Hose." They got a good laugh out of it. But that was probably the first and last laugh Donnie shared with anyone at Corvettes. After several weeks of serving as Ted's target of abuse, he started calling off work. After not showing up one day and not calling, he was fired. When Vivian found out, there was hell to pay. "I knew it! I knew it! You worked just long enough to get your money for a new record player. Then you quit. You planned it that way, didn't you? Now you think you're just going to sit in your room and play records all day? You eat my heart out! You'll put me in an early grave!" Donnie escaped to his room; I escaped to the library.

One memory from my summer at Corvettes sticks with me. It was the time Sherman Johnson, the head janitor, walked into the sign shop to tell us that he had just bought a new Oldsmobile. We congratulated him and asked him about the color, the engine size, and all the new features on it. He answered somewhat unenthusiastically. He didn't seem too happy about the whole situation. Turned out that he had paid for the car completely in cash, and he told us, "When I saw all that money disappear at once, I just sat down and cried like a baby." Even when you achieve a long sought after goal, sometimes it just doesn't turn out the way you imagined it.

64

Art was watching an old Marx Brothers movie on TV and laughing. Chico had just been hired by a hotel manager. "Do you have a job for my grandpa too?" "I don't know. What does he do?" "He puts-a cheese in da mousetraps." "Mousetraps! We don't have any mice here!" "It's-a alright, he brings his own." I didn't know Art was a fan of the Marx Brothers. Maybe he didn't know either. He didn't have much time for movie watching over the years. He was too busy trying to make a living. I remember that he liked Groucho, though, on the TV quiz show he ran, *You Bet Your Life*. Groucho with his nonstop, verbal riffs, attacking everything and everybody including himself. Groucho to contestant: "How old are you?"

"I'm 80 and I feel like 40."

"I feel like 40 too. Like 40 elephants just dragged me through a knothole." I remember Art liked that one. Nonsensical but self-effacing. Groucho didn't take himself too seriously, or seriously at all, for that matter. In fact, that was the Marx Brothers in a nutshell – nothing is to be considered serious. All sacred cows will be methodically and systematically deconstructed. Chaos will reign. Do you feel oppressed by society's rules and regulations? Burdened by responsibilities? Watch Groucho, Chico, and Harpo make them all disappear. They will be revealed as mirages, hallucinations, figments of your own imagination. Pay them no heed. Dispense with them all. It's not difficult. All it takes is an attitude adjustment.

Harry believed that Art's illness, tragic though it was, enabled Art to shed the burden he carried as a lifelong worker. From the time he was a kid he was the designated laborer. It was his role in life. His lack of a formal education made the job all the more difficult. Now for the first time he could escape all that. So Harry reasoned. Maybe there was something to that, but it seemed a little too simple. It was as if Art had nothing to do with the way he dealt with his failing health. It was all arranged for him. An automatic psychological reaction had kicked in, and Art just went along for the ride. No, there had to be more to it. There were no easy answers to something like this. Art deserved a ton of credit for working so hard all his life. He was never one to knock off work early and spend a few hours at the local bar. He didn't gamble. He worked six or seven days a week to eke out a living for his family. Sometimes it wasn't enough, but he tried his best. Now I had to believe that he was still trying hard. He was working at holding his emotions together so that we didn't see a broken man wallowing in self-pity. Life at home could have been a lot worse if Art displayed all the pain, anger, and misery he had to be experiencing at times. Art deserved credit for this too.

It wasn't long before Art was spending time in the local hospital. His cardiologist worked out something through Medicare where Art could be treated there for various complications of his ALS. Eventually, he would live there fulltime, coming home only on Sundays when we would take him back to the apartment for the day. Doctors remarked about his exceptional attitude toward all this. Why wasn't he depressed? This was an interesting case study indeed. They arranged a meeting with Art where they questioned him about his feelings toward his impending death.

There were four docs there: neurologists Alvin Cummings and William Beddeker, psychiatrist Lenore Krakower, and occupational therapist Marvin Peeler. Cummings began the interview by praising Art's stoicism in the face of such hardship. "Mr. Feldman, we find your positive attitude to be inspirational, and wanted to ask you a few questions regarding the source of your strength. Do you find religion to be your comfort?"

"I'm not very religious, actually. I mean I do believe in God, but beyond that…" (Art shrugged).

Krakower: "Do you ever feel sad or hopeless about your situation?"

"Sure, sometimes. More than sometimes. But what am I going to do about it? It doesn't get you anywhere to dwell on it."

"But how do you avoid dwelling on it? You see, many of our patients become very depressed, and we were thinking they, and we, might learn something from your experience."

"It's hard to say. I wake up every day and think about things I want to do, that I can still do, and I look forward to doing them. Seeing my wife and kids. Maybe keeping up with news and sports. Seeing how things will turn out."

Beddeker: "But you know how your illness will turn out. Doesn't that cast a pall over everything else?"

"To some extent."

Peeler: "You know, I think this is a good example of a patient being able to mentally overcome his disability by envisioning all the things he can still do. Did you ever consider taking up bookkeeping, Mr. Feldman?" The other docs looked at Peeler questioningly.

Art thought, "Peeler? Is this the same guy who screwed up my back?" Then he answered Peeler's question, "No, it didn't occur to me."

"Well, I had a patient once who used to be a custom tailor. He made some exquisite clothing. In fact, he made this tie I'm wearing. I admired it and I asked him if he would consider giving it to me when he got tired of it and he did. Anyway, he became ill with multiple sclerosis and he took up accounting."

At this point Art interjected, "Do you have a brother who's a chiropractor?"

"Me? Oh, no, why do you ask?"

Cummings attempted to get the discussion back on track. "Surely, Mr. Feldman, you realize that all the things you enjoy will soon be gone, that even with the best of care you do not have all that long to live."

"Of course, I know that."

"Yet you can carry on so well. How is that possible?"

"If I feel good, I just go with it. I don't ask why."

Krakower: "You know that's a wonderful philosophy. It doesn't have to be explained."

Beddeker: "But when you feel depressed, how do you prevent getting stuck with that?"

"Well, like I said, I start thinking about things that interest me."

"But many patients in your situation find it impossible to be interested any longer in matters that used to provide enjoyment for them. They are completely preoccupied by their terminal status." Art had no reply.

Krakower: "Mr. Feldman, your sister is here today to visit you, and you can see her as soon as we are finished. We talked to her a bit about your childhood together. She told us that you were your mother's favorite child, and about how you used to help your father in his shop. She said you even saved your young brother's life by pushing him out of the way of a truck. And she spoke about how you were a star on the high school track team. It sounds like you had a very active childhood. How do you feel reflecting back on all of that?" Again, Art had no reply, but he gave a shrug and lowered his head. "Mr. Feldman? What do you think?"

When he lifted his head, there were tears in his eyes. "Ancient history."

Of course it wasn't such a very long time ago. Art was 53, pretty young to die. But the docs called a halt to the interview shortly thereafter. They had demonstrated that even an upbeat, congenial guy like Art was capable of realizing the tragedy of his own situation, and reacting in a manner they considered appropriate. Was that what they were after? In any case, Art's sister Rita had made the long trip from Jersey, and was waiting to see him.

65

Rita, the oldest, was the one who always paid visits. She didn't drive, so she would take buses and trains into the city. She had lost two husbands and had a grown son and daughter who lived out-of-state. She was well-fixed financially, her second husband having been a successful architect, but she was alone and she didn't know quite what to do with all the time on her hands. At sixty she was still trim and attractive. She had always been considered the pretty one – blonde hair, slim, fine features, fair complexion, and very self-possessed. She still kept her hair a light blonde color, and you could never be sure if she was discreetly dyeing it or if she had just not gone gray at all.

Naturally, Art was glad to see her. Rita walked to his bedside and gave him a hug. "Artie, it's good to see you."

"How was your trip?"

"Oh, alright, how can it be? I read." She held up a romance novel.

"I hear you've been telling the doctors all about me."

"They were so interested. What are they doing, psychoanalyzing you?"

"They think I'm too happy about dying."

"What? And look, you're not dead yet. Don't even talk that way." Rita sat down and opened a package she had been carrying. "Here, I forgot you don't like chocolate, but you can give it to the nurses. They'll take better care of you." Rita gave Art the rundown on the rest of the Jersey siblings. Sol was on the road selling pharmaceuticals.

"When is he going to take it easy already? His two boys are growing up without him." David was so successful as an engineer that he now owned half the town of Long Branch, but his wife was still a brassy loudmouth (but they liked her just the same). His three kids are getting big. Ida was still a stickler for her housekeeping. "You have to remove your shoes before entering, but let her enjoy her little home and be well. She took good care of ma all those years, and still looks after pop." Art told Rita that Saul was going with a woman and they were planning to move to Florida. "Good for him. May he live and be well." They both considered the irony of Saul, "the sick one," having outlived two wives and about to embark on a third marriage. "You never know what life has in store for you," said Rita.

"That's for sure."

"Oh, here, before I forget." Rita opened her pocketbook and removed a packet of old photos. "I had these negatives developed. They're from the last time we were all together with ma." She handed them one at a time to Art who held them up with his good hand.

"Ma looks so old," Art said.

"She was old."

"But older than I remember. You can't see her eyes through those thick glasses. And she's not smiling in any of them."

"They never smiled in the old days. Taking a picture was serious business."

"But she was a good ma."

"The best. And you were her favorite, Artie. You know that. I was going to bring you something else but forgot. You know how ma always had Ida go to the bank to get a roll of quarters right before the grandkids visited? Well, she had two rolls sitting on her nightstand the night she died. I know one of them was for your kids. I was going to give it to you as a remembrance."

"That's OK, these photos are good enough."

Art asked Rita what she was doing these days. "What is there to do? Mostly I just rattle around in the house, doing this and that. Nothing that amounts to much."

"You could do a lot. Look how you came all the way out here to see me."

"Maybe I'll volunteer."

"That's what you should do. There's lots of organizations that need help."

"You're right, Artie." And that's how they left it. But when Art reflected on it, it seemed that they had had that same conversation before.

As Rita was leaving, the hospital rabbi stuck his head in the door. Art never did learn his name. "Mr. Feldman, how are you doing?"

"Living the life."

"God willing."

The rabbi waved and was about to move on to the next room when Art added, "Rabbi, pray for me."

"I pray for everyone." And he was gone. "Lucky for him I'm already a Jew." Art thought. "He'd never sell me on the religion."

Ironically, Art developed a much better relationship with the young Catholic priest who visited patients. When Art returned 29-year-old George Dempsey's greeting one day, George asked if Art felt like some company. Art invited him in, and before long they were talking about their shared experiences in the Bronx. George's family grew up on Bainbridge Avenue, and he attended nearby St. Ann's School then went on to Fordham University as his older brothers had done. Art brought up Vince Lombardi and the Fordham football teams of the 1930's. Eventually, they got around to discussing Art's illness. Art could see that the young priest was sincere in his compassion and hoping to provide some comfort but what could he offer? The answer came shortly before he was about to leave. Father Dempsey offered Art some literature, and asked if he would read it before his next visit. Art accepted it and said that he would. When George returned a few days later, he asked Art if he had read the material. "I did."

"And what did you think of it?"

"It seems like it's saying that I was chosen to suffer."

"Yes, and what do you think of that idea?"

"I think that if I ever find the SOB who chose me, I'll kick the shit out of him." George just smiled and dropped his head. Perhaps he thought that Art had failed to consider the larger significance of his predicament, or that he was somewhat lacking in spiritual sensitivity. To his credit, the young Father was not completely put off by Art's response. Although he realized a conversion was not likely, he continued to visit on occasion, sit and enjoy Art's company. They connected in a fundamental way, both sharing their observations and insights honestly, appreciating the willingness of the other to listen, and enjoying the candid feedback received – all benefits accruing to those who take the time to make the effort. Religion, however, was not one of the conversation topics.

One day when I visited Art, he mentioned to me that he'd been talking to a new student nurse who was working in the hospital. "She's a nice girl, pretty. And I told her I had a son about her age." If I'd considered Art's comment objectively, I would have been interested, but instead I felt a little humiliated that my father felt he needed to fix me up on a date. I hadn't been seeing anyone, and was self-conscious about it, as if every guy my age should have a girlfriend. So I ignored Art's offer. That was until I happened to be present a week so later when Pam Laurens entered Art's room in her blue scrubs to take his vitals. She had light brown hair, a nice smile, and a gleam in her eye. Art did the introductions. "This is the son I was telling you about." Ordinarily, I would have found it difficult to make conversation with a stranger, especially when being watched by someone who was anxious to observe my reaction. Pam's attitude was so open and welcoming, however, that before I knew it, I found myself warming to this kind of situation as Art usually did. "I hear you've been taking care of my dad. Is he giving you any trouble?"

"Oh, not much." She smiled at Art like they had some kind of secret.

"Yeah, he's a pretty nice guy," I said, "never gives me any trouble either."

"Do you ever give people trouble?" she asked.

"Me? Impossible." I was surprised at her boldness, but liked it. It made things easier for me, someone who found it hard to come up with a line for girls who were reluctant to engage. I asked her if she might like to go to dinner next week.

"Me? It's possible." And she smiled. After she left, Art asked me if he'd been to right to recommend her. "I'll let you know after our dinner date." Art nodded in agreement. I could tell that he was pleased I had asked her out. It turned out to be a good move. Pam was a bright light, full of fun and adventure. Oh, she liked to drink a little too much, and got a little too loud sometimes. But her heart was in the right place, and she was the first girl with whom I became physically intimate. She also made me see life from a different perspective, and I needed that experience in order to grow as a person.

Art received one memorable visit from a former co-worker, Itchy Green. He showed up one afternoon with a small bouquet of flowers in his fist, tan sport coat over a polyester, multi-colored Hawaiian shirt featuring a palm tree pattern, buttoned low to reveal curly black chest hair. Sparse black curls were scattered over his swarthy head. "Hey, Itchy, what's with the flowers? I'm not dead yet," Art said.

"Just good manners, Art, like what do you always bring to someone in the hospital? Flowers, right? Or candy, and I'm not into sweets, and you probably shouldn't be either in your condition. Am I right or wrong?"

"Right, right, you're always right Itch, sit down. How did you hear I was in the hospital?"

"Hackley told me."

"You've been seeing Hackley?"

"Oh, sure, in fact me and him are doing some work together."

"Don't tell me you're selling Bibles again."

"No, no, none of that. We work together over at Yonkers Raceway."

"What, did Hack get chased out the city with that tout scheme of his?"

"Nah, he's had some close calls, but he still hits the local places too on occasion. We're doing good at Yonkers though. Lots of takers."

"Just make sure you take yourself out of action before they get wise to Hack's racket."

"Oh, sure, we play it safe. Anyway, how are you doin'?"

"How can I be doin' layin' here?"

"I know it must be rough. I had a cousin had the same thing."

"Really?"

"Oh, yeah, he was a piano player too, a real good one. Got a lot of work playing weddings and bar mitvahs until he got sick. Then he lost everything. A damn shame. A funny guy too. Always with the jokes. Made everyone laugh. But there was nothing to laugh at in the end. You know, it got him in the throat."

"What do you mean?"

"That's how it does you in, you know. You can't breathe no more."

Art flushed red. He'd felt a bit short of breath lately. "You stupid bastard! You come here to tell me that?"

"What?"

"Thanks for the visit. Now get the hell out of here!"

"Jeez, what the hell. I thought you knew. Don't the docs tell you nothin'?"

"Don't let the door hit you on the way out."

"Hey, I didn't know, Sorry. Didn't mean no harm." Itchy rose and headed toward the door. Art waved him out, shaking his head.

Later, Art began to regret throwing Itchy out of his room. "He didn't mean any harm. That's just the way he is," Art thought, "always speaking without thinking. Besides, isn't that the way we all go? Cause of death: he stopped breathing."

It turned out Itchy Green had it right. In Art's case, as in his cousin's, it was a weakening of the diaphragm that was posing a deadly threat. We could see the signs when we visited Art. Vivian came every day. She was helping feed him now, and when she didn't time the spoonful of nourishment just right, Art would give a weak cough, flush and start to choke. Just a little spoonful that didn't go down exactly the right way would start him off, and it was hard for him to recover. He just didn't have much wind. Sometimes it seemed like he might expire right then and there, but he didn't. He kept on going, at least for a little while.

Art was by himself for a few weeks, but he was given a roommate eventually – a young man named Dan Boling who was under observation for extremely high blood pressure. It seemed to be an unusual pairing – a middle-aged man nearing the end of a terminal illness and a kid like Dan. Maybe they didn't give it much thought. Perhaps it was just chance or convenience. It wasn't that they didn't get along, because they did. Art was a natural conversationalist, and he could talk to just about anybody about anything. His illness didn't affect his intellectual or social abilities at all. If he wasn't well-informed on a topic, he could at least ask the right questions. Plus he had three sons so he had some idea of the interests and attitudes of someone like Dan. And Art liked having company. I was thinking more about how it was for Dan. I'm sure he found Art to be a congenial roommate, but still it was apparent that he was a very sick man. It had to be scary enough being in a hospital with dangerously high blood pressure without having a dying man lying in the next bed.

One evening Vivian returned from the hospital looking a bit upset. It turned out that Art's cardiologist had told her it could be anytime now. I guess he wanted to prepare her. Funny, but just a few days before, I remembered Art making a crack about how his cardiologist had told him his heart was now in great shape because he was getting so much rest. And here the doc was telling Vivian that Art's respiratory system was just about done. It turns out that there might have been some heroic measures that could have been taken. We saw that later on because one of New York's senators, Jacob Javits, came down with ALS several years later and survived much longer because he was put on a respirator. But would Art have wanted to be on a respirator? I doubt it. Would the family have wanted him kept alive that way? Probably not.

In any case, it wasn't more than a few weeks after the cardiologist's warning that we got a phone call in the middle of the night, summoning us to the hospital. It wasn't clear immediately that Art had died, but all of us – Vivian, me, Donnie, and Harry who met us there – feared that it must be the case. And that's what it was. During the night, Art had started gasping for air and that awakened Dan who called for help. I don't know if they had a "do not resuscitate order" on file, but Art had stopped breathing when help arrived, and that's the way it ended. After we arrived, some doc came in and asked Vivian if she would give her consent to have Art's body submitted for post-mortem examination. Vivian was adamant in her refusal, breaking into tears. This set Harry off and he told the doc, "I want you to guarantee that we will never be asked that question again!"

No matter how prepared one might think one is for a moment like this, it still feels unreal. Your father is no more. Your mother, so strong and composed, is broken. Harry steps in as man of the house. He and Vivian provide information for the required paperwork, begin the process of making funeral arrangements. Back at the apartment, me and Donnie don't know what to do with ourselves. Soon Sam and Bessie were there, quiet, subdued. Sam kept repeating, "The good die young." A nice tribute to Art, I guess, or was it just something to say under the circumstances? No, I think it was an honest sentiment. Art had never had any conflict with his in-laws, as far as I can remember. And who could really have harbored any animosity toward Art anyway? I couldn't think of anyone who considered him an enemy. I remembered Art once completing the statement Sam made, "The good die young," by adding the phrase "and bastards live forever." I think at the time he was referring to old ex-Nazis who were still being discovered trying to escape retribution for their murderous deeds. But it raises the question of whether living to a ripe old age is a stigma rather than a blessing. Does it indicate an unwillingness or inability to take responsibility for actions performed during one's life? Sam was an old man. When he said, "The good die young" was he condemning himself? Maybe Bessie would do that for him, given the difficult times she had as his wife. I was thinking too much, analyzing everything. Maybe that's what happens when you are the first in your immediate family to attend college. It was useless. There were no real answers to these type of questions in the end. Even if you were learning what the great thinkers of history wrote about such subjects, it might not help. Someone once said that intelligence was like four-wheel drive. It just got you stuck in more remote locations.

There was a surreal quality about the rest of the day. We had never experienced one like it. We felt numb. Just doing what had to be done. That night when I went to the bathroom to prepare to wash up, I suddenly burst into tears, crying uncontrollably. Why would it hit me then? Donnie was already in bed when I emerged. He commented on how terrible the whole thing was. I confessed to having broken down a few minutes ago. Neither of us slept much that night.

67

Art hadn't been a member of any synagogue. Despite his early religious upbringing (or maybe because of it?) he didn't even attend religious service on the High Holy Days. He would be out beating the pavement, trying to drum up more sales just like Itchy and

Whitey and Hackley and all the other guys. That meant that when he died, we also had to find a rabbi who would officiate at the funeral even though he did not know Art at all. This was not difficult as much as it was awkward. Just like with Aunt Fran, we had to sit down with the rabbi and introduce Art to him after the fact. The rabbi would learn something about him so that he could speak intelligently about Art at the funeral, and, at the same time, apply some scriptural message that was appropriate to the individual. It's good that rabbis, like other clergy, are well-versed in composing these kind of messages. The Bible gave them a lot of raw material to work with. They had stock phrases and anecdotes that they could use time and again, and this rabbi came through as expected. The fact that Art was no longer an observant Jew was omitted. The rabbi stressed Art's dedication to his family, his hard work, his sense of responsibility and trustworthiness, and related all this to traditional Jewish values that honored such men. He also called attention to all the grieving family that were present paying tribute to Art as evidence of the fact that he was a beloved man.

That's all I really remember of the rabbi's talk. The event still had an aura of unreality about it. The sense of strangeness was compounded by the fact that I hadn't slept all night. I did wonder, after the fact, why we could not have called upon Rabbi Appelman or Rabbi Perlmutter to do the service. At least they had met Art, even if just briefly, when me and Donnie were Hebrew school students. They could have added a little bit of a personal touch. On second thought, maybe it was better this way. If you know someone a little bit, your impressions may be way off. Your impressions won't take into account complete aspects of the person about which you are unaware. Plus, when a rabbi sees someone only once or twice, and notices that person never shows up the rest of the time, there's a chance that they might hold it against him for not being involved enough with the congregation. Then there might be some animosity entering into the situation, even if unconsciously.

In any case, this whole aspect of the funeral pales in comparison with the experience of encountering Art's open casket. I know you are supposed to make the deceased look good for the funeral, and that this might be difficult when someone has suffered through a wasting disease. But the truth was that Art's disease had not taken a toll on his face, and that's the only part that was visible. You'd think that whoever prepared the body could make Art look like himself as he was in life. Don't they work from a photograph or something? I don't even remember what clothes were selected, hopefully something he wore regularly. All I can recall is the face. It had this completely unnatural smile fixed on it, a smile Art never in his life ever made. Kind of a smirk. As if the undertaker had completed the job, and as an afterthought had swiped a couple of fingers over the edge of Art's lips and flicked them up, thinking, "There, that's it, bring me the next corpse." The effect was that Art didn't look anything like himself. Oh, I'm sure anyone who didn't know him well might think, "Gee, he looks happy. What a nice job." But to me it was a travesty. There was nothing to be done at that point either. Besides, this whole thought process I am describing was overwhelmed by a sense of sadness that pervaded the whole experience. I felt pretty upset about it, but I didn't make a scene.

There was a scene anyway, but for a different reason. Aunt Ida was beside herself with grief. Ida was always a very demonstrative woman. Her emotions were always readily on display. She was the kind of person who might throw herself on a grave. She didn't do that here, but her sobs and wails were clearly audible throughout the ceremony. Personally, I didn't see anything wrong with it. After all this was her baby brother, her second sibling to die at a relatively young age. It was a natural reaction. But to others it was uncouth. In particular, it didn't measure up to the standards of current, polite society where every tragedy is to be met with perfect equanimity. To display one's grief in such a manner was to be considered an embarrassment, a sign that one's family had not risen to the desired level of civility. It stigmatized one, revealed that they had not succeeded in leaving behind them the medieval, superstitious behaviors that characterized their ignorant ancestors. This, no doubt, is how Harry felt when it was revealed that he had an aunt who dared to carry on so scandalously in front of him and his patrician co-workers. (Actually, few, if any of them, were true patricians. They were all, more or less, social climbers, or would-be elites, like Harry.) Harry kept staring at Ida with dismay, no doubt thinking, "Why doesn't someone shut her up?" As if it would be entirely appropriate for anyone to tell her not to cry at a funeral, or even eject her for displaying actual grief. Before the service Ida had walked over to Harry to personally express her condolences. She hadn't noticed me and Donnie yet, so she asked Harry how we were doing. I thought this was a very nice gesture, but apparently Harry felt her naked display of sorrow later on outweighed any earlier personal gestures of empathy.

I was glad to see that Harry was ultimately frustrated in his attempt to silence Ida in any way. In fact, I found her behavior the most appropriate of anyone present that day. Vivian was equally distraught although more quietly so. If she didn't find Ida's behavior to be out of place, why should Harry? Later on, Harry started to ridicule Ida. "Did you see the pulsating vein in her neck, how fire-red her face was?"

"It was her brother, she's entitled," I answered. It didn't go any further. One welcome face at the funeral belonged to Daniel Darrow. I don't know how he found out about it. Maybe he read the obituary. In any case, Daniel could be depended upon to show up at all such occasions to express appropriate sentiments. Dressed in a familiar brown suit one would expect to see on a gentleman at least a generation older, he slumped toward us, placing a hand on my shoulder. "May you know no further sorrow." Then he shook everyone's hand gently. His long, solemn visage reflected honest concern and respect. As we left the funeral home I noticed a clump of men gathered on the sidewalk near the street. They made no effort to approach us but were talking among themselves, watching everyone file out. I looked more closely and was able to identify Whitey O'Connor and Les Altman among them. Whitey saw me looking at him and gave a wave. I waved back. But none of them ever came over to say a word. Did they feel like they were outcasts of some kind? Not fit to mingle in polite society? Could salesmen be shy? Maybe they weren't confident in this particular kind of situation. Probably they hadn't had many of their friends die yet, and they didn't know how to approach it. I don't know, but they remained on the fringe. They were there but they kept their distance. When we stepped into the limo for the ride to the cemetery, they were still standing there watching.

Back at the apartment we prepared for *shivah*. Even though we were not very observant Jews, the traditions of mourning were to be maintained. Mirrors were covered. Hard benches were delivered upon which we were supposed to sit. It was once prescribed that mourners should rend their clothing as a visible sign that they were in mourning. That had given way to the practice of wearing a black ribbon that was partially cut. We pinned our ribbons on. Uncle Saul, not yet relocated to Florida, joined us every evening as we walked over to the closest synagogue to say mourner's kaddish for Art. "Consider me an uncle," he told us. He had no children, and had never functioned as a father. It was his way of letting us know that we could count on him if he was needed, and we appreciated it. Gun Hill Jewish Center was a small congregation that was gone ten years later. Most of the congregants were elderly men. I noticed Al Weinberg the former proprietor of the local delicatessen where we used to buy our corned beef and pastrami sandwiches on Saturday nights. He had recently sold his business and retired. Unlike many of his contemporaries, he did not relocate to warmer climes.

Even the most sincere mourners begin to emerge from their immediate shock and sorrow as time goes on. Even in the early stages of mourning a glimmer of hope, a hint of joy, a sense of moving on emerges now and then. So it was that one evening during services, as we took our seats, the curly blonde head of a young girl three or four years old popped up before us. She was sitting in the row directly in front of us next to an elderly gentleman who may have been her grandfather. She peered intently, brows knitted, over the back of the bench at us. Saul was the first to point at her and break into a smile. When she noticed that we were paying attention to her, she immediately ducked down again, disappearing from view. Services began, we rose to our feet for the some prayers, sat down again for others. Saul no longer remembered how to read Hebrew. Maybe that's why the prayer book did not distract him much from the girl's playful antics. I tried to follow along but found myself drawn to the girl as well. She wasn't hiding as much now. She would look at us with a deadly serious expression for a few seconds then break into a broad smile before briefly ducking down again to continue her game. We were all enjoying her playfulness now – Saul, Harry, Donnie and me. Distracted as we were, we did not forget to rise for the intonation of mourner's kaddish. After resuming our seats, the girl pointed her index finger at us and said the only words she uttered that evening, "Handsome boys." Walking back to the apartment, we kidded skinny, bald-headed Saul about being a handsome boy. "Your Aunt Edith thinks so," Saul said. Our gloom had been lifted for a bit by a little girl. Life goes on. Art would have wanted it that way.

68

A couple of weeks later New York experienced an unusual wave of warm weather. It was mid-February but temperatures had soared into the 60's. I didn't remember what the groundhog had predicted, but it couldn't have been anything like this. I decided to grab my basketball, head over to the courts in the nearby park, and shoot some baskets. The courts were empty despite the mild weather. Most people are taken by surprise when it's not freezing in February, and it takes them a day or two to realize that they can act like spring has already arrived. By the time they figure it out, winter has returned and it's too late. I shed my light jacket and draped it over the chain link fence surrounding the playground. The sun was peeking out from behind a puffy cloud pretty low on the southern horizon. A few sparrows darted around pecking at crumbs and seeds near the park benches. I started bouncing the ball off the blacktop. The sound echoed off the nearby the concrete administration building and surrounding rock formations. I drove to the hoop and attacked the backboard in my shirtsleeves, my black mourner's ribbon still pinned above the pocket. Before long another guy came over and asked if I wanted to play some one on one. We went at it and sweat began to flow. We both commented on how great it was to be able to be out shooting hoops in February. We didn't keep score, but I had one shot that was almost automatic that day. I would spin either to my left or right and bank a right hand jumper in off the backboard. The ball would rattle around in the naked, iron rim and drop through. I couldn't miss for some reason. It was unusual, because I was never that great a shooter. I was always more of a rebounder and defender. The points I scored were usually off offensive rebounds, following somebody else's missed shot. The guy I was playing with was a banger. He played tough but clean. But that day, even when well-defended, I managed to clear enough space to get the shot off and it went in. Once or twice, when completely covered, I threw the basketball overhand like a baseball and still sank it. We both laughed about that. There was an angry rhythm to the way I was playing. It wasn't pretty. I was just slamming that ball off the backboard and having it bang around the rim and in. The unseasonable warmth, my thick winter shirt with sleeves rolled up, the mourner's ribbon flapping, the sweat running down my face – there was never another day quite like it.

By mid-afternoon there were some old men playing bocce ball in the court covered with red clay adjacent to the playground, and a couple of guys were carrying sticks and disks they had just borrowed at the administration building, walking toward the concrete shuffleboard courts. I decided to take the long way back to the apartment, cutting across the track and football field that occupied the center of the park. A park employee with a pointed stick was slowly gathering up discarded gum wrappers and cigarette packets that had been left around by those who had turned out to watch the semipro football game the previous weekend. I looked around half expecting to see mothers leading their little tykes into the bushes so they could take a leak, and the arthritic, old gent who pushed around the ice cream cart from April to October each year. But no, there were no leaves on the bushes that would provide some privacy, and no moms with kids. The wading pool was dry, the metal swing sets and seesaw were unoccupied, and there wasn't even any water coming out of the drinking fountains. It was still February after all.

When I got back to the apartment there was a small stack of mail on the kitchen table. Tossing aside the flyers and bills, I found one envelope that was addressed to Mr. Art Feldman in a very simple, neat handwriting. I took the liberty of opening it. It was a small, Hallmark, thank you card that read. "Thank you very much Mr. Art for the encyclopedias. I wanted to let you know that it helped me make the honor roll at my school. I hope you are doing good. My grandpa sends his regards. Thanks again. Yours truly, Lester Rollins."

www.ingramcontent.com/pod-product-compliance
Lightning Source LLC
Chambersburg PA
CBHW022023240626
47154CB00007B/2242